P9-DML-120

For
Edward and Richard
Liz and Anne
with all my love

ACKNOWLEDGMENTS

A big thank-you to Jackie Cantor and all at Berkley for their enthusiasm and sensitive editorial support, as well as their elegant artwork. Also to Amy Schneider for her fine attention to the detail of the manuscript.

Special thanks to my agent, Teresa Chris, for always being there and always knowing when to listen or encourage or bully—depending on which I need at the time.

I am deeply indebted to the lovely Elena Shifrina for her dedicated research in Moscow and her help with the Russian language.

Finally, my love and thanks to Norman for everything else.

PRAISE FOR THE NOVELS OF

KATE FURNIVALL

THE RED SCARF

"This romantic confection can make a reader shiver with dread for the horrors visited on the two heroines imprisoned in a labor camp and quiver with anticipation for their happy endings. Furnivall shows she has the narrative skills to deliver a sweeping historical epic."

—*Library Journal*

"Furnivall again pinpoints a little-known historical setting and brings it vividly to life through the emotions and insights of her characters. Beautifully detailed descriptions of the land and the compelling characters who move through a surprisingly upbeat plot make this one of the year's best reads." —*Booklist*

THE RUSSIAN CONCUBINE

"I read it in one sitting! Not only a gripping love story, but a novel that captures the sights, smells, hopes, and desires of Russia at the dawn of the twentieth century, and pre-Revolutionary China, so skillfully that readers will feel they are there." —Kate Mosse

"The kaleidoscopic intensity of British writer Kate Furnivall's debut novel, *The Russian Concubine*, compellingly transports us back to 1928 and across the globe to the city of Junchow in northern China. . . . Lydia is an endearing character, a young woman with pluck and determination. . . . With artistry, Furnivall weaves a main plot that hinges on Lydia's love affair with Chang An Lo, a Chinese youth who is a dedicated Communist at a time when Chiang Kai-shek's Nationalists are gaining ground. . . . Furnivall's novel is an admirable work of historical fiction." —*Minneapolis Star Tribune*

"Furnivall vividly evokes Lydia's character and personal struggles against a backdrop of depravity and corruption." —*Publishers Weekly*

"The wonderfully drawn and all-too-human characters struggle to survive in a world of danger and bewildering change . . . caught between cultures, ideologies—and the growing realization that only the frail reed of love is strong enough to withstand the destroying winds of time."
—Diana Gabaldon

"This stunning debut brings the atmosphere of 1920s China vividly to life. . . . Furnivall draws an excellent portrait of this distant time and place."
—*Historical Novels Review*

The
Girl from
Junchow

Kate Furnivall

BERKLEY BOOKS, NEW YORK

THE BERKLEY PUBLISHING GROUP
Published by the Penguin Group
Penguin Group (USA) Inc.
375 Hudson Street, New York, New York 10014, USA
Penguin Group (Canada), 90 Eglinton Avenue East, Suite 700, Toronto, Ontario M4P 2Y3, Canada
(a division of Pearson Penguin Canada Inc.)
Penguin Books Ltd., 80 Strand, London WC2R 0RL, England
Penguin Group Ireland, 25 St. Stephen's Green, Dublin 2, Ireland (a division of Penguin Books Ltd.)
Penguin Group (Australia), 250 Camberwell Road, Camberwell, Victoria 3124, Australia
(a division of Pearson Australia Group Pty. Ltd.)
Penguin Books India Pvt. Ltd., 11 Community Centre, Panchsheel Park, New Delhi—110 017, India
Penguin Group (NZ), 67 Apollo Drive, Rosedale, North Shore, 0632, New Zealand
(a division of Pearson New Zealand Ltd.)
Penguin Books (South Africa) (Pty.) Ltd., 24 Sturdee Avenue, Rosebank, Johannesburg 2196,
South Africa

Penguin Books Ltd., Registered Offices: 80 Strand, London WC2R 0RL, England

This is a work of fiction. Names, characters, places, and incidents either are the product of the author's
imagination or are used fictitiously, and any resemblance to actual persons, living or dead, business
establishments, events, or locales, is entirely coincidental. The publisher does not have any control
over and does not assume any responsibility for author or third-party websites or their content.

Copyright © 2009 Kate Furnivall
Excerpt from *The Russian Concubine* copyright © 2007 Kate Furnivall
Cover design by Richard Hasselberger
Cover photos: Cathedral: Panoramic Images / Getty Images; Woman: Titus Lacoste / Getty Images;
Chinese fabric: IMAGEMORE Co., Ltd. / Getty Images; Flowers: Jupiterimages Unlimited
Book design by Kristin del Rosario

All rights reserved.
No part of this book may be reproduced, scanned, or distributed in any printed or electronic form
without permission. Please do not participate in or encourage piracy of copyrighted materials in vio-
lation of the author's rights. Purchase only authorized editions.
BERKLEY® is a registered trademark of Penguin Group (USA) Inc.
The "B" design is a trademark belonging to Penguin Group (USA) Inc.

First edition: June 2009

Library of Congress Cataloging-in-Publication Data

Furnivall, Kate.
  The girl from Junchow / Kate Furnivall. — Berkley trade pbk. ed.
    p. cm.
  ISBN 978-0-425-22764-0
  1. Russians—Fiction. 2. Political refugees—Soviet Union—Fiction. 3. Young women—
Travel—Russia (Federation)—Fiction. 4. Political prisoners—Soviet Union—Fiction.
5. Fathers and daughters—Fiction. 6. Reunions—Fiction. 7. Soviet Union—History—
1925–1953—Fiction. I. Title.

PR6116.U76G57   2009
823'.92—dc22

2008051515

PRINTED IN THE UNITED STATES OF AMERICA

10 9 8 7 6 5 4 3 2 1

One

LYDIA IVANOVA COULDN'T SLEEP. TINY RATS WERE taking bites out of her brain. Ever since she'd arrived in Soviet Russia the nights had been hard, and through the long dark hours it felt as though sharp yellow teeth were gnawing through her skull. Sometimes she could smell them. Worse, sometimes she could hear them. *Chip, chip, chip.*

She was angry with herself for listening to them. At seventeen years old she should know better. She sat up in the narrow bed and dragged her fingers through her tangled mane to rid herself of the noise, yanking any rats out by their tails. She had to keep her mind clear. But nights were never quiet in this hotel, one of Stalin's new breed of concrete rabbit warrens that she found impossible to navigate. She was always getting lost in it, and that startled her. She couldn't afford to get lost. She tucked her chin tightly to her chest and closed her eyes, trying to find the bright warm place she kept in there, but tonight it was impossible. Snores were rattling in from the next room and a couple were arguing farther up the corridor.

Lydia was impatient now for the morning to

arrive. She was tempted to leave her bed and prowl up and down the scrap of floor space in her room, eager to push on to the next step. But she was learning to keep herself in check, to curb her instinct to seize each day by the throat. So to fill the dead time she unzipped the money belt at her waist, which she didn't take off even at night. It felt warm and soft to the touch. From it she extracted first her Russian passport. In the trickle of yellow light that spilled through the window from the gas lamp outside, it looked genuine enough. But it was forged. It was a good one and had cost her more than she could afford to pay, but every time she had to hand it over for inspection her heart clawed at her chest.

Next she pulled out her British passport and ran a finger over its embossed lion. It was ironic. This one really was genuine because of her English stepfather, but it was even more dangerous to her than the Russian one. She kept it well hidden in the money belt among the roubles because all foreigners foolish enough to set foot on the black soil of Soviet Russia were at best watched like hawks, at worst interrogated and interned.

Finally she took out the bundle of rouble notes and considered counting them yet again but resisted the temptation. Instead she weighed them in her hand. The bundle was growing lighter. She made a low sound, almost a growl, in the back of her throat and thought of what it would mean if they ran out. Quickly she pushed everything back into the money belt and zipped it up hard, as if to zip up her fear.

Her hand slid instinctively to the thong around her neck and the amulet that hung there. It was a quartz dragon. A powerful Chinese symbol, rose pink and nestling against her flesh. She circled her fingers around it.

"Chang An Lo," she whispered.

Her mouth curled into a smile as she saw the bright warm place rise into view. She closed her eyes and her feet started to run, flying over ice and snow, feeling the morning sun reach out its golden fingers to stroke her skin, her toes suddenly bare in soft treacly sand, and beside the shimmering sheet of water a figure . . .

A door banged and the image slipped from Lydia's grasp. *Chyort!* Outside, the sky was still as dark and dense as her own secrets, but she'd had enough of waiting and rolled out of bed. She pulled on her long brown coat, which she used in place of a dressing gown, and padded barefoot down the hall to the communal washroom. With a yawn she pushed open the door and was surprised to find the overhead light already on. Someone was standing at one of the washbasins.

The room smelled. An odd mix of lavender, disinfectant, and layers of something more unsavory underneath. But Lydia wasn't complaining because she'd smelled worse. Much worse. This was better than most of the communal bathrooms she had trawled through recently. White tiles covered the walls right up to the ceiling, mottled black ones on the floor, and three white basins lined one wall. Yes, one was chipped and the other had lost its plug, probably stolen, but everything was spotless, including the mirror above the basins. In the corner a tall cupboard door stood half open, revealing a damp mop, bucket, and disinfectant bottle inside. Obviously a cleaner had been in early.

Brushing back her unruly hair, Lydia headed toward one of the three cubicles and glanced with only casual interest at the figure by the basin. Instantly she froze. The other occupant of the room was a woman in her thirties. Average height, slender, wearing a burgundy woolen dressing gown, her feet in stylish little maroon-and-gold slippers. On her finger a thick gold wedding band looked too heavy for her narrow fingers. But Lydia saw none of that. All she saw was the swirl of dark silky hair that was twisted into a loose knot at the back of her head. A narrow neck, long and fragile.

For one blinding moment Lydia believed it was her mother. Returned from the dead. Valentina, come to join in the search for her missing husband, Jens Friis.

An ice pick of pain under Lydia's ribs wrenched her back to reality, and she turned away abruptly, hurried into the first stall, locked the door, and sat down. It wasn't Valentina, of course it wasn't. Reason told her it couldn't be. Just someone of similar age with similar hair. And the neck. That same creamy vulnerable neck.

Lydia shook her head and blinked hard. Valentina was dead. Died in China last year, so why was her mind playing such tricks? Her mother had been the victim of a hand grenade meant for someone

else; she'd been just a beautiful innocent bystander. Lydia had cradled her shattered and lifeless body in her arms. So why this? This
sudden confusion in her mind? She placed one hand over her mouth
to hold in any screams that rattled around inside her lungs.

SHE HAD NO IDEA HOW LONG SHE REMAINED LIKE THAT IN
the stuffy little stall, but it felt like forever. Eventually she unlocked the
door, walked over to one of the spare washbasins, rinsed her hands, and
splashed cold water over her face. Her cheeks were burning. Beside her
the woman was still washing her hands. Lydia avoided looking in the
long mirror above the basins because she didn't want to see her own face,
never mind the other woman's. But her eyes were drawn to the movements the woman was performing next to her. They were hypnotic.

With firm rhythmic strokes she was dragging a wooden nail
brush down her arms from elbow to fingertips, over and over again.
Smooth and unhurried, but relentless. Slowly she rotated each arm
so that the soapy bristles scraped over the soft underside as well as
the upper skin, first one, then the other. Then back to the first one.
Strong, stern strokes. Lydia couldn't make herself look away. The
woman was using a bar of lavender soap that scented the air, and
the water in the basin foamed with bubbles. Not Russian soap then,
that was certain. Bubbles were almost impossible to create with the
greasy Soviet utility soap. More likely French from one of the shops
open only to the Communist Party elite. On a smattering of the
bubbles gleamed tiny specks of scarlet. Her skin looked raw.

Without looking up from her task, the woman asked, "Are you
all right?"

The voice was completely calm, totally composed, and it took
Lydia by surprise.

"*Da,*" Lydia said. "Yes."

"You were a long time in there."

"Was I?"

"Have you been crying?"

"No."

The woman sank one whole forearm into the basin, let the soapy
water swirl over it, and murmured a long, drawn-out "Aah!"

Lydia wasn't sure whether it was pain or pleasure. The woman flicked a glance in her direction, and for the first time Lydia saw her eyes. They were dark brown, deep set, and not a bit like Valentina's. She had pale skin, as if she had lived her life indoors.

"Don't stare," the woman said in a sharp tone.

Lydia blinked, leaning back against the washbasin. "We all do things," she said, and folded her coat tight across her chest. The room was chill. "To make ourselves feel better, I mean."

"Like shutting yourself in a lavatory?"

"No. Not that."

"So"—the speculative eyes slid again to Lydia—"what does a young girl like you do to make herself feel better?"

"I steal." Lydia hadn't meant to say it. She was appalled that the words had crept out. It had something to do with the unreal hour of the morning.

One dark arched eyebrow shot up. "Why?"

Lydia shrugged. It was too late to take the words back. "The usual. My mother and I were poor, so we needed money."

"And now?"

Lydia shrugged once more, a gesture her brother was always pointing out made her seem unthinking. Was he right? Did it? She stared thoughtfully at the neat maroon slippers.

"It became a habit?" the woman asked.

"Something like that, I suppose." She glanced up and caught the woman's gaze intent on her, saw it slide away self-consciously from Lydia's smooth pale hands to her own scuffed ones. In the mirror reflection, she saw something falter deep in the dark eyes, a crack opening up somewhere. Lydia gave her a smile. At this unearthly hour of the morning, normal rules of conduct didn't quite apply. The woman returned the smile, lifted her arm from the water, and gestured toward a smart leather bag on the windowsill.

"Feel free to steal from me, if it helps," she offered.

"Don't tempt me," Lydia smiled.

The woman laughed and reached for a pristine square of white toweling that was draped ready over one shoulder, but in doing so, she tugged too hard and it tumbled to the floor. Lydia watched the pale face crumple in panic.

"It's all right," she reassured the woman quickly and stooped to pick it up. "The floor's clean. It's just been washed."

"I know. I washed it. I washed everything."

Lydia spoke soothingly, in the same tone she had used with her pet rabbit when he was nervous. "Don't worry, no harm done. You can use the other side of the towel, the side that didn't touch the floor."

"No!"

"There's a hotel towel on the wall over there."

"No. I can't touch that . . . thing." She said the last word as if it were covered in slime.

"Do you have another one?"

The woman breathed out. Nodded and pointed to her bag. Lydia immediately went to it, removed a small paper package from its depths, and opened it up to reveal another pristine square of white. Without actually touching the material anywhere, she held it out to the woman but kept a good arm's length away from her. Any closer she knew would be too close. For both of them.

"Thank you. *Spasibo*."

She patted her dripping arms, meticulously dabbing at each spot, and Lydia noticed scarlet hairline cracks in the skin.

"You need cream on them," she said matter-of-factly.

"I have gloves."

The woman walked over to the leather bag and, using only fore-finger and thumb, carefully extracted a pair of long white cotton gloves. She slid her hands into them and released a soft sigh of relief.

"Better?" Lydia asked.

"Much."

"Good. I'll say good night then." She moved toward the door.

"*Do svidania*. Good-bye and . . . thank you." Lydia had opened the door when the woman asked quietly, "What's your name?"

"Lydia. And yours?"

"Antonina."

"Get some sleep, comrade."

Slowly the woman's head started to swing from side to side. "*Nyet*, no, I have no time to sleep. You see . . ." For an awkward moment no words came, then she murmured, "I am the wife of the camp commandant, so . . ." The words stopped again. With an uncertain frown, she stared for a long moment at the pure white gloves.

In the silence Lydia whispered, "The camp? You mean Trovitsk prison camp?"

"*Da*."

Lydia shuddered. She couldn't help it. Abruptly she left the washroom. But as the door closed behind her, she heard the taps start to run once more.

Two

THAT EVENING NOTHING HAD CHANGED. THE same confusing hotel, the same people moaning about the cold when really all they wanted to complain about was the lack of a reliable railway system. All waiting for the same train that never came. Lydia's feet ached from standing on a frozen station platform all day, but now she pushed it from her mind. It was time to concentrate.

In the heart of the hotel the room stank. Stank like a camel pen because there had been a delivery of dung today to burn on the fire. It was a big shambling place, a gloomy bar of sorts, packed with too many vodka-stained eyes and too much greed. Lydia drew a slow breath and watched carefully. She felt the greed throb in the air around her, crawling like a living thing from one man to another, creeping through their mouths and nostrils down into their empty bellies and their crusted lungs. She had to time it right. Just right. Or Liev Popkov's arm would break.

Money was thrust into hands. Men shouted across the room and spirals of cigarette smoke rose, turning the air as gray and thick as rabbit fur. In one corner a forgotten dog hurled itself forward to the limit of its stubby chain, choking off its bark. Its scrawny rib cage heaved with excitement.

All eyes were focused on the struggle taking place at the center table. Chairs had been kicked roughly aside. Bodies jostled to find a place close, close enough to see the sweat burst forth and veins rear up like serpents under the skin. Two men were seated opposite each other. Big men. Men who looked as if they chewed the heads off weasels for fun. Their heavy bearded features were contorted with effort and the greasy black eye patch of one of them had slipped out of place, revealing a sunken twisted socket the color of overripe plums. Their massive forearms were locked in battle.

The arm wrestling had been Liev Popkov's idea. Lydia hated it at first. And yet in a strange insidious kind of way she loved it at the same time. Hate. Love. She shrugged. A hair's breadth between them.

"You're out of your crazy Cossack mind!" she responded when he came out with the idea. He'd just downed half a tankard of rotgut vodka.

"*Nyet*. No."

"What if you lose? We need every rouble of the money we have left."

"Hah!" He shook his big shaggy bear's head. "Look, little Lydia."

He jerked up the sleeve of his filthy shirt, seized her hand in his paw, and placed her fingers on his massive bicep. It didn't feel like a piece of human anatomy. It felt more like a winter log that had been warming in front of the fire. She had seen him break a man's face with it.

"Popkov," she whispered, "you are a devil."

"I know."

His white teeth flashed at her above the black beard and together they had laughed.

Now she glanced quickly up at the gallery landing above them. It coiled round two sides of the room and led to the corridor of shoeboxes that the hotel chose to call bedrooms. A tall figure was up there, leaning forward, alert and staring down on the scrum beneath him, his arms resting on the banister rail, his thumbs linked as if he couldn't bear his flesh to touch its grimy surface.

Alexei Serov. Her half-brother.

They shared a father, if it could be called sharing. Which Lydia doubted.

His brown hair was swept back from his face, emphasizing the arrogant forehead inherited from his aristocratic Russian mother, the Countess Serova. But his fierce green eyes came straight from the Viking father Lydia could only dimly remember. Jens Friis was their father's name, a Danish name neither of them bore. Jens had worked as an engineer until 1917 for the last tsar of Russia, Nicholas II, and now more than twelve years later he was the reason that she and Alexei had spent months travelling with the unruly Popkov in tow all the way through the mountains of China to this godforsaken dead-and-alive hole in Russia.

A shout dragged her attention back to where it should have been, and her young stomach swooped with a sudden flutter of panic. Popkov was losing. Not just pretend losing. Really losing.

She felt sick. Coins were pouring into the grubby green kerchief where the bets were held on the bar, and all of them were now against Popkov. That was exactly what she and he had planned, but she'd left too late her signal to him to start fighting back. The burly black hairs on his forearm were only a hand's breadth from the surface of the table as his opponent forced him down and the bulging muscle started to twitch and shake.

No, Popkov, no.

Damn it, how could she have left it so late? She knew he would see his arm break before he'd allow it to collapse in defeat.

"God damn you, Popkov," she yelled at the top of her lungs, "are you some kind of *babushka* or what? Put a bit of effort into it, will you?"

She saw his teeth flash, his shoulder swell. His fist lifted a fraction, though he never took his one good eye off his opponent's face.

"He's done for!" someone shouted.

"*Da,* I'll drink well tonight." Raucous laughter.

"Finish the job. You've got him . . ."

Sweat dripped onto the stained table, and the dog in the corner barked in time to their rapid heartbeat until someone slapped it down. Lydia elbowed a path through the crush of bodies to stand right behind Popkov, desperately rubbing her own right forearm as if by doing so she could rub fresh life into Popkov's tearing muscle.

She couldn't let him lose. Couldn't.

To hell with the money.

UP ON THE LANDING ALEXEI SEROV LIT A BLACK CHEROOT AND flipped the dead match down on the drinkers below.

The girl was impossible. Didn't she realize what she was doing?

He narrowed his eyes against the pall of smoke that clung to his hair and his skin like dead men's breath. There were probably thirty men down there in the bar, plus a handful of women in dark dreary clothing, heavy gray skirts, and brown shawls. That was one of the things he loathed most about this new Stalinist Russia, the dreariness of it. All the towns the same. Depressing gray concrete, gray garb, and gray faces, dull eyes that slid away from you to the gray shadows and mouths that stayed firmly shut. He missed the exuberant colors of China, the same way he missed its swooping rooflines and vibrant songbirds.

Lydia was proving harder to deal with than he'd expected. When he'd sat her down and explained the dangers here, she'd just laughed that effortless laugh of hers, tossed her flaming hair at him, and assured him with eyes wide that she might be only seventeen, but she'd lived with danger before and knew how to handle it.

"But this danger is different," he'd explained patiently. "It's everywhere. In the air you breathe, in the black bread, the *khleb* you eat and in the pillow that lies under your head at night. This is Josef Stalin's Russia. It's 1930. No one is safe."

"*Davai, davai, davai!*"

"Come on, come on, come on!"

The gamblers in the bar were chanting the words, and to Alexei it sounded dismally like the bleating of sheep. The locals had bet their petty kopecks on their own man and now crowded round the pair, who were locked together as intimately as a couple in the throes of sexual frenzy, mouths open and spittle in silver threads between their lips. There was nothing more than a shiver between Popkov's arm and the table. You couldn't slide a goddamn knife between them.

Alexei felt his heart kick up a pace, and that was when Lydia leaned down to the Cossack and whispered something in his ear. She was a small slender figure among the bulk of broad swarthy faces and thick padded waists, but her hair stood out like a fire down there in the dim light as it drew close to the greasy black curls and stayed there.

It took a moment. No more. Then slowly the massive arm began to rise, to force the other arm back, a whisper at a time, until the crowd began to howl its anguish. The local man flared his broad flat nostrils and roared a battle cry, but it did him no good. Popkov's arm was unstoppable.

What the hell was she saying to him?

A final roar from Popkov and the battle was over, as he drove his opponent's meaty fist flat onto the surface. The force of the impact made the table screech as if in pain. Alexei pushed himself back from the banister, turned on his heel, and set off for his room, but not before he'd seen Lydia dart a glance in his direction. Her wide tawny eyes were ablaze with the light of victory.

ALEXEI LEANED HIS BACK CASUALLY AGAINST THE CLOSED DOOR of Lydia's room and looked around the tiny space. It was no better than a cell. A narrow bed, a wooden chair, and a metal hook on the back of the door. That was it. He'd say this for her, she never moaned about the conditions however bad they were.

It was dark outside, a wind rattling a bunch of loose shingles on the roof, and the naked overhead lightbulb flickered every now and again. In Russia, Alexei had learned, you never take anything for granted. You appreciate *everything*. Because you never know when it will disappear. You may have electricity today, but it could vanish tomorrow. Heating pipes shook and shuddered like trams on Nevsky one day dispensing a warm fug of heat, but lay silent and cold the next. The same with trains. When would the next one arrive? Tomorrow? Next week? Even next month? To travel any distance across this vast and relentless country, you had to have the patience of Lenin in his damn mausoleum.

"Don't grumble."

Alexei's gaze flicked to Lydia. "I'm not grumbling. I'm not even speaking."

"But I can hear you. Inside my head. Grumbling."

"Why would I be grumbling, Lydia? Tell me why."

She pushed back her hair, lifted her head, and gave him a sharp glance. She had a way of doing that which was always catching him off guard, making him feel she could see inside his head. She was sitting cross-legged on the bed, the thin quilt pulled around her shoulders and a square of green material between her knees. Her busy fingers were counting out her winnings into small piles.

"Because you're angry with me about the arm wrestling for some reason." Lydia studied the money thoughtfully. "It does no harm, Alexei. It's not as if I'm stealing."

He refused to accept the bait. Her thieving activities of the past, snatching wallets and watches the way a fox snatches chickens, were not something he cared to discuss right now.

"No," he said, "but you took something from them downstairs and they won't thank you for it."

Lydia shrugged her thin shoulders and returned to her miniature coin towers. "I took their money because they lost."

"Not the money."

"What do you mean?"

"Their pride. You took away their pride, then you rubbed their noses in it by emptying their pockets."

Her eyes remained firmly on the money. "It was fairly won."

"Fairly won," he echoed. "Fairly won." He shook his head angrily but kept his voice low, his words deliberately measured. "That is not the point, Lydia."

She twirled one of the coins between her fingers and flashed him another quick glance. "So what is your point?"

"They won't forget you."

A shimmer of a smile touched her full lips. "So?"

"So when anyone comes asking questions, the people here will take pleasure in recalling every detail about you. Not just the color of your hair or how many vodkas you fed into Popkov or your name or your age or the names of your companions. No, Lydia. They'll remember carefully the numbers on your passport and on your travel permit and even what train ticket is hidden away in your body belt."

Her eyes widened and a blush started to creep up her cheek. "Why would anyone bother to remember all that? And who would come asking?" Suddenly her tawny eyes were nervous. "Who, Alexei?"

He pushed his shoulders away from the door and only one half-pace took him to the bed, where he sat down next to her. The mattress was bullet hard and the three piles of coins shifted slightly in her lap.

She treated him to a surprised smile, but her gaze was wary. "What?"

He leaned close, so close he could hear the whisper-soft clicking of her teeth behind the smooth curve of her cheek. "First of all, keep your voice down. The walls are paper thin. That's not just to save money on materials; they're designed to be like that." His voice was the faintest trickle in her ear. "So everyone can eavesdrop on everybody else. A neighbor can report a muttered complaint about the cost of bread or about the incompetence of the rail system."

She gave him that direct look again and rolled her eyes so dramatically he almost laughed out loud, but stifled it with a frown instead.

"Damn it, listen to me, Lydia."

She took his hand, scooped up one of the piles in her lap, and dribbled twenty coins onto his palm.

"I don't want your money," he objected.

But she gently wrapped his fingers round the little heap, one by one.

"Keep it," she whispered. "One day you may need it."

Then she turned her face to him and kissed his cheek. Her lips felt feather-soft and warm on his skin. His throat tightened. It was the first time such an intimate gesture had passed between them. They'd known each other for eighteen months now, much of it unaware of the fact that they were brother and sister, and he'd even seen her stark naked that terrible day in the woods outside Junchow. But a kiss. No, never that.

He stood up awkwardly and flexed his legs. The room was suddenly claustrophobic, and silent except for the vibration of a woman snoring next door.

"Lydia, I'm just trying to protect you."

"I know."

"Then why do you make everything so . . . ?"

"Difficult?"

"Yes. So damn difficult. As if you prefer it that way."

She shrugged and he studied her for a long moment, the mane of fiery hair that she refused to cut, the delicate heart-shaped face with candle-pale skin, and the firm chin she was in the habit of picking at when nervous. She was seventeen years old, that's all. He needed to make her understand, but he knew she had long ago learned to be stubborn, learned to be strong enough and difficult enough to deal with the hardships of her life. He knew that. Something in him wanted to reach out to her, to bridge the gap between them and touch her, to pat her shoulder or her undisciplined hair, to reassure her. But he was certain she wouldn't welcome it, would regard it as pity.

Instead he said gently, "We have to work together, Lydia."

But she didn't look at him, didn't answer.

Just a faint murmur escaped her lips, and it struck him as a wretched and lonely sound. Alexei saw her eyes unfocused and her lips moving silently. She'd gone. Sometimes she did that. When things became too much. She would disappear, leave him and float away into her own private world, somewhere in her head that brought her . . . what? Joy? Comfort? Escape from this dingy room and this dingy life?

Alexei's back stiffened. He could guess where she'd gone. And with whom. Abruptly he opened the door to leave.

"I'll see you at the station tomorrow," he said in a brisk voice.

No reply.

He walked out and shut the door with a sharp click behind him.

ALEXEI STEPPED OUT INTO THE GLOOMY CORRIDOR AND stopped dead. Right in front of Lydia's door loomed Liev Popkov, that crazy Cossack of hers. Alexei himself was tall and unused to looking up at people, but Popkov was considerably taller and as broad-chested and bad-tempered as a water buffalo. Popkov didn't back off. He was rooted to the scuffed floorboards, deliberately in Alexei's way, huge arms folded across his chest so that he seemed to swell with every breath. He was chewing something vile that turned his teeth the color of old leather.

"Get out of my way," Alexei said quietly.

"Leave her alone."

Alexei gave him a long cool stare. "Leave who alone?"

"She's young."

"She's dangerous because she's impetuous. She has to learn."

"Not from you."

"You let her take a risk tonight in that bar."

"*Nyet*. You are the danger. You, not her. You, with all your fancy talk and your aristocratic stiff neck. I tell you, each day that dawns in this land, *you* are the risk to us, not . . ."

"You're a brainless fool, Popkov."

"I'm here to protect her."

"You?" Alexei dragged out the single word and gave the Cossack a slow insulting smile.

"*Da*." Popkov's black curls were as unruly as his temper and sprang over the ragged scar that sliced across his forehead into the eyepatch. "*Da*." Popkov spat it out more vehemently, his breath escaping in a foul-smelling hiss.

"Frighten her," he growled, "and I will rip your fucking balls off."

Alexei's eyes narrowed. He spoke softly. "Touch me and I'll snap your windpipe before you even open your ignorant mouth to cry for help. Now tell me what she said to you."

"What?"

"Tell me, ox-brain, what she said to you when you were arm wrestling. What words, when you were dead in the water, did she whisper in your ear that made you find the strength to win?"

"You'll never know."

Alexei dropped his voice. "Did she promise to fuck you, is that it?"

The big man bellowed.

A door slammed open. The sound of it cracking against a wall reverberated down the corridor and bounced off the gray walls, jerking both men's attention off each other and onto the woman who was standing in the doorway of the room next to Lydia's. Her hands were planted firmly on her hips, feet wide apart, apparently unaware that her striped cotton nightshirt was unbuttoned to the waist, allowing an intimate, if partial, glimpse of the curves of her abundant breasts.

"Shut up, you braying donkeys!" she yelled at them. "I'm trying to sleep here and all I get is two oafs banging their heads together."

Alexei took in her broad flat feet with toenails that seemed structured out of moose horn, the loose hang of her stomach under the nightshirt, her tangled hair that may once have been a luxuriant brown but now had the color and texture of last year's hay bales. With an effort he kept his gaze firmly away from her breasts.

He gave a small stiff bow of his head. "My apologies."

"Piss on your apologies, comrade," she snapped. "Just let me get some sleep."

Alexei glanced across at Popkov and nearly burst out laughing. The big bearded ox was standing there with his mouth gaping wide open, his one good eye focused without the slightest embarrassment on the pale half-moons on display. Little grunting noises escaped from his throat.

The woman was having none of it. Her dark eyebrows shot up and she darted forward, jabbing the Cossack in the stomach with a thick finger, not once but three times. Instantly Popkov recoiled, lurched back against the opposite wall as though prodded with a rifle butt, and Alexei took the opportunity to stride off down the corridor without another word. He needed some peace. Some quiet. Needed to think. *Dear merciful God, protect me from the insanity of these peasants.*

Three

BREATHE, MY LOVE, BREATHE.

The voice was Chang An Lo's, and it echoed as strong and clear in Lydia's head as Junchow's temple bell.

Don't snatch at bites of air like a dog snatches at crumbs. You must learn to breathe with exactly the same concentration with which you learned to walk.

She smiled, alone in her room, dumped the coins on the bed, and rose to her feet, so that she could straighten her spine and lift her ribs out of their slump. She inhaled slowly, like pulling on a long reel of fishing line the way he'd taught her, so deep and so smooth that her skin prickled as the inrush of oxygen brought it to life.

"Like just the thought of you, Chang An Lo, brings me to life."

She'd had no idea it would be like this. This bad. Being parted from him, not knowing where he was or even whether he was still alive. No word of any kind. Five months and eleven days it had been. Of this. This agony. She'd known it would be hard but not that it would be this . . . unbearable. That she'd forget how to think, to breathe, to be. How could she still be Lydia Ivanova when all that was best in her was with him back there in China?

Chang had saved her life. It happened in the colorful old town of Junchow on the wide open plains of northern China. In an alleyway she'd got herself caught between an old man latched like a leech on to her wrist and a painted lady, both intent on kidnapping her, but Chang had come flying like a black-haired dragon through the air. And after that, she'd belonged to him utterly. It was as simple as that. Despite the anger and tears of those around them who'd fought to break them up, they had fallen in love. But now he was away from her and in the kind of danger she couldn't bear to think about.

Oh my love, take care. Take great care. For my sake.

He was a Communist revolutionary fighting in Mao Tse-tung's rebel Red Army in China, and time and again when she lay awake in the dark hours before dawn she brooded over whether she should be there at his side. Instead of traipsing across Russia, searching for a father she hadn't seen since she was five years old. But she and Chang had agreed. It wasn't possible. She would be as much a danger to him as one of Chiang Kai-shek's bullets. If she were in China with him, she would always be his weak spot, distracting him, the pressure point his enemies could use. *No, my love, even though it was like watching blood flow from my own artery, I had to let you go.*

Her fingers brushed the rose-colored talisman he'd given her and she recalled the last time he came to her, standing tall and strong in the doorway of the old shed. His black hair tousled by the wind, an air of wildness about him, a grubby green blanket thrown over his shoulders in place of a coat. His eyes wanting her.

I must leave you here, the light of my soul, he'd said. *Leave you safe.*

Safe? She started to prowl back and forth across the narrow space. What was the point of being safe, if it meant being without the one person who made her blood sing? Was that why she kept taking the risks that Alexei so hated? Poor Alexei; she knew she drove him mad at times. Her half-brother had been brought up as part of a privileged elite, first in the scented salons of Russia and then in China. He was used to order and discipline. Not this uncertainty, not this chaos. And it didn't help that he and the Cossack loathed each other, while she was caught in the middle between them. It was Liev Popkov who had brought the news from Russia to Junchow, to her mother, Valentina, news that the husband she thought had died in 1917 during their escape as White Russians from the fury of the Bolsheviks was in fact alive in a prison camp.

How he discovered this she never found out, but Lydia believed him implicitly. He'd helped her in China when she'd been searching for Chang An Lo in the dangerous docklands of Junchow. Popkov had protected her fiercely, throwing her money back at her when she'd offered it for his services as a bodyguard. It was only later when she learned that he—and his father before him—had been devoted servants to her grandfather in St. Petersburg in the days of the tsar that she understood. She felt a rush of affection for the big Cossack. His devotion touched her. Deeply. She trusted him, and that was something she valued above all else, it was so rare. Trust.

Can I trust Alexei?

Lydia shivered and moved over to the narrow window in her room, where she stared out for a long time at the vast winter sky. Watching the stars glitter in the darkness and the lights shimmer in the houses as the small town of Selyansk settled down for the night. Once again she felt the landscape of Russia slide into her heart, calming her and chiming with some image already deep inside her. She loved this country, loved its magnificent tortured soul. Just to have her feet stamping on Russian soil after the long absence in China satisfied some intense need that she hadn't even realized was there.

Did Alexei feel it too? That need? She wasn't sure. He was hard to read. But she was getting better at it, and even though he believed he kept his thoughts hidden behind that veil of indifference—using that rigid self-discipline of his that she both envied and loathed—she was learning to spot a faint rise of an eyebrow. Or a tightening of a cheek muscle. Or a fractional twitch of the lips when amused.

Oh yes, Alexei, you're not as inscrutable as you would like. I hunt around inside you, sniffing out the secrets you try to hide. We may have the same father, but our mothers were very different. Nor am I as blind as you think. You hated it when I kissed your cheek tonight, didn't you? You couldn't get out of this room fast enough. As if I'd bitten you. Don't you want me as a sister? Is that it? Am I not what you would have wished for? Have I spilled too much of our aristocratic blood out of my veins and filled them instead with the instincts of a wild alley cat, as my mother used to claim?

Though Lydia and Alexei had been living in the same town in China for many years, they had moved in very different circles and their paths had never crossed. It was only when her mother's new fiancé had introduced her to the sophisticated glamour and bright lights of the elite society in Junchow that Lydia had met Alexei. In a French restaurant, she recalled. And she'd thought him arrogant and cold.

Yet he'd been generous with his help when she needed it, and after her mother's death last year she'd learned the truth in a letter Valentina had left for her. That Alexei's mother might be the wealthy Countess Serova, but his father was Jens Friis, the Danish engineer. The affair happened in St. Petersburg long before he married Valentina, but Alexei had been as shocked as Lydia herself by the discovery that they were related. She knew it had shaken his world as much as it had shaken hers. They had each been an only child until that point, dealing with the loneliness in their own different ways, but now . . . She conjured up the image of his straight back, his neat brown hair, and controlled smile . . . now she had a brother. One who was as committed to finding their father as she was.

A sudden ache in her throat caught her unawares at the thought of her father locked in one of Stalin's brutal prison camps. She rested her forehead against the icy pane, and the shock of the cold glass jerked her mind away from places it didn't want to go. She focused on tomorrow. The station. Another long day for her between Alexei and Popkov. It was wrong what she'd done in the bar, using whispers about Alexei to bait the Cossack.

"See him up there, Popkov? Watching you."

Her words blew hot on the black hairs in his ears.

"He wants you to lose, he's laughing, Popkov, sneering."

"*Da,* you're winning now . . ."

"He's gone. Couldn't bear to watch you win."

But she couldn't have let him lose. He'd have just set about getting himself drunk out of his skull for a week, refusing to travel, refusing even to speak. It had happened before. Just grunts would come out of his mouth and just vodka would go in.

She turned abruptly to the bed, where the remaining coins lay in two equal heaps. One pile she tipped inside one of her mittens, burying it deep in her pack the way a fox stores food for the winter.

The other she folded up in the green cloth, ready for Popkov in the morning. The morning. Another dawn to get through. She never felt lonelier than when she woke up to find that Chang An Lo wasn't there in bed beside her, but maybe tomorrow they would at last get out of this tired little town. She tapped a finger impatiently on the black windowpane as if to wake up whatever forces were out there and uttered the words she had whispered every single night for the last five months.

"Jens Friis, I am coming for you."

And as always Chang An Lo's warning whispered into her ear: *You will step into the dragon's jaws.*

THE RAILWAY STATION OF SELYANSK WASN'T IN THE CENTER OF the town, but perched on the western edge as an afterthought. The ticket office and nicotine-stained waiting room were built of good straight pine, though the brown paint was peeling away in strips. The winter air was brittle, and a chill wind stiffened Lydia's cheeks as she walked onto the crowded platform, her eyes darting from face to face, alert for new travelers. The family huddles were familiar now, cocooned in their padded *fufaikas*, gazing along the lines of the silvery rails as if willpower alone could summon up a train with its smoky breath.

She spotted the strangers immediately. Six men and one woman. Her pulse gave an uneasy kick, but she allowed herself no more than an indifferent glance as she walked past. Nevertheless she took in every detail.

What were they doing here in Selyansk station?

Three of the men looked innocent enough, one a lone laborer in rough homespun trousers and rubber boots, while two others had the air of government apparatchiks dressed in well-cut overcoats. They looked sleek and contented and spoke in loud voices instead of the usual whispers. Lydia was sick to the pit of her stomach of words hidden behind hands and eyes that clung to the floor so that there was no danger of thoughts spilling out for anyone to see. Or report on. She smiled at the men and their laughter.

"What's so funny?" It was Alexei.

He was at the end of the platform, leaning against an empty oil drum and smoking one of his foul black cheroots. She was glad he had discarded the expensive winter overcoat he'd arrived with in Russia and replaced it with a coarse black woolen one. It swung around his ankles and had a small tear in the collar as if someone had yanked it too hard in a fight. Yet even in plain workman's clothes he still managed to look elegant and somehow untouchable, dangerous even, she sometimes thought. There was a controlled coldness in his eyes that warned others against approaching too close. Well, she was his sister. She'd come as close as she damn well pleased.

"Good morning, brother. *Dobroye utro*," she said cheerfully. "Let's hope we'll get out of this rat hole today," she added and swung her canvas bag on top of the oil drum.

His mouth curved into an obliging smile. "Good morning, *sestra*, sister. Did you sleep well?"

"Like an overfed cat. And you?"

"Very well, *spasibo*. Thank you."

Both knew they were lying, but it didn't matter. It was their morning routine. She looked around her.

"Where's Popkov? I thought he'd be here by now."

Alexei shook his head. He was wearing an old *shapka* with ear-flaps, and its softness emphasized the sharpness of his facial bones. Lydia abruptly realized he had grown thinner. She stared at the hollows that had appeared under his cheekbones and felt an unease press on her chest. Were they so short of money already?

He gave her a close-lipped smile. "Popkov has gone off in search of food for the journey."

The Cossack was their scavenger when supplies were scarce. Lydia wanted to help him—she was quick with her fingers—but Alexei wouldn't permit it. They'd argued, but he was adamant.

"This country is not like China, Lydia. If you steal here, even just a handful of bread or a couple of eggs, you will be sent to a prison labor camp and die there."

"Only if you're caught."

"No. It's too dangerous."

She'd conceded with a shrug, unwilling to admit that his warning had frightened her. She knew what it was to be locked up.

"Any word on the arrival of a train?" she asked.

"The usual."

"*Maybe today.* That's what the stationmaster always bleats."

"So this time it could be true."

She nodded and let her glance roam casually over the straggly trees on the far side of the track, their skeletons etched in ice. Then as if in no hurry, she turned to the headscarves and flat caps of her fellow travelers. Casually. It took an effort, but she kept her expression neutral as she sought out the three other figures who had joined the usual crowd. Two men, one woman. The two men wore uniforms she didn't recognize, and both possessed an air of authority that made her wary of eye contact, but she noticed them glance her way. A couple of paces to one side of them stood the woman.

"Don't stare." Alexei's voice was gentle.

"I'm not staring."

"You are."

"Of course I'm not. I'm just admiring her fur coat."

"Admire something else."

Lydia dragged her eyes from the woman's long dark hair, from the way it curled softly on her collar and swayed like a delicate glossy wing across her cheek as she moved her head. Exactly as Valentina's used to. Bile, bitter tasting, rose in Lydia's throat.

"From the back the resemblance to her is striking," Alexei murmured, his breath billowing white in the chill air.

"Resemblance to whom?"

Alexei gave Lydia a long unblinking stare, then dropped the subject. He took a drag on his cheroot and slid a glance in the direction of the two uniformed men.

"They know the train is coming or they wouldn't be here."

"You think so?"

"No question. It'll come today."

"I hope Popkov hurries up. I don't want him left behind."

Even as she said it, she sensed it was a mistake. Alexei gave her a look but made no comment. She knew there was nothing he'd like better than for Liev Popkov to be left behind in Selyansk. He cast another glance over in the woman's direction. "I wonder who she is," he said under his breath. "She sticks out like a sore thumb in a place like this."

Lydia allowed herself another look, a lingering stare this time at the woman's silvery fur coat that seemed to shine in the dull wintry light. She noted the stylish matching hat perched at an angle, the pale gray boots as soft as kittens' paws, and the flash of a creamy cashmere scarf at the throat. The woman looked as if she'd strolled off Leningrad's Nevsky Prospekt and found herself in a farmyard by mistake.

"Her name is Antonina," Lydia said quietly.

Alexei looked at Lydia with surprise. "How in hell's name do you know that?"

"I learn things."

"And how exactly did you learn that?"

"She told me herself."

"When?"

"Yesterday. In the hotel bathroom."

Alexei stubbed out his cheroot under his boot and took a deep breath. Lydia could see he was thinking hard, working out the odds of his sister having blundered. She touched his sleeve with her fingers.

"It's all right, brother. I did no harm. I was careful, I told her nothing."

"So what else did you learn about this woman?"

Lydia let her gaze be drawn back to the ripple of dark hair and the arrogant lift of the chin.

"She's the commandant's wife."

ALEXEI STUDIED THE WOMAN. THE CAMP COMMANDANT'S wife. Now that was interesting. No wonder the uniforms hovered so close.

He experienced a sudden unreasonable rush of hope. He knew it was totally unwarranted, ridiculous even, but he was powerless to crush it. Last summer in China he'd jumped on a train with Lydia without a backward glance, and together they'd headed hundreds of bone-shaking miles north across the border to Vladivostok to find a father neither of them had seen or heard of for more than twelve years. Alexei had done it for a whole handful of different reasons, but expectation of success was certainly not one of them.

In his heart he was certain their search for Jens Friis was doomed to failure, but he never uttered a word of this to Lydia. The Soviet

State was too massive and too resolute a fist to prize open, and anyway their father was surely dead by now. Few could survive in those terrible camps where conditions were so harsh. The slave work in mines or on railways or canals or roads in freezing Siberian temperatures was brutal. Worse than brutal. Life out there was too thin, a brittle thread too easily snapped. The death rate was unimaginable.

Nevertheless, Alexei had come. Why?

Night after night on their long journey into Russia, he'd lain awake in bed in the early hours of the morning in some flea-bitten hostel or other smoking cigarette after cigarette. He'd been forced to listen to the snores and loose farts of the other men in the Soviet communal dormitories while he considered and discarded one plan after another. In reality he knew planning was pointless. They had no way of knowing what lay ahead, so what purpose did it serve?

None. Absolutely none. But he was military trained and could no more stop his thoughts making precise preparations than he could prevent this sudden burst of hope at the sight of the commandant's wife. He looked across at his sister on the station platform. She was totally unaware of how she drew eyes to herself, envious eyes. Not for her drab brown coat or her straight young back. Not even for her flame-colored hair, which she'd tucked under her woolen hat as he'd instructed, but which crawled back out in rebellious tendrils as soon as she wasn't paying attention.

No. Not for any of those did the eyes follow her. It was because there was an irrepressible air about her, an energy that they all envied, all craved. There was something unbroken, untamed in the way she swung her head or darted her eyes. They envied her that. However much he clothed her in drooping coats and stuck ugly hats on her head, he couldn't hide it. He lit himself another cheroot and saw Lydia turn her head, give him a soft, almost shy, smile.

He knew why he'd come. He'd come for her.

"WE'RE CLOSE NOW."

Alexei's words caught Lydia by surprise. They were about to climb on to the train. Just when it seemed they'd be stranded for yet another interminable day, the train had announced itself with a belch of smoke. The crush of passengers surged around them on the platform but the big Cossack grinned, holding them back from the steps to make space for Lydia. Alexei offered a hand to help her up the steps into the train, and that was when he said, "We're close now."

"It's taken us long enough." She felt a rush of affection as she gripped his hand.

"It's just a matter of narrowing the distance, day by day."

"I know, and we're getting better at it, Alexei. We're close now and we'll stay that way."

He hesitated, but he returned the pressure of her fingers. Only then did it occur to Lydia that she may have misunderstood. Alexei may not have been talking about them—about himself and her. He could have been referring to the fact that they were getting closer to the camp. Suddenly she felt mortified at her blunder.

"Lydia." Alexei leapt up on the step behind her and touched her shoulder. "I'm glad I came."

She turned and looked at him. "I'm glad you did too," she said.

LYDIA TUCKED THE RUG TIGHTLY AROUND HER KNEES AND SANK deeper into her seat between Alexei and Popkov. The train carriage was full but most of her fellow travelers were dozing. An old man over by the door was snuffling into his moustache.

"What part of Russia do you hail from, girl?"

Lydia felt pleased by the question. It made all the aching hours of hard work worth the effort. For months now she'd spoken nothing but Russian and was even finding herself thinking in Russian now. The words seemed to fit inside her mouth as if finally they belonged there. From the moment they left China, Alexei and Popkov adamantly refused to speak anything but Russian to her.

She'd groaned and moaned and whined, but Alexei wouldn't budge. It was fine for him. He'd lived in Leningrad until he was twelve years old and had the advantage that even in China after the Bolshevik Revolution his mother, Countess Serova, had insisted on speaking her native tongue within the home. So no problems for him. The words flowed from him like black Russian oil, and even though he spoke English as elegantly as any English country squire, he refused to let even one word of it pass his lips.

Lydia had cursed him. In English. In Russian. Even in Chinese. "You bastard, Alexei, you're enjoying this. Help me out here."

"*Nyet.*"

"Damn you."

He'd smiled that infuriating smile of his and watched her make a mess of it again and again. It had been a lonely start for her, isolated by her lack of words, but now, though she hated to admit it, she realized he'd been right. She'd learned fast, and now she enjoyed using the language her Russian mother had refused to teach her.

"Russian?" her mother, Valentina, would say in their Chinese attic with a scowl on her beautiful fine-boned face, her dark eyes flashing with contempt. "What good is Russian now? Russia is finished. Look how those murdering Bolsheviks destroy my poor country and strip her naked. I tell you, *maleeshka*, forget Russia. English is the language of the future."

Then she'd toss her long silky hair as if tossing all Russian words out of her head.

But now in a cold and smelly train rattling its way across the great flat plain of northern Russia, Lydia was cramming those words into her own head and listening to the woman opposite her asking, "What part of Russia do you hail from?"

"I come from Smolensk," she lied and saw the woman nod, satisfied.

"From Smolensk," she said again, and liked the sound of it.

Four

China

THE CAVE WAS COLD. COLD ENOUGH TO FREEZE the breath of the gods, yet too shallow to risk a fire. Chang An Lo had hunkered down in the entrance, still as one of the brittle gray rocks that littered the naked mountainside all around him. No movement. Nothing. Gray against the unrelenting gray of the winter sky. But outside the cave a thin dusty crust of snow swirled off the frozen scree and formed stinging tumbles of ice in the air that clung to his eyelashes and nicked the skin of his lips till they bled. He didn't notice. Behind him water trickled down the lichen-draped walls, a whispery treacherous sound that seeped into his mind sharper than the cold.

Hold the mind firm.

Mao Tse-tung's words. The powerful new leader who had wrenched control of the Chinese Communist Party for himself.

Chang blinked his eyes, freeing them from ice, and felt a rogue kick of anger in his guts. *Focus.* He fought to still his mind, to focus on what was to come. Let the gutter-licking gray dogs of Chiang Kai-shek's Nationalist Army learn what he had in store for them, discover what was waiting on the rail track in the valley below. Like an alligator waits in the great Yangzte River. Unseen. Unheard. Until its teeth tear you apart.

Chang moved, no more than the slightest flick of his gloved hand, but it was enough to draw a slender figure from the back of the hollow that the wind and rain had carved out of the rock. The figure, like Chang, wore a heavy cap and padded coat that robbed it of any shape, so only the soft voice in his ear indicated that his companion was female. She crouched beside him, her movements as fluid as the water that seeped into his mind.

"Are they coming?" she whispered.

"The snowdrifts across the valleys will have delayed the train. But yes, it's coming."

"Can we be certain?"

"Hold your mind firm." Chang echoed his leader's words.

His sharp black eyes scanned the mountainous landscape around him. China was an unforgiving land, especially harsh on those who had to scrape a living from its bleak treeless terrain up here where the relentless winds from Siberia raked the surface free of soil like fingernails scraping dirt off the skin. Yet something about this place satisfied his soul, something hard and demanding, the mountains a symbol of stillness and balance.

Not like the soft humid breezes that he had grown used to in recent months down south in the provinces of Hunan and Jiangxi. That was where the Communist heartland lay. There in Mao Tse-tung's own hideout near Nanchang, Chang had smelt a sticky sweetness in the air that turned his stomach. It was in the paddy fields. On the terraces. In the Communist training camps. That smell of corruption. Of a man crazed by power.

Chang had spoken to no one about his awareness of it, told none of his brother Communists of his sense that something at the heart of things wasn't quite as it should be. They were all, himself included, willing to fight Chiang Kai-shek's ruling Nationalists and die for what they believed in, yet . . . Chang inhaled sharply. His friend Li Ta-chao had been dedicated to the cause and had died with his sixty comrades in the heart of Peking itself. Chang spat his disgust onto the barren rock. His friend had been betrayed. Executed by slow strangulation. There was nothing definite Chang could point to and say, *This is where the corruption lies.* Just an uneasy rustle in his soul. A cold wind that cut deep and made him wary.

It was certainly nothing he could mention to Kuan. He turned to her now and studied her intense young face with its straight brows and high broad cheekbones. It wasn't what any man would call a pretty face, but it possessed a strength and determination that Chang cared for. And when she smiled—which was rare—it was as if some dark demon vanished from her spirit and let the light inside her glow bright as the morning sun.

"Kuan," he murmured, "do you ever think about the lives we take when we commit ourselves to an action like this? About the parents bereaved? About the wives and children whose hearts will break when the knock comes to their door with the news?"

Her body shivered close beside his shoulder and she turned her head quickly to face him, the soft pads of her cheeks red with cold. But he could sense the shiver was not one of horror, could see it in her eyes, hear it in the shallow rhythm of her breathing. It was a shiver of excitement.

"No, my friend, I don't," she said. "You, Chang An Lo, are the one who planned this operation, who guided us here. We followed you, so surely you're not . . ." Her voice trailed away, unwilling to give life to the words.

"No, I'm not altering my plan."

"Good. The train is coming, you say."

"Yes. Soon. And Chiang Kai-shek's dung eaters deserve to die. They massacre our brothers with no hesitation."

She nodded, a vehement jerk of her head, her breath coiling in the gray air.

"We are at war," Chang said, his eyes on the gun at his belt. "People die."

"Yes, a war we will win so that Communism can bring justice and equality to the people of China." Up on the godforsaken icy mountain ledge, Kuan smiled at Chang and he felt the heat of it warm just the outer edge of the cold void that lay black and empty in the cavern of his chest.

"Long live our great and wise leader, Mao," Kuan said urgently.

"Long live our leader," Chang echoed.

The doubts were there in those four words. His own ears could hear the weakness in them, little worms of disbelief burrowing deep, but Kuan's eyes sparkled with conviction, satisfied with his echo. Her neat little ears had not detected the worms.

Chang rose to his feet and drew a long slow breath, stilling the unsettled beat of his heart. In front of him the mountain fell away steeply to the narrow gully below and rose again in a sheer bleak rock face on the opposite side. No villages or cart tracks or even wild goat trails in sight, just the empty treeless landscape strewn with rocks cocooned in ice, and the twin snakes of silver metal that cut through the base of the valley. The rail track.

For a brief moment he allowed himself to wonder how many Chinese lives had been lost, how many rockfalls had come crashing down on their heads, turning the rails red as they were laid on the ground. It was the *fanqui*, the Foreign Devils, who dynamited its path through the valley. They'd come and stomped all over China. They laid down their metal roads, indifferent to the voice of the land itself, their big elephant ears deaf to the anger of the spirits of the mountain.

First the European uniforms marched over the land, swarming like flies across the yellow dust and stealing its wealth, but now it was the Nationalist Army of that strutting peacock, Chiang Kai-shek. He was tearing everything from under the feet of the Chinese people, even the grass in their fields and the green shoots in the paddies. It made Chang An Lo's heart ache for them and for this vast and beautiful Middle Kingdom.

"Kuan," he said, tasting ice on his lips. "Contact Luo, then Wang. Tell them to lay the charges."

The young woman at his side slid the khaki canvas burden from her shoulder to the ground and began to unbuckle its straps and turn the dials with efficient skill. Kuan had trained as a lawyer in Peking but now was a radio expert, and it was her job to keep the various Communist cadres in constant touch on this mission. She worked well, with no fuss. This pleased Chang and made her an easy companion to him. He trusted her. Her only weakness was her stamina in the mountains.

As she murmured into the mouthpiece, he closed his eyes and opened his mind. He turned his face northward, directly into the bitter wind that raced down from Siberia, and he breathed it deep into his lungs, let its teeth bite at the soft tissue within him.

Was she there? His fox girl. Somewhere across the border in that foreign land?

Could he taste her in the Russian wind?

Smell her?

Hear the clear bell of her laughter?

He wouldn't say her name, not even inside his mind. For fear that the whisper of it would betray her and bring the forces of vengeful spirits down on her copper-fire head inside Russia itself. She had stolen something from the gods and they did not forgive.

"It is time," he said with an abruptness that took Kuan by surprise.

"Now?" she asked.

"Now."

Quickly she buckled up the canvas straps, but by the time her cold fingers had finished the job Chang was already moving fast down the mountainside.

DEATH. IT SEEMED TO STALK HIM. OR DID HE STALK IT?

All around him bodies lay torn to shreds, limbs and torsos blasted to limp chunks of flesh and bone that were attracting crows before they were even cold. One head, a young man's with black blood-streaked hair and one eye missing from its socket, perched on a boulder ten meters from the wreck of the train and stared straight at Chang. A head, no body. Chang felt the finger of death touch his heart till he shivered, turned away, and walked down the broken line of the train. Glass crunched under his feet.

Carriages at both ends had been blown apart by the dual explosions. Ripped open into a raw and tangled twist of metal and timber, bodies spewed out like wolf bait on the icy ground. As Chang prowled past the carnage, he hardened his heart against the screams and reminded himself that these men were his enemies who were traveling south with the sole purpose of slaughtering Communists, determined to destroy Mao's Red Army. But somewhere deep beyond his reach, his heart wept for them.

"You."

He pointed at a young soldier in the gray uniform and red arm-band of the Chinese Communist forces who was dragging a bleed-ing figure from the wreckage. The wounded man was a Nationalist Army captain, judging by the uniform he wore, and his gut had been torn open by the explosion. He was trying to hold in his bloody innards with his hands, cradling them, but one end of his intestines had slipped from his grasp and trailed behind him. It was unwinding as the young Communist pulled him free, yet the Nationalist cap-tain didn't scream.

"You," Chang said again. "Stop that. You know the orders."

The young soldier nodded. He looked as if he would vomit.

"Only those who can walk will travel with us. The rest . . ."

In a slow, reluctant movement, while Chang stood over him, the young soldier slung the rifle off his back. Despite the ice in the air, sweat formed on his brow. He had the heavy features and broad hands of a farmer's son, a peasant away from home for the first time in his life. And now this.

Chang recalled his own first killing, seared into his soul.

The soldier nestled the rifle to his shoulder exactly as he'd been taught, but his hands were shaking uncontrollably. The man on the ground didn't beg, just closed his eyes and listened to the wind and to what he knew would be the last beats of his heart. Abruptly Chang drew his own pistol, leaned down to the captain, placed the muzzle at his temple, and pulled the trigger. The body jerked. Chang bowed his head for a split second and commended the man's spirit to his ancestors.

Death. It seemed to stalk him.

THE TRAIN'S MASSIVE STEAM ENGINE HAD BUCKED OFF THE damaged track and plunged nose first down the bank, but just man-aged to stay upright. Behind it lurched the baggage wagon at an odd angle, but the only baggage it was carrying came in twenty long wooden boxes, four of which had splintered open in the crash. Chang's heart raced at the sight of them. He leapt inside the wagon, feet braced against the buckled slope of the floor, and rested a hand possessively on one of the open boxes.

"Luo," he called.

Luo Wen-cai, the young commander of the small assault force, clambered up awkwardly after him. A slow-healing bullet wound in his thigh hampered his usual quick movements, but nothing hampered the grin that shot across his broad face.

"Chang, my friend, what treasure you have found for us!"

"Tokarev rifles," Chang murmured.

This was even better than he'd expected. This haul would please Chou En-lai at Party headquarters down south in Shanghai and put rifles where they were needed—in the military training camps, in the fists of the eager young men who came to fight for the Communist cause. Chou En-lai would preen himself and sharpen his tiger claws as if he'd hunted them down himself. This success would gain him even greater support from the *mao-zi*, the Hairy Ones.

The *mao-zi*. The words stuck in Chang's throat. They were the European Communists, the ones who held the purse strings of the Chinese Communist Party. They were represented by a German called Gerhart Eisler and a Pole known as Rylsky, but both were mere mouthpieces for Moscow. That's where the funds sprang from and where the real power lay.

Yet here was a train carrying troops and arms from Russia to Chiang Kai-shek's overstretched Nationalist Army, who were sworn enemies of the Chinese Communists. It didn't make sense, whichever way Chang turned it. Like a dog humping a goose, it wouldn't fit together. He frowned, feeling a sudden unease, but nothing could dampen his companion's delight.

"Rifles," Luo crowed. He scooped one out of a box and ran a hand down its length, lovingly, the way he would down a woman's thigh. "Beautiful well-oiled little whores. Hundreds of them."

"This winter," Chang said with a grin for his friend, "the training camps in Hunan province will be stocked as tight as rice in a *tu-hao's* belly."

"Chou En-lai will be more than satisfied. It'll do us no harm either to be the ones to bring him such a harvest."

Chang nodded, but his thoughts were chasing each other.

"Chou En-lai is a genius," Luo added loyally. "He organizes our Red Army with an inspired mind." He lifted the rifle and sighted down its barrel. "You've met him, haven't you, Chang?"

"Yes, *xie xie*, I had that privilege. In Shanghai, while I was attached to the Intelligence Office."

"Tell us what the great man is like?"

Chang knew Luo wanted big words from him, but he could not find them on his tongue, not for Chou En-lai, the leader of the Party headquarters in Shanghai.

"He has the charm of a silk glove," he murmured instead. "It slides over your skin and holds you firmly in his grasp. A thin handsome face with spectacles that he uses to cover his . . . thoughtful eyes."

Slavish eyes. Slavish yet ruthless. A man who would do anything—anything at all, however brutal to others or demeaning to himself—for his masters. And his masters were in Moscow. But Chang said none of this.

Instead he added, "He's like you, Luo. He has a mouth as big as a hippo's and likes to talk a lot. His speeches run on for hours." He banged a hand down on one of the boxes. "Now let's get these loaded on the pack animals before—"

A sudden explosion silenced his words. A dull thud outside that rattled the boards of the wagon. It came from somewhere close and both men reacted instantly, springing from the wagon, pistols in their hands. But the moment they hit the ground, feet scrabbling for grip on the ice, they halted because immediately ahead of them, lying helplessly on its back among the rocks like an upturned turtle, was a tall metal safe. Its door had just been blown off and around it huddled an excited group of Luo's troops.

"Wang!" Luo barked out to his second-in-command. "What in the name of a monkey's blue arse are you doing?"

Wang was a stocky young man with thick eyebrows and a short bull neck that angled forward and made him look as though he were always just about to launch into a charge. He broke free from the group and marched over to his senior commander with a fistful of papers extended in front of him.

"The safe came crashing out of that carriage." He pointed to a mound of mangled metal.

The third carriage had borne the brunt of the first explosion that derailed the train. It had twisted upside-down on the valley floor and emptied its contents—uniformed officers and a dark green safe—across the rocky surface before lurching into a tangled heap that crushed whatever or whoever was left inside it.

Respectfully but with a triumphant spark in his eyes, Wang held out his fist. "I took the liberty of removing its door."

Chang An Lo seized the sheaf of papers from the soldier's hand. His eyes skimmed the first page and abruptly the world seemed to slow down around him. Soldiers were still moving, herding their prisoners into battered lines, but it was as if they had lead weights in their boots, each step a slow effortful blur on the edge of Chang's vision. He tightened his grip on the papers.

"You were right," Luo Wen-cai growled. "There *were* documents on board."

Chang nodded. He stepped forward, lithe as one of the mountain leopards, and seized the front of Wang's jacket in his fist. The second in command's eyes widened and his head sank farther into his shoulders.

"Did you read them?" Chang demanded.

"No, sir."

"Do you swear? On the word of your ancestors?" The jacket was ready to tear.

"I swear."

A heartbeat. That's all. And a knife would have slid between the tendons of Wang's throat. He saw it in Chang's black eyes.

"I can't read," the soldier whispered, his voice barely scratching the air. "I never learned."

Two more heartbeats. Then Chang nodded and pushed the man away.

"So," Luo said quietly, "your intelligence information was accurate. The train was carrying more than just military personnel to the Nationalists." He directed a scarred forefinger at the gaping mouth of the safe. "Look."

Chang moved across the rocky terrain, his eyes no longer seeing the shattered bodies that crisscrossed his path. In the back of the safe, solid enough to remain undisturbed by the explosion that blew off the door, lay three burlap bags. He reached in and lifted one. It was heavy enough to strain the muscles of his forearm, and on the outside of it in dark brown ink was a string of words stamped in Russian Cyrillic script.

Chang shook the bag and heard its metallic clink. He knew what was inside without even looking. It was good Russian gold.

Five

"TELL ME, ALEXEI, WHAT DO YOU REMEMBER?"

Lydia tried to keep the hunger out of her voice as she asked the question, but it was hard. The train had stopped. It felt strange to be standing here with her brother, in the middle of the night and the middle of nowhere under a dark and starless Russian sky. But anything was better than remaining cooped up in that compartment for hour after hour. The novelty of train travel had worn off long ago; all that initial excitement and sense of discovery had been buried under a mountain of delays and disappointment. No, not disappointment exactly. Lydia shook her head and pulled her hat down tightly in a useless attempt to keep out the cold that crept relentlessly under her skin. She stamped her boots on the icy gravel and felt her blood kick briefly into her toes.

No, not disappointment. That was the wrong word. Carefully she sifted through her newly acquired Russian vocabulary and came up with *dosada* instead. *Frustration*. That was it. *Dosada*. It was new to her.

"I wondered when you'd ask," Alexei said quietly. "It's taken you a long time."

There was something in his voice, something that dragged at the words.

"I'm asking now," she said. "What do you remember?"

In the darkness she couldn't make out his expression, but she sensed a tension in the way he shifted his shoulders, as though something tight were rubbing against them. Something he wanted to be rid of. Was it her? Did she rub and fret and cause him pain?

Blackness had swallowed the landscape around them, so that Lydia had no idea whether mountains hunched over them or flat open plains spread ahead. Somewhere she could hear the murmur of a river. Several other passengers had climbed down from the carriages to stretch their legs while the train took on water, but their voices were muted. Lydia ducked her head against the wind and in doing so caught sight of Alexei's gloved fingers down by his side, clenching and straightening, clenching and straightening. When she'd asked *What do you remember?* she hadn't specified which memories, but she didn't need to. They both knew. Yet now, staring at his fingers, it occurred to her for the first time that maybe he had no wish to share his memories of Jens Friis. Not with her.

Was that space in his head where his father lived too intimate? Too private?

She waited, aware of the shouts of the rail workers calling to each other as they swung the spindly arm back against the metal water tower on its thin spidery legs. A lamp hung from a high wire above it and was swaying in the wind, sending shadows like ghosts skittering around their feet. She shifted her boots carefully to avoid stepping on them. Specks of soot were landing on her skin, soft as tiny black-winged moths. Or were they night spirits, the ones Chang had warned her about?

"For months," she said, "we've been traveling together, yet never have we talked about our memories of Jens Friis. Not *really* discussed them, I mean. Not even when we were stranded for three weeks in Omsk."

"No," Alexei agreed, "not even then."

"I wasn't . . ." She hesitated, uncertain how to explain to him. ". . . I wasn't ready."

A pause. The sides of the engine seemed to heave, sighing as it released its hot breath. Lydia brushed the soot from her cheek, while out of the darkness Alexei's voice came to her with a gentleness she wasn't used to.

"Because your Russian wasn't good enough?"

"Yes," she lied.

"I wondered."

"Tell me now."

He took a deep breath, as if about to plunge under water. What was it he feared down there? What dangerous current from his past? She let her glove brush his sleeve, and at that moment on this icy scrap of dirt in the middle of this land that was theirs, yet not theirs, she had never felt closer to her brother. She felt something melt as her glove touched his sleeve, fusing them so tightly that she experienced a curl of surprise that her hand could move away from him without effort.

"He used to visit," Alexei started quietly. "Jens Friis. In St. Petersburg. My mother and I lived with her husband, Count Serov—the man I always believed was my father—in a grand mansion with a long graveled drive. I'd watch for Jens from the upstairs salon window—it gave the best view of the approach."

"Did he come often?"

"Every Saturday afternoon. I never questioned why he came so regularly. Or why he always made such a fuss of me. Sometimes he brought me presents."

"What kind?"

"Oh"—he let his hand drift casually through the freezing air—"stamps for my stamp album or a new model for me to build."

"Model of what?"

"A ship. A wooden schooner to sail to the Far East. But sometimes he would cover my eyes, spin me around, and present me with a book."

"What kind of book?"

"Poetry. He liked Pushkin's poetry. Or Russian folk tales. Though he was Danish, he was keen for me to know my Russian heritage."

She nodded.

"So I'd rush over to the window seat"—his voice was growing warm with the memories—"whenever Mama told me Jens Friis was coming to visit and I'd crouch there, ready to jump up and wave to him." A self-conscious laugh pushed its way between the words. "Just a small boy at one of thirty or more windows."

"But did he see you when he came up the drive?"

"*Da,* always. He would lift his hat to me and sweep it through the air with a great flourish to make me laugh."

"In a carriage?"

"Sometimes, yes. But more often he was astride his horse."

His horse.

A memory came rushing into Lydia's head from nowhere, barging its way through the thin bones of her skull. A horse. A magnificent high-stepping chestnut with a black mane that she used to hang on to with stubby fingers. A horse that smelled of musty oil and sweet oats, a horse called . . .

"Hero," she said. "*Geroi.*"

Alexei's face was suddenly closer to hers and she could smell tobacco on him. "You remember Hero too?"

"Yes," she whispered. "I loved his ears."

"His ears?"

"The way they twitched and pricked when he was happy. Or flattened when he was irritable. I thought they were so magically expressive. I wanted ears like that."

She could hear, rather than see, Alexei's smile in the darkness. "Jens used to take me riding. I would perch like a monkey in front of him on Hero's saddle, and later when I was big enough to have a pony of my own, we'd go off for the afternoon together, just the two of us."

A small sound escaped Lydia.

"We'd ride out along the banks of the Neva River." Alexei was speaking to her, but she could tell that he'd slipped far away. "We'd canter all the way to the woods."

We. Always this *we.*

"We used to laugh a lot on those days out. I especially loved it in the autumn when the trees were so full of burning color it was as if they were on fire. Until one day—I must have been about seven years old—he stood me in front of him like a stiff little soldier, holding my arms to my sides, and told me he couldn't visit me every Saturday anymore."

Lydia listened to the silences that stretched between the words.

They both could guess the reason for the abrupt change in Jens' routine, but Alexei was the one who voiced it.

"He must have become involved with your mother, Valentina. Obviously he had to stop seeing my mother."

"Was that the last you saw of him?"

"No. For a whole year I lost him and I had no idea why. I'd heard him quarrel with my mother behind closed doors, so for a long time I blamed her. But without warning he came back."

Lydia stared at Alexei, surprised.

"Don't look so shocked," he said. "It wasn't often. He came just for birthdays and for Christmas sleigh rides. And an occasional canter through the forest again. That's all."

"What did you call him?"

"I called him *dyadya*. Uncle. Uncle Jens."

Lydia said nothing.

"He taught me to jump. First the boughs on the forest floor, I'd pop over them on my pony, no trouble, but then he put me to bigger obstacles, the fences and streams." Alexei tipped his head back and she saw a ripple of something flow up the line of his throat. "He used to roar with laughter whenever I fell off and sometimes"—he gave a chuckle deep in his chest—"I used to tumble out of the saddle just to hear that sound."

Lydia could see them. A boy. His green eyes alight with excitement. His red-haired father leading the way on the chestnut horse, the sun low in the sky painting them both golden. Leaves forming a bright brittle carpet under the hooves.

She thought her heart would crack with envy.

THE RAILWAY CARRIAGE WAS COLD. NEVERTHELESS MOST OF THE ten occupants managed to sleep in their seats, heads askew, as the train hauled itself through the night. At times Lydia's exhausted mind convinced itself of strange certainties as she sat wrapped in a rug, Alexei beside her, his body upright even in sleep. She could hear the throb of the train's heartbeat in each turn of its wheels, but outside the black windows it seemed to her that all existence had ceased. She closed her eyes. Not because she was sleepy but because she couldn't bear the sight of all that nothingness. It was too oppressive. Tapping at the windows. Seeping through the cracks. Curling around her ankles.

Sleep eluded her. She found herself irritated too by the moodiness of the train, by the way it stopped and started for no obvious reason, so that the hours of darkness crept past slowly. But as soon as her eyes closed, pictures painted themselves on the insides of her eyelids, images of Chang An Lo, dark eyes intent, watching her stitch his foot together after it was savaged by a dog. Or wide with astonishment when she carried a white rabbit to his bedside to make him laugh when he was sick in Junchow. Those same eyes black with anger . . . or bright with love. They snagged in her mind, always there.

What were they gazing at now? At whom?

Lydia snapped her own eyes open.

"Nightmares? *Koshmaryv*?"

It was the woman in the seat opposite who'd spoken, the one who'd asked her earlier what part of Russia she came from and who had snored in the room next door at the hotel. Conversation was the last thing Lydia wanted right now. The woman was plump and middle-aged, with a flowered scarf tied too tightly round her head, making her cheeks puff out like a hamster's. Her eyes must once have been blue but now were as colorless as tap water, and they were studying Lydia with lazy interest. No one else seemed awake. The man on the woman's left was wearing a pale sable fur coat that had fallen open as he slept, and she had taken the opportunity to peel back a section of the coat from his lap and spread it over her own for added warmth.

Lydia liked that. "No," she said. "*Nyet.* No nightmares."

"Boredom?"

"Something like that."

The woman blinked and for a while said nothing more, so that Lydia believed the conversation was at an end, but she was wrong.

"Who's your friend?"

"Why do you ask?"

The woman let her mouth drop open and licked her lips with a slow, deliberate lascivious movement of her tongue. "I'm always looking for a man."

"He's not interested," Lydia said flatly.

"Interested in you? Or me?"

"He's my brother."

"Hah! Not the handsome long-legged one, *durochka*, you idiot. *Dermo!* He's too young for me. The other one."

Popkov? This woman was interested in Popkov?

Lydia leaned forward and politely tapped the woman's fur-draped knee with a firm finger. "Stay away from both of them."

"You don't need two of them," the woman laughed. "That's greedy." Her pale eyes studied Lydia in a way that made her uneasy. "And you, *maleeshka*," the woman added, "are no more from Smolensk than I am from"—she paused, showing a glimpse of a fat pink tongue—"China."

Lydia sat back. Heart thudding. How could she possibly know?

Lydia remembered what Alexei had said about people in this Soviet State knowing your secrets almost before you did yourself. With an indifferent shrug as though bored with the conversation, she removed the wool rug from her own knees, took her time folding it neatly, and rose to place it up on the luggage rack above her head. Then without a glance at the woman, she slid open the internal door of the carriage and stepped out into the gloomy corridor.

I'm breathing, my love. I'm still breathing.

Six

THE CORRIDOR OF THE TRAIN WAS EVEN COLDER than the carriage. Lydia looked in both directions and was relieved to see no one else plagued by insomnia or feeling the urge to stretch their legs, though it stank of pipe tobacco, as if someone had been out here recently. The corridor was brown. Like climbing inside a long brown tube with only one dim light set high up on the wall. Lydia liked the gloom. It soothed her. Helped her think more clearly.

The train shuddered to the monotonous rhythm of its wheels and Lydia pressed her face to the cold glass, but she could see nothing outside, except the night itself under its thick black blanket. No lights out there, no towns, no villages. Just a frozen never-ending wilderness of trees and snow.

How on earth did they build the railway out here? The scale of Russia, like the scale of China, took her breath away and she struggled to cram the size of them into her head. Instead she'd learned to focus on the small things. She was good at that, seeing the things others missed. Like the sun flaring on a man's pocket watch or the corner of a wallet jutting out of a jacket or a lady's gold lipstick case left for no more than a second on a shop counter. Lydia couldn't help a faint smile. Yes, she'd been good at that.

Abruptly she shifted her gaze from the blackness outside to her own reflection in the glass. She grimaced. The hat was truly hideous, a brown wool thing with a wide peak that made her look like a baboon. She was glad Chang An Lo wasn't here to see her in it. She sighed and could hear her fears crackle like biscuit crumbs in her breath. She was seventeen, he was nineteen, nearly twenty. Would a man wait indefinitely? She didn't know. He loved her passionately, she was certain of that, but . . . A dull flush of color rose to her cheeks at her own naïveté. How long could a man be without a woman? A month? A year? Ten years?

She knew she'd wait a lifetime for him if she had to. Is that what her father had done? Waited year after year in a labor camp for her mother to come?

Suddenly Lydia yanked off the hat and tossed her head so that the tumble of copper waves leapt into life and framed her face, rippling over her shoulders. It gave her a look of wildness that satisfied something in her. A lioness, someone had once called her. She dragged her fingernails down the glass, ripping tracks through the film of mist that her breath had painted on it, sharpening her claws.

IT WAS JUST BEFORE DAWN AND LYDIA WAS WATCHING THE light shift from the intense darkness that cloaked northern Russia, black as the coal that was hauled up from its depths, to a pale translucent gray. Trees began to emerge like icy skeletons. The world was becoming real again.

She headed up the gloomy corridor toward the tiny washroom at the end. A line of three passengers had already formed outside it. Russians, she'd noticed, were good at lining up, unlike the Chinese. As she leaned against the wooden paneling and felt the constant turn of the wheels echo through her bones, her thoughts centered on the woman back there in the carriage, the one who'd asked where she came from. She made Lydia nervous.

Suddenly there came the sound of quick light footsteps hurrying toward the washroom. Lydia had shuffled her way up to second place in the line. Not that she was in a rush to use the squashed little facility, but she wanted to delay her return to the carriage. The footsteps stopped. Lydia looked behind her and was astonished to see a line of four women and a child—when had they arrived?—all waiting patiently, clearly rural workers, with headscarves and shawls and big-knuckled hands that labored hard in the potato fields. Their faces were uncommunicative, their thoughts private. The child, a small boy in a cap, was nibbling at his thumb and making little mouse noises to himself. Behind him stood the new arrival. Lydia felt a jolt of surprise, though she shouldn't have. It was Antonina, the wife of the camp commandant, and she was wrapped up warm in the silver fur coat.

"*Dobroye utro*, comrades," the newcomer said brightly. "Good morning to you." She nodded at Lydia.

The women stared at her the way they would at a gaudy magpie. One muttered, "*Dobroye utro*," then looked at the floor. The others remained silent. The child touched a grubby hand to her coat and she stepped away from it. She was wearing the white cotton gloves and started to rub them together awkwardly, fingers curling around each other.

"Comrades," she said, but her brightness was cracking at the edges, "I'm desperate." She gave them a smile that reached nowhere near her eyes. "Do you think I could . . . ?"

"*Nyet*."

"Wait your turn."

"My boy needs to go, but he doesn't complain. You should know better."

Antonina's deep-set eyes blinked. Her mouth looked fragile. She shook her head and as one hand started to scratch the back of the other, a tiny thread of crimson appeared on the white cotton.

"Comrade," Lydia said pleasantly, as she stepped out of the line, "you can take my place."

The mother of the child gave her a quick look of disapproval. "Comrade," she said to Lydia, her tone quiet and reasonable, "we no longer have to let worthless parasites like this woman in her bourgeois finery steal our rights from us. She is clearly not a worker. Just look at her."

Everyone stared at the pale pampered face, at the ruby earrings nestling in the dark hair and at the luxurious fur coat.

"It's obvious she is—"

Lydia interrupted. "Please, comrade. *Pozhalusta.* This is not harming you. I'm giving her my place in the line, so—"

"Young girl," the child's mother said with interest, "what is your name?"

Lydia's mouth went dry. "My name doesn't matter. It is no concern of—"

The woman pulled a small blue notepad from her pocket. Attached to it by a rubber band was a pencil.

"Your name?" she repeated.

The commandant's wife said abruptly, "Enough of that, comrades."

She half-turned her head, raising a gloved hand, and immediately one of her uniformed traveling companions detached himself from the wall and appeared at her side. He said nothing. He didn't need to. The women stared at the floor. Lydia didn't wait for more. She squeezed past his bulk and headed back toward her compartment, but as she approached it she saw the second of the woman's uniformed guardians blocking her path.

"Excuse me," she said politely.

He didn't move. Just rested his hand on the gun holster at his hip. He was tall with fine Slavic features and a high color to his cheeks. His dark eyes were amused.

"Tell me, girl," he asked, standing too close and scanning her coat, her shoes, her ugly hat, "what is your interest in our Comrade Commandant's wife?"

Lydia shrugged. "She's nothing to me."

"I'm here to make sure it stays that way."

"That's your business, comrade. Not mine."

His eyes were no longer amused, but after a long stare he stood aside to let her pass. His uniform smelled stale, as though it had been slept in too many times. She felt his eyes bore into the back of her head as she scurried on down the corridor.

BY MIDMORNING IT WAS RAINING HARD, A GRAY SLEETING downpour that rattled like buckshot against the windows. Without warning as they were crossing a wide flat plain, the train started to slow with disconcerting jerks, the brakes shrieking and clouds of steam swirling alongside. Outside, the world blurred.

A small station with wooden roof boards and rusting iron railings slowly slid into view, and Lydia felt her pulse quicken the moment she caught sight of the sign. Trovitsk. This was the station for Trovitsk labor camp. No one was allowed off the train here under the eagle eyes of the armed soldiers unless in possession of an official pass. Nevertheless Lydia rose from her seat.

"Where are you going?"

"Don't worry, Alexei. I'm just stretching my—"

"You can't get off here."

"I know."

"It's raining. She'll be in a hurry."

Lydia glanced down at her brother, at his intelligent green eyes. He knew. It dawned on her that he knew what she was going to do.

LYDIA STOOD ON THE TOP STEP OF THE TRAIN CARRIAGE. THE heavy door hung open, but she knew better than to attempt to descend to the platform below. The rain gusted into her face as she leaned against the door frame, looking out with an unhurried gaze and wishing she smoked. Leaning and smoking went together; they made a person appear unthreatening. And more than anything right now she wanted to appear unthreatening.

Three soldiers were busy off-loading a string of men from the baggage wagon at the far end of the train. Lydia watched them. The men were prisoners. She could see it in their hunched shoulders and tight pale faces, in the way they moved, as if expecting a blow. Some wore coats, several in suits, collars turned up against the rain, one in nothing more than shirt sleeves. All were bareheaded.

She made herself study them carefully, refusing to look away however much she wanted to. It felt too intimate. There was a nakedness about the hunched figures, their fear and degradation too huge and too exposed for everyone to see. It sickened her stomach.

Papa, is this what it's like for you? This kind of humiliation?

It was hard to keep her mouth closed, to jam the words inside. She could tell by their clothes and their air of bewilderment that these men must be new prisoners. It showed in their nervous glances at the guards, even in the way one of them looked for a brief moment at Lydia herself. The shame in the eyes. One man with a small bundle wrapped in a scarf under his arm managed an odd little smile at Lydia, fighting to pretend this was all a hideous mistake. That they'd been snatched from warm beds for . . . what? The dropping of an unwary word, the voicing of a wrong thought?

Using rifles like cattle prods, the three soldiers were herding them into a long line that stumbled toward the station entrance. At the very back a small plump man started sobbing in a loud outpouring of grief. To Lydia it sounded more like a sick animal than a human being.

"Get back inside."

It was a guard patrolling the platform. He jabbed at the open carriage door to slam it shut.

"Comrade *soldat*." Lydia smiled at him and pulled off her hat, letting her hair fall loose. He was young. He smiled back.

"My lungs aren't good," she said, "and there's always smoke in my compartment. I need some clean air." She inhaled noisily to emphasize the point and felt the sleet nip at the back of her throat. It made her cough.

"Well, shut the door and open its window instead." His tone was friendly.

At that moment she spotted an elegant figure descending the steps farther along the train. It was Antonina. She ducked her head against the rain that glistened on her furs like a shower of diamonds. Behind her the two uniformed companions were wrestling her luggage off the train, but Alexei had been wrong about her. She didn't hurry. She took her time. She smoothed her soft gray leather gloves over her fingers, adjusted the angle of her hat, and then with expressionless eyes she studied the wretched line of prisoners. She murmured something to one of the uniforms and instantly a small black umbrella was produced for her. She accepted it but held it too high above her head, indifferent to the sleet streaming in under it.

Lydia took a deep breath. She had a few brief seconds, a minute at most. No longer, before the train moved on. The soldier had his hand on the door, ready to slam it shut.

"Antonina," she called.

The pair of deep-set eyes turned toward her, narrowed against the rain, and she gave a faint nod of recognition.

The soldier started to shut the carriage door. "Move back there."

Lydia didn't move. "Antonina," she called again.

With neat unhurried steps, the dove-gray boots crossed the wet platform and Antonina stood in front of her, appearing small from Lydia's view high up on the steps of the train. The soldier moved away instantly with a smart salute. Clearly he knew who this woman was. In her furs and her carmine lipstick she looked much less approachable than in her maroon dressing gown.

Lydia tried a friendly smile, but the only response was a distant little grimace.

"Before you even ask, young comrade," the woman said briskly, "the answer is no."

"The answer to what?"

"To your question."

"I haven't asked a question."

"But you were going to."

Lydia said nothing.

"Weren't you?" Antonina tipped back her umbrella and gave Lydia a long scrutiny, her beautifully groomed eyebrows arching into a mocking curve. "Yes, I can see you were."

Her manner rattled Lydia. It was dismissive; it made her feel clumsy and childish. She wasn't sure of her footing any more. There was something so sleek and slippery about this woman today that Lydia could feel herself sliding off with nothing to hold on to.

"I just wanted to say good-bye," she murmured.

"*Do svidania*, comrade."

"And . . ."

"And what?"

"And yes . . . you are right, I want to ask something."

"Everyone always wants to ask me for something." Her dark gaze slid off to where the prisoners on the platform had bunched up, awaiting further orders. Their hair was plastered to their heads by the incessant rain and the man who had been sobbing noisily was quiet now, his face in his hands, his shoulders trembling.

Lydia looked away this time. It was too much.

"Everyone," Antonina continued in a voice that sounded amused, though her eyes were sad and serious, "wants me to convey a parcel, to pass on a message, to beg my husband, the commandant, for this or that for their loved one."

Lydia shifted uneasily on the steps. "Mistakes are sometimes made," she said. "Not everyone is guilty."

The woman gave a short hard laugh. "The OGPU decisions are always right."

Time was running out.

Lydia said quickly, "I am searching for someone."

"Isn't everybody?"

"His name is Jens Friis. He was captured in 1917, but he shouldn't be in a Russian prison at all because he's Danish. I just need to know if he's here in this camp. That's all. Nothing more. To hear that . . ."

The woman's eyes turned to her, smooth and cold as black ice, but the palms of her pale leather gloves were fretting against each other fiercely. She noticed the way Lydia glanced at them and for the first time she smiled, a small angry smile, but still a smile.

"Is this man your lover?"

"No."

"So what is he to you?"

"Please, Antonina? *Pozhalusta*?" Lydia said in a rush and climbed down one step in her eagerness. The guard nearby was moving closer. "All I need is just one word from you."

The train suddenly shuddered beneath her and heaved a great sigh, sending steam billowing down the platform. For one startling moment, the commandant's wife was enveloped in a cloud that obscured everything but her two hands in their ceaseless motion. When the steam cleared, Antonina had turned her back on Lydia, her long fur coat swaying as if the skins were still alive.

"*Nyet,* Lydia." She started to walk away, calling over her shoulder, "My answer is no."

The soldier closed the door and the train began to move. Quickly Lydia opened the window and leaned out. "I'll be in the hostel in Felanka," she shouted after the retreating woman. "You can leave a message for me there."

Slowly the figures on the platform grew smaller. Lydia continued to stare at where they had been, long after the rain swallowed them.

Seven

"YOB TVOYU MAT," LIEV POPKOV SWORE SUDDENLY
and pushed his huge fist toward the window. "Look
at that. It's the stinking hellhole."

Alexei saw Lydia elbow him hard in the ribs to
silence him, but it was too late. Every head in the
carriage turned to stare at what he'd indicated, and a
young woman with a baby asleep in her arms started
to weep silently. It was the camp. Trovitsk labor camp.
It couldn't be anything else, though from this distance it looked harmless enough, more like four dog
kennels rising above the flat winter horizon. Those
must be the tips of the watchtowers, but the rest of the
camp was lost in a faint blur, secretive and secluded,
too far away to make out anything of the communal
huts or barbed-wire fences.

"God help the bastards," Alexei muttered.

The big woman on the opposite seat grimaced.
"He hasn't done much of a job of it so far."

Lydia looked around at them both and frowned.
Her tawny eyes were huge. A straggle of hair had
crept out from under her hat and lay like a lick of
flame on the collar of her coat. "The Soviet State is

looking after those people," she said in a curt voice. "It does what is best. For all of us."

Oh, Lydia. But Alexei made a show of nodding agreement. "*Da,* we must never forget what we owe the state."

"As if we could," the big woman chuckled, and the chuckle grew until it was a loose rollicking laugh that shook her abundant bosom and sounded too loud in the tight confines of the carriage. Alexei eyed her with increasing caution.

At the other end of the carriage a man with a pipe and a bushy Stalin mustache banged his hand flat on his knee. "Those prisoners are here for good reason. Don't let's forget that, comrade."

Alexei let his eyes stray again to the window, and a small shock ran through him. The landscape was monotonously flat, a naked terrain that betrayed the scars and stumps where a forest had once stood, but way off to one side along the edge of a stand of pine trees that had somehow escaped the ax, eight men were bent double hauling a wagon. It was stacked high with bare tree trunks, and the men were yoked to it by chains. Beyond them, so small and colorless they were scarcely visible against the icy wasteland, other figures scuttled like ants across the Work Zone.

"Yes," Alexei murmured, not taking his eyes off them. "That's why they're here. It's the raw materials we need."

"For industry?" the woman asked.

He nodded. "For Stalin's great Five-Year Plan."

"So what is it the prisoners do all the way up here?"

Still he watched them. Saw a man fall. "Mining. This region is rich in ore and coal."

An uncomfortable silence descended, while the passengers pictured the prisoners, black-faced somewhere deep under the train's wheels, swinging picks at a brutal coal seam, lungs filling up with heavy choking dust.

"And timber," Alexei added softly.

Dear God, let Jens Friis be good with a saw.

"THIS PLACE IS TOO TIDY FOR US," LIEV POPKOV GROWLED UNDER his breath. "Too clean."

For once the ox-brain was right. The town of Felanka was not what Alexei had been expecting and not what he wanted. They were walking down the main street, Gorky Ulitsa, with Lydia tucked safely between them, taking a careful look at their surroundings. Where were the usual rows of ugly concrete apartment blocks? Most of the towns up here in the north were sprawling indifferent places that had sprung into being to accommodate the recent enforced migration of Russia's dissidents into these sparsely populated areas. No one would notice an extra few travelers in one of those. But this was different. This town felt loved.

Elegant buildings lined wide graceful boulevards, and everywhere there was an abundance of scrolled ironwork. Balconies and streetlamps, door and window settings, all curled and twined in an outbreak of wrought iron. Felanka was built on iron ore. It lived and breathed it. Some way off to the west of the town lay the massive brick-built foundry. It loomed like a giant black turtle on the horizon, belching foul-smelling smoke that turned the air into something you could touch. But today the east wind was keeping the smoke at bay and the town was parading its charms under a brittle blue sky.

"Popkov." Alexei nodded toward a shop front they were passing. "In here."

He wanted to get Lydia off the street. She'd been silent since leaving the train, and all through their registration at the hostel where they were shown into rooms that smelled of laundered sheets, she'd looked pale and listless. He wondered if she was sick. Or sick at heart.

He pushed open the door off the street. It was a printer's shop with heavy iron presses on the left and a huddle of men in deep discussion around them. The air held the tang of metal and ink, but on the right side of the gloomy interior a high counter ran across the window, and this was what Alexei had spotted from outside. Here customers could buy a hot drink and stand while they waited for their print order. An old *babushka* with sparse gray hair scraped back into a bun sat sharp-eyed at the back of the shop, one hand resting possessively on the claw foot of the samovar beside her.

"*Dobriy den,*" Alexei greeted her politely. "Good afternoon."

"*Dobriy den,*" she nodded, and gave him a toothless twist of her mouth that he assumed was a smile. He bought tea for himself and

Popkov, hot chocolate for Lydia. They carried the glasses over to the wooden counter by the window and stood looking out at the street.

"It's too tidy," Popkov muttered again. "For us."

"What do you mean?" Lydia asked.

She was again positioned between them—that's how it always was—but didn't look at him, just wrapped her gloves around the hot glass in its metal *podstakanik* and stared at the flurry of trucks trailing past. There was no one else in their section of the shop, and the noise from the printing press meant there was no danger of being overheard.

Popkov rummaged his fingers in his thick black beard. He was chewing a wad of tobacco and his teeth were so stained they merged with the black bristles. "They don't need us."

"You mean our money?" she asked.

"*Da.*"

She sank back into her silence, sipped her chocolate, and blew steam at the window. Alexei could sense the shreds of hope slipping from her grasp. He placed his *podstakanik* down on the scratched surface with annoyance.

"People always take money," he said firmly. "People always take money. Don't you know that yet?"

Lydia shrugged.

"Listen, Lydia." Alexei leaned an elbow on the counter and concentrated on her face. It looked tired, dark shadows circling her eyes. "We've come this far. To Trovitsk camp. We've even laid eyes on some of the wretched prisoners, poor bastards." He saw her flinch, a tiny movement of the muscle beside her eye. That was all. She said nothing. He lowered his voice. "We always knew the next part would be difficult."

"Difficult?" Popkov snorted. "Fucking dangerous, you mean."

"Not impossible, though." Alexei was irritated and gave a sharp rap with his knuckles on the wood, as if he could knock some sense into their heads. "Jens Friis could still be there."

He saw her tremble. Sometimes he forgot how vulnerable she was, how unguarded. He had to remind himself that he'd had years at a military training establishment in Japan where he'd learned levels of self-control, but she'd had . . . nothing. He took a mouthful of his *chai*. It was hot and burned a path down inside him, but couldn't warm what lay deep in there, cold and untouched. He pushed himself upright, stretched his shoulders, and faced the one-eyed Cossack.

"Popkov, I thought you were a man who liked danger. Drank it in with your mother's milk, I heard."

He saw the one black eye flicker and dart quickly across to the girl between them. In that moment Alexei knew that if Popkov possessed any fear of danger—which he seriously doubted—it was not for himself. Alexei detested the man. Could never understand what bound Lydia to this lazy, stupid, drunken Cossack who stank like a bear and farted like a horse. But right now he needed him.

"So, Popkov, I think it's time you and I get going tonight. With a wad of roubles in our pockets and a vodka bottle to crack over a few heads."

Alexei's voice was amiable enough, but the look he gave the big man was cold and challenging. Popkov turned, eyeing him over the top of Lydia's hat and baring his teeth in what could have been a smile or a snarl.

"*Da.*"

It was the way they'd done it before. A few bottles on offer, a few new friends in the back streets of a strange town. It was amazing what you could discover, what secrets tumbled off a loose tongue. Which officials were clean and which were dirty. Which one was fucking his boss's wife and which one liked to pick up little boys in the dark alleyways. That's what Popkov had meant when he complained Felanka was too tidy, too clean, but nowhere was *too clean*. Such places didn't exist.

"You see, Lydia, it's far too soon to . . ."

But she let out a moan and dropped her head into her hands. Her hat fell to the floor and her hair tumbled like a fiery curtain around her pale face, shutting him out. Alexei glanced at Popkov. The big man was staring at the girl with an expression of such dismay, as if her moan had frightened him far more than any prospect of being arrested for bribery of a Party official. Neither of them had ever seen her like this. Alexei put out a hand, tentatively touched her shoulder.

"What is it, Lydia?"

Tremors were running through her body. He waited. She made no sound. At least she wasn't crying. He hated women who cried.

After a full minute he gently squeezed her shoulder. He could feel the shape of her bones, small and fragile, under the padding of her coat, but he continued to squeeze until he knew the pressure must be hurting her. He heard Popkov grunt and emit a rumble from his chest, but still he didn't release her shoulder.

With a murmur she raised her head and blinked slowly, turning to face him. Her eyes, usually so bright and curious, were dull and flat, a sad muddy brown, but her mouth curved into an affectionate smile.

"You can stop now," she said softly.

He stopped but didn't remove his hand. He left it there on her shoulder.

"All right now?" he murmured.

"Just fine." She gave him an unconvincing smile and he wanted to shake her.

"What was that all about? Tell me."

She reached up and for a brief moment rested a hand, light as a bird, on top of his, but then she gave him one of her damn shrugs and picked up her hot chocolate. "Just scaring you," she murmured and sipped her drink.

"You succeeded."

"So tonight, Liev, you . . ."

But Popkov's attention had moved elsewhere. His gaze was fixed on something in the broad street outside, a stupid cockeyed grin on his face. Alexei scanned the street for whatever it was that was so absorbing the Cossack but at first saw nothing out of the ordinary. People were striding quickly along the sidewalk, hurrying to escape the wind, *fufaikas* buttoned tight to the neck, and a heavy truck trundled down the road making the glass vibrate in the window. As it drove past, Alexei caught sight of a figure standing squarely on the sidewalk opposite, waving both hands and smiling back at Popkov. It was the big woman from the train, the one in the headscarf who had been in the hotel in Selyansk. The one with the breasts. What the hell was she doing here? Instantly he swung around to confront the dumb Cossack, but Lydia got in there first.

"Liev," she hissed, "what are you doing?"

He blinked at her mildly. "Waving to—"

"She's following us, don't you realize?"

"*Nyet.*"

"*Da*."

"*Nyet*."

"What does she know?"

"Nothing. *Neechevo*."

"You told her, didn't you?"

His scarred brow hunched into a scowl at Lydia's sharp tone. "Told her what?"

"That we've traveled here from China."

"So?"

"Oh, Liev, you stupid fool, what else have you told her? She could be an OGPU agent."

The big man snorted. "She's not a spy, nor an informer."

Alexei decided to deal with this quickly before the argument drew too much attention from the huddle of men at the printing bench on the other side of the room. However much he was enjoying seeing these two at each other's throats for a change, now was not the moment. "Ignore the woman, Popkov. Keep well away from her. We can't take the risk that—"

The Cossack snatched the filthy *shapka* off his own head and threw it on the counter, knocking over Alexei's *chai*. All three ignored the brown pool of hot liquid that trickled over the edge.

"Don't you ever give your fucking orders to me, Alexei Serov!" Popkov shook his head, thick shaggy black curls rising like horns, and growled, "I tell you she is not a spy. She thinks *you* are following *her*." He spat noisily on the floor, an evil black jet that skidded across the boards.

The old *babushka* at the back screeched a complaint but was silenced by a glare from Popkov's single eye.

"Liev!" Lydia said.

But inexplicably, there was suddenly a smile on her face. Where the hell had that sprung from? There was just no telling with these two what cliff they were going to jump off next. Alexei righted the spilled glass, folded his arms across his chest to hold in his annoyance, and watched how his sister intended to deal with this. Where Popkov was concerned, he had to admit her instincts were good.

"What's her name, Liev?" Lydia asked.

"Elena Gorshkova."

"What is she to you?"

"A friend." A red flush rose above his beard and crept up the sides of his nose.

"Something more than a friend?" She scrutinized his face. "Where did you first meet her?"

"In Selyansk."

"At the hotel?"

"*Da.*"

She paused and drew a long breath, then scooped up his hat off the counter and thrust it against his massive chest. "Go," she said with a laugh, "if that's what you want."

Popkov looked at her for a long beat, then shook himself vigorously. For a moment Alexei thought he was going to crush her between his huge arms, but instead he lumbered toward the door. Alexei stepped into his path before he could reach it.

"Popkov, be careful."

A nod from the big man.

"Why is she here? In Felanka."

Popkov grunted something inarticulate, but Alexei couldn't let it go at that.

"Do you know why?" he insisted.

Another grunt, deep in his oily throat.

"Tell me."

He expected another grunt, but instead the Cossack rummaged a fist through his beard once more, narrowed his one good eye, and said evenly, "Elena Gorshkova is in Felanka to visit her son's grave."

Lydia reached out and caught his shoulder. "Liev, spit out that bloody tobacco before you speak to her."

Popkov thumped her hard on the back in what was obviously meant to be a gesture of affection and barged out of the shop. Together and in silence, Alexei and Lydia watched through the window as he crossed the broad boulevard in ten massive strides, after threatening to rip the bumper off a timid saloon car that didn't want to stop for him. They saw him eject the wad of tobacco into the gutter, wipe his mouth on the *shapka* and jam it back on top of his shaggy mane, then greet the woman with a delicate bow that surprised them both. The unlikely couple ambled off together as if taking a leisurely stroll in a park, ignoring the bite of the wind and the bustle of the crowd around them.

Lydia sighed, elbows on the counter, chin in her hands. Alexei hated the wistful expression in her eyes. It meant that Chinese Communist of hers, Chang An Lo, was eating into her brain again. He pushed himself away from the counter.

"Come, Lydia, let's walk. It'll do us good."

Eight

THEY WALKED UNTIL THE SKY LOST ITS BRIGHT sheen and turned a muted crimson, the color of molten metal as it cools. Its light washed everything with a soft pink hue that belied the harshness of the landscape, but it suited Lydia's mood. She was sick of sharp edges, sick of black and white, sick of right and wrong. She thought she knew herself, knew where she ended and others began, knew where to stop and where to start. But now . . . now she didn't seem to know anymore. Was she trying to do too much? Was she not as strong as she believed herself to be? As Chang An Lo believed her to be?

"You have the heart of a lion," he'd whispered to her once, as he ran a lock of her coppery hair through his fingers, "as well as the mane of one."

He'd lifted the curl to his lips and she'd thought he was going to kiss it, but he didn't. Instead he closed his teeth over the end and slowly and deliberately bit through it, so that a finger's length disappeared into his mouth. His black eyes fixed on hers as he swallowed it, and a shiver of excitement had rippled through her. She watched his throat work as the hair from her own head slid into the tunnels within him.

"Now you are a part of me," he'd said simply, and gave her that slow smile of his that stopped her heart. "Now I can listen to you roar inside me."

She'd laughed and lain in his arms, growling at him, nipping his collarbone with her teeth, dragging her nails across the taut skin of his chest.

"Lydia?" It was Alexei. His head was tipped to one side so that he could peer up into her face. "Are you still with me?"

He said it lightly, with an easy laugh, but behind the words she could hear the concern, the uncertainty. He was doubting her too. From the moment they set foot on the sidewalk outside the printing shop, Alexei had hooked her arm through his own and set a good pace as he strode through the town. He'd steered her past the imposing pillars of the Lenin Library and into a quiet park that was laid out with gravel paths, edged with hoops of decorative ironwork. To Lydia they looked like open mouths begging for food. They forced images of the labor camp into her head.

She locked her arm tight against her brother's. The place was deserted. Yet it felt busy because there was so much movement and commotion around them as the wind battered the bare branches or chased a newspaper around the central statue on its plinth. Empty Belomor cigarette packets and a trail of abandoned peanut shells swirled under their feet and all the time that they walked, Alexei talked. His words soothing her, quieting her. The flow of them creating firm footholds in her mind as, with infinite delicacy, he fed the words into the silence. Step by step he retraced their plans, bringing her with him, reminding her, leading her, not letting her slip away.

Alexei patted his waist, where his body belt lay securely fastened next to his skin, and smiled at her, for once without that look of detachment that so often guarded his thoughts. They had left the park and were heading down a road through an area where the houses were smaller but showily decorated with carved shutters.

"We have money," he reminded her. "We have diamonds and we have new identity papers for our father. We are well prepared, Lydia."

"I know."

"We always knew it's going to be dangerous to attempt to bribe the guards at the camp. To find the right one, a guard so greedy he will sell his soul and risk anything—even execution—to have—"

"I know." A pause. "I know."

The wind snatched at her words.

"It will take us time," he said quietly. "We can't—you mustn't—rush into any risks that—"

"I know."

He let a silence drift between them but still held her arm laced through his. She could feel the strength in his hand where it was fastened on her wrist and the strength of the mind that controlled it.

"Alexei."

"What is it?"

"Do you think Jens was one of those prisoners?"

She felt a muscle tighten in his hand, heard his intake of breath. "Pulling that timber wagon, you mean?"

"Yes."

"It's unlikely." His voice was as calm as if discussing the possibility of rain.

"I thought one man seemed to have red hair."

"No, Lydia, we were much too far away. You couldn't possibly see that. It's wishful thinking. Anyway it may not be red anymore."

They looked at each other, then walked in silence, the street growing narrower, the neighborhood rougher. The well-built brick homes gave way to shapeless wooden houses that were looking tired and shabby. A honey-colored mongrel in a doorway whined at them as they passed.

Wishful thinking.

I wish. I think. Oh yes, Papa, Alexei is right. I wish for you and I think of you . . . and I am frightened for you. My blood runs cold when I picture you, a green-eyed Viking, condemned to exist underground in one of the mines.

"The man who built this town was a visionary," Alexei interrupted her thoughts. He had turned away, so she could see only his profile with its high forehead and straight uncompromising nose, but his mouth was curved into a line of approval.

"What do you mean?" She had no interest in the town.

"His name was Leonid Ventov."

"How do you know that?"

"I did my research. When preparing for battle, you reconnoiter the land."

Lydia loved him for that, the way he kept them safe. She squeezed his arm. "Tell me about this Leonid Ventov of yours."

"He was an industrialist from Odessa at the end of the last century. He grew fat and rich on what he discovered lay under this cold black soil, huge deposits of coal and iron ore, but he was a fiercely religious man. So instead of just stripping the land bare and leaving it raped and useless, he built this town of Felanka as a beautifully designed thank-you to his God. He tried to persuade others of the growing breed of wealthy industrialists to do the same throughout Russia, but . . ." His voice trailed away.

Lydia felt his attention focus abruptly elsewhere. She glanced ahead as they emerged from the shadow of a row of houses and saw what it was that had drawn his interest. Ahead of them at the edge of town stretched a flat dull landscape, deserted except for one wide rutted road that ran straight to the iron foundry about a kilometer away. The brick building was hunched and forbidding, as if waiting for night to fall, when it would stalk closer to the town under cover of darkness. Its stacks stretched upward, like fingers raking the crimson sky, and belched a thick black smoke that today was swept away from the town by the east wind. But still the air tasted sour and stung the nostrils.

Lydia examined it with interest. "So this is where we'll bring him?"

"*Da*. As soon as we've got Jens out of the camp, we'll need to hide him. What better place than in a foundry, where blackened faces and constantly changing shifts are the norm? Among that vast throng of metal workers, he would pass unnoticed, but first . . ."

". . . we have to find a worker willing to take him in there."

"Exactly. That's what your Cossack and I will start work on tonight."

"Alexei?"

Their footsteps slowed and finally halted on the edge of the frozen landscape that ranged for miles in every direction. Only the foundry itself was built in a sunken hollow, as though its creator had endeavored to keep it as much out of sight as possible, its ugliness an affront to the splendor of his God. Now, with religion nothing more than a dirty word, just something the Politburo wiped its Communist boots on, the factories and foundries of Russia had become the new churches.

"Alexei?" Lydia said again, her finger tapping his arm insistently.

He nodded to indicate he was listening, but his eyes still scrutinized the approach road to the foundry. Somewhere unseen, the sound of a truck starting up drifted to their ears.

"I've thought of an idea," she said.

She felt his arm stiffen. He looked at her quickly.

"What idea?"

"I need to help. At the moment it's just you and Popkov sniffing out a guard and a foundry worker who will take a bribe, while I sit twiddling my thumbs, just waiting for you to—"

"For God's sake, Lydia, what do you expect? If you start putting your face about and asking questions, you'll throw us all in danger." He tightened his grip on her hand. "Don't!" he said. His green eyes probed hers intently. "Whatever it is, don't! Do you hear me? Don't!"

There was a long silence between them, broken only by the truck engine approaching. Lydia was the first who looked away, not because she was nervous of him but because she didn't want him to see how angry she was. She tried to remove her hand from his arm, but he refused to release it. The sky was losing its color, and the first wings of darkness were gliding in from the west.

"Let's go back," Lydia said.

They turned and retraced their steps along the narrow streets in silence.

THE TRUCK OVERTOOK THEM. IT WAS EMPTY AND BOUNCING along at speed, kicking up dust and trailing a foul odor in its wake, but just ahead a handcart had tumbled onto its side in the middle of the road, spewing out cabbages that rolled into the gutter like loose heads. The truck sounded its horn, then juddered to a halt. As Lydia and Alexei approached, the blond young driver of the truck wound down his window, leaned out, and treated Lydia to an inviting smile that displayed perfect teeth under the sparse beginnings of a mustache. He was wearing a navy woolen cap pulled down at an angle over one eye, giving him the air of an adventurer.

"Hello, beautiful," he called, "*ti takaya krasivaya.*"

Lydia felt Alexei bristle, but nevertheless she looked up into the cab of the truck and gave the driver an answering smile. "*Dobriy den*," she responded. "Good afternoon."

"Want a lift?"

She let the question hang in the air and felt both men alert to her answer. Alexei still held her hand on his arm but made no attempt to speak, looking deliberately straight ahead at the cart being man-handled out of the way.

"*Nyet*. But thanks anyway." She gave the driver a slow sideways glance and heard him laugh delightedly.

He leaned down in his cab and brought up something small in his hand, which he tossed out the window to her. It arced between them, spiraling and twisting, until Lydia snatched it out of the air with her free hand. It was just a metal disk, no bigger than a coin but polished to perfection, with the name *Niko* engraved on it. The driver waved to her and drove on over the cabbages, leaving them with a belch of exhaust fumes and a long blast on his horn.

"I bet he keeps one of those in his truck for every girl he passes," Alexei muttered, and it amused Lydia to see that he was irritated by the little gift. She twirled the flat disk between her fingers, and the last rays of sunlight turned it to fire.

"It's an omen," she laughed, and swept off her ugly hat, letting her hair leap free.

She had learned about omens from Chang An Lo, how the gods sent them as a sign. Westerners had lost the skill of recognizing them, but Chang had taught her how to feel for them with her fox spirit.

"Lydia, there's no such thing as—"

"Of course there is." She spun the gleaming disk. "See the fire in it. It matches me. Don't you see, it means I'm meant to be here. The omen burns so bright, it shows we're destined for success."

Alexei had stopped in the middle of the street and was staring at her, disbelief written all over his face. But she didn't miss the laugh-ter in his eyes.

"Now," she said, "shall I tell you my idea?"

"THE ANSWER IS STILL NO."

Lydia stood alone in her bedroom in the hostel, her limbs too stiff and unyielding to let her curl up on the bed and seek refuge in sleep. It was as if they took orders now from Alexei instead of from herself. She heard his words still rattling round inside her skull with a persistence that drove her to fret at the hat in her hands, pulling threads out of it when really what she wanted to do was pull threads out of Alexei.

The answer is still no.

That's what he'd said, over and over again. "I will not allow you to go wandering off on your own. The answer is no."

Her plan was straightforward, simple really. While he and Popkov spent the next few days or weeks—however long it took—combing through the detritus of the back streets, prodding and poking at it to find the weak points, she would return to the railway station and endeavor to buy a ticket for herself on a train going back the way they'd come, in the direction of Selyansk.

"Why?" he'd asked, eyes narrowed. "What would be the point of that?"

"To travel past the prison camp's Work Zone again."

He exhaled sharply through his teeth, a low whistling sound she'd noticed he made only when caught off guard by a sudden strong emotion. It should have warned her.

"You see," she rushed on, "I might be able to find a way to pass a message into the camp. Now we know that these trains carry prisoners in transit as well, I might find a way of contacting one and"—she slowed the words to make him listen; she knew her brother hated disorder—"he might seek out Papa . . . Jens Friis . . . and tell him he might—"

"That's a lot of *mights*."

She felt a dull flush rise up her cheeks. "You and Popkov *might* not have success in bribing officials who *might* just chuck you both straight into the prison camp instead, leaving me stranded here on my own. That," she'd said, snatching her hand away from his arm, "*might* happen. And then what?"

They were standing still in the narrow street outside a house where the shutters hung on broken hinges and the roof was patched unevenly. Darkness was beginning to roll down the center of the road with long strange-shaped shadows, and a straggle of horse-drawn carts was trundling along behind them.

"Lydia." He did not attempt to retrieve her hand. "We must all three of us take care. Listen to me. I cannot do my task here properly if all the time I am looking over my shoulder, worried about what antics you're getting up to."

"Antics?"

"Call them what you will, but can't you see that I have to be the one who asks the questions to—"

"Why? Because you are a man?"

"Yes."

"That's not right."

"Right or wrong doesn't come into it, Lydia. It's the way it is. You are *ranimaya* just because you are a woman and—"

"What does *ranimaya* mean?" She hated asking.

"It means vulnerable."

"Well I think maybe the Communists have got it right."

He studied her face with such concentration that she almost turned away.

"And what exactly," he asked, "do you mean by that?"

"That Communists give women greater equality, they recognize them as . . ."

A tiny child, impossible to tell whether girl or boy, with a mop of greasy curls and mucus encrusted under its nose abruptly materialized at Lydia's knee. Round brown eyes stared up at her with the moist hopefulness of a puppy's, but when she smiled at the child it tottered backward and stuck a filthy thumb into its mouth.

"We're becoming a spectacle," Alexei murmured.

He released a long exasperated sigh that annoyed Lydia and glanced farther along the street to where a man was propped against a windowsill and smoking a pipe. His eyes, behind a pair of spectacles bound together with black tape on the bridge of his nose, were observing them with quiet interest. Alexei took hold of Lydia's upper arm and tried to propel her forward, but she refused to move. She pulled away from him and squatted down on the sidewalk in front of the child. From her pocket she extracted a coin, took the grubby hand that wasn't otherwise occupied into her own, and wrapped the little fingers around the rouble. They felt as cold and slippery as tiny fish.

"For something to eat," she smiled gently.

The child said nothing. But the thumb in the mouth suddenly popped out and ran down Lydia's hair past the side of her jaw and onto her neck. It was repeated twice. She wondered if the child expected the strands to be hot like fire. With no sound the curly creature turned and waddled with surprising speed toward an open door three houses away. Lydia rose to her feet and rejoined her brother. Side by side but no longer touching, she and Alexei continued up the street at a brisk pace.

"If you hand out money to every filthy urchin we stumble over in the streets," he muttered, "we'll have none left for ourselves."

For a long while they walked on in stiff silence, but just when they passed the park once more, where the wind was still chasing its tail and pursuing the sheets of newspaper, Lydia suddenly snapped, "The trouble with you, Alexei, is that you've never been poor."

AT THE HOSTEL THEY PARTED WITH FEW WORDS. IT WAS ONE of the new buildings, deprived of any iron scrollwork, faceless and totally forgettable. They were springing up throughout the town to house the expanding workforce, but it was clean and anonymous, which suited them both.

In the entrance hall someone had hung a large mirror, flecked with black age spots like the back of an old man's hand, and in it Lydia caught sight of the refection of Alexei and herself. It took her by surprise, the image of the two of them. They both looked so . . . she struggled for the word, then abandoned thinking in Russian and settled for *so inappropriate*. With a jolt she realized they didn't blend in at all. Alexei was taller than she'd realized, and though his heavy coat was right in every respect and the way his gloves were patched on two fingers was perfect—she suspected he'd purposely torn and then sewn them up himself—nothing else about him fitted in with the dreary little entrance hall. Everything here was plain and utilitarian, whereas Alexei was elaborate and elegant even when clothed in a drab overcoat. He was like that wrought ironwork outside, carefully crafted and irresistible to the eye.

The thought bothered her. For the first time she wondered if Liev Popkov was right. Alexei could be a danger to them because people noticed him. Yet tonight he was venturing out among the town's lowlifes to start asking questions, and she wanted to tell him not to do it. *Don't. You might get hurt.*

"Alexei," she said in a low voice, "make certain you keep Popkov close by you tonight."

He raised one eyebrow at her. That was all.

"You might need him," she insisted.

But he took no notice, and she knew he was still angry with her about her plan to return to Trovitsk camp on her own. He was just too damn arrogant to let his little sister tell him what to do. Well, to hell with him. Let him get himself strung up by his thumbs for all she cared. She looked away and once again bumped into her own reflection in the mottled mirror. She swore under her breath.

"*Chyort!*"

The girl inside the mirror wasn't her. Surely it wasn't. That girl looked utterly dejected, her heart-shaped face thin and nervous. Her eyes were watchful and her hair far too colorful for her own good. Lydia quickly yanked her stupid hat from her pocket, pulled it on her head even though they were now indoors, and jammed her hair up under it with sharp little jabs that scraped her ears.

"Alexei," she said, and found him observing her with that cool scrutiny he was so fond of, "if you keep Popkov at your side this evening, I promise I'll stay shut in my room and not put a foot outside the door until you're back."

Would he thank her? Would he appreciate that for once she was offering him peace of mind?

His slow infuriating smile crept up on one side of his mouth, and for a split second she was foolish enough to think he was going to laugh and accept her offer. Instead the green of his eyes turned a chilly mistrustful grayish shade that reminded her of the Peiho River in Junchow, which could catch you out in the blink of an eye just when you thought it was looking warm and inviting.

"Lydia," he said, so softly no one else would have been able to detect the carefully controlled anger, "you're lying to me."

She spun on her heel and stalked off down the stubby brown corridor that led to the stairs, her boots clicking on the floorboards. He made her so mad she wanted to spit.

Nine

LYDIA STAYED IN HER ROOM JUST AS SHE'D promised. She didn't want to but she did. It wasn't because she'd given her word—yes, Alexei was right about that: in the past she'd never let something as trivial as a promise cramp her activities—but because Alexei didn't believe she would. She was determined to prove him wrong.

The room was lugubrious and chilly, but clean. Two narrow single beds were squashed into the small space, but so far no one else had come to claim the second bed. With luck it would remain empty. A mirror in an ornate metal frame hung on one wall but Lydia was careful to avoid it this time. Still wearing her hat and coat, she paced up and down the narrow strip of floorboards between the beds and fretted at her thoughts, the way she'd fretted at the hat earlier.

She tried to concentrate on Alexei, to picture him donning his coat ready for the evening sortie, staring into his own ornate mirror with that look of eagerness, almost wantonness, that sprang into his eyes whenever there was some action in prospect. He always tried to hide it, of course, and she'd seen him disguise it with a yawn or an indifferent flick of his hand through his thick brown hair, as if bored by the world around him. But she knew. She recognized it for what it was. She'd seen it flare in the green depths. Just like her father.

She paced faster and kicked her foot against the bed frame to drive a jolt of pain up her leg. Anything to keep her thoughts away from Jens Friis. Instead she crammed images of the commandant's wife into her brain, of her slender mistreated arms and the graceful swing of the fur coat as she turned her back and walked away along the railway platform.

Walked away. How can you do that? How can you walk away?

A rush of rage swept through Lydia. She wasn't sure where it came from, but it had nothing to do with Antonina. She felt it burn her cheeks and scour her stomach, her fingers seizing one of her coat buttons and twisting so hard it came off. That felt better. She clung to it and tried to sweep away the misery that had driven a spike right through her from the moment on the train she laid eyes on the prisoners in the Work Zone today. The men hauling the wagon over icy boulder-strewn ground, no better than animals. No, worse than animals because animals don't die of shame. Even from so far away she'd felt it, that shame, and tasted the acid of it in her mouth. And then one of the men had fallen and not risen.

Papa, I need to find you. Please, please, Papa, don't let it be you crumpled inside that heap of rags.

And suddenly the rage was gone and all she had left were the tears on her cold cheeks.

A KNOCK ON THE DOOR MADE LYDIA LOOK UP. SHE'D REMOVED her coat and hat and was kneeling beside her bed, engrossed in removing every single item from her canvas bag.

"Come in," she said. "*Vkhodite.*"

The door opened and she expected it to be a another overnight resident come to claim the spare bed, but she was wrong. It was Popkov's friend, the big woman with the straight straw hair, the one from the train, the one with the tongue that asked too many questions. What did he say her name was? Elena, that was it.

"*Dobriy vecher*, comrade," Lydia said politely. "Good evening."

"*Dobriy vecher.* I thought you might be bored here on your own."

"No, I'm busy."

"So I see."

The woman didn't attempt to enter the small room. Instead she leaned a hefty shoulder against the door frame and continued to smoke the stub of a cigar, balancing it delicately between her fingers. Lydia paused in arranging her possessions neatly on the quilt and studied her visitor.

"I'm sorry about your son."

The woman's face folded into a scowl. "Liev talks too much."

"*Da.* He's a real blabbermouth," Lydia said with a straight face.

The woman blinked, then smiled. The aroma of the cigar drifted across the room. "Don't worry, he's told me nothing that need give you sleepless nights. Just that you've traveled from China and are searching for someone."

"That's more than enough. It's one more fact than I know about you, so I'll ask you a question."

"Sounds fair."

"What do you want with Liev Popkov?"

"What does any woman want with a man?"

She swung her hips lasciviously and pushed the cigar into her mouth, sucking hard on it so that the tip glowed brightly. Lydia looked away. She folded her two skirts, one navy and the other a heavy green wool, and placed them in an orderly pile beside two pairs of rolled-up socks, a pair of scissors, three handkerchiefs, a book, and a small cotton drawstring bag.

"Was your son in the camp?" she asked without looking up.

"Yes."

"I'm sorry."

"Don't be."

Something about the way she said it drew Lydia's glance to her face. It was totally expressionless.

"He was one of the guards," Elena explained in a flat voice. "One of the prisoners killed him with a piece of glass. Cut his throat open."

Lydia's head filled with the image of blood bursting from the son's severed flesh, the young man clawing at his throat, eyes glazing. Was Jens there? Did he see it happen? Did he wield the weapon? Because whoever had done it would be dead by now. A pain started up in Lydia's throat. She unfolded and refolded one of the skirts, then pulled out a hairbrush from her bag. It wasn't special to look at, just plain and wooden with a cracked handle, but it had belonged to her mother. She placed it in line with the scissors and drawstring bag.

"Your son was a guard," she whispered, turning her head to one side. She spat on the floor with a sharp little hiss.

The woman nodded, all softness emptied from her eyes. "I know, he had it coming." She gave a little growl of despair in the back of her throat. "God only knows what the bastard did to those men."

Outside, a truck roared past, its headlamps carving through the darkness and flaring briefly into the room.

"But it must be hard to lose a son," Lydia said. "I'm sorry."

"I'm not."

"No parent would want to lose a child."

"Don't be so sure."

Lydia concentrated on her canvas bag and removed a pad of writing paper and a pencil. *Papa, would you want to lose a child?* She started a new row on the quilt and added an unopened bottle of rosewater that her widowed stepfather had presented to her for the journey. Dear Alfred. He was back in England now, but if he could see her now he would die of embarrassment. For an Englishman to hold a conversation about the loss of a son with a complete stranger would be tantamount to torture. Unthinkable. But here in Russia things were different. There was a raw edge that Lydia was starting to appreciate because it made doors easier to push open.

"Elena," she said with a sudden smile, "let's drink to your son."

From the bag she extracted a half-bottle of vodka, a small pewter cup upturned over its neck.

Elena's eyes lit up. She tossed the cigar butt onto the corridor floor and stamped on it. While Lydia unscrewed the cap, her visitor kicked the door shut and plonked herself down on the spare bed with a force that set the springs twanging.

"Right, little comrade, hand it over."

Lydia filled the metal cap to the brim, but instead of passing it across to the woman, she took a sip of it herself and proffered the bottle to Elena, who seized it with relish.

"*Za zadorovye*," Lydia said. "Good health."

Together they drank, Lydia from the cup, Elena from the bottle. The liquid scalded a path to Lydia's stomach and made her feel instantly sick. She took another sip.

"Don't hurt him, Elena."

"Who? My son? Too late for that."

"No, I mean Liev."

"Hah! What are you? His mother?"

"*Da.* Yes. His mother, his sister, and his nanny all rolled into one."

Elena laughed and took another swig. "He's a lucky man, then."

Lydia leaned forward. "Is he, Elena?"

"Of course. He's got you to fuss over him, he's got your brother to fight with, and he's got me to . . . well, to spice up his life, shall we say?" She flexed and rolled her shoulders, making her bosom dance. It was expertly done.

"Comrade Gorshkova," Lydia said with a sweet smile, "are you by any chance a whore?"

Elena blinked, inhaled noisily, looked affronted for a moment, then threw back her head and laughed so hard her breasts seemed in danger of bursting.

"Those eyes of yours are sharp as a snake's, Comrade Ivanova." She wiped her eyes on the back of her wrist and tipped another mouthful of vodka down her throat. "How did you know? A young creature like you should not be aware of such things."

"It's the way you look at men. As if they're . . . usable. Tools instead of people. I've seen the same look in the eyes of the painted ladies in Junchow."

"So you think I'm using your Cossack?"

"*Da.* And I wonder what for."

"Well, this time you're wrong, little comrade. My whoring days are just about over." She leaned back against the wooden headboard swinging her legs up onto the quilt. "Hardly surprising, is it? Look at me now."

They both looked at her, at the thighs broad as pillows under her skirt, the stomach billowing in soft folds, and the blue knots of varicose veins beneath her stockings. They studied her body as if it belonged to someone else. Lydia had never been invited to take part in such an intimate scrutiny before and found it appealing in an uncomfortable sort of way.

"Some men," she said, "like big women." Lydia was far from certain whether this was true, but she offered it anyway.

"*Chyort!* You are far too young to know what men like."

Lydia ducked away from the pale eyes and cursed the steady flow of color rising up her neck to her face. She hoped the woman would think it was the drink.

"Hah! I see." Beaming with anticipation, Elena linked her hands behind her head, which made her bosom rise alarmingly. "So who is he?"

"Who is who?"

"The one who sends flames into your cheeks and makes your eyes melt like butter in sunlight. Just the thought of him and your bones turn soft."

"There's no one. You're mistaken."

"Am I?"

"*Da.*" For a moment their eyes were fixed in a mildly hostile stare, then Lydia turned once more to her belongings on the bed and lifted the hairbrush. "There's no one," she said again.

She could hear the woman drinking more vodka, the swish of the liquid in the bottle, but it was followed by the sound of the cap being screwed firmly back in place. That surprised her. For a while neither spoke, and Lydia began to hope she might leave.

"I gave him away." Elena was speaking with her eyes shut, her lashes long and thick on her cheeks. They were much darker than her hair. "Then I let them take him. What kind of mother does that?"

"You mean your son, the one in the camp. What was his name?"

"Dominik."

"That's a nice name."

Elena smiled, her eyes still closed, and Lydia was certain she was picturing him.

"Was he handsome?"

"You young girls, you're all the same, always wanting your perfect man to be tall, dark, and handsome."

An image of Chang An Lo sprang into Lydia's mind and her mouth went dry.

"I'm forty-two," Elena said. "I was sixteen when I had Dominik, already a year in the brothel. They let me keep him for four weeks, but then . . ." She opened her eyes abruptly. "He was better off with a proper family."

"Did he know?"

"About me, you mean?"

"Yes."

"No, of course not, but"—Elena's pale eyes brightened—"I found out where he was living and I watched him grow up. Hung around outside his school and later saw him parade through town first as a Young Pioneer and later as one of Stalin's *Komsomol*."

Lydia reached across the gap between the beds and touched the woman's hand, just a brief brush of skin. "You must have been proud of him then."

"Yes, I was. But not now. I want to forget him now."

"Can parents ever forget their children?"

"Oh yes. You have to get on with your own life. What are children anyway? Just an encumbrance."

"I thought that . . ." Lydia stopped. She knocked back the remainder of her drink and asked instead, "Does Liev know?"

"Know what?"

"About your . . . occupation?"

The woman smiled, and this time it possessed a warmth that made Lydia realize why men might like her.

"Of course not," Elena scoffed.

"So why tell me?"

"Why indeed? I must be a fool."

"You may be many things, but I think a fool is not one of them."

Elena laughed and sat up, eyeing the array of possessions on the bed. Her inspection made Lydia suddenly aware of how meager they must look.

"So what book are you reading?"

"The poems of Marina Tsvetaeva. Do you know them?"

"No."

"Would you like to borrow it?" Lydia picked up the book, which was soft and battered from all the traveling, and offered it to her visitor.

Elena closed her eyes and sighed. "I'm too tired."

It occurred to Lydia that maybe Elena, like many women in Russia, had never learned to read. "As you're tired," she said, "would you like me to read some of it to you?"

"*Da*," the woman smiled. "I would like that. Your Russian is excellent."

Lydia opened the book and started to read.

SOUNDS CAME TO HER IN THE ROOM. OF BREATHING. OF A CAT yowling. The ticking of water pipes. The rumble of cartwheels. Sounds that told Lydia she was alive, but sometimes she wasn't sure. Silently, so as not to wake the sleeping woman on the next bed, she repacked her traveling bag. Each evening it was the same, the unpacking, the tidying, the repacking, and when it was finished she patted the bag like a sleepy old dog.

"There. All done," she said softly.

Then she lay down on her own bed and curled up tight around the bag, as if its neatness could keep the chaos inside her at bay. She pressed her cheek against its canvas side, inhaled its smell of soot and cigarettes.

Alexei didn't want her with him. Popkov would be consumed by this woman. Her father might not even remember her. And Chang An Lo was two thousand miles away. She crushed her cheek harder against the rough material, wrapping both arms around the bag so fiercely she could feel the handle create grooves in her skin. She tightened her grip even more. Her life was in splinters, but she was determined to hold it together.

Ten

China

CHANG AN LO HAD NOT EXPECTED TO SEE BLOOD, not here, not now.

Alone with his own thoughts, he had been taking pleasure in the long ride through the jungled mountains of Jinggang. His horse, a small and attentive mare, picked its way with skill along the rough tracks up toward the town of Zhandu. The air was heavy and humid, thick with insects and the sound of whirring wings, the temperature rising with each mile south. He brushed aside the thick undergrowth that stank of decay and rode at a gentle pace that satisfied both his horse and himself. Neither was in any hurry. Underfoot the trail was treacherous, as muddy and slippery as a monkey's arse, so that time and again a hoof skidded from under them.

"Calm your spirit, little one," he murmured to the horse.

He laid a hand on her muscular neck and clicked his tongue at her. Only once had he needed to dismount and lead her off the track, down into the dense vegetation of a steep hollow shrouded in mist. She had made no sound but stood silently at his side, ears laid back, his grip steady on her mane while a troop of riders passed by. They might be Red Army soldiers, but Chang took no chances. This was bandit country.

It was on the dirt road just outside the mountain stronghold of Zhandu that he reined his horse to a halt. A fork-shaped wooden frame had been driven into the ground at the side of the road and a man lashed to it with rawhide thongs. He was naked above the waist and his head hung down, eyes closed, as if he had dozed off, bored by the enforced inactivity and the unrelenting glare of the sun. But Chang knew he wasn't asleep. Flies had settled in a black iridescent crust that moved like a spill of oil over the man's chest.

How long he'd hung there as a warning to other Red Army deserters before he died was impossible to tell, but the three wounds in his chest where sharp-pointed *suo-biao* had been thrust in must have put a welcome end to his agonies.

Chang breathed deeply to still the rising tide of anger and commended the worthless soldier's spirit to his ancestors. Up here in the mountains the gods were close, almost visible in the mists, their voices echoing in the bamboo forests. When a man's time came, this was a good place to die. He bowed his head to the dead soldier, picked up the reins, and heeled the young mare onward into the town.

THE MAIN STREET OF ZHANDU WAS COBBLED AND BUSY. ALONG it rolled a cart laden with boulders among which scuttled lizards, shiny yellow like leaves. As Chang rode past, the stink of the two oxen hauling it drew clouds of flies to their moist muzzles, while the rumble of the wooden wheels sounded like thunder in his ears. He had grown too accustomed to silence.

The small town had been carved out of the mountain's rock face, and its people fought a daily battle with the jungle for possession of the surrounding land. Precious crops of rice and papaya tumbled over terraces in splashes of vivid green in sharp contrast to the more somber hues of the jungle that encircled them. Its hot breath scorched their young shoots.

The houses were single-story, constructed of wood and bamboo with gray clay tiles on the roofs, a bustling jostling jumble of them clustered around the cobbled streets. A clutch of rickshaws trundled past Chang, the pullers sweating under their wide coolie hats and glancing with interest at the stranger on the horse. Chang ignored them. It was always the same when he entered a new town or tasted a dish that was new to him, that sharp tug under his ribs, as if someone were trying to pull out his liver. He knew what it was.

It's you, my love, my fox girl. You. Your small fist inside me, giving me no peace.

Anything new, he felt the need to show her. To let her see the elements of China she didn't know. To watch her tawny eyes widen, her *fanqui* nose wrinkle up in delight at the sight of the wild sweeping curves of the rooflines, at the carvings of gods leering out from the beams, the fretwork painted a gaudy scarlet and gold. Everything in the south of China was brighter, more elaborate, fiercer than anywhere else, and he longed to see it through her eyes.

Abruptly he sat straighter in the saddle and surprised his horse with a sudden jab of heel. His loose black tunic clung to his back with sweat and he pushed the images of her out of his mind, closed his eyes to her full warm lips. Such desire weakened him. But he could not stop her laughter, like the song of a river, flowing into his head and making his heart float.

CHANG DISMOUNTED AT THE STONE WATER TROUGH. HE TOSSED a coin to one of the bristle-haired street urchins to hold the reins and watch over his horse. He doused his head under the water pump, hitched his saddlebag over one shoulder, and moved away down the street.

A barber was wielding his razor with grinning delight over the jaw of a customer on a stool outside his shop, and next to him a storyteller's booth was keeping them both entertained with tales of a rat king. Chang liked this town. The feel of it was . . . settling. He imagined staying here. His fears that it would be in turmoil were groundless; it was clearly more robust than he'd expected. He walked with a smooth easy stride, not disturbing the hum of workers and traders that ebbed and flowed around him. He had learned that the way you walk can make you visible or invisible, whichever you chose.

Today he was invisible.

"YOUR FINGERS GROW AS CLUMSY AS AN OLD WOMAN'S, MY friend."

The shoemaker was middle-aged, seated in the shade on a bamboo seat outside his shop and engrossed in sewing a long strip of leather with exquisitely intricate stitches. His fingers were figuring in fine detail a scene of a snake coiled around a monkey and, at the end of the strip, a lion waited patiently with open jaws. The shoemaker looked up from under his wide-brimmed hat woven from bamboo leaves, and for no more than a second his sharp black eyes were taken by surprise. They gleamed with pleasure as he peered at the figure against the sun, but then his long-boned face drooped into a frown.

"Chang An Lo, you piece of dog meat, where have you been all this time? And to what does this worthless town owe the honor of a visit from one of our leader's trusted servants?"

"It is not this worthless dung heap of a place I come to see. It is you, Hu Tai-wai, I need to speak with." In a movement as silky and silent as a cat's, he crouched down on a patch of dirt next to the shoemaker and lifted the tail of the strip of leather, running it through his fingers. "I hope I find my good friend in fine health."

The needle resumed its work. "I am well."

"And your family too? The honourable Yi-Ling and the beautiful Si-qi?"

The lines of the man's face softened. "My wife will be overjoyed to welcome you to our humble house. She has not seen you for two years and berates me that you stay away so long. She blames me."

Chang laughed softly. "A wife blames a husband for everything, from a plague of rats in the paddies to the loss of an elegantly painted fingernail while cooking his meal."

Hu Tai-wai grinned and treated Chang to a long affectionate inspection, taking in the state of his clothes and the stillness of his eyes. "And what do you know of wives, my friend?"

"Nothing, thank the gods."

But his voice must have betrayed him because the shoemaker didn't laugh. For a while neither spoke, but the silence lay comfortably between them while they observed the needle flying in and out of the leather as if it had a life of its own. A woman with pox scars shuffled past in the street, a yoke balanced across her drooping shoulders, cutting into her flesh. In each of the two buckets that dangled from it squirmed a black piglet, both squealing as piercingly as if someone had stepped on the toes of the gods. The heat and the noise lay heavy on Chang, and he leaned back against the wall behind him.

"The town has recovered?"

Hu Tai-wai turned and studied him intently. "From the honor of Mao Tse-tung's visit, you mean? You've seen the dead soldier?"

Chang nodded.

Hu Tai-wai sighed and Chang felt the weight of it. "There were more of them." The shoemaker gazed out in the direction of the wooden frame, hidden from their sight by a brightly decorated tearoom. "We took them down, but one had to remain."

"A warning to other soldiers who think of deserting the Red Army. Yes, Mao Tse-tung insists on it. But it is an army of peasants who cling to the belief that Mao will bring about the redistribution of land throughout China. That's why they fight for him. They long to own the fields they work, fields they want to pass on to their children and their children's children. When they discover that our Great and Wise Leader is more interested in power than in people, they try to return to their villages to harvest their crops but . . ." Chang silenced his tongue. Let his heart bleed in private. "Was he here long?"

Though seated, the shoemaker gave a deep bow over the leather work on his lap. "Yes, Mao was here long enough."

Chang glanced at the guarded face and murmured, "Tell me, my friend."

Hu Tai-wai resumed his stitching, meticulously outlining the twitching tail of the dying monkey. "He stayed here a month." His voice was low. "A section of his army camped outside on the terraces, spoiling our crops, but the men had nothing to do while their leader lazed in the best house in town, so they drank *maotai* and swaggered through the streets. They scared the girls and took whatever they wanted from the shops."

Chang hissed through his teeth. "Mao Tse-tung was a schoolteacher. He is not a military man and does not know how to control an army."

"No, unlike Zhu. With Zhu in command, that army was disciplined."

"But Mao stole Zhu's army from him. He humiliated Zhu and lied to Communist Party headquarters in Shanghai. You have to admit, old shoemaker, our leader is clever. His lust for power is so great and his ways so devious, he may yet conquer China."

Hu Tai-wai grunted.

"Was his latest wife, Gui-yuan, with him?" Chang asked.

"Yes, she was. As delicate as a morning flower. Together they took over the grandest and biggest house in Zhandu, spent each day in bed supping rich stewed beef and drinking milk." Hu Tai-wai abruptly snapped his thread with disgust. "Who in their right minds drinks milk? Milk is only for babies."

Chang smiled. "In the West I believe everyone drinks milk."

"Then they are sicker in the head than I thought."

Chang chuckled. "They say it is good for you." He had a moment's flash of a cup at his lips. The unpleasant fatty taste of milk in his mouth. A gentle *fanqui* voice telling him, "Drink." For her, he drank.

"It is better," he told the older man, "when Mao travels with his wife. Better for the towns he stays in."

"Why better? She was an expense to us each day she was here, demanding the best of everything."

"Even so, it is better." He stared at a young woman sweeping the doorstep of the rope seller's shop on the opposite side of the road. Her hair was long and braided prettily. "It is better for the town's girls," he said.

"I'd heard rumours," Hu Tai-wai scowled, his thick eyebrows swooping together in a black line. "I kept Si-qi locked in the house."

"A wise decision."

"So." Hu Tai-wai jabbed his needle into a scrap of leather that was tied around his wrist and left it there. "Tell me, whelp of the wind, why has the Chinese Communist Party sent one of their best code breakers to the lazy town of Zhandu?"

"No one knows I am here."

"Ah."

"I have come to speak with you in private."

"About what?"

"The Russians."

Hu Tai-wai gave him a slow amused smile. "Then you are a fool. You're too late, my young friend. The years when I was an adviser and negotiator with the Russians, the bearded ones, are long gone. You know I gave it up. Now I am just a poor country cobbler." His black eyes glittered, the lines around his mouth contented in the sunshine. "I value my life and my family too much. With Mao, as with Josef Stalin, that other power-crazed *vozhd*, you never know when he will tire of you. You blink and the next thing you know your head is raised on the point of a stick."

"But you've been to Soviet Russia."

"Many times."

"I fear we all dance to the tune of roubles now. So tell me about them, Hu Tai-wai. Tell me what I must prepare for."

HU TAI-WAI'S HOUSE WAS MODEST. NOTHING LIKE THE ELE-gant home Chang recalled that he used to possess in Canton, with its numerous courtyards and an abundance of jade and ancient carved furniture that had once belonged to his father and his father's father. Here everything was plain, sturdy and adequate for a shoemaker's family. Only in the hallway the shrine to his ancestors boasted of what once had been. Pearls and gold adorned the paintings of his parents and his grandparents. Silver platters offered up carefully cooked slices of veal and dolphin along with colorful fruits and sweetmeats. On a marble stand an engraved glass goblet, so fine it was barely there, contained thick ruby wine.

Chang experienced a tug of envy when he set eyes on the shrine, and a spill of guilt flowed into his mind that he had created nothing similar for his own dead family. He dipped his hand into an onyx dish of azalea petals and sprinkled them over a bowl of pomegranates and mangoes, murmuring words that bound him to his father's spirit. He lit an incense burner and watched the fragrant smoke coil up in a thin wisp of faith.

Communism decried faith. Just as it decried the individual. It was designed to train the human mind to produce a new and improved version of mankind. That was the future task of Communism and that was the battle that Chang was committed to. He loved China with all his soul and was convinced that Communism was the only way forward for his country. He believed its ideals could bring peace and equality to an unjust society in which fathers were forced to decide which child to sell in order to feed the others. At the same time glossy fat overlords bathed in goat's milk and burdened their tenants with land rents that crippled their backs and shortened their lives.

Chang gazed at the flame in the burner. His black eyes swallowed its fragile flicker, and he felt the familiar flame of rage in his gut flare alongside it. It was a fire he fought to control, but time and again it blazed unchecked, beyond his reach. Scorching him.

"Chang An Lo, you bring light to our humble home and joy to my unworthy heart."

Chang bowed low to Yi-Ling, wife of the shoemaker. "It is an honor and a pleasure to see you again. I have traveled far and your home is as always a bed of rose petals for my weary bones."

He bowed again to emphasize his regard for her. He was always tongue-tied and awkward in her presence, uncertain of how to express his gratitude to this woman. She was broad hipped and broad cheeked, with a high forehead, but it was the warmth in her eyes that made her beautiful. He would not presume to guess her age, but she was old enough to be his mother and kind enough to have taken him into her home when his parents were beheaded in Peking when the Republic was declared.

Yet it was Yi-Ling's husband, Hu Tai-wai, who widened his world. He was the one who had introduced the young Chang, son of a court adviser to the Empress of China, to the ideals and aims of Karl Marx and Communism, the very reverse of all he had previously been exposed to. But Chang had not stayed long, unwilling to endanger their lives by association with him. So he had moved on and it had become the recurring pattern of his life, but a part of his heart had always remained in this woman's pocket.

She poured tea for him now into small handleless cups. "The gods have kept you safe. I thank them for that and will take a gift to the temple."

"They have been kind to you too. I have never seen Hu Tai-wai so fat and relaxed. He sits out front there at his work, as contented as a cat in the sun."

She smiled. "I wish I could say the same for you, Chang An Lo."

"Do I look so bad?"

"Yes. Like something a dog has spat out."

"Then I'll take a bath, if I may."

"You're welcome. But that's not what I meant. I was looking only in your eyes, and what I see there tears at my heart."

Chang lowered his gaze and sipped his tea, and for a moment silence settled in the small humid room, where the air moved sluggishly and reluctantly each time they spoke. Eventually Chang raised his eyes, and they both knew that part of their conversation was over.

"How is Si-qi?" he asked.

"My daughter is well."

Yi-Ling's face lit up, as if the sun had rolled over it. Her eyes met his, intent and hopeful, and instantly he realized what plans blossomed behind them. Si-qi was sixteen, of marriageable age.

"Go," she said, and flicked a delicate hand to urge him on his way. "Go and speak to her. She's in the courtyard."

He stood and bowed with respect. She snorted gleefully.

"Before I go, Yi-Ling, I would like to give you a gift."

Her thin straight eyebrows rose, and she brushed at her black skirt uncomfortably. "That is not necessary, Chang An Lo."

"I think it is."

He opened his leather saddlebag and removed something bundled up in an old shirt. He held it out to her. She rose to her feet and accepted it, but when she felt its weight, her smile grew full of curiosity and she unwrapped the gift.

"Chang An Lo," she whispered. Her breath shuddered.

In her hand lay a gun.

"Yi-Ling, I know that your husband refuses to own a firearm anymore because he says he is finished with violence. But I fear violence has not yet finished with him, nor with China, so I want you to have . . ."

Her eyes darted to the door, but Hu Tai-wai was still outside with his leather and needles. Deftly she rewrapped the pistol and slid it into the embroidery workbox beside her chair.

He stepped nearer to her. "This is just between us," he said. "For you."

She nodded and for the first time in his life she leaned close, smelling of sandalwood, and kissed his cheek. An intense little brush of her dry lips.

"And for Si-qi," she breathed.

SI-QI WAS TALL WITH LONG SKINNY LEGS AND ONE WOODEN foot. But it was hard even to notice her foot because her face drew men's eyes the way a pot of honey draws bears. Whereas her mother's face was broad, hers was slender and delicate with skin pale as fresh cream and eyes that were soft and patient. She was wearing a pale blue dress, seated on a bench under a fig tree in the courtyard behind the house, her dark head bent over sheets of paper.

At the sight of Chang she started to cry.

He bowed a greeting to her. "No tears, my beautiful Si-qi, look what I have brought you." He laughed and took out a book from his saddlebag. "It's to improve your English."

Each time he'd visited Hu Tai-wai during the years spent in Canton, he had labored diligently on teaching Si-qi to speak English. Without a strong foot, lost as a baby to a snakebite, her choice of work would be limited and neither he nor her father wanted her to be dependent on a husband. So their plan was that she would become an interpreter. She was quick, her mind retentive, eager to learn. Though sometimes he wondered if she was doing it for herself . . . or for him.

"*Xie xie*," she said shyly. "Thank you. *The Jungle Book* by Rudyard Kipling." Her eyes shone with pleasure and he wished he'd brought her more than one book.

"It's about a boy who is brought up in the jungle by wolves."

She slid a glance at him under her long black lashes. "Is that what you feel happened to you? Brought up in our household by Communist wolves?" She laughed, and something about the sound of it shortened his breath.

"If your parents' house was a jungle, then you were always the golden flower that enchanted us all with your perfume."

She laughed again, delighted, swaying her long hair in a luxurious ripple of velvet, and opened the book. He sat down beside her and together they began to read, word by word, page by page, and all the time he was aware of the nearness of her, the softness of her, and what a perfect wife she would make for him.

Only once did she turn to him and inquire in a whisper, "Have you news of my brother, Biao?"

"No. None."

Her eyes clouded with disappointment and she returned to the book.

A FLICKER OF MOVEMENT INSIDE HIS MIND. THAT WAS ALL. AS though Kaa, the snake, had slid off the pages, silent and stealthy. Chang raised his head, listening.

"What is it?" Si-qi asked softly.

He shook his head, attentive to every sound. The sky was leaking colors onto the roofs, reds and yellows and secretive misty purples. The day was changing, preparing for evening, insects thickening the air, strange harrowing sounds rising like ghost spirits from the jungle.

Was that what he'd heard? That shift in the day?

Si-qi touched his hand, warm and weightless on his skin. "What is the . . . ?"

But Chang was on his feet, saddlebag over his shoulder, and moving fast to the far end of the courtyard toward a black wooden door that would open onto a back alleyway. He turned the handle. It was locked. As he took two steps backward to give himself the impetus to spring to the ridge tiles on top of the wall, the door to the house burst open. Hu Tai-wai and Yi-Ling were marched into the courtyard by a troop of five soldiers. The red band of Mao's army was emblazoned on their sleeves.

"Chang An Lo," the leader of the soldiers said firmly but with unmistakable respect. "I apologize for disturbing you, but you are summoned to Guitan."

"Summoned by whom?"

"By our Great Leader, Mao Tse-tung."

Eleven

THE DOOR BANGED OPEN. A BLAST OF ICY AIR TORE through the tavern. It carved chunks out of the solid pall of smoke that hovered like death over the heads of the drinkers. Alexei glanced up from the playing cards in his hand. So. Popkov had at last turned up. The big Cossack was brushing snow from his shaggy beard, but his movements were unsteady, swaying on his feet, his single eye already bloodshot as a pig's heart.

You stupid fucking bastard. We were meant to be watching each other's backs tonight. What good are you to me in that state?

Alexei returned his attention to the game in hand. His mind was struggling to concentrate. This was his fourth session of cards in as many bars, each one buried in a back alley that stank of cat's piss and despair. The bare wooden tables were stained with beer, the floor etched with vodka and waxed with tears. These places were strictly all male. Not a smooth cheek or a shapely leg in sight. Just a huddle of men determined to drown their day's cares and the screech of their women's voices in the glorious oblivion of a glass.

"Get on with it, will you? Haven't got all night, you know."

Alexei ignored his opponent's grousing. He'd selected this man deliberately out of all the ones who were shuffling cards at the tables. He chose him because he was fat. Fat means food, plenty of it. The card player must be stuffing himself on a diet of kickbacks and bribes, a feast of fistfuls of roubles. Clearly the man was an informer. A whisperer. He sold information.

A chair crashed to the floor nearby, and out of the corner of his eye Alexei caught sight of Popkov weaving a path toward him.

"Where the hell have you been?" Alexei snapped without looking up from his cards.

Popkov shuffled his ungainly frame around the table and stood behind Alexei's chair. He laughed out loud as he spotted Alexei's hand, and the alcohol on his breath spilled over his shoulder.

"Better give up while you're losing," the big man mumbled in Alexei's ear, then chortled at his own joke.

The fat man opposite joined in the merriment. "Your friend is right." He held up his own cards in a fan and waved them to and fro, as if waving Alexei's chances good-bye.

"Game's not over yet," Alexei responded with irritation.

He was about to toss another few roubles onto the pile in the center when he received a nudge in his side that was so violent his fingers jerked open and he let go of his hand. The cards slid across the dirty tabletop and four of them tumbled to the floor, three face up.

"What the hell . . . ?" Alexei reached for the fallen cards. But it was too late. The fat man had moved fast despite his paunch and had already scooped them up.

"A seven, nine, and ten, that's no winning hand." The man grinned and dipped his heavy mustache into his glass of beer. "Now give up, like your fine friend said." His eyes shone gray and greedy.

Alexei threw up his hands in surrender, letting his opponent sweep up the roubles and pocket them. He looked up at Popkov. "You crazy drunken idiot. You've bloody lost me . . ." But then he saw the look in Popkov's eyes. "Okay, okay. Game's over." Alexei rose from his chair and gave a mock salute to his card partner. "It's not my night, it seems."

But the fat man wasn't listening. He was already trying to ensnare another player from the group huddled around the bar. Alexei reluctantly obeyed Popkov's hand on his shoulder and allowed himself to be propelled toward the back of the room, where there was a spare table. They both sat down. Alexei thought about the lost roubles and sighed, but he lit himself a cigarette, inhaled deeply, and looked across at Popkov.

"You're not as drunk as you appear, are you?"

Popkov's face broke into a sly smile. "I never am. You should know that by now."

"So what's the great hurry that you have to break up my game?"

"I think the game I've been playing may be worth far more to you."

"So?"

"So I've been having a drink."

"Correction. Drinks."

"Of course. If it hadn't been more than one, I would have learned nothing. Just listen to me, will you, for a change?"

Alexei sat back in his chair, avoiding the Cossack's fumes. "All right. Go on. Where were you?"

"I was in a brothel."

"Oh shit. Don't tell me you've got the clap."

"Just shut up. I wasn't there to touch any of the girls, I was on the lookout for a guard from the camp. They'd be desperate, see? I reckoned the place would be crawling with them."

Alexei took a drag on his cigarette to hide his surprise. The Cossack wasn't as dumb as he looked.

"And did you find one?"

"You bet I did. Almost as big as me, he is, and none of the girls wanted him, you could tell." He lowered his voice and dropped into a disconcertingly confidential tone. "Sometimes these girls are too small, you see, for our—"

"Enough, *spasibo*."

Popkov scratched at his eye patch and resumed his tale. "The man was staggering about the room, knocking into everything and everyone in sight. The madam was yelling, 'Someone take this fucking guard back to his camp. Get him out of here!' So I did."

Alexei offered the Cossack one of his cigarettes and lit it for him. It was a small gesture. "Okay, so what then?"

"He's a big guy, like I said. Kept collapsing in the street, so I had to—"

"—pick him up. Being such a gentlemanly character."

"Let me finish, will you?" Popkov scowled at Alexei. "At least I didn't sit around playing cards all night, losing good roubles to—"

"The trouble with you, my friend, is that you don't have a strategic mind."

The single black eye glared at him through the smoke. "Meaning?"

"Meaning that the loss of a few roubles was necessary to discover . . ." Alexei paused, making the big man wait. ". . . that there are going to be heavy troop movements through Felanka in the next few weeks. That means trains. Frequent trains coming and going, a constant stream of new faces creating confusion." He leaned forward, elbows on the filthy table, gaze intent on Popkov. "If we can finish our business quickly, we can be out of here sooner than I expected. But"—he hesitated, finding the next words hard—"I need you to watch out for Lydia."

"I always watch out for Lydia Ivanova."

"I think she might try to ride one of the trains back to Selyansk." The thought of his sister on one of those troop trains packed with soldiers, traveling on her own, turned his stomach.

The Cossack stabbed out his cigarette in one of the spills of beer on the tabletop. It hissed as he lumbered to his feet with a sudden urgency. "Let's get moving."

Together they wove a path to the door. "It's not Selyansk she'll be aiming to get to," Popkov muttered as he yanked it open.

THE NIGHT WAS STARLESS, THE WIND A SLAP IN THE FACE. FRESH snow lay soft underfoot. Alexei followed the Cossack down a narrow back street where there were no lights, just a dreary row of warehouses whose doors rattled like dead men's bones in the buffeting of the wind. The smell of something burning caught at Alexei's nostrils and grew stronger when Popkov took a turn into an open yard. Flames were leaping from inside a metal container drum that stood in front of a small stone storage shed. Popkov headed straight for it.

"What have you done to him?" Alexei asked with foreboding.

Popkov's chuckle told more than Alexei cared to know.

The big ox kicked open the door. The shifting glow of the flames leapt inside and curled up on a pale face that looked dead. It was attached to an extremely large male body stretched out on its back on the floor with a chain looped several times around its neck. Each end of the long chain was hooked onto one of the metal shelf brackets that lined the walls on both sides of the shed. The man couldn't move his head more than a fraction either way. It was no wonder his eyes were closed. Could he breathe?

Alexei asked coldly, "Popkov, did you have to? What was wrong with bringing him to the bar and asking him questions over a few more vodkas? Tell me, you ox-brain, what was wrong with that as an option?"

The Cossack looked taken aback. He held both hands out like plates to the warmth of the flames and shrugged mildly. "He might not have wanted to give us the answers. This way is . . . surer."

That was probably true. But it was not the point.

With a snort of disgust Alexei stepped into the storehouse and unhooked one end of the chain from the wall. A faint choke like a dog's cough issued from the man on the floor. At least the poor devil was still alive. With no apparent damage other than a telltale swelling on his jaw, he rolled over on his side, muttered something incomprehensible, and started to snore.

"*Podnimaisa!* Get up!" Alexei barked. He backed it up with a prod of his boot.

This produced a grunt. He bent down and hauled the man to his feet, and they staggered out of the shed into the night air. Its icy blast instantly froze the alcohol in their blood and the big guard shuddered but sobered up enough to stand alone, listing precariously toward the heat inside the drum. He was younger than Alexei had at first thought, a clean-shaven, good-looking face, early thirties probably.

"Now," Alexei said. The sooner this was over the better. "I need to ask you a few questions."

"Piss off."

The guard started out with an odd sort of flat-footed gait toward the yard entrance. It was like watching a duck on ice. Popkov stepped away from the fire and tapped him on the back, except that one of Popkov's taps was like anybody else's full-bodied thumps. The man went sprawling to the snow-covered ground, facedown, arms and legs splayed, and before he could even think about what had happened to him, Popkov was sitting astride his back. He yanked off the guard's hat, tossed it into the fire, and seized a handful of thick fair hair in his fist. He wrenched the man's head back and waited for Alexei to begin.

The Cossack was efficient, Alexei had to give him that, but this was a way of doing business that disgusted him.

"What's your name?" Alexei demanded.

A dry croak issued from the guard's tortured throat.

"Ox-brain," Alexei snapped, "let the man speak."

The grip on the hair loosened a touch, so that the guard could swallow.

"Your name?"

"Babitsky." A hoarse whisper.

"Well, Babitsky, it's quite simple. I want to know whether a certain person is a prisoner in the Trovitsk labor camp."

Babitsky grunted.

"So if I give you a name, you will tell me whether he's—"

"*Nyet.*"

Without hesitation Popkov bounced the guard's face on the ground. Up and down. Just once. But it came up with a nose covered in blood.

"For fuck's sake, stop that!" Alexei exploded. "Babitsky, just answer my question and then you can go."

The man moaned and spat out blood. "I only know the prisoners by numbers. Not names."

Fuck.

"So who would have the list of names?"

"The office."

"Who works in the office? A name this time."

The man's eyes were growing hazy and he was having trouble breathing. With a mountain crushing his lungs, it was hardly surprising.

"Get off him," he said to Popkov.

For a moment their eyes met, and Alexei prepared to deliver that punch he'd been promising himself all evening. But Popkov wasn't stupid. He gave a flash of teeth, released the hair in his fist, and raised himself up on his knees so that he was still astride the guard but no longer resting his weight on him.

Babitsky dragged in air and said in a rush, "The camp office is run by Mikhail Vushnev. He knows them all."

"Where will I find this Vushnev when he comes into town? Where does he drink?"

"The bar"—he spat more blood onto the snow—"down by the tire factory. It's a dump but it's always got some fuckable girls serving the beer."

Alexei removed a handkerchief from his coat pocket, wiped the man's bleeding face, and rose to his feet, thankful to be at a distance from him. He dropped the scarlet cloth into the fire. He wished he could drop the whole of tonight into the flames as easily.

"Okay, let him go."

For once Popkov did as he was told.

The man staggered to his feet, cursing. Alexei took out a packet of cigarettes, shook out two, lit them both, and handed one to Babitsky. He watched the man's blood drip onto the cigarette.

"Fuck you," Babitsky groaned, drawing smoke into his lungs. "Fuck the lot of you. I'm off tomorrow out of this freezing shit hole."

"Where are you going?"

"What's that to you?"

"Nothing."

"I've been posted to Moscow." His split lips curled in a bitter smile. "So fuck you and your questions."

Alexei turned away. He'd seen enough. He had a name: Mikhail Vushnev. That's where he'd start. Without the damn Cossack this time.

Twelve

LYDIA LAY BACK ON HER BED AND THOUGHT about the bargain she had struck with Alexei. She had promised to stay in her room in exchange for keeping Popkov at his side tonight, but would he stick to his word? Her nerves were tight and her eyelids burned. That was the trouble with making deals with people; you never knew whether they'd let you down. She stared up at the ceiling, at a damp patch on it that had oozed into the shape of a giraffe, probably a few leaky pipes up there. Like leaky tongues, they couldn't be trusted.

Your Russian is excellent. Elena's words drifted back into her head and brought with them similar words she had once said to Chang herself. She murmured them now. *Your English is excellent.* It had been summertime and the Chinese sky was huge that day, a bright peacock-blue sheet of silk shimmering above them. She smiled at the memory and let her mind spiral down into it as readily as a bee spirals down into the sweet overpowering scent of an orchid. She didn't struggle against it. Not this time. Day after day here in this cold Russian landscape she was fighting to mold a future, but this time, just for tonight, she allowed herself the sweet fluid pleasure of slipping back into the past.

Chang An Lo had led her down a dirt track to Lizard Creek, a small wooded inlet to the west of the town of Junchow. The morning sun lazed on the surface of the water and the birch trees offered dappled shade to the flat gray rocks.

"I am honored that you think my English acceptable," Chang had replied politely.

Her heart had been racing. It was a risk, coming here alone with a young man she scarcely knew, and to make matters even worse he was Chinese *and* a Communist. Her mother would tie her to the bedpost if she knew. But already their lives, his and hers, had become entwined in a way she barely understood. She could feel the hooks like tiny little darts sinking into the soft and tender parts of her body, into her stomach and the thin white flesh of her thighs. Tugging at the strong beat of her heart. His stillness was as elegant as his movements in his black V-necked tunic and loose trousers. Horrible rubber shoes on his feet. Earlier he had waited for her outside the English church where she had greeted him very formally, hands together and eyes on the ground, bowing to him.

"I wish to thank you. You saved me in the alleyway and I am grateful. I owe you thanks."

He did not move, not a muscle shifted in his face or body, but something changed somewhere deep inside him, as if a closed place had opened. The warmth that flowed from him took her by surprise.

"No," he said, eyes fixed intently on her. "You do not owe me your thanks." He came one step closer, so close she could see tiny secret flecks of purple in his eyes. "The people-traffickers would have cut your throat when they were done with you. You owe me your life."

"My life is my own. It belongs to no one but me."

"And I owe you mine. Without you I would be dead. That Foreign Devil policeman's bullet would be in my head now and I would be with my ancestors, if you had not come out of the night and stopped him." He bowed very low. "I owe you my life."

"Then we're even." She'd laughed, uncertain how serious this was meant to be. "A life for a life."

Now at the creek she noticed the way he squatted down on a patch of grass at the edge of the water, keeping his distance from her, and she wondered if he was being careful not to alarm her. Or was it because he couldn't bear to be near a Foreign Devil, yet another *fanqui*. She was lazing on a slab of rock, stretching out her bare ankles in the sun, ducking her face under the brim of her straw hat. Her hat was battered and her dress was old. They embarrassed her. She stared at a small brown bird attempting to extract a juicy grub from a fallen branch and hoped Chang An Lo wouldn't look at her.

"I had an English tutor for many years in Peking," he continued. "He taught me well."

She peeked at him from under the shade of her hat and was shocked to see him unwinding a blood-soaked cloth from his foot. Oh God, the guard dog last night. Its teeth must have done far more damage than she'd realized. She felt a wave of nausea at the sight of his skin hanging in scarlet strips from the bone. A physical pain in her chest. How could he walk on a foot in that state?

He glanced up and caught her staring open-mouthed at his wound. Her gaze rose to his face, and for a long moment their eyes met and held. He looked away. She watched in silence as he placed his foot in the swirling flow of the river and rubbed it with his fingers, so that clots of blood drifted to the surface, making the water speckled with brown spots like a fish's back. Quickly she rose and knelt on the grass beside him. In her hand lay the needle and thread he had asked her to fetch for him. Now she understood why.

"You'll need these," she said and held them out.

But as he reached for them, she made a decision and lifted them away from him. "Would it help," she asked, "if I did it?"

A spark of something she couldn't decipher leapt into his eyes. Their blackness seemed to be consumed by something bright and untouchable. She swallowed. Appalled at what she'd just offered.

The first time she pushed the needle in she expected him to cry out, but he didn't. She darted a look of concern at his face. To her amazement he seemed to be staring at her hair and smiling, his black eyes full of secret thoughts. After that she just kept sewing. In fact she became bolder, concentrating more on making the work neater than on whether it hurt, aware of the scars it would leave. All the time she rinsed away the blood with her handkerchief so that she could see what she was doing, and carefully avoided thinking about the white glimpses of the delicate bones underneath.

When it was over, she pulled off her underskirt, used Chang's knife to cut it into strips, and bound up his foot. It looked clumsy but it was the best she could do. *Chyort!* She was no better at bandaging than she was at sewing. Without even asking, she cut his shoe open and tied it on the underside of the bandage with two more strips of cloth.

"There," she said when she'd finished. "That's better."

"Thank you."

Chang gave her a deep bow as he sat on the grass, and she had the feeling he didn't want her to see his face. Why? What was it that he was holding back from her?

"Don't thank me. If we go around saving each other's lives, then that makes us responsible for each other. Don't you think?" She laughed lightly.

She heard him inhale sharply. Had her words annoyed him? Had she presumed too much? She felt suddenly out of her depth, uncertain where to place her foot in these unfathomable and unfamiliar Chinese waters she had entered. She scrambled to her feet, kicked off her sandals, and waded into the shallows. The creek rippled against her legs, cooling her skin, and she splashed water over the hem of her dress to remove the blood from it. His blood. Entwined in the fibers of her clothes. She stared at it, touched one of the smears with the tip of her finger, and stopped rinsing it away into the river.

"Lydia Ivanova."

It was the first time he'd spoken her name. On his tongue it sounded different. Less Russian. More . . .

"Lydia Ivanova," he said again, his voice quiet as the breeze through the grass, "what is it that is such trouble to you?"

She felt a tremor. She didn't know if it was in her own blood or in the water, but in that bright sunlit moment she knew she'd got it wrong. He could see right through her, her thoughts as transparent to him as the water droplets that trailed behind her hand. That intake of breath she'd heard wasn't annoyance. It was because he knew, as she knew, that they *were* responsible for each other now. As she looked across at Chang An Lo where he was resting on his elbows, watching her with his black gaze, their eyes fixed on each other and she was aware of something tangible forming between them. A kind of thread, shimmering through the air. It was as elusive as a ripple in the river, yet as strong as one of the steel cables that held the new bridge over the Peiho.

"Tell me, Lydia, what lies so heavy on your heart?"

She released the hem of her dress and as it floated around her legs, she was again acutely aware of how shabby it was. She made her decision.

"Chang An Lo," she said, "I need your help."

"I STOLE A NECKLACE FROM A MAN'S COAT POCKET LAST NIGHT." She was back on her rock, perched on it like one of the orange lizards, head up and limbs tense, ready to flee. "In the Ulysses Club."

The Ulysses Club was the haunt of the British colonials in the International Settlement in Junchow, a place that was absurdly grand and stuffy and utterly desirable to Lydia. Try living in a drab airless attic, she had once scolded her friend Polly, and then see if the Ulysses Club holds any charm for you.

"That's why the police arrived at the club last night," she explained to Chang. "The loss was discovered before I could get out. So I had to hide the necklace." She was talking too fast. She made herself slow down. "I had to leave without it after we'd all been questioned and searched."

She kept darting glances at Chang, but his face remained smooth and unshocked. That was something, at least. Never before had she admitted any of her thefts to anyone, and they had been nowhere near the value of this necklace. She was nervous.

"It was horrible," she added.

Despite the cumbersome bandage, he uncoiled from the grass with ease, sat up, and leaned forward, black gaze intent on her. "Where did you hide the necklace?"

Lydia swallowed. She had to trust him. Had to. "In the mouth of the stuffed bear outside the gentlemen's cloakroom."

Light seemed to leap from the surface of the river and fill his face. He laughed and the sound of it created a strange contentment in her chest.

"You want me to get it back for you." His words were not a question.

"Yes." She added a deep bow.

"Why me? Why not you?"

"I'm not allowed into the club. Last night was a special occasion." In the silence that followed she felt the full weight of what she was asking.

"I am not permitted to enter either," he reminded her. "No Chinese. So tell me how I am supposed to slip my hand into the bear's mouth."

"That's up to you. You've already proved you are . . . resourceful."

"You realize that if I'm caught, I will be imprisoned. Or worse." She closed her eyes. Sick of herself.

"I know," she whispered.

"Lydia."

She opened her eyes and blinked, astonished. With no sound he had crossed the stretch of grass between them and was standing in front of her, tall and lithe and yet so still he barely seemed to breathe.

"I could be executed," he said softly.

She threw back her hair and met his gaze. "Then don't get caught."

He laughed and she heard in it a wild rush of the energy that was usually so controlled in him. He touched her hand, the briefest brush of skin, but it was all it took to make her understand. He was like her. Danger made his blood flow faster. What others saw as risk, he saw as enticement. They were the mirror image of each other, two parts of the same whole, and that moment of skin against skin was the drawing together of the splintered pieces.

"Chang An Lo," she said firmly, "make certain you are not caught." She tilted her head at him. "Because if you are, I won't get my necklace."

He smiled at her, his mouth gentle. "Is it so valuable?"

"Yes. It's made of rubies."

"I meant," he paused, studying her face, "is it so valuable to you?"

"Of course. How else can I ever make a life, a proper life I mean,

not this miserable scratching on the edge of survival? For me . . .
and for my mother. She's a pianist. How else can I buy her the Erard
grand piano she craves?"

"A piano?"

"Yes."

"You'd risk everything . . . for a piano?"

Abruptly a chasm widened between their feet, so deep its bottom
lay far out of sight in the shadows beneath. A chasm neither of them
had even noticed was there.

Thirteen

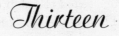

THE KNOCK ON THE DOOR WAS SHARP. THE sound dragged Lydia back to Russia and the present with a jolt, and a familiar nausea flooded her stomach, making it ache as the wisps of remembrance were wrenched away. She rolled off the quilt, her bare feet chill on the boards though she was wrapped in her coat. It surprised her to find Elena heavily asleep on the other bed. She'd forgotten her. The woman's mouth hung open, yet in sleep she looked younger, prettier, less formidable somehow.

Another rap shook the door. Lydia didn't need to ask who it was. She debated whether to answer it at all, but she knew he wouldn't give up. Her brother didn't ever give up. She opened the door and Alexei was standing outside in the corridor, his long face pinched with cold and worry. He wasn't quite quick enough to hide the look of relief that flicked through his green eyes at the sight of her, and she didn't know whether to be pleased or insulted by it. Right now she was too lonely to care.

"You're here," he said.

"Yes. I promised I would be."

"Good."

There was nothing more to say. He'd checked up on her; she was here; that was it. In the next room behind the paper-thin wall a woman suddenly started to laugh, but Lydia felt no urge to smile. The hole inside her was too big, too consuming; it had swallowed everything she had.

"Alexei." She whispered her brother's name as something to hold on to. "Alexei." Her eyes focused on the third button of his coat. She couldn't bear to look at his face because at the moment she had no armor. It had all disappeared down the hole.

"Take me with you."

"*Nyet*. It's too dangerous. I'll work better without you. Stay here."

She nodded and, still without looking at him, quietly closed the door. She leaned her back against it and listened to her brother's footsteps walking away from her. Fast. As though he couldn't wait to leave her behind. Slowly she slid down to the floor and wrapped her arms around her shins, balancing her chin on her knees.

THE FIRST PERSON ALEXEI SPOTTED AS HE ENTERED THE BAR near the tire factory was the blond truck driver, the one who had flirted with Lydia so outrageously on the road back from the foundry. What was his name? Niko. He was trying to build a precarious tower of full vodka glasses on a table. Alexei elbowed his way to the long counter at the back of the smoke-filled room.

"Vodka," he ordered.

A bottle and a glass appeared in front of him.

"*Spasibo*." He poured himself a drink and threw it down his throat. "And one for yourself."

The barman was small with tough no-nonsense eyes and a broken front tooth. He nodded and filled a glass for himself but left it untouched on the bar. Alexei could smell the sweet odor of almond oil on him.

"What is it you want?" The man spoke with a strong Muscovite accent.

"I'm looking for someone."

"Got a name?"

"Mikhail Vushnev. I'm told he drinks here. Do you know him?"

"Maybe."

"Is he in tonight?"

He didn't even bother to look around. "*Nyet.*"

Alexei knew he was lying. He shrugged, poured himself another drink, and pretended to watch the truck driver's antics, all the time checking out the room. A dump, Babitsky had called it. He was right about that. Airless, gloomy, and needing the attentions of a scrubbing brush but warm and comfortable in a lazy sort of way. There was the usual clutch of dedicated drinkers huddled around the tables, a thin child on one man's knee, while a dog lay under another man's chair with watchful eyes. In one corner two men were playing chess, totally engrossed.

Alexei picked up his drink and ambled over to them, keeping a respectful distance from their table but close enough to observe their moves. For ten minutes he stood there, absorbed in the game. During that time two girls in colorful Uzbek dress materialized from a back room, flashing dark southern eyes and smooth olive skin as they balanced beer on trays. The atmosphere in the place changed with their arrival as if an electric switch had been flipped. Even one of the chess players was distracted enough to lose his rook foolishly, and his king fell soon after. One of the girls brushed her hip invitingly against Alexei as she squeezed past and pouted her full crimson lips at him, but he shook his head and lit another cigarette.

"Don't turn her down, comrade," the younger of the chess players laughed. "You never know when you'll get another offer."

"I'll take my chances," Alexei replied and held out the cigarette pack toward him. The man accepted and stuck one behind his ear for later. "You play well," Alexei commented, nodding at the *shakhmatnaya doska*, the chessboard.

"*Spasibo.* Do you play?"

"Badly."

The older player scrutinized him from deep-set eyes. "I doubt that," he muttered.

Alexei leaned down and righted the white king. "I was told I could find an excellent player here. Mikhail Vushnev was the name. I'm in the mood for a good match. Do you know him?"

"If you want a good match, comrade, Mikhail is not your man," the younger one laughed scornfully. "He's as much use on a chess-board as one of those girls in a nunnery, so—"

"Leonid," the older one interrupted, "maybe a chess match is not the kind of match our friend here has in mind."

Fuck. The man was sharp. Alexei gave him a careful smile. "Is he here, this Vushnev?"

"*Nyet.*"

The younger one looked at his companion in surprise. "Boris, have you gone soft in the head or something . . . ?"

"*Nyet.*" This time even Leonid heard the emphasis in the word and kept his mouth shut.

"Thanks anyway," Alexei said pleasantly.

Aware of eyes on his back, he moved over to the bar where Niko was fondling one of the girls and getting his hands smacked for his trouble, ordered another vodka, then turned as if he had all the time in the world and no thought in his head other than where his next drink was coming from. He let his gaze skim the tables, his eyes narrowed against the smoke, and settled for no more than a heartbeat on a lean man with brilliantined hair, smoking a long-stemmed pipe over by the stove.

Alexei's gaze moved on indifferently. But he had his man. Young Leonid had betrayed him without even knowing it with just a glance at the mention of Vushnev's name. But it was enough.

ALEXEI PLACED A BOTTLE OF VODKA AND TWO GLASSES ON THE man's table.

"*Dobriy vecher.* Good evening, comrade. May I join you?"

He didn't wait for an answer but pulled up a chair and sat down. The fact that the man's angular face registered no surprise was not lost on him. Alexei poured them both a drink.

"*Za tvoye zdorovye!*" He raised his glass. "Good health!"

"*Za tvoye zdorovye, tovarishch,*" Vushnev responded, but he didn't touch the glass.

His gray eyes were thoughtful and curious, but he asked no questions. In Soviet Russia, questions could get you into trouble. He was a man of around forty and contented himself with chewing on the stem of his pipe, shadows shifting in the hollows of his face, light skidding off the gleam of his hair. Something about the shininess of the man grated on Alexei's nerves, but he dug up a smile of sorts and asked, "You're Comrade Vushnev, I believe?"

"I wondered how long it would take you to find me."

"You knew I was looking?"

The man snorted with amusement. "Of course."

"Word travels fast in Felanka."

Alexei picked up his drink and stretched his legs out toward the stove. At the far end of the bar two men broke out in song while another clapped a fast rhythm. Alexei took time to enjoy it because he recognized it as a tune from his childhood that he hadn't heard in fifteen years. Memories of Jens Friis with his beloved fiddle, which he cursed and cajoled in equal measure in Danish each time he rested a bow on its strings, came flooding into Alexei's head, and he downed the vodka in one throw.

"They sing well," he commented. "Exceptionally well."

"They used to be professionals. Now they're sheet metal workers, poor devils." Vushnev balanced his pipe on his knee, and for the first time a hint of real interest tightened the curve of his shoulders. "We're all workers now for our great Soviet Motherland."

This was the moment. Alexei slipped a hand into his coat pocket as if to keep it warm, casually jingling the coins there. He made the first move.

"You must grow weary of people coming to you, comrade, interested in your work for the Soviet Motherland."

A pause. A slight smile. Nothing more. "You wouldn't believe how many. From all parts of the country they come knocking on my door." He puffed on his pipe, in no hurry.

Alexei lit himself another cigarette. His throat was dry as the dirt on the floor. The room was growing noisier; another man was singing an old folk song that had other drinkers swaying and joining in. The electric lamps on the walls were flickering, in danger of plunging them all into blackness.

"Comrade, you must work hard," Alexei said, just softly enough for his words to slip under the barrage of noise but still reach his companion's ears, "so hard you must make our Great Leader proud of your dedication to the reconstruction of Soviet society. All of us benefit from what you do." He let the words hang there. "You are trusted with much information."

At last the greed was there, naked in the gray eyes. Vushnev was on the hook. Alexei slid the second vodka glass across the table toward him. This time the office manager of Trovitsk camp picked it up, tossed the liquid down his throat in one hit, and smacked his lips with satisfaction.

"Not here," he warned. "Too many eyes."

"Where?"

"On Kirov *most*. The bridge on the east side of town. There's a stone arch in the middle of it."

"In half an hour."

"I'll be there."

Alexei exhaled heavily, the muscles in his neck starting to loosen. Now why did he feel this wasn't the first time Vushnev had said those exact words?

THE BRIDGE WAS EMPTY. SNOW WAS DRIVING THROUGH THE darkness as if it had to get somewhere. The lethal ice on the road and sidewalk, which had been churned up by traffic during the day, was now freezing hard once more, and that made it impossible to walk silently.

Alexei arrived early. He hung back in the dense black huddle of buildings on the riverbank, a row of workshops locked up for the night. He watched the bridge closely, but other than one solitary truck trundling over, it remained empty. He wondered whether Vushnev was watching from the other side. Kirov *most* was a stone bridge with carved creatures rearing up at intervals along its parapet, and in the center the stone archway that Vushnev had mentioned. No sign of life.

At each end of the bridge an elaborate wrought-iron lamp attempted to shed a circle of light, but it was losing the battle and they were barely visible in the sheets of snow that clogged the air. The wind snatched at Alexei's hat and drove fingers into his eyes, but he didn't move. He breathed in shallow gasps behind his scarf. When something brushed against his shin he jumped, heart in his throat, so focused was he on the bridge, but it was only a scrawny cat seeking warmth.

Half an hour passed. An hour. Still no one on the bridge. He and the cat kept each other company, but his thoughts grew chill and slippery, so that he almost missed it. A figure was moving on the bridge. It was leaning into the wind, hunched in a *fufaika* with a scarf wound tightly around its head and much of its face. It might be Vushnev. Or it might not. More to the point, the figure was alone. Alexei scratched the cat's head in farewell and moved out from his spot. He covered the ground quickly with long strides, coming up behind his quarry and tapping the snow-draped shoulder. The man swung around, startled, eyebrows heavy with ice above frightened eyes. It was Vushnev.

"For fuck's sake, you scared me!"

"You're late," Alexei pointed out.

"So what? I was busy. I had to . . ."

The gray eyes were wary but no longer frightened. Alexei didn't like that. It made him nervous.

"Let's get this over with," Alexei interrupted. "I'm too cold to hear your bloody life story."

The man backed off a step and glanced the length of the bridge. That made Alexei even more nervous.

"I'm looking for someone," he said quickly.

"Name?"

"Jens Friis."

"Russian?"

"No, he's Danish. Remember it?"

"Do you realize how many names I . . . ?"

"Do you recognize it?"

Silence, except for the howl of the wind. Alexei brushed snow from his face.

"I might," the man muttered at last.

"How much to remember?"

"What are you offering?"

From an inside pocket Alexei drew out a flat leather jewelry box. He flicked it open. An exquisite sapphire necklace nestled in a creamy satin bed, and he heard Vushnev's intake of breath. He snapped the case closed. The necklace had been his grandmother's, worn to Tsar

Nicholas's grand balls at the Winter Palace. The thought of it in this man's grubby hand made him angry.

"So do you know Jens Friis?"

"I know the name."

"He's in Trovitsk camp?"

"What's he to you?"

"That's none of your damn business."

"Sometimes I like to know why my"—he smiled—"why my clients are so keen to extract one of the inmates, when very often the prisoner has become a different person from the one they used to know. Are you ready for that? Years of hard labor and degradation change them, you see. Life in the camp makes them hard and selfish and only interested in . . ."

He's stalling me. Keeping my attention off . . .

He swung around but it was too late. Shit! A blow thudded into his kidneys, another into the side of his head. He staggered but kept his foothold on the ice. He jammed an elbow into a face and a knee into a groin and gained himself some breathing space, but in front of him stood four men. Two more behind him and another crumpled in a groaning mess on the ground. Vushnev was smiling, standing well clear of any violence.

"My friend," the office manager said softly, "you have no choice. I shall take the necklace anyway. And anything else you are hiding. Don't refuse," he chuckled, "or I shall have to unleash my friends here. Surely you don't want that."

With no more than a small movement of his wrist, a gun appeared in Alexei's hand and he pointed it directly at Vushnev's face. "You didn't think I'd come unprepared, did you?"

Vushnev edged backward. The other men stood their ground.

"Vushnev, don't be a fucking fool. You can take the jewels. But in exchange I want—"

The knife came out of the darkness behind him. Pain tore through his body and it was so total, so mind-scouring, he couldn't work out where it was hurting. Hands and feet were suddenly all over him, beating and kicking, hammering his body to the ground. He pulled the trigger twice, three times, and heard screams but the hands were still burrowing through his clothes, tearing at them, and he couldn't stop them. He fought till he felt someone's wrist snap and fingers go limp, but suddenly he was hoisted up into the air and launched over the edge of the bridge parapet. Out into the night air above the river.

All he felt at first was a rush of relief. He was free of those bastards on the bridge. The night was so dark he was barely aware of plummeting, but his mind kicked in and told him to prepare. He drew in his flailing arms and legs, clutched at one last fading image of his sister. Then the water rose up and smacked into him like a brick wall and its freezing force squeezed him so hard his lungs jammed. He sank like a stone.

Fourteen

SIX DAYS. NO WORD FROM ALEXEI FOR SIX LONG days.

It was obvious her brother had abandoned her. Lydia felt utterly bereft. She prowled the streets of Felanka in search of his tall upright frame with its neat brown hair and long arrogant stride, but there was no sign of him. As each day passed, her fears hardened. Lydia became certain that he'd gone out to the prison camp after he'd discovered some information the evening he trawled the bars. He was acting on it without her.

I work better without you.

That's what he'd said. He'd made it clear when he stood in her doorway, irritated by her request to join him, so he'd sneaked off to the prison camp, probably in some truck whose driver he'd bribed. He would find their father and somehow whisk him out of Russia before she'd even contacted him, and Jens Friis would think she didn't care and would go riding on horseback with him in the woods again, while she . . .

She put a hand over her mouth to stop the words.

She needed to find Jens before he disappeared, urgently needed to ask him things. *Papa, wait for me, please. I haven't abandoned you.*

"DON'T GO."

"I'll be all right, Elena."

"Huh!"

"I can take care of myself."

Elena responded with a scowl. "You're good at pretending you can, you mean. But not as good as you think you are."

Lydia blew out a puff of impatience, her breath coiling in a long lazy loop into the cold bright air. They were at Felanka railway station, squeezed onto a platform that was thick with uniforms as soldiers in transit awaited a train with a degree of patience that left Lydia baffled. Her own limbs were restless, her heart beating with an urgency that kept her on the move, up and down from one end of the platform to the other, squirming a path through the crush of bodies. The place had been transformed into male territory, with deep voices and loud masculine laughter stamping ownership on the platform. It even smelled different.

Soldiers were sprawled on the ground or seated on their army packs when Lydia passed them, and their eyes were at the level of her hips. They stared hard. Some even put out a hand and fingered her ankle or tipped a head back to brush against her skirt as if by accident. But it was no accident that Elena trudged behind her and whacked her umbrella down on the head of anyone who touched Lydia. It made Lydia smile. Even her own mother wouldn't have done that. It took nerve.

"You certainly know how to handle men," Lydia said.

"I'll need to know how to handle Liev when he finds out you've gone off on a train on your own."

"I stood in line three days for this ticket."

"Tell him that yourself."

"I never see him now except when he's asleep."

"That's because he's out day and night searching for news of your blasted brother."

"I know."

Lydia could imagine him trawling the bars, drinking and fighting in the lonely back streets in order to glean a whisper of what had happened to Alexei. *Oh Popkov, you don't even like the man.*

"I'll be back," she promised, "before he even notices I'm gone."

THIS TIME LYDIA WAS PREPARED. SHE KNEW WHAT TO EXPECT. Her breath misted the train's window and she dragged her coat sleeve down it to rid the glass of moisture. She wanted nothing— *neechevo*—to come between herself and what lay out there. Last time she had fallen apart, but this time would be different.

Dense waves of pine forest rolled past, the dark branches edged with fingers of snow that sparkled in a million ripples of sunlight, deceiving any casual observer into believing the air outside was warm. But Lydia knew better. There were many things she was learning to know better.

The train compartment was full and she was the only female. *You knew that's how it would be. So don't moan, don't whine.* Nevertheless it was claustrophobic. There were two rows of seats facing each other, and above their heads the luggage nets were weighed down with bulging army packs that looked far too heavy for the flimsy mesh. Most of the occupants were soldiers, wrapped in their greatcoats that smelled of tobacco, all too cumbersome for the small space. Their boots were too big and their jokes too loud. Only two of the men were not in uniform, but one was asleep and had pulled his flat cap down over his face, seemingly deaf to the noise. The other, seated directly opposite Lydia next to the window, was wearing a smart pinstriped suit and a stylish fedora. He checked his fob watch at regular intervals, but Lydia had a feeling it was more to display its jeweled face than to discover the time. The fifth time he lifted it from its home in his waistcoat pocket, looping its heavy gold chain around his thumb as he inspected its jeweled face, Lydia could resist no longer. She leaned forward.

"Excuse me, may I see it?"

"Of course, young comrade."

Both of them knew it wasn't the time she was interested in. He shifted forward in his seat and cradled the watch in his gloved hand in the small space between them. Quietly, thoughtfully, she studied its engraved dial, raised a hand, and ran a finger along the curve of its gold case.

"*Ochen krasivye*. It's beautiful."

"*Spasibo*."

In the dingy carriage the watch gleamed like a splash of sunlight, and other eyes observed it with interest. The man was a fool to flash it around. It wouldn't take much. She could stand up when the train was entering her station, stumble against him as it jerked to a halt and have the watch neatly in her pocket as she slipped onto the platform. Easy as taking coins from a blind beggar.

She sat back and closed her eyes, feeling an unexpected warmth seeping into her blood, so intense she could feel her cheeks start to burn. Where was it coming from? She thought about it carefully and decided it was the watch. Not this passenger's watch but another one, even finer, years ago. The memory of the weight of it in her hand tumbled into her mind, a memory she didn't even know she possessed, and she found herself smiling without knowing why. And then the memory opened, blurred around the edges but still there.

Papa in his heavy traveling cape, the collar turned up around his ears, the lining of dark green silk swirling like pond water as he paced the room. *What room?* She tugged at the memory and at first nothing came, but then she had the impression of a high ceiling, heavy furniture, and books. *That's it*. Books climbing all the way up the walls. Papa's library. Papa with his watch in his hand, green eyes impatient, fiery curls creeping over the cape's collar, every part of him eager to be on the move. Even now all these years later she could feel that swirl of energy and the ache in her own small chest.

"Don't go, Papa," she'd begged, fighting tears, pushing them away. Cramming them back where they came from.

Immediately he was at her side, kneeling, arms around her. She'd breathed in quickly to keep the scent of his wood-smoke cape safely inside her.

"I'll be back soon, *maleeshka*," he crooned and soothed her unruly hair, the mirror image of his own. "Just a couple of weeks." All the lines of his face melted into a wide smile for her and he kissed her forehead. "It's work," he said. "I have to go to Paris. But if your mother doesn't come downstairs soon, I'll have to go to the station without you."

"No!" she'd wailed.

Waving good-bye to Papa was a ritual.

"Listen," he said to comfort her and held his watch to her ear.

The tick, she could suddenly remember the sound of the gentle tick. Its voice was a soft whisper that enchanted her, so that her eyes grew wide and her heart-shaped face became absolutely still as she concentrated.

"It talks," she whispered.

"Here, feel it."

He placed it in her hand, filling the whole of her palm, and she was astonished at the weight of it.

"It's gold," he explained.

She studied it carefully, the intricate engraving, the filigree work as fine as one of her hairs, and when he turned it over and opened the back she was entranced by the movement of the tiny cogs. This was where it hid its voice.

"I thought you had a train to catch, Jens."

It was her mother's voice, teasing him, holding a hand out to him as if her skin could not bear to be without his touch for a moment longer. Her dark hair danced loosely around her shoulders, just the way he liked it. Papa stood up straight and tall, and Lydia watched it happen. Just as it always did. Papa would come home grumpy or impatient or weary and then he'd lay eyes on Mama and it set something alight inside him. It burned away the grumpiness and the impatience and the weariness.

Her mother gently removed the watch from her grasp and gave it back to Papa, murmuring, "She's too young to play with it." But Papa gave Lydia a secret smile and winked at her. And then everything was a rush and a bustle and they were at the station, full of sounds and smells, shouts and mountains of luggage. And tears. Lydia realized that this was where adults came to cry. Papa hugged them, kissed them, and climbed onto the train, calling out last words from the open window as it hauled itself down the track in a giant bellow of steam. Something red. She pulled at the memory but it was hazy, yet she was sure she could recall something red. And then it came to her. A red handkerchief fluttered from his hand, up and down, until it became no more than a tiny spot. Like a tiny speck of blood.

Mama was crying, dabbing at her tears, but Lydia refused to. In Papa's pocket the cogs were still turning. The cogs of time, little teeth clinging to each other and moving the hands of the watch. The cogs would bring him back to her. She clenched her tiny fists and listened to their voices ticking inside her head.

THE WORK ZONE WAS STILL THERE.

It hadn't moved.

That had been her fear. That they'd have gone. Packed up their saws and their axes and their timber wagons and transferred to another part of the forest far away from the railway line. She shivered, but it wasn't from the cold in the rail carriage, it was with relief. She felt the golden hairs rise on her arms and she leaned her forehead against the icy pane of glass as if it brought her closer to him. Outside, the landscape was flat as the glass and frosted with patches of snow. Large swathes had been completely stripped of trees, so that rocky stretches were now visible, shifting the color of the terrain from a thousand shades of green and russet brown to an unrelenting battleship gray.

Had that happened to Papa too? That shift to Soviet gray? She rested the fingertips of one hand on the window, averting her eyes from the monochrome uniforms that surrounded her.

Papa, I'm here. The cogs have brought me to you. The wheels are turning.

LYDIA ROSE TO HER FEET AND YANKED ON THE LEATHER STRAP, so hard the train window slid all the way down with a clunk. The rush of freezing air wrenched her breath away and an outburst of moans and complaints scrambled around her.

"Shut that window!"

"It's fucking freezing."

"Are you out of your mind, girl?"

"My bollocks are falling off!"

She scarcely heard the outcry. Every scrap of her attention was focused on the terrain out there as the tips of the watchtowers slid into view far in the distance, tiny gray matchsticks against a crisp blue sky. At first she could make out no figures laboring on the edge of the forest. Her heart slumped in her chest, but as the train billowed its way along the track it swept past a huge stack of pine trunks that lay on the ground like dead people's limbs. Lydia had assumed the timber was floated downriver somewhere, the way she'd seen it done in China, but no. Not here anyway. This small mountain of tree trunks was clearly intended to be loaded onto flatbed wagons and hauled into the timber yards by rail.

Lumbering along the flat terrain at a painfully slow pace, still distant but heading in the direction of the dead limbs, a wagon was approaching loaded with another consignment. Lydia struggled to count the number of miniature figures yoked to the transporter, but it was too far away. She blinked and counted again. There had to be at least twenty. Her eyes fixed on them and wouldn't let go.

"Comrade." It was the man in the suit, her watch companion. This time his voice was curt. "Close that window, *pozhalusta*."

Still she didn't hear. He touched her elbow to gain her attention and made as if to rise to his feet to perform the job himself, but before he could do so Lydia pulled from her shoulder pack two small scarlet bundles. Each one consisted of a headscarf tied in a knot, and inside lay something of weight.

"Look here . . ." The suit was losing patience.

She'd seen a working party of prisoners up ahead, just four of them, no more than a few hundred meters away from the track. They were digging with spades, shifting rocks it seemed, maybe clearing a path for the wagon. Lydia snatched off the red scarf that was around her neck, leaned out of the window as far as she could, and waved the vivid smear of material at them. Back and forth, back and forth, to gain their attention.

Pozhalusta, she breathed, *please look up.*

Smuts from the engine smacked into her face. The figures were coming closer. Not one of them looked up from his shovel. Don't they want to see human faces at the train windows? Is the sight of freedom too painful to contemplate? One hundred meters. It was as close as she was going to get. She drew back her arm and hurled one of the scarlet bundles out of the window. As it arced through the trembling air like a bright red bird, she watched the men closely and emptied her lungs in one long banshee shriek. Not one of them looked her way.

Don't they hear? Or don't they care?

The red bird landed on the edge of a rock, rebounded, and fluttered to rest on an open stretch of ground where it fell against the stump of a tree and nestled among the dead roots. *No, no, no.* Lydia's mouth gasped open, and her tongue was stung by ash from the engine.

"Stop that, comrade." This time it was the man who'd been asleep under the cap. He was awake now all right, alert and angry. "What you're doing is against the law. Stop that right now or . . ."

"Or what?" The young loose-limbed soldier, who up till now had been sitting quietly next to Lydia and whom she had given barely a glance, unfolded himself from his seat and stood behind her in the narrow space between knees. "Or what?" he repeated.

A chuckle rippled around the other soldiers and one warned, "Don't cross him, comrade. He's our boxing champ."

Lydia raised the second bundle, ready to throw.

"Allow me?"

The soldier was holding out his big-knuckled hand, palm uppermost, and waited with a polite smile on his face. Lydia noticed that his nose had been recently broken, and the bruise had spread to a muddy yellow. She hesitated for no more than one turn of the wheels, then entrusted the little parcel into his hand and edged back into her seat to allow him room. He grinned at her, tossed his army cap onto his seat, pushed his broad shoulders through the window as far as they would go, and took careful aim. He launched the red bundle with a grunt of effort.

It sailed through the air as if it didn't know how to stop. Lydia's eyes didn't leave it, her hopes all tied up inside the knotted scarf. It flew up and over the rocks until it finally hung in the air and curved gracefully down to earth. It didn't even bounce, just landed flat right in the middle of an expanse of gleaming white snow. Lydia could have kissed the soldier.

"*Spasibo*," she offered instead. "Thank you. Thank you so much."

She gave him a grateful smile. He blushed and sat down. Cheers rose from a few of his comrades and one crowed like a cockerel. The man in the flat cap scowled but had enough sense to say no more, while the suit stood up and yanked the window shut, ignoring the boisterous laughter with a degree of dignity.

It was done.

As the wheels turned and the prisoners were left far behind in the freezing wind, Lydia let her thoughts race over the words crouched inside the scarlet bundles: *I am the daughter of Jens Friis. If he is here, tell him I've come. I need a sign.*

Inside each one lay five shiny silver dollars from China.

Fifteen

CHANG AN LO MOVED THROUGH THE DARKNESS like the breath of a shadow. Unseen, unheard. The air was moist in his lungs while the call of frogs vibrated the night the way a concubine's fingers vibrate the strings of a *guqin*.

The village of Zhumatong was alive with light and noise, spilling from the windows, tumbling through the doors and into the streets. The Red Army had descended like flies. Soldiers lurched from one house to another, trying to remember where their billets were, a bottle in one hand, a girl in the other. The village councillors bowed politely, hands stiff together in front of them, but steered the crumpled uniforms into the drinking house and the gambling room where they could be fleeced of the few yuan in their pockets.

Chang remained patiently under the black overhang of a rear wall and listened to the soldiers leaving a building that was decorated with delicate fretwork and lanterns swaying from the eaves. Their voices were thick with *maotai* and complaining loudly at the speed with which they were back on the street with-

out the mah-jongg tiles falling even once their way. One soldier with
hair cropped brutally short and long spindly legs detached himself
from a group and picked his way into a side street, where he opened
his trousers and urinated against a wall with a contented sigh.

Chang allowed for him to finish before he approached silently
from behind and slipped an arm around his throat, a hand placed
firmly over his mouth. The soldier grew rigid and tried to turn.

"Quiet, Hu Biao, or you are in danger of snapping your worthless neck." Chang spoke the words softly in the young man's ear, letting them sneak out under the night's breeze. He released his grip.

The soldier spun around. "Chang An Lo, you scared the shit out
of me."

Chang tipped his head in a lighthearted bow. "Stop bellowing
like a stuck pig, Biao. That's why I put a hand over that ever-open
mouth of yours, to silence it."

Hu Biao thumped the side of his own head with his knuckles.
"My apologies, brother of my heart." He leaned close, fumes of
something more than just alcohol rising from his angular frame, and
lowered his voice to a murmur. "What in the name of the gods are
you doing here in this piss-hole village?"

"Searching for you."

"Why me?"

"I was told your unit was billeted here. I heard that the fighting
was fierce in the valley, so I came to see if your miserable ears were
still attached to your hide."

Their enemies counted the dead by slicing off ears and threading
them on a wire.

"They're both still mine," Biao laughed, and swung his head to
display them, leaning back against the wall.

But Chang could hear the tension in it, the nerves that had to be
deadened with a night of *maotai* and a whiff of the black paste before
the next march into battle.

"So you've done well, my friend."

"What are you doing all the way down here, Chang? I thought
you were somewhere up north."

"I was, but I've been summoned to Guitan." Even in the shadows
his sharp eyes took in the hollow cheeks and scarecrow limbs of Hu
Biao, and he feared for Yi-Ling's son. "My escort troop sleeps even

now the sleep of drunken monkeys, ten *li* away from here. Tomorrow I will arrive at Guitan to do Mao's bidding."

Biao pushed himself off the wall, suddenly sober, and gave a deep respectful bow. "I am honored that one so distinguished chooses to spend time with an unworthy army dog like myself."

Voices in the main street shouted out Biao's name, searching for him. Chang took hold of his shoulder and led him farther into the shadows, drawing away from the dancing lanterns.

"Biao," he said urgently, "my time is short. I have to return to my escort before they wake."

Biao nodded. "I'm listening."

"I've come to ask you to be my aide." His eyes scanned his friend for a reaction, and he was satisfied by what he saw. A quick flicker of excitement. "Good. I shall order the escort to request your presence in the morning."

Their eyes met, and something in Biao's changed. His exhausted gaze didn't move from Chang's face. "This is for Si-qi, isn't it? Not for me. Did she ask you to do this?"

"No. This has nothing to do with your sister." He smiled and treated Biao to another lighthearted bow. "Believe me, times are hard. I need a good man I can rely on at my back. You are that man."

"But it's fortunate for me that I have a beautiful sister. She could steal any man's soul, couldn't she?"

"As easily as a butterfly steals nectar from a blossom."

Biao clapped Chang on the back and released a pungent belch. "She'll love you forever after this. That's what you want, isn't it?"

Chang An Lo stepped back into deeper shadow and when Biao spoke again, he was gone.

CHANG AN LO HAD NOT ANTICIPATED THIS. THIS DECADENCE. Despite all the whispers that flitted through the sultry air more numerous than bats on a summer's evening, this was worse than he had expected. His spirits sank as he contemplated the knowledge that the leader of the Communist movement within China was a man of such total self-indulgence.

Mao Tse-tung sprawled in a giant four-poster bed. His large

round head, with its receding hairline exaggerating the height of his forehead, rested back on a tumble of pillows as if the thoughts inside were too weighty for the short stubby neck. Elaborate silk canopies hung from above in vivid turquoise and magenta folds, while scarlet sheets flowed around him echoing the color of the Communist flag, chosen to give the impression that this great leader had spilled his blood for the cause. But Chang knew differently. When he traveled with his armies he enjoyed a level of comfort and safety his soldiers could only dream about.

Mao lay on the sheets and conducted this meeting with his observant eyes narrowed as he watched the individuals he had summoned to attend him in his bedroom. The immense bed was raised up on a double step so that his head remained higher than those belonging to the nervous men seated in the seven chairs that encircled him. The chairs were elegant but deliberately hard and were placed at least six feet from the silk coverlets, so that the occupants had to strain to hear when Mao chose to lower his voice.

The atmosphere was tense. Chang was aware that the official next to him had a trickle of sweat running down his temple, and he had no doubt that Mao's quick eyes had spotted it too. He had seized leadership of the army from men like General Zhu, a sullen figure who sat silent in the room, by being both intelligent and bold. Men followed him because, despite being just a schoolteacher and adopting a peasant's plain dress, he was astute at manipulating people and situations and, above all, knew how to win. Chang had to remind himself not to be fooled by the soft moon face and the rough rural dialect with which he spoke. This man was nobody's fool. He had no problem with inflicting terror on his own people. "Power," he had stated, "comes out of the barrel of a gun." Chang even breathed carefully so as not to create a ripple in the flow of the great man's thoughts.

"Chou En-lai informs me," Mao said with a guttural emphasis on the word *me*, "that our bearded neighbors, the Russians, are playing both hands still, one against the other. That is foolish of them."

"Yes, as our young comrade across the room discovered," said a sharp faced Party official whom Chang did not recognize. But with Mao, people fell in and out of favor with a speed that set a man's head spinning.

Mao had listened with close attention to Chang's account of the train raid and the acquisition of the Russian Tokarev rifles. He'd clearly relished the details of the discovery of the papers that revealed the secret Russian orders to Chiang Kai-shek. In exchange for the weaponry and the gold, the Chinese Nationalist leader was supposed to lay siege to a list of towns and strongholds, and even give his wholehearted support to Russia's invasion of Manchuria.

"Tell me, young comrade," Mao asked, "how you knew the contents of that train were destined for the hairless hyena, Chiang Kai-shek?"

"From my intelligence sources."

"And what sources are these?"

Chang drew a slow breath. "My humble apologies but it's not possible for me to reveal them, Honored Leader." He looked directly into Mao's dark gaze. It was like looking into the eyes of a snow leopard he had once stumbled across up in the mountains—insatiably greedy, unwilling to let any prey pass without leaving claw marks on its back. "There are too many loose tongues in a place like this." Chang gestured round the room. "Not these honorable men, but the ears that listen outside and the unseen eyes that are fixed to spyholes. The invisible traitors who take Chiang Kai-shek's silver."

Mao's expression hardened and he nodded, satisfied. "You are wiser than your years, comrade. For you are right. It is the same wherever I go, always surrounded by those I cannot trust."

He turned away, fingering the huge pile of books that lay spread out on one side of the bed as if he had dismissed further discussion of the point, but Chang felt the vibrations soft as drumbeats in the room. He knew it wasn't over.

"When we catch them," Mao said quietly, so quietly two of the older men had to lean forward to hear, "we deal with these traitors. Is that not so, Han-tu?"

Han-tu smiled, as if his lips had been oiled. He wore a military uniform and nodded his head sharply in salute. He didn't speak.

"Tell him, Han-tu. Tell our fresh-faced comrade what we do, so that he can tell others."

"The punishment is severe: death by a thousand cuts."

"Tell him more."

Han-tu didn't look at Chang, just at the Buddha figure in the bed. He spoke as though describing how to take apart a piece of machinery. "The traitor is stripped naked. His wrists and ankles are tethered to stakes, so that he is upright but immobile. He cannot fall to the ground or turn in any direction."

"And then . . . ?" Mao urged.

"A knife is wielded by an expert butcher. One thousand cuts into his flesh. It is a slow and painful death. By the time the treacherous snake loses consciousness he will have told all he knows, who he works for, who he has betrayed, and what secrets he is hiding."

Still Mao wasn't satisfied. "Tell him of the warning of the lizard skin."

"Ah, Comrade Commander, the lizard skin is a specialist art." Han-tu puffed out his chest like a pigeon. "Few can perform it well."

A sad-faced elderly man was seated on the opposite side of the room. He had a throaty smoker's cough and his flesh bore the telltale yellow tinge of opium, but his fierce eyes were glaring at Chang, his papery skin creased in lines of disapproval. Chang had been ushered into this inner sanctum an hour after the meeting had started and he knew it would drone on long after he left. He had not been told the names of the other men but felt the hostility of many of the looks cast in his direction, sharp as wasp stings on his face. He was young. He had Mao's ear. He was a threat.

Mao smoothed a hand over his large square forehead, as though feeling the shape of the thoughts inside his skull. The hands of a girl, Chang noted, soft and milk-fed.

"How is it performed, this lizard skin?" Mao demanded of Han-tu.

As if he didn't know.

"The blade is sharpened to the width of a hair," Han-tu explained in the same flat voice, "and sliced under the skin on face and body in a thousand shallow round cuts, so that when it heals it has the appearance of a reptile's scales. It is a sign to others. A blood warning that . . ."

Mao licked his lips, his tongue quicker than a snake's. Chang blocked Han-tu's words from his ears and breathed out slowly to flush the images from his mind. Addicted. That was the rumor. It was whispered in dark corners of Communist hideouts and in the sultry air of interrogation huts. Mao was addicted to violence. Even between his sheets with the young maidens who were lined up for his bed at night when his fragrant wife, Gui-yuan, was not at his side. None of his wives had yet lasted long, despite producing a clutch of sons for him.

What kind of ruler would this man make when he finally held the whole of China in his grip? Because Chang had no doubts that the Communists would oust the Nationalists and send Chiang Kai-shek fleeing like a whipped cur into the sea, tail between his legs. Not this year, maybe not even next year. But eventually it would happen. Chang believed it passionately with his heart and soul, but would Mao bring to China the justice and equality it craved? The peasants in the fields yearned for freedom from the yoke of feudal landlords of the Manchu dynasty, and this was what the Communists promised them.

But would Mao Tse-tung deliver it? He was an intelligent man, well read, sharp-eyed, a bed full of books beside him, but . . .

"Chang An Lo, are you no longer with us?"

Chang bowed his head low and cursed his foolishness. "Forgive my distraction, Honored Leader. I am overawed in the presence of such company."

Mao snorted and Chang knew he must tread with infinite care.

"But my mind is still chasing in and out of the Russian maze, seeking the twisting path of their reasoning."

"And what conclusion did you reach, young comrade?"

"That either the Russians are trying to destroy China by prolonging the civil war, providing finance to both sides so that the Soviet army will be free to invade not only Manchuria but also other northern provinces of our country. While we busy ourselves with snapping at each other's tails here in the south."

"Or?"

"Or there is a traitor at the heart of the Politburo in Moscow."

A hiss and an intake of breath trickled round the room. Han-tu thumped the palm of his hand on his knee with a loud slap. "Our last delegation to Moscow reported that it found Stalin eager to commit greater resources to our struggle against the Nationalist despot. I cannot believe that they would betray us to—"

Mao sat up abruptly. Han-tu fell silent.

"The Russian bear has always been a dangerous and unreliable ally." Mao's moon face was stern. "I remind you all that at one time it had such control over our Chinese Communist Party that it tried to force us to merge with Chiang Kai-shek's treacherous Nationalists. Stalin believed we were too weak to seize control of China but"—a cold smile tilted his lips and he smoothed the red sheet in front of him with his small hands—"the *Vozhd* of Soviet Russia was wrong."

"He underestimated you, our Great Leader."

"You are leading us to victory."

"Your army will die for you if you ask."

Mao nodded, satisfied, and then his eyes sought out the one man who so far had said nothing. "Is that true, General Zhu? Will my Red Army die for me?"

Everyone in the room studied the man who had been outmaneuvered by Mao for control of the military. Zhu was an army man to his core, and his men loved and respected him.

"My Comrade Commander," Zhu growled, "the army is yours to command. They have already died for you."

Silence hit the room. Was the general implying that Mao had commanded them unwisely? Chang felt the air shudder and saw the eyes of the five other men drop to the silk carpet beneath their feet. The stench of their fear was sharp as cow dung in his nostrils. Mao let the silence lengthen, held the general's gaze until Zhu also was forced to lower his eyes, then lifted a small brass handbell at the side of his bed and rang it. Immediately a young girl servant entered the room, bowing almost to the floor.

"*Chai,*" Mao ordered with a dismissive flick of his wrist. "Tea." He leaned back among the pillows as she left the room, his eyes tracing the swing of her slender hips. "Perhaps," he said with a sudden burst of energy, "our young comrade here is correct. Perhaps Josef Stalin himself is lying to us with a whore's smile on his face while he still hands out arms and Soviet gold to our enemies."

Mao looked again at Chang, thoughtfully studying this young newcomer who seemed to know too much.

"Chang An Lo," he said softly, "do you speak Russian?"

Sixteen

ALEXEI MOVED. NOTHING MUCH AT FIRST, JUST a slight shift of his body. Pain. Bright and bloody. It gathered in his lungs and reached out to portions of his flesh in sharp malicious handfuls. *Dermo!* Shit! Even his thoughts hurt. They felt as though they were being crushed like walnuts under a flat iron till their shells split and splintered. The pieces lodged in his brain.

"Awake, are you?"

Alexei opened his eyes. His eyeballs felt dry and gritty, as if they hadn't been used in a long time. The light that greeted them was yellow and smelled of kerosene. He was lying flat on his back, that much he registered, so with an effort he rolled his head to one side and slowly the world around him shivered into focus. A low planked ceiling, wooden walls, a table bolted to the floor, cupboards with delicate fretwork, the strong aroma of coffee.

"Coffee?"

Alexei attempted to sit up. Not a good move. The pain in his lungs sank its teeth in and set off a vicious spasm of coughing, but a strong arm supported him and a deep laugh gusted warm air on his skin.

"Take your time, comrade."

Alexei took his time. *How in hell's name did I get here?* He eased himself so that he was propped up on the narrow bunk he was lying on, his head resting against the wall. Someone had lit hell's fire inside his chest.

"*Spasibo*," he murmured. Throat as dry as ash.

He focused on the fair-haired man sitting on the edge of the bed and received an impression of a handsome face, neat features clean-shaven but with a hesitancy in his blue eyes. Eyelashes too long for a man but large masculine teeth, full lips more than ready to laugh. In his forties, perhaps a little younger.

"*Spasibo*," Alexei said again, and this time he made it more robust.

"You're welcome, friend. Ready for coffee?"

Alexei nodded, regretted it, and waited for the room to reassemble. The man moved away to a stove in the corner and lifted a coffeepot that was stewing there. It was at that exact moment that it dawned on Alexei's sluggish mind that this new world of his was rocking. The movement wasn't just inside his head. A gentle sway, but definitely rocking.

"We're on a boat," he said.

"Correct. The *Red Maiden*."

"Yours?"

"She certainly is."

The word *she* was spoken with affection. The man patted the wall with his palm, the way Alexei would a horse, and poured coffee into two metal cups. He was wearing a thick fisherman's jersey that looked as if it hadn't been washed in a while, and for the first time Alexei realized he was clothed in a similar one himself, as well as rough socks and trousers he'd never seen before. He watched warily as his host returned to sit on the side of the bed and wrapped Alexei's hand around the cup.

"Here, drink, *tovarishch*. It'll put iron in your veins."

To Alexei's shock, his arm felt like a dead weight when he tried to lift the cup. His hand shuddered and spilled some liquid on his sweater, but eventually it reached his lips. The coffee was black and strong and seemed to kick a hole in the fog in his brain as it scalded his tongue, but it tasted good. Where the hell did a fisherman get his hands on coffee like this in Stalin's Russia where the shop shelves were covered in nothing but dust? He felt his senses returning one by one and breathed cautiously.

"Your name, comrade?" he asked.

"Konstantin Duretin. Yours?"

"Alexei Serov."

"Well, Comrade Serov, what were you doing swimming in the river with the fishes in the middle of winter?"

"Fishes?" Alexei frowned. Images battered his brain. A game of chess, a long-stemmed pipe. The curve of a road to a bridge.

Dear God, the bridge. Men coming at him from all directions. With a jolt of memory he slid a hand down to his side and felt the bulk of bandages there.

The blue eyes were still smiling at him, but more thoughtful now. "I did the best I could for you. As good as dead, you were. I found your carcass clinging to a scrap of wood in the middle of the river like a drowning kitten. Lost all but a cupful of blood, I'd guess, and near frozen to death."

"*Spasibo*, Konstantin. I owe you . . ."

"Hush, rest now. I'll cook us some fish and we can get some food into you at last. You've not eaten for weeks."

"Weeks?"

"*Da.*" He stood up.

"Weeks?"

"*Da.* I managed to get some water into you and a little soup but nothing more."

"Weeks?" The word had stuck in Alexei's mind.

"Yes, nearly three weeks it's been. You've had a fever. Thought I'd lost you more than once." He thumped a hand on the table. "But you must be made of good strong oak like my *Red Maiden* here." He laughed.

The noise of it set up a vibration in Alexei's head, and he closed his eyes to stop his brains spilling out.

THE SMELL OF GRILLED FISH PERMEATED THE DUSTY CABIN, ousting even the stink of the kerosene. They ate slowly and in companionable silence, the job of maneuvering a fork to his mouth taking all of Alexei's concentration. Konstantin left him to it but when they had finished and coffee was once more in his hands, Alexei rested back and scrutinized his host.

"Why did you take care of me?"

"What was I supposed to do? Chuck you back in the river like a poisoned fish?"

Alexei smiled. The muscles of his cheek felt stiff, made of cardboard. "Some would have. Under Stalin's system of informers, people have become afraid of strangers."

Konstantin returned the smile. "I was glad of the company."

"Where are we now?"

"Downriver."

"South of Felanka, you mean?"

"*Da.*"

"How long have we been traveling?"

"Ever since I picked you up."

"Three weeks. *Chyort!*"

"Wrong direction for you?"

"Yes. I have to return to Felanka."

Konstantin looked away and there was a moment of awkwardness that made Alexei feel ungrateful. To cover it, the boatman reached into a drawer under the tabletop and pulled out a small knife and a piece of wood, then proceeded to whittle away at it, his blond eyebrows knit in concentration.

"What's in Felanka that is so important?"

"Some business I have to attend to."

His gaze lifted to Alexei. "Girl business, you mean?"

"Not *that* kind of girl business. It's my sister. She's in Felanka."

"Ah, my friend, then there's no rush. A sister can wait."

Can you, Lydia? Can you wait?

LYDIA WAS FORCED TO WAIT. DESPITE HER CONSTANT DAILY hammering on the stationmaster's hatch, it was two weeks before she was allocated a seat on a return train to Felanka. What surprised her was how easily she filled the days. She expected herself to be pacing the sidewalks with impatience, frantic and fretting, but no, it wasn't like that. She sat quietly. On a station platform, in a park, in a hotel room.

She taught herself stillness.

When finally the train heaved itself into the station, the compartment was full but this time with more women than men. Conversations concentrated on the lack of goods in the shops despite rationing and the length of the bread lines. Before boarding, Lydia had seen a chain of prisoners loaded at the last minute into the baggage van, but so carefully guarded that she had no chance to get anywhere near them. Their heads were already shaven against lice. That came as a shock. The idea of Papa without his flowing fiery locks. The image just wouldn't stay inside her head. She became aware of a young girl next to her, small and slight. She was traveling alone, much the same age as Lydia herself, but her fragility made her seem younger. Lydia took out a cone of sunflower seeds that Elena had thrust into her bag and offered it.

"Hungry?" she asked the girl.

"*Da.*" She took a handful. Her face was thin and nervous. "*Spasibo.*"

"Traveling far?"

"To Moscow."

"That's a long journey. But it must be exciting for you."

"Yes, you see, I won a prize. I was the fastest maker of copper pots in my factory. So I am to receive a medal."

Lydia blinked. "That happens?"

"Oh yes, of course. Workers are always rewarded for dedication. Sometimes even by Stalin himself." Her young eyes gleamed with anticipation. "It's to be awarded in a big ceremony in the Hall of Heroes."

"Congratulations. You and your family must be very proud."

"We are . . . but I'm told Moscow is dangerous."

Lydia looked at her with interest. Didn't the girl know that in Stalin's Russia, everywhere was dangerous?

"In what way do you mean?" she asked.

The girl leaned closer, eyes wide. "The city is riddled with criminals."

Lydia laughed; she couldn't help it. "Every city is riddled with criminals, no matter where you go. It's always the same." She noticed that a man in workman's clothes farther along the bench seat was openly listening to her. She added quickly, "But I know Comrade Lenin has taught us all to share what we have, even our apartments. Crime is no longer necessary. Not like it was under the bourgeois system of exploitation."

She almost smiled. Her brother would be proud of her. *You see, Alexei, I'm learning. Really I am.*

The girl said nothing, just chewed on the seeds, then glanced sideways at Lydia from behind her thin blond hair. "They are well known," she murmured. "With tattoos. A criminal fraternity. The *vory v zakone*, they're called." She lowered her voice to a faint whisper. "That's why I'm nervous of going to Moscow."

A criminal fraternity? Tattoos?

No. Not again. Not China all over again. Lydia's pulse thudded in her throat. Thank God she wasn't heading for Moscow.

"I'm sure you'll be well cared for." She smiled reassuringly and patted the girl's arm. "Someone as special as you will be kept safe."

The look of relief on the thin face was worth the lie.

THE RAIN HAD STOPPED AND THE LANDSCAPE STRETCHED AWAY into the mist, dismal and damp. Everything looked different. How would she know when the train was close to the Work Zone? There was nothing here that marked out one featureless place from another, and now that the clouds had descended so low it was impossible to see where the forest had been leveled. This mist had swallowed all signs, a gray thief that had stolen her hopes.

Lydia was standing at the carriage window, fingers wiping away the moisture of her breath on the glass. The Work Zone had to be here, somewhere here, she was sure. She peered out intently, searching for even a hint of the matchstick watchtowers, but all she saw was a dead blanket of low cloud that, as the train raced past, curled and swayed like a drunk unsteady on his feet. The red handkerchiefs, the bright scarlet birds? Would they be visible? But no. Nothing broke the colorless monotony. She rested her forehead against the glass, felt the vibrations rattle through her brain.

She closed her eyes, remembering Chang's words: *You must focus, my love, draw the parts together into a whole. Then you will be strong.*

Focus.

She opened her eyes, forgot the mist and the forest, and focused on the stretch of rocky ground nearest the track. For the next twenty-five minutes she didn't let her gaze stray but kept it riveted on the few meters of terrain that bordered the rail as the engine thundered through the damp air. Slowly she felt her mind change. It grew lighter. The weight of other thoughts and fears slid away until all that existed was the rock and the earth speeding past. They threaded dark lines through her mind.

Then it was there. The sign.

She blinked and it was gone. But she'd seen it and didn't need to see it again. Rocks had been placed in a pattern, an arrangement of stone that spelled out a word and a number. The word was *Nyet*. The number was 1908.

Nyet. 1908.

Lydia didn't know whether to laugh or cry. She had no idea what it meant.

Seventeen

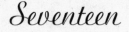

ALEXEI WOKE IN TOTAL DARKNESS. THE TIMBERS creaked around him and he could hear the slap of the waves on the bow.

"Konstantin!"

He heard movement in the cabin.

"What is it, my friend? Wait while I strike a match."

A flame flared and a lamp hissed. In the sudden gleam of yellow light Alexei focused on the jumble of blankets on the floor on the other side of the table and realized it was Konstantin's own bed he had usurped. The boatman was naked, his long back well muscled, blond curls on his thighs. He turned and studied Alexei, unabashed by his own nakedness, his blue eyes still heavy with sleep.

"What is it, Alexei? A nightmare?"

"No. Where is my money belt, Konstantin?"

The long eyelashes blinked. "Money belt? What money belt?"

"I was wearing one when . . ."

"My friend, I am no thief."

"I'm not accusing you."

"That's what it sounds like to me." He spread his broad hands as if to show there was nothing hiding in them. "When I dragged you out of the water, you were in a mess. Bleeding over everything, your clothes cut and torn, but there was definitely no money belt." He chuckled softly. "Do you think I wouldn't have noticed?"

Alexei collapsed back on the pillow and closed his eyes. "I apologize, Konstantin. Please go back to sleep."

Immediately the light went out. Alexei heard his companion's bare feet pad across the boards, felt a hand touch his hair in the darkness and slide gently down to brush the skin of his neck.

"How old are you, Alexei?" Konstantin's voice was a whisper.

"Twenty-six."

"So young. And so . . . untouchable."

A silence, black and sticky as pitch, dropped into the gap between the two men. Alexei rolled onto his side, turning his back on the boatman, so that the hand fell away. "Good night, comrade. *Dobroi nochi, tovarishch.*"

Quietly the footsteps padded away.

EVERYTHING WAS GONE. THE MONEY, THE JEWELS, ALL THAT HE had secreted away from prying eyes. How they must have laughed at his naïveté.

Alexei felt bile rise in his throat because he knew it wasn't his naïveté that had caused this. It was his own blind arrogance. He'd known what to expect, what Mikhail Vushnev was likely to try on that freezing cold night on the bridge. But he had been so confident that he could handle whatever a dumb camp apparatchik thought up and still extract the information he needed.

How wrong could he be? How unforgivable was the mistake?

He forced his eyes closed. But the images remained there under his eyelids, etched sharper than acid into his brain. Everything of real value was gone. Everything.

A STRING OF BEADS OF SUNLIGHT THREADED THEIR WAY through a line of holes in the curtain that hung across the small cabin porthole. Bright tears of regret. That's what they looked like to Alexei when he opened his eyes and saw them spilling over his blanket and onto the table. The sun had scarcely climbed above the eastern horizon, the dawn light still drifting lazily down the surface of the river, in no hurry to get anywhere.

But I am. In a hurry to get back to Felanka.

Alexei threw off the blankets and swung his legs over the edge of the bed. His head threatened to split wide open when he pushed himself to his feet and nausea hit. Stale fevered breath escaped from his lungs in a rush. He swore. Swaying dangerously, he fought to catch his breath and that was when he saw Konstantin watching him in silence from his nest of blankets on the floor.

"You're weak as a kitten," the boatman said. "Where do you think you're going?"

"Time to leave."

"*Nyet.*" It came out as a soft moan. "Not yet. You are not well enough."

"I have to go."

Alexei straightened up. The boards were cold under his feet and he looked around the cabin for his boots. They were by a bucket in a corner and they had been polished. He shuffled over to them, picked them up, and put them on. The effort left him trembling. Konstantin said nothing.

"My clothes?" Alexei asked.

"I told you, they were torn to rags, so I threw them away. You can keep my old ones that you're wearing and your coat is in that cupboard."

Alexei retrieved it. The heavy material had one long cut down the front that had been meticulously mended.

"How can I thank you?"

Konstantin wrapped himself tightly in his blankets. "There's bread and some cold pork in the—"

"No. But thank you. You've done more than enough for me already."

"I have no money to offer you."

"A knife is all I need."

A brief nod of the head toward a cupboard. Alexei chose the sharpest and thinnest blade, then approached his rescuer and held out his hand in farewell.

"Thank you, Konstantin. *Spasibo*. You have been a true friend." He felt an urge to do more, to bend down and embrace this man, to hold him close the way he would his own father, to utter more words than just *spasibo*. "I am more grateful than I can say for what . . ."

"Not grateful enough, it seems." The blue eyes closed. "Just go."

Alexei bent down, squeezed his shoulder, and left.

POPKOV SWORE AT HER. IT CAME AS A SHOCK TO LYDIA.

He started cursing the moment she stepped off the train in Felanka. She hurried down the icy platform toward him, but he just stood there without moving, swearing at her in his booming voice. He loomed big and bulky, a bear on its hind legs, so black-eyed and dangerous that other passengers on the station platform swerved to avoid him. His hat was missing, so that his greasy curls launched out at angry angles, and his black eye patch lay askew where he'd been picking at it.

How many times had he waited here for her?

How many trains had he met?

How many hours had he wasted in the snow and the rain?

"Liev!" she called out and started to run, her coat catching at her legs.

The Cossack bunched up his massive eyebrows and scowled harder at her, looking ready to kill something, and as she drew near she heard his hot words clearly in the chill air.

"Fuck you, *suka*! Where have you been? Why the devil did you leave without me? Why? You stupid little chit, you could be lying in fucking shit in a gutter somewhere by now or—"

"Hush," she murmured and stood still in front of him. "Hush." She looked up into his face with a wide affectionate smile.

His black eye glittered at her. "Damn you," he said.

"I know."

"Go to hell."

"I probably will."

"You stupid little fool." His big paw landed on her shoulder, crushing it.

He'd never sworn at her before. Never. That's how bad it was for him.

"I'm sorry," she said, and her words were almost lost in the great sigh of the steam engine as it belched out smoke.

She stood close to him. Slid her arms around his chest as far as they would go and laid her cheek on his stinking coat. The bristles of his beard prickled her forehead as he kissed the top of her head. His huge arms wrapped around her, grinding her slender frame against his ribs till she couldn't breathe. She could hear him swallow, over and over again.

"Put him down," a woman's voice chuckled just behind Lydia. "Stop mauling him. That Cossack is mine."

It was Elena.

ALEXEI PUSHED THE TIP OF HIS KNIFE INTO THE BOTTOM OF HIS boot and twisted. Nothing happened.

Chyort! He was too damn weak even to flick the heel off a shoe. He dropped the knife and sank down with relief on the rain-soaked grass, indifferent to the chill and the wet creeping through his coat. Since leaving the boat he'd walked north through the flatlands, following the line of the river, forcing his legs to march hour after hour. Only now did he allow himself to collapse onto the riverbank.

He was drenched in sweat despite the bitter wind that skidded off the surface of the water. Flecks of ice in the air nicked at his skin like minuscule ice picks. His mouth was dry as sand and his hands shaking. Up ahead appeared a village, its wooden cottages breathing out coils of smoke from metal chimney pipes, and the smell of cooked meat swirled on the wind. He needed money. Without it he wasn't going to get far, which was why he was now hacking at his boot in an attempt to remove the heel.

Under a steel-gray sky he rested his cheek on the grass to cool the fire that was raging under his skin. *Oh, Lydia. Damn it, just wait. Be patient. I'm coming back, I promise.* He felt again the sudden rush of shame. He'd let her down. He forced himself upright and started in with the knife once more. He'd lost the money belt to that Felanka bastard, but safe inside the heel of each boot lay a neat roll of white rouble notes . . . not much, maybe, but enough to get him back to Felanka and to . . .

The heel popped off, hanging on by just one cobbler's pin. Inside the gap he had specially created lay nothing. It was empty. Alexei stared at it. Shook the boot ferociously as if the money would materialize from some other hole. He snatched up the other boot and with one angry jab jerked the heel onto the grass. Empty. He didn't even bother to shake it this time.

Cold despair slid into his gut. He tried to think straight. *The coat?* He twisted out of it and sliced the knife into the hem, into the collar, into the cuffs. All empty. All gone. No roubles, no silver dollars. No hope of buying his father's freedom.

He bent to one side and vomited last night's fish onto the grass.

"Oh, Konstantin, you bastard, you thieving fucking bastard. You . . ."

Rage robbed him of words. He knew it was over. He lifted the knife. Without hesitation he cut through the material of his trousers and stabbed the blade into the spot high on his thigh where there was already a rough scar. A flow of blood spilled down over the pale muscle to form a pool on the grass. Using the knife tip he extracted something small and hard, covered in blood, from within the flesh and put it into his mouth. When he spat it out onto his palm, it was clean. A diamond. Too small to be worth much. Even less in a dog-shit place like this. But hopefully enough to get him to Felanka.

It was the last. There was nothing left after this.

He cut a strip off the bandage on his side and knotted it tightly around his thigh. Blood still oozed, but Alexei ignored it. He welcomed the pain in the wound at each step. It deadened that other pain, the one in his chest, the one that was trying to suffocate him as he limped into the village.

"1908?"

"Yes, that's what it said. The stones spelled out *Nyet* and *1908*." Lydia frowned and turned to Elena. "I don't understand what it means. What happened in 1908?"

On the train back to Felanka she had cudgeled her brain into trying to work out the significance of the number. *1908*. But however meticulously she trawled through her knowledge of Russian history, nothing came to mind that made the slightest bit of sense.

"1908?" Elena asked again. "Are you sure it wasn't 1905? That's when the first revolution started in St. Petersburg with the Bloody Sunday massacre. Maybe it's telling you he's in St. Petersburg."

"No, it was definitely an eight, not a five. I'm sure of it. 1908."

They were walking back from the station and had stopped at a roadside stall that sold hot *pirozhki* to passersby. Lydia was holding her hands out to the heat of the brazier, eyeing Popkov's broad uncommunicative back as he waited for the little pies to be fried. Since leaving the station he hadn't spoken to her. She stamped her feet on the hard compacted snow, frustrated by his silence and by the cryptic message from the camp. She rubbed her gloves together hard to bring blood to her fingers and turned to Elena. "The Tunguska event happened in 1908, didn't it, the explosion over Siberia?"

"*Da*, but I don't see a connection."

"Neither do I, except that it flattened millions of trees, just like the prisoners are doing." She looked at the older woman hopefully. "I thought you might think of something."

Elena shook her head regretfully. "Yet it must be obvious or they wouldn't have left you that message. Can you think of any connection to yourself?"

"No, it's four years before I was born."

"And your parents?"

"They weren't married then, but they both lived in St. Petersburg. Do you think it's referring to something that happened in St. Petersburg that year?"

"Like what?"

They stared at each other blankly and shook their heads.

Popkov took a bite out of one of the *pirozhki* and breathed hot air at the two women as he thrust a pie at each of them.

"It's not a date," he growled and turned to the pie seller for more.

"What?" Lydia demanded.

"You heard."

She prodded his back. "What do you mean, it's not a date?"

He shoveled another pie into his mouth. How could he do that without burning his tongue?

"How do you know it's not a date?"

Popkov lumbered around to face her, and she could still feel his anger at her, bristling on his clothes and lurking in his thick shaggy beard. She wanted to tell him she was sorry, to promise she wouldn't stray again. But she couldn't do it.

"Tell me, Liev," she said softly, "if 1908 isn't a date, what is it?"

He glared at her and plucked at his eye patch with a greasy finger. "When the prison guards are drunk, they blurt out things. I've heard from several of them about the places so secret the authorities don't give them names, just numbers. 1908 is one of them. I've heard it mentioned."

"So what is it?"

"It's a secret prison."

"A secret prison?" The bones of Lydia's face seemed to freeze.

"*Da.* I have no idea where, except that it's somewhere in Moscow."

Lydia seized the front of his coat and hugged it to her. "Then that's where we'll go. To Moscow."

Eighteen

THE SILENCE. THE STILLNESS. THE SAMENESS. They rob you. Steal your sense of self.

In a set of bright basement rooms deep under the streets of Moscow, a tall man leaned over a clutch of technical drawings spread out over the surface of his desk and for a moment wondered whether he was dead or alive. Sometimes he couldn't tell.

Week by week, the days scarcely varied. The electric light was never switched off and the concept of darkness became a luxury he craved. He worked at his desk whenever he chose, whenever he could concentrate his mind, unaware of time or routine. Right now, was it day or night? He had no idea. He released the pair of calipers from his hand and let them clatter onto the wooden surface of the desk, just to hear a noise of some kind other than the hum of the hot-water pipes that trailed along the walls.

He rested his chin on his hand. What were other people doing? Eating? Singing? Best of all, talking? He allowed his mind to create a world up there above his head, a city where snow fell onto its golden church domes in a thick lacy curtain. Where sounds were muffled and there was the swish of greased runners, and hopeful young street urchins touted firewood for sale, hauling it along the gutters on sledges.

Moscow was alive above him. Living and laughing. He could smell the dough in the ovens and taste the sour cream on his tongue . . . but only in his dreams. In his waking hours there was nothing but silence, stillness and sameness.

"SO YOU HAVE A DAUGHTER."

Jens Friis made no response. He was sharpening a pencil when the guard rattled his keys, unlocked the heavy metal door, and entered the workroom with a grimace on his face. It was the fat one, Polia-kov. He wasn't so bad. Better than some of the other bastards. And this one liked to talk, even if it was just to poke and prod the prisoners out of their carefully constructed shells. Jens didn't mind that. He'd developed a knack of letting the taunts slide past and responding with comments that sometimes succeeded in enticing the warder into conversation.

But this. *So you have a daughter.* This was different.

He sat back in his seat, a padded comfortable armchair in which he did most of his thinking, and showed no hint of surprise.

"What do you mean, Poliakov?"

"Your daughter."

"You've got it wrong. I have no family. They were lost in the terrors of 1917."

The guard leaned against the door frame, his belly straining at the buttons of his shirt, his round brown eyes full of amusement. That was a bad sign.

"No daughter?"

"*Nyet,*" Jens repeated.

"Are you sure?"

"Yes." But his heart stopped.

Poliakov pulled out a cigarette, lit it with a match that he dropped on the floor, and took a long drag on it before letting loose a conspiratorial smile. "Now what's the point of lying to me, Friis? I thought I was your friend."

At least here they were called by their names. In the camp it had been just impersonal numbers. Jens dismissed the guard's words as another attempt to provoke him, so he refused to rise to the bait.

"Any chance of a smoke?" he asked instead.

"I tell you, Friis, you're going to love listening to this. Your daughter has turned up at your last camp, it seems. Don't look so shocked. She's searching for you in the wrong place, thousands of miles away from here. Isn't that funny?" He chuckled at first, but when he saw the expression on his prisoner's face, he burst out laughing. "What chance does a stupid kid have of tracing you here?"

What chance?

Jens wanted to strangle him, to squeeze that thick lardy neck. He stood up abruptly, and as he did so a flash of fiery curls roared into his brain. A dainty heart-shaped face. A mischievous smile that could pulverize his heart. Lydia? *Is it you? My Lydia?*

Could it really be her?

Sweat broke out on his skin. Was his daughter alive? After all these years that he'd believed her dead. And his wife?

"Oh, dear God, let my beautiful Valentina be alive. Let my little Lydia be . . ." He choked.

For twelve long barren years he'd lived without them, without even the memory of the two people he had loved most in the world. Because to think of them, of their smiles and their clear voices, would destroy him. So for twelve lonely years he'd lived without love and without hope. Only now when Poliakov said so slyly, *She's searching for you,* did the images of the moment he lost them come crashing back into his head.

He pictured once more the icy wasteland of Siberia, white and monotonous. The gray frozen slats of the cattle wagons that were packed with fear and fury, as the train with its cargo of fleeing White Russians growled its way across Russia in search of freedom. Valentina's breath on his cheek, the weight of their child asleep in his arms. Then came the rifles, the men on horseback with hate in their eyes, the cries as the women and children were snatched from the train by the Bolsheviks. In flashes he recalled again the pitiless gaze of the Red Army commander as the men were herded away to be shot. Valentina's eyes huge with an agony of despair. Lydia's thin piercing scream. The terror spread around them as solid as the frozen snow under their feet.

He jerked his mind away from that moment, the way he would jerk his hand away from red hot metal.

"Valentina?" he whispered.

"Who the fuck is Valentina?" Poliakov snapped.

Jens suddenly hated this guard, loathed and detested him for enticing hope back into his life. Hope was dead. Long ago he had slain it, a many-headed monster that made life in the prisons unbearable. But now it had risen from the dead to torment him again. The pencil in his hand snapped.

Nineteen

"SHE'S NOT HERE."

"When did she leave?" Alexei asked.

"A while ago."

"A week? A month? Longer?"

The concierge shook her head unhelpfully. She was a sturdy comrade who took her job seriously. "I don't keep track of everyone's movements, you know."

I bet you do, comrade. I bet that's exactly what you do.

But she wasn't going to share the information with him. He couldn't blame her. He looked a mess; his filthy clothes and unshaven appearance didn't exactly inspire confidence.

"I'm her brother."

"So?"

"I was delayed elsewhere. I thought she'd still be here in Felanka."

"Well, she's not."

"Did she leave anything? A note perhaps?"

"*Nyet.*"

Alexei rested his elbows on her desk and leaned so far forward it occurred to him that she might think he was trying to kiss her. He smiled, but it wasn't friendly. "I believe she did," he said evenly.

The woman thought about that. "I'll check."

She backed away, rummaged in a drawer, and, after a show of considerable effort, produced an envelope. Scrawled across it in large looping letters was his name, Alexei Serov. He realized he'd never seen his sister's handwriting before in all the time they'd been traveling together. It surprised him. It was bold—but that much he would have guessed. What he hadn't expected was the softness within it, the uncertain ends to the words and a carefulness in the forming of the capital S. *Oh, Lydia. Where the hell are you? Why didn't you wait?*

His fear was that she'd gone to the camp and been arrested.

"And the man we were with? The big—"

"I remember him." For the first time she smiled, and it made her almost pretty. "He's gone too. They went together."

Her memory was improving, so he decided to try again. "I left a bag in my room. Is it . . . ?"

"Any possessions remaining in the room are kept for three days and then sold to cover any unpaid rent."

"But I'm sure my sister would have paid anything owing."

The woman shrugged carelessly. She was growing bored.

"Thank you," he said politely and smiled at her. "*Spasibo.*"

"You're welcome."

"Could you make sure my bag is not also hidden away somewhere and forgotten?" He said it pleasantly enough, but one look at his eyes made her hesitate as she started to shake her head. She moved over to a dark cubicle behind her, disappeared for no more than one minute, and returned empty-handed.

"*Nyet,*" she said. "*Neechevo.* Nothing."

"Thank you, comrade. For your . . . help."

My dear Alexei,

I'm writing in the hope that you may return here to Felanka. I want you to find this letter. I waited for you, Alexei. Three whole weeks— with no word. But you didn't come back. Where are you? I swing between being frantic with worry one moment and angry with you for deserting me the next. Don't you care if you hurt me?

To practical matters:

1. *I enclose some money. In case you are in any trouble.*
2. *Your bag is missing from your room. So I must assume you planned your leaving. Popkov has haunted the bars to hear any word of you, but no one is saying anything. Maybe they know nothing.*
3. *Now for the big one. I am going to Moscow. With Popkov and Elena. I'm not sure about Elena, why she is sticking so close, but she and my beloved bear seem to have taken a liking to each other.*
4. *Why Moscow? Papa is there. Think about it, Alexei. Papa in Moscow, not in a coal mine. I could cry with joy. I was given a number— 1908. I thought it was a date. It's not. Popkov tells me it is the number of a secret prison in Moscow. Thank God for Popkov.*

We leave by train today. I wish you were with us. Take good care of yourself, my only brother. If you find this letter and decide to come to Moscow, meet me at noon outside the Cathedral of Christ the Redeemer. I'll try to be waiting there each day.

From your sister with love—and fury,
Lydia

"Niko."

The blond young truck driver lifted his head from his copy of *Pravda* and regarded Alexei with interest. He had the kind of eyes that would always be interested. In anything.

"What can I do for you?" He tossed his newspaper into the cab of his truck and watched as Alexei approached.

Alexei had tracked him to an open concrete yard alongside the road to the foundry. Drivers gathered there with their trucks, waiting in line to make deliveries or to collect a new load from the ironworks, and the line was sometimes so long that a stall supplying *kvass* had been erected and another selling *chai* and *blinis* beside it.

"Let me buy you a drink," Alexei offered, and gestured to the stalls.

Niko grinned. "I'd prefer vodka."

"So would I." Alexei pulled a bottle from his pocket. He took a swig from it himself and handed it across to Niko, who did the same.

The day was dull, the cold not as intense as a month ago, and snow was shoveled into oily mounds round the edge of the yard. For a moment Alexei held his breath, considering the risk he was about to take. He had to judge his man well. He was in no doubt that OGPU secret police had informers in every corner of Felanka. When a handsome bird suddenly rose from somewhere downriver, a Siberian crane spreading its black-tipped wings and circling effortlessly above the truck yard like an extra pair of eyes, Alexei laughed out loud. He turned to Niko and slapped him on the back.

"Okay, comrade, drink up. Fancy a bit of action?"

"Yes. This town is like a morgue." The young driver flashed his teeth.

"Then let's talk business."

THERE WAS NO MONEY IN THE LETTER. OF COURSE THERE wasn't. Concierges were expert at steaming open sealed correspondence. It was a fact as well known in Soviet Russia as the color of the snow after the wind blows in from the factories on the edge of town; everyone was aware of it, took it for granted—except Lydia, it seemed.

The money was gone and he had no way of proving it was ever there. But that was the least of his concerns. He sat alone on an iron bench in the deserted park with its elaborate wrought-iron lampposts and finished off the last of the vodka. He wanted the liquid to burn away the hard lump that had lodged somewhere just below his throat.

My beloved bear.

Thank God for Popkov.

That's what she'd said.

To hell with the dumb Cossack. That bastard must be so pleased with himself. Just because he'd been a servant on her grandfather's estate and had now shifted that doglike devotion to Lydia herself, it didn't give him any right to take over now, whisking her off to Moscow on some wild and dangerous goose chase. Of course Jens Friis wasn't there. It was just a terrible waste of their time and resources. And the plague of it was—should he remain here in Felanka? Waiting for their inevitable return. Or chase after them and drag them back.

Don't you care if you hurt me?
I care, my little sister. I care.

IT WAS THE HAIR THAT DID IT FOR HIM. THE WAY IT HUNG IN a dense glossy swathe around her shoulders with a handful of dark waves pinned up into an elaborate coiffure on top of her head. Alexei recognized it immediately, though for a moment he had no recall of who the woman was.

Midafternoon and the day was gray. Iron gray, he told himself with a wry smile, suitable for an iron town. He was making his way down Felanka's main street, avoiding the grander buildings and the snow heaped in the gutters, heading straight for the more run-down areas where the street traders would have their cheaper wares on display. He was weary. Sore and hungry. He hadn't eaten for two days, trying to preserve the few roubles that lay secreted in his pocket.

That was when he saw the woman's hair, and the long silver fur coat that swung as she moved. She was standing at the edge of the curb attempting to cross the busy road at one of the spots where the gutter had been cleared of snow to allow pedestrians passage. As she flicked her head from side to side, watching out for the traffic in both directions, for one fleeting second their eyes met.

His brain was sluggish. Infections and fever had taken their toll, so his reactions were slow. If he'd had something to eat, something to give him the strength to clear his mind, maybe what followed might have worked out differently. The woman stared at him, then abandoned the curb and walked briskly toward him across the frozen pavement, so purposeful in her stride that he knew she wanted something from him.

"Well, you're certainly a mess, aren't you?"

This was not exactly the greeting he'd expected. She didn't smile, just looked him up and down the way she would a homemade dress on a hanger, and that was when he remembered who the dark hair belonged to. The camp commandant's wife.

"*Dobriy den*, good afternoon," Alexei responded. "I'm surprised you recognize me." He rubbed a hand over his rough beard. "But you," he said gallantly, "are unforgettable."

She gave him a look. "Don't lie. At first you had no recall of who I was."

"You're quick," he smiled, meaning it as a compliment. "I apologize. I've been unwell."

"That's obvious."

"But you are looking even more elegant than ever."

"I've just had my hair done. Like it?" She patted the pinned loops and her carmine lips curved, inviting praise.

"It looks delightful." He gestured vaguely up the street. "Especially here. You add color." He studied her carefully groomed face with its narrow bones and deep-set eyes that seemed to hide in shadows, "You bring style to the streets of Felanka."

She laughed, but it was a practiced effort that fooled neither of them. Alexei guessed she was about five years older than himself, probably in her early thirties, but there was something fragile about her that was at odds with her glossy smile and confident walk. He slid a hand into his pocket and prodded the pathetic huddle of roubles.

"Comrade," he smiled, "let me have the pleasure of buying you a drink."

"I'M LOOKING FOR THE GIRL YOU WERE WITH IN SELYANSK."

"She's gone," Alexei said.

"So it seems."

"Why the interest in her?"

"She asked me for something. This is the third time I've tried to trace her but she appears to have"—she twiddled her fingers in the air as if tracing a puff of smoke—"vanished."

"I'm her brother. You can tell me and I'll pass it on when we—"

"So she's not your lover?"

"*Nyet.*"

The question irritated him. As did the place they were in, the Leninsky Hotel. It was lavish beyond his expectations and certainly beyond his means. It wasn't exactly designed for the use of the working proletariat either. A spacious hotel lounge with high corniced ceilings and comfortable silk brocade sofas that would not have been out of place in the Leningrad of his youth. Gold-framed mirrors lined the walls, reflecting light into every corner, and Alexei was shocked to catch sight of his own appearance. He looked terrible, even worse than he'd feared. The hotel manager would not have even let him up the front steps if it had not been for Antonina at his side.

"Don't fuss, Vladimir," she had beamed, dismissing the startled manager with a wave of her hand. "Bring us tea . . . and two brandies," she ordered, and breezed into the salon.

Alexei was acutely aware of his filthy homespun clothes and his unkempt appearance. He inspected his black fingernails with disgust. Why had she brought him here? He looked around. In one corner a lone pipe smoker was bent over a stack of manila folders, and down one side of the room a handful of well-dressed women were sipping *chai* and staring with open curiosity at Alexei. Antonina waved to them but nothing more. At the far end beside a small dance floor an elderly man with an impressive walrus mustache was playing a grand piano, utterly wrapped up in his own world, producing sad unfamiliar tunes that drifted through the air with a melancholy that suited Alexei's mood.

"Relax." She sipped her brandy, eyes serious.

"Do you bring men here often?"

She frowned. "Of course not. Don't be insulting. But I have an account here for when I'm in town. I would remind you that my husband is an important figure in these parts." She gave him a slow smile and indicated her brandy glass. "So don't worry about these. Would you like me to order you a cigar with it?"

"No. But thank you."

They were sitting opposite each other, a low mahogany coffee table between them, and he enjoyed observing her. It was a long time since he'd been alone with a woman. Lydia didn't count. She was his sister and anyway, just a girl. He found himself wanting to reach out and touch the silkiness of this woman's dress, slate blue and close fitting at the hips. It revealed very little, with its long sleeves and high neckline, and would have looked demure if it had not been so artfully cut that it emphasized the slenderness of her body and the full curves of her breasts. The only thing he didn't like was that she kept her gloves on, beautiful pearl-gray doeskin, because he liked to see hands. They told a lot about a person.

He leaned forward and raised his brandy to her. "To fortunate meetings," he smiled.

"I'll drink to that."

He tasted the golden liquid, remembering other brandies on elegant terraces and in other civilized smoking rooms. Now look at him. In secondhand clothes. He snorted with a sudden sense of the absurdity of it.

"What are you laughing at?" she asked.

"At the strangeness of life. You never know what—or who—is coming next."

She smiled, and for the first time her eyes became less guarded. "Isn't that what puts the spice into it?"

"No, not for me. I prefer to be prepared, and for that you need information."

"Ah! I see. You want something from me."

He sat back and gave a low laugh. "Just like you want something from me."

She didn't react, except to sharpen her deep-set gaze.

Abruptly Alexei emptied his glass and stood up. "Come," he said, holding out his hand, "dance with me."

Her eyes widened with surprise and flicked to his filthy clothes.

"Don't worry," he said. "I won't contaminate you."

They both knew that the word *contaminate* was a Soviet word. Subversives *contaminate* the proletariat. Dissidents *contaminate* their families and friends. For one moment he thought she would refuse, but he was mistaken. She was clearly a person who liked a challenge. With a brief glance in the direction of the other women in the salon, she rose to her feet and accepted his hand. Her gloved fingers were warm in his as he led her onto the dance floor and took her into his arms. The pianist looked up, surprised, and immediately struck up a waltz.

Alexei didn't hold her too close but close enough. He could inhale her musky perfume and see the way she had tried to cover the dark shadows under her eyes with makeup.

"You smell," she said, smiling.

"I apologize," he laughed.

"That's all right. I like it actually. You . . ."

"Hush," he murmured and drew her a fraction closer, his hand light on her back, aware of the delicate curve of each rib under his fingers. "Just dance."

Twenty

"ALEXEI, WHY ARE YOU CHASING ACROSS RUSSIA like a madman?" Antonina rubbed her cheek against his shoulder where she lay among the pillows. "What on earth drives you to this idiocy?"

Alexei sat up and cursed that his movement was still hampered by his wounds. He swung his legs off the bed and perched on the edge, feet brushing over satin sheets that lay tangled on the floor. His back was turned to her. After a moment he heard a rustle and felt the bed stir behind him, as gently her gloved fingers started to trail down his naked back from his neck to his buttocks. Soft and insistent.

"Tell me, Alexei."

Her lips found the exact spot between his shoulder blades where a nerve throbbed unrelentingly. He tipped his head back, resting it against hers, and immediately she wrapped her arms around him, her bare breasts tight against his spine, her hands cradling the scar on his side. For a while there was nothing but silence and the tick of their heartbeats.

"I was born and brought up in Leningrad, though I still think of it as St. Petersburg," he said. "The person I believed to be my father was part of the government there, always at the beck and call of the duma or the tsar. I hardly ever saw him." He paused before adding thoughtfully, "I certainly never knew what kind of man he was." ·

One of her fingers, so oddly erotic in its doeskin sheath when the rest of her was naked, reached out and found the scar on his thigh, which it started to circle gently. Watching the movement made him feel dizzy.

"My mother," he continued, "led an extremely social life, constant balls and soirées, and I had a tutor for my lessons. No other children. Just adults."

"A lonely life for a little boy."

"Except there was one man. I knew him as Uncle Jens. Every week he came and showed me what a boy's childhood should be."

"You're smiling," she laughed, though she couldn't see his face. "I like this Uncle Jens already." She brushed her hair like velvet against his skin, and he felt his loins stir once more.

"My mother took me to live in China when I was twelve." He made no mention of the Bolsheviks. "But as soon as she heard my father had died in the civil war, she married a French industrialist."

"Don't tell me you went to live in Paris. I am green with envy. All those dresses."

"No, you frivolous creature," he laughed. "We stayed in China. There's a large Russian community there, and as soon as I was old enough I became part of the liaison advisory delegation because I could speak both Russian and Chinese."

She tugged a strand of his greasy hair and teased him. "So there's an intelligent brain lying somewhere under all this good Russian dirt."

He laughed again and it felt good. He'd forgotten how much laughing helps. He turned and wrapped his arms around her naked body as she knelt on the bed, kissing her lips and taking a lingering pleasure in the soft pliant response of them. But after a moment she pushed him away, leaving only her hand on his chest.

"So?" she demanded.

"So what?"

"So how did you get from liaison officer in China to filthy tramp in this backwoods town of Soviet Russia?"

He brushed his lips along the soft angle of her cheekbone and wondered how much of this would be passed on elsewhere, but he couldn't stop his tongue now.

"That's simple. I discovered I had a half-sister." He looked deep into Antonina's dark troubled eyes and didn't want to lie to her, to add to the shadows that haunted her lovely face. But nevertheless he did. "I was sick of the bourgeois life. At the time I was considering returning to Russia for good."

"Why?"

"Because I wanted to be a part of this great undertaking that is occurring here. This sculpting of a whole new nation, this transformation of thought processes to an idealistic instead of materialistic society."

She eased her slender body out of his arms and lay back on the pillows, her long naked legs stretched out, her gloves stroking them as though they belonged to someone else. There was something unself-consciously sensual about the slow ritualistic movements.

"So you came here together," she said without looking at him, "you and your Lydia, to find this Jens Friis?"

"Yes."

"He's no longer at Trovitsk camp, you know."

"Are you certain? Is that what you came to tell Lydia?"

"Yes."

"So where is he now?"

"Moscow."

"Fuck!"

Moscow. Damn the Cossack for being right.

She regarded him solemnly. "So now you have the information you wanted. Are you going to leave me?"

"Antonina," he said teasingly, "where else am I going to get a bath and a shave? Of course I'm staying."

She laughed, delighted, and ran a toe all the way up his arm and into his beard.

HER SKIN TASTED OF OLIVES. OF WARM SUNLIGHT ON GOOD French burgundy with plump ripe olives. It tasted civilized. It's what

Alexei had missed. He was sick to his soul of grayness and dirt and utilitarian living. He wanted olives.

He kissed Antonina's throat and felt the flutter of her pulse as his tongue traced the fragile line of her collarbone, heard her excited intake of breath. Like a child when it spies the Christmas tree. His own breath quickened as he ran a hand along the length of her naked thigh, caressed her slender waist where a small blue scar broke the smooth perfection of her skin, and let his fingertips trail softly over her breasts and down into the valley between them. She moaned and murmured something inaudible, shutting her eyes, her lips opening in a smile of secret pleasure. He touched her teeth with his tongue. They tasted of brandy.

"Is this dangerous?" he murmured.

"Of course it is. That's why you're here."

"And you?" He kissed each eyelid. "Is that why you're here?"

"I'm here because . . ."

A pause, nervy and tense, seemed to take over the room, and then reluctantly her eyelashes lifted and he could look into her eyes. They were dark and confused. Slowly they began to fill with tears.

"Oh, Antonina, what are you doing?"

Gently he took her in his arms, rocked her against his chest as he lay back on the pillows and enveloped her shuddering body in his arms. He kissed her dark glossy hair and tightened his grip on her. He didn't know this woman or what was hurting so fiercely inside her. But he did know he didn't want to let her go. If he were married to someone who routinely sent starving men out to haul wagons like slaves or dig coal with little more than their bare hands, he too would come looking for ways to ease the pain. He might even wear elbow-length gloves in bed the way she did. Quietly he breathed in her perfume and felt an unexpected connection with Antonina. He rested his head on hers, cradling her to him, feeling the warmth of her body flow into his.

How do any of us know what we will do until we do it?

ALEXEI PUSHED OPEN THE DOOR. THE BAR WAS THICK WITH bodies. The air clogged with cigarette smoke that hung in a lifeless pall near the ceiling, where it mingled with fumes from the stove. At least the place was warm. That was something. Alexei stamped his feet to rid them of ice, while outside in the darkness snow was falling in soft flurries.

He elbowed his way through the crush and reached the bar, where he ordered vodka and beer for two. The pretty young Uzbeki girl with the embroidered blouse and the wayward hips served him his drinks and rolled her black eyes at him invitingly, but he shook his head. He scooped up his drinks and made his way over to a table at the back where Niko was already seated.

"*Dobriy vecher.* Good evening," he greeted the truck driver.

He placed the vodkas and beers on the stained surface, and in return Alexei received a grin of gleaming strong teeth and the offer of a smoke. He declined it because despite the bath and shave, he could still smell Antonina's perfume on his skin and he liked it there. He wasn't ready to coat it in nicotine. Leaving her had been hard, dislocating something inside him because he didn't know when he would see her again.

"*Dobriy vecher*, comrade. *Spasibo.*" Niko accepted the drinks and knocked back the vodka with relish. The beer he nursed fondly between his hands. "Now, tell me, who is this wretch who stole your money?"

Alexei leaned forward. "We have an agreement, you and I."

"*Da.* I get to keep half of everything I get back for you."

"Just as long as you remember that."

"Don't worry, comrade, I'm not a thief. Nor are my friends."

Niko nodded meaningfully toward a group of men in truckers' heavy outfits and with a certain look in their eyes; they all had it. The look of a loner. Alexei knew he'd think twice before crossing them. Hopefully Vushnev would as well.

"So?" Niko took a mouthful of his beer. "His name?"

"It's Mikhail Vushnev, the camp—"

"I know him. Thin as a weasel and smokes a pipe."

"That's the bastard."

Niko slumped back in his chair and drained half his beer. "The shit has gone."

"Gone?"

"He came swaggering in here a few weeks back, buying everyone drinks. Said he was off to Odessa to start a new life with his money, so . . ."

"With *my* money," Alexei corrected. "And it won't be Odessa. He'll have the brains to cover his tracks."

"The bastard."

"No success for either of us, it seems, comrade."

"The bastard," Niko repeated mournfully, as if the loss of the money had frozen something in his thought processes.

Alexei drank the vodka. What the hell else was there to do? Except smash the glass on the table. He sat in silence, stiff and stern, his thoughts crashing into each other.

"Niko, where are you heading with your next load?"

"Novgorod."

"When?"

"Day after tomorrow."

"I'll see you then. At the truck stop. Be there early." Alexei threw his last handful of coins on the table. "Buy your friends a drink from me."

He pushed himself to his feet, and once outside in the darkness he said the bastard's name.

"Mikhail Vushnev."

He said it only once and spat in the gutter to rid himself of it. He began to walk, slowly at first, letting the snow settle on his skin, then faster, feet skidding in the snow. His mind started to clear. Twenty-four hours. Twenty-four precious hours to smell her perfume on his skin, to feel again the gentle weight of her body on his and see the thoughtful brown-eyed gaze that did something to the dark cold places inside him. Up ahead the lights of the Leninsky Hotel shone brightly.

Twenty-one

❦

IT WAS THE MIRROR THAT BROUGHT LYDIA BACK to Chang. He was being driven in a large black sedan that smelled of new leather and shone with polished chrome. Seated alone in the back with just the cap of the driver in front of him, a young soldier who knew how to remain silent, Chang glanced up with no real interest at the rearview mirror. He caught sight of a rectangular slice of one of the driver's black eyes, and a sudden lurch in his chest stole his breath away.

Another car. Another driver. Another city. Another rectangle of a mirror. Yet it was as if she were here right now beside him. Her presence was so strong. He turned his head, expecting to see Lydia's bright smile, and instead saw nothing but the chaos outside on the busy streets of Canton, rain-soaked rickshaws dodging the bumpers of the heedless cars and vans that clogged the thoroughfares. He lifted a hand, letting it touch the empty air next to him on the bench seat, curling his fingers through it, feeling for her. He listened intently for her breathing.

Slowly his hand drifted down to the seat till it was resting, palm down, on the leather. It was maroon and the thought that slipped into his head was that it wouldn't show the blood from his hands. He blinked, startled. Where had that come from? His hands were long healed where the two fingers had been removed.

Did it come from her? From Lydia? Was she in need of his hands? The thought caught at his throat.

Each morning and each night he prayed with bowed head to the gods to keep her safe. He offered them bargains, his safety for hers; he made them promises that were extravagant and ever more costly, every one of which he swore to honor if only Lydia was returned to him unhurt, unharmed, undamaged. He vowed eternal devotion to the shrines and burned candles in the temples, as well as incense and paper images of fearsome dragons. He slaughtered a bullock. To give her strength. All this despite his Communist ideals that dismissed such beliefs as a fool's superstition. All this to keep her safe. To keep her safe he would even give up his fox girl and spend eternity in tears.

But now today it was as though she were suddenly here. With him. On the maroon leather. And his heart for one fleeting moment flew back to that other day when she sat beside him in a car, and he had looked up at the rearview mirror to seek out the eyes of the driver. To learn whether he had stepped into a trap.

Her hands had curled around Chang's, cradling his bandages to her breast as she might cradle an infant, and despite the raging fever that made his eyes dull as pond water and his brain as sickly as a rabid dog's, he knew he would remember this moment. For a brief second she'd rested her cheek on his shoulder and her hair had crept like flames over his shirt front. Just to look at her was enough, at her pale cheek and her clear amber eyes. It drew him back from the edge.

She seemed fragile. Frightened. Yet she'd pulled him forcibly into Theo Willoughby's car on the snowy streets of Junchow, whisking him from under the nose of the police just when the Nationalist authorities believed they had captured him at last. She'd looped her arm around his shoulders, holding him upright on the seat, and the last thing he wanted was to topple over in her teacher's car. She would lose face.

"Thank you, sir," Lydia said politely to the man driving. "Thanks for giving us a ride."

The schoolmaster glanced quickly in the mirror, his gaze seeking Chang. Even in his sick state Chang knew the signs. The yellowish skin around the mouth. The eyes not quite in this world. This Englishman was smoking the pipe of dreams at night and could not be trusted.

"So what have we here?" Willoughby had asked with more curiosity than Chang cared for.

"This is my friend, Chang An Lo."

"Ah! The young rebel I've heard about."

"He's a Communist fighting for justice."

"It's a fine line, Lydia."

"Not to me."

After a moment Willoughby said, "I'm sorry."

"Sorry for what?"

"For you."

"Don't be."

"You are crossing a divide that is too wide for your young legs."

"Just help us. Please."

"How? He looks almost dead."

"Take us somewhere where the soldiers will not come."

"Where, Lydia? A hospital?"

"No, they'll find him there. Your school."

The teacher had snorted as if he'd swallowed a frog.

Lydia had turned to Chang and with her touch as gentle as a moth's wing, she'd taken his face in her hands and he'd breathed her sweet strong breath into his lungs.

"Don't die on me, my love," she'd whispered. He could feel her trembling.

He was not far from taking the path to join his ancestors, he knew that. He could hear their voices rustling in his ear. One slip of his foot and he'd slide into . . . His eyes closed, their lids like lead coins, but instantly her lips brushed each eye.

"Open," she murmured.

They opened and her eyes were no more than a finger's width from his own, pinning him to life. Not allowing him to leave this world.

"Chang An Lo, what color is love?"

He wanted to speak, but there were no words inside his head.

"He's gone," the schoolmaster said.

"No," she hissed, and she squeezed the bones of his skull between her palms. "Tell me, tell me."

"It's too late, Lydia," the teacher insisted, though his voice was not unkind. "You can see he's gone."

She ignored him, listening to nothing but Chang's breath sighing from his lungs. "It's the color of my eyes," she whispered, "of my lips, of my skin. It's the color of my life. Don't you dare leave me, my love."

He didn't leave her. Not then.

Twenty-two

"COME HERE, GIRL. I HAVE A CLOCK FOR YOU, A good marble one with—"

"*Nyet*, I don't need a clock." Lydia shook her head and backed away from the stall.

She liked street markets. The shouting and the pushing and the manhandling of goods. They reminded her of home. *No,* she pulled herself up sharply, *get it right.* What she meant was they reminded her of China, but China was no longer her home. *Face it.* Her mother was dead, her stepfather had scuttled back to England, and Chang An Lo was . . . was where? *Where? Where?*

She looked around at the hustle and bustle of the market. At the vegetables spread out next to a jumble of old shoes, at the neat pile of homemade preserves between the books and the bread. She even spotted an ancient microscope, all brass and knobs beside a hank of brightly colored embroidery silks. The traders were bundled up against the cold while haggling and arguing over kopecks as if they were as precious as bars of gold.

Moscow had come as a shock. Not at all what

Lydia had expected. The Bolsheviks had made the right move, she decided. They had shifted the capital city of Soviet Russia right away from the decadent bourgeois elegance of Leningrad—the city of her own first five years of childhood. Instead Moscow became the hub. Forever turning. She could almost hear its wheels.

The moment she stepped off the train, she fell in love with the place. Alexei had told her that it lacked the grace and beauty of Leningrad, that Moscow was a dirty industrial dump. But he was wrong. What he'd omitted to mention was that the new capital was bursting with infectious energy. There was a kind of spark in its streets. An eagerness. It made the hairs rise on the back of her neck. And hanging over it all was the unmistakable smell of power in the air.

Moscow was the future. No question.

But was it her future? More importantly, was it Papa's?

"I'm here, Papa," she whispered. "I'm back."

"I DON'T KNOW WHAT YOU'RE LOOKING SO DAMN PLEASED about." Elena was staring with annoyance at Lydia.

"I was thinking," Lydia said as she inspected the shabby room they'd just entered, "thank goodness Alexei is not with us. He would hate this place."

"I hate this place."

"It'll do us. It's our first step. Now we're here, we can start searching properly. Anyway I've seen worse," Lydia laughed. "I've actually *lived in* worse."

"More fool you," Elena grunted and plonked herself down on a bed. The springs pinged with a metallic screech.

"The room is small, I admit." Lydia started to pace slowly around it, trying to find something positive to say. The air was musty, heavy with the long-lost hopes of past occupants. The wallpaper was stained and peeling in places. One of the windowpanes was cracked and an electric cable stuck out of the wall above one of the beds, ending in a spray of naked wires. It looked to Lydia horribly like a snake with its head cut off.

"The ceiling's nice," she said. It was high and decorated with elaborate cornices. "And the floor. It may be battered but it's solid parquet."

Elena rolled her eyes in disgust. "Look at the rugs."

"Okay, so the *poloviki* are a bit old. But what do you expect in a *communalka*?"

"*Neechevo*," Elena groaned. "Nothing."

"Well, that's what we've got. *Neechevo*."

That wasn't strictly true. They had a roof over their heads. That's what mattered to Lydia and she wasn't fussy about what was under that roof. She'd learned the hard way. While living from hand to mouth with her mother in Junchow, the sight of the rent money ready in the blue bowl on the mantelpiece made the difference between eating and not eating, between sleeping and not sleeping, between being warm and being cold. She craned her neck back now and gazed up at the ceiling. It was solid. Yes, its prettiness was an extra bonus when you lay in bed. But its solidity was what mattered.

"Don't complain, Elena."

"I'll complain if I like." She put her hands on her broad hips. "You think all three of us, you, me, and Popkov, can live in this shoebox without killing each other?"

Lydia swished the dividing curtain across the middle of the room, shutting off Elena and the big bed, creating the illusion of privacy.

"Don't fret, Elena," she laughed. "I'll wear earplugs."

"THREE HUNDRED, THREE HUNDRED AND TWENTY, THREE hundred and forty . . . four hundred, four hundred and ten."

"Little Lydia, you can go on counting it all night, but it's not going to change." Popkov was leaning against the windowsill, his intimidating bulk in a long black coat, its collar up around his ears. He was watching her empty out her money belt onto her bed.

"Four hundred and ten roubles," Lydia said flatly. "It's not enough."

"It will have to be. It's all we've got."

"The residence permits and ration cards cost us far too much."

"We had no choice."

"I know. You said."

"It's what they charge. On the black market. I tried, Lydia, but . . ."

"It's not your fault."

She shuffled the remaining notes together, patting them, chivvying them, as if she could persuade them to increase in number. It was why they'd given up even the cheapest hotels and moved into one of the crowded communal apartments on a run-down street, but they were lucky to get it. She and Elena had stood in line for days outside the Housing Committee office in the freezing wind and were allocated the room only when the man in front of them dropped to his knees with a heart attack the moment he was told he could have the room. Now each rouble that passed through Lydia's fingers seemed to burn a hole in her stomach, and no amount of the black doughy *khleb* could fill it. She shivered, wiped the back of her hand across her mouth, and picked at her chin. Her lips were dry.

"What's the matter?" Popkov asked. Behind him the sky was shifting its choice of gray, slipping into the colorless shade that came just before sunset. Pigeons began to settle on the roofs. "What's the matter?" he asked a second time when she didn't respond.

"Nothing."

"It doesn't look like nothing."

"Well, it is. But thanks for asking."

He growled, an indistinct rumble in his chest. She made herself concentrate on the room, on its four square walls. They were still here. They were going nowhere. She could rely on that. The three-story house overlooking a central courtyard had once been smart, but some years earlier had been taken over by a housing committee that had carved the living space up into small chunks and allocated a few square feet of it to each person. Enough for a bed and, if you were lucky, a chair and a cupboard. Lydia wasn't lucky. She had a bed but Popkov got the chair.

Washing and cooking facilities were communal at the end of the landing, and the rotation system was supervised with hawkish efficiency by a housing manager named Comrade Kelensky. He prowled around with an ill-fitting suit and an air of reproach. Lydia had already been in trouble for not cleaning the communal stairs thoroughly enough. She'd scrubbed them twice, as instructed, but as soon as her back was turned a bored little child from downstairs bounced a muddy ball on them. Kelensky made Lydia perform the task again. While she did it, Popkov had sat himself down on the top step of the steep flight of stairs like a dark-eyed St. Peter at the gates, elbows on his knees, humming *chastushki*, peasant songs, to himself and munching sunflower seeds from his pocket. She wasn't sure if he was guarding her from others or from herself.

She packed the roubles neatly back into the money belt and zipped it up. It was stained with sweat and rubbed thin in places.

"Your brother should have had the sense to divide the funds equally between you," Liev grumbled.

"He didn't trust me enough."

The window rattled as a sudden gust of wind fingered the broken pane and the daylight outside took another step toward the solid shadows of a winter's afternoon. Silence drifted into the room. Lydia buckled the belt firmly around her waist once more, tucked her legs under her on the bed, and pulled the quilt over her shoulders. She watched the big man take out his battered old tin of tobacco and roll himself a smoke with the smooth ease of long practice. His thick fingers dwarfed the cigarette he stuck between his lips.

"It's a waste of time," he growled. "Waiting outside the church each day."

"Don't, Liev."

"I mean it, Lydia. He's not coming."

"He will."

"I don't want . . ." He stopped.

"Don't want what?"

"I don't want to see you hurt. Again." He lit the cigarette, took a drag on it, and inspected its glowing tip so that he didn't have to look at her.

Lydia swallowed awkwardly, both touched and angry at the same time. Damn him for doubting Alexei.

"Liev, Alexei will come, I know he will. Tomorrow or the day after or the day after that, but one day soon I'll walk up the steps to the Cathedral of Christ the Redeemer and he'll be waiting there for—"

"No. He's gone. Good riddance to the bastard."

"Don't, Liev," she said again.

He jerked his bull frame away from the windowsill and seemed to fill the small room. Elena had gone out on some mission of her own, but still the place felt overcrowded, its drab walls pressing in on them. Lydia unzipped her money belt, pulled out one of the notes, and threw it on the bed in front of the Cossack.

"Go buy yourself a drink, Liev. That filthy temper of yours is—"

"Why are you so fucked up by Alexei's disappearance?" he demanded. "You and he were always at each other like cat and dog. The man is an arrogant prick. We're better off without him."

Lydia threw off the quilt and leapt to her feet, a tiny figure next to his bulk. She thumped a fist on his granite chest.

"You stupid Cossack," she shouted at him. "Take that back."

"*Nyet.*"

"Take it back."

"*Nyet.*"

They glared at each other.

"He's my brother. Can't you see? Are you so blind with your one eye? Alexei means everything to me. He's all the family I've got until we find my father. Don't ever say I'm better off without him, you ignorant peasant."

"*Chyort*, little Lydia," Popkov said. "He's not worth—"

"He is to me." She was struggling for breath. "I owe him. Everything."

"Don't talk rot, girl. You owe that bastard nothing. He's deserted you now the going is tough, and before that all he ever did every step of the way was to complain."

"You're wrong."

"Hah! Tell me how."

A long sigh crept out of Lydia's lungs and she slumped down on the edge of the rumpled bed, her arms snaking tightly around her thin body. Her hair fell forward, curtaining her face.

"Don't you remember?" she murmured through her hair. "How he issued the order that saved Chang An Lo's life when he was in the hands of the Nationalists. That was the reason Alexei had to flee Junchow. The Nationalists wanted revenge on him. He gave up everything to help me. To save Chang An Lo for *me*."

Popkov uttered one of his dismissive grunts. "He's still a bastard."

Lydia raised her head and dug up a lopsided smile for him. "Okay, you're right, you old bear. I'm sorry I shouted. He *is* a bastard—in more ways than one."

Liev laughed and the windowpane fell out.

★ ★ ★

ROOMS WERE SCARCE. PEASANTS WERE FLOCKING INTO THE city. Lydia had been astonished by their numbers, and they all wanted rooms. She had watched them wandering the streets, up and down the Krasnoselskaya, a blanket under one arm, a pair of boots or a sack of tools slung over their shoulder, anything that they could sell or barter in exchange for food. She'd learned to recognize them. It wasn't just their homespun clothes and their big-knuckled hands, but the bewilderment in their eyes. Is that what hers were like too? Uncertain. Nervous. Rolling loose in her head.

"Why did they leave their villages?" she'd asked Elena as they waited in line with their ration cards.

"Why do you think? They're starving out there in the communal farms and they've heard there are jobs to be had here."

"It must be true because there are factories going up all around us. It's part of Stalin's Five-Year Plan."

"Exactly." The woman lowered her voice. "But they're peasants, for God's sake, they don't know the first thing about operating machinery. If they can press the *on* and *off* buttons, they're doing well."

"Aren't they trained?"

"If you call losing a finger training, yes. When they've lost one, they don't make the same mistake again."

"How do you know all this?"

Sometimes it astonished Lydia how much this woman knew. Lydia had heard little about her life except that she'd had a child and fallen into whoring.

"It's the one bloody thing I'm any good at," Elena had chuckled one night when they passed a prostitute parading the street. She'd slapped Lydia on the back with relish. "Don't get any ideas. No one would want a skinny runt like you."

"That's not true," Lydia had retorted.

Elena had slid her gaze over her companion's bony hips and small breasts and snorted disparagingly. Lydia's cheeks had burned.

As they shuffled forward on the sidewalk outside the bakery, ice seeping up through the thin soles of their boots, Lydia pointed across the street.

"Look," she said.

In the doorway of a boarded-up shop opposite, a small makeshift cardboard shelter had been thrown together, drooping sideways like a bird with a damaged wing. A pair of feet wrapped in rags stuck out one end. But they'd remained immobile for too long. Was the man asleep? Dead? Injured? Or just sliding down the crack in his dreams?

"Leave it," Elena said, and placed a restraining hand on Lydia's arm. "It's dangerous."

"Elena, I remember what it's like to be so hungry you'd eat your own toes." She shook off the hand. "Communism is supposed to make society fairer. For everyone."

Elena brushed the straw wisps of hair off her face with irritation, tucking them into her hat as if tidying her thoughts. "This world isn't fair, don't you know that yet? Look around you."

Lydia looked. At the women waiting hours in line for a few grams of heavy black bread and at the feet in the cardboard shell. But Elena hadn't finished.

"The trouble with you, girl, is that you think you can construct a new world for yourself with a father and a brother of your own, all wrapped up cozily together in a fair society. And you're frightened that it will come crashing down around your ears and then you'll be left with nothing and no one."

"No." Lydia gazed directly at her. "No, you're wrong."

The lines of the older woman's face grew gentle. "Don't look so desperate. I know what it's like to have nothing and no one. It's not so bad." She smiled, a sad little upward twist of her lips. "When you get used to it. Because then you've got nothing to lose."

"But I still have"—Lydia felt something delicate tremble inside her chest—"everything to lose."

She pulled away from Elena and launched herself across the road toward the cardboard shelter.

THE DOORWAY SMELLED AND LYDIA ALMOST TURNED AWAY. OLD newspapers were piled in a sodden yellow heap behind the cardboard, and a mess of something slimy lay in the corner. As if someone had been sick and left it there to freeze. She knew Elena was right when she said this was dangerous. She wasn't a Muscovite and didn't know this city's ways. Nervously she prodded the foot with her own.

"Are you all right?"

Instantly the foot withdrew. It wasn't a corpse. That was something.

"Do you need help?"

The cardboard shifted. In the street people hurried past, heads averted. Wary, Lydia bent over to peer inside the shelter.

"Hello?"

"Fuck off."

"Are you all right?"

She rested a hand on the cardboard and it was wet and soft, and as cold as a dead man's cheek. She wiped her hand fiercely on her coat. She was tempted to turn and cross the road to her place in the line where Elena was waiting, still glaring at her.

"Hello?" she said again and tapped the front flap of the cardboard, which was acting as a door. It immediately caved in.

A pair of blue eyes stared back at her. For a fleeting second neither reacted, each of them in shock at the unexpected confrontation. The eyes moved before she did, as the figure threw itself out the back of the shelter and hunched like a cornered rat against the brickwork at the rear of the doorway's arch.

"I'm not here to frighten you," Lydia said quickly.

No response. Just feral eyes and skin stretched so tight over bones it looked ready to split. Lydia realized with relief it was only a boy, around twelve years old. Despite the icy temperatures, sweat trickled down his neck. She smiled to show she meant him no harm.

"I thought you might need help."

"Fuck off."

"You don't look . . . well."

"So what?"

"So I came across to—"

"Fuck off."

His rudeness was starting to annoy her. "Shut up, will you? I'm offering help."

"Why?"

Suspicion was mutual. The dismal doorway was thick with it.

"Because . . . well, just that I remember."

His hair was a strange color. Milk white. As if he'd been shocked almost to death by his life. His face and hands were black with grime, and he reminded her of an old-fashioned chimney sweep's boy, though on his chin a small round patch of skin shone pink. She took a step backward, unwilling to unsettle him further, and almost slipped on the ice. His expression didn't change.

"Remember what?" His breathing was labored.

"It doesn't matter. Are you ill?"

"What's it to you?"

Lydia almost gave up.

"Here," she said.

She reached into her coat pocket and tossed him a coin. His quick eyes, heavylidded and sunken in his skull, darted along the coin's arc through the murky gloom, and he snatched it from the air with a speed that turned Lydia's heart over. She remembered. Having that level of need.

"Eat something," she said.

He bit the coin. She grinned.

"Some *khleb*, I mean."

Abruptly he crouched down to the ground, and she saw a rip all the way down the back of his ragged jacket, as if someone had tried to grab him and he'd torn away. His attention was no longer on her but on the sodden heap of cardboard that had collapsed when he rolled out of it.

"Misty," he whispered.

A tremor shook the pile. Then a blur of movement as something leapt out, something disturbingly like a rat. Lydia shot back onto the sidewalk, crashing into a pedestrian who was passing. He swore at her clumsiness that made him drop his umbrella.

"I'm sorry," she said and swung around to look again at the boy.

In his arms curled a puppy, its fur a smoky gray. The creature seemed to be made of nothing but brown eyes, long feathery ears, and bony ribs so fragile they looked as if they would snap at a touch. It was licking the boy's chin with frantic joy, but before Lydia could even smile, the boy and dog were gone, a faint ripple in the crowd.

Twenty-three

❧

THE METAL SANG TO HIM. IN THE PRISON'S engineering workshop Jens Friis could hear its voice as he worked it. He listened to its hiss of laughter as he welded one bar to another, felt its tremor as he inserted rivets, making it stronger, more structured. He'd forgotten how he loved handling different metals, searching out their qualities and watching out for their weaknesses. Like people. Each one unique.

For ten years in the labor camp he'd handled nothing but wood. Felled unending forests of it. The smell of pine became so much a part of himself that he was no longer capable of differentiating between the smell of wood and the smell of his own skin. At times—desperate times—he had gnawed the rough bitter bark. It stained his teeth a strange russet color and lay hard and indigestible in his gut, but it had granted him the illusion of food when he most needed it. For that he was grateful.

Some mornings when he woke in the stale odor-heavy air of the crowded prison barrack hut, he'd inspected his fingertips intently, convinced they would start to sprout tiny green buds one day soon.

The buds would grow into whippy little twigs and eventually into massive branches that he would have to drag out through the forest with him each day to the Work Zone.

Starvation does strange things to the mind.

"FASTER. THE WORK *MUST* PROGRESS FASTER."

The words were spoken by Colonel Tursenov, but the two men standing either side of him nodded vehement agreement. The colonel was a reasonable man in his position as controller of the Development Center, but he was under heavy pressure. Lazar Kaganovich himself, a leading member of the Soviet Politburo, telephoned each Friday evening to question progress. That meant each Saturday the team of six senior engineers was summoned to stand in a rigid line in Tursenov's office at seven o'clock in the morning and ordered to speed up their work rate.

Jens Friis took one step forward. The sign that he wished to speak.

"What is it, Prisoner Friis?"

"Colonel, we are working all hours already and the construction is making steady progress—which is what we are all aiming for," he added solemnly. "But the reason the test last week was aborted was because the metal supplied for the rear support struts proved to be of poor quality. It was too brittle and so it snapped under the weight of—"

"Silence!"

Jens forced himself into silence. But he didn't step back into line. The other engineers, prisoners like himself, were wiser. They said nothing, just fixed their eyes on Tursenov's highly polished shoes and nodded each time he spoke. The colonel was a big man with a big voice that he kept reined in, most of the time, speaking softly and deliberately, but occasionally on the rare occasions when he relaxed he forgot and let it boom out like gunfire. Today it was soft. The colonel's mouth settled into a familiar line of disappointment and Jens feared he was suspecting sabotage, but nothing was said. When the silence in the room had lasted so long it became painful, Tursenov turned to the stocky woman with iron-gray hair behind him who was clutching a notebook and a red pencil.

"Comrade Demidova," he said, "check the supplier. Report them."

"*Da,* Comrade Colonel." She scribbled something on the paper.

"No more stoppages," he said curtly.

"No, Comrade Colonel."

"How long before I can see a demonstration?"

"It will take at least a month," Jens began, "before—"

"Two weeks." It was Elkin who had spoken at the end of the row. "It will be ready in two weeks."

"Are you certain?"

"Yes, Colonel."

"*Otlichno*! Excellent! I shall inform Comrade Kaganovich. He will be pleased."

Elkin smiled and concentrated on the polished shoes. Tursenov took his time scanning the men in their khaki overalls, noted that Jens was still forward of the line, and frowned. "Anything more, Prisoner Friis?"

"Yes, Colonel."

"What is it you wish to say?"

"If a demonstration is conducted before the problems are fully overcome, the canister could open prematurely and that would be highly dangerous to—"

"Two weeks," Tursenov interrupted in his softest voice. "Overcome them in two weeks, Prisoner Friis."

Their eyes met for no more than a second, but it was enough. Jens knew now. He couldn't delay the project any longer. Tursenov's suspicions were roused. Without another word he stepped back into line.

Twenty-four

❧

"WAIT HERE," LYDIA SAID.

"Don't worry, girl, you wouldn't get me in there if you paid me."

Elena folded her arms comfortably over the bulk of her bosom and positioned herself to one side of the large double doors like an incongruous sentry in a headscarf. She faced out onto the busy road, and her eyes became stubborn slits in her broad face. Lydia wasn't yet good at reading this woman's expressions, but she had the feeling Elena preferred to keep it that way. Today she noticed Elena looked tired, the lines sinking into ragged crevices around her eyes, but she was careful not to mention it—or the new navy coat Elena was wearing.

The brass plaque outside on the wall stated in discreet lettering: COMMUNIST PARTY LIAISON OFFICE.

"I'll be quick," Lydia promised.

"The words *quick* and *Communist Party* aren't even on speaking terms," Elena muttered, stamping her feet to keep warm.

Lydia darted up the steps.

"Papers?"

A uniformed middle-aged man with receding fair hair and kindly eyes stood just inside the door. He stepped in front of Lydia, shoes squeaking on the marble floor, and held out an expectant hand.

"*Dobroye utro*, comrade," she said, and tipped him a smile.

"Back again?"

"*Da.*"

"You must like it here."

"Not as much as you," she joked, and was pleased when he laughed.

It made her feel safer. She handed over her precious residence permit and identity document and immediately started chatting. "It's not so cold today," she said, and waved a hand at the window where the mist outside hung like a gray secretive curtain. He started to examine her papers. This was the moment when her heart skipped. Forgot to beat. It was always the same. "Do you think it's going to snow later?" she asked.

He glanced up and smiled at her. "Why? No umbrella today?"

She yanked off her hat and saw him watch her hair tumble to her shoulders. "I was in too much of a hurry to get here," she laughed.

"How many times is it you've come here now?"

"Not enough yet, it seems."

He handed back her documents without further scrutiny. "Well, I look forward to tomorrow then," he chuckled.

She touched her throat with a slow soft stroke, a gesture she'd seen her mother use when in the company of men. His eyes followed the movement.

"I'll be here," she said.

"So will I."

They both laughed. She didn't think he'd even bother to look at her papers next time.

THE MAN AT THE DESK WAS NOT SO EASILY ENTERTAINED.

"You again," he said. He didn't hide his irritation.

"Yes, comrade. Me again."

"Comrade Ivanova, I told you yesterday and all the other days that I have no way of contacting this person."

"But this is the International Liaison Office. That's what you do. Liaise. So you must liaise with Communist Parties across the world."

"That is true."

"So why not with . . . ?"

"I've told you already that it's not possible. Stop wasting my time, comrade."

He was one of those men who fiddle a lot, always twitching and straightening and tapping with his fingertips. It was the turn of his mustache today. He combed its luxurious growth with the long fingernail of his little finger, and she wondered if he grew both the facial hair and the nail especially to satisfy this inner need. What was it he had to feel so nervous about? Maybe his own papers were no more convincing than hers. She tried a smile. Sent it winging across the icy gap between them, but it fluttered and died. She'd tried it before and found this apparatchik totally smileproof.

"Is something amusing you?" he demanded sharply.

"No, comrade."

"Then I suggest you go home." He plucked up a pen and started tapping the end of it on his desk.

Lydia's cheek flushed. She should leave. She was getting nowhere. She looked around at the vast domed entrance hall with its acres of marble flooring, designed to intimidate. Fat marble pillars were draped with blood red flags and slogans that read, TOGETHER WE SHALL FIGHT. TOGETHER WE SHALL WIN THE VICTORY.

Fight. Win. Victory. Communism seemed immersed in a constant exhausting battle. Even within itself. Footsteps clicked back and forth across the polished floor as clerks and neatly dressed secretaries scurried like worker ants to and from their offices, arms heaped with brown faceless files, and Lydia felt horribly out of place.

She gripped the front edge of the desk to keep her feet exactly where they were. She didn't trust them not to turn and run.

"*Pozhalusta*, please," she urged politely.

He sighed, twitched at his tie, and raised bored eyes to hers.

"His name is Chang An Lo," she said. "He is a member of the Chinese Communist Party, an important member of—"

"So you said."

"I want you to contact the Chinese Communist's Party's headquarters in Shanghai and leave a message with them for him."

"That's not my job."

"Then whose job is it?"

"Not mine."

"Please, it's important. I must contact him and . . ."

A blast of cold air swirled in from the street, nipping at bare skin with icy pincers. The man behind the desk shed his air of indifference and jumped to his feet faster than a buck rabbit, startling Lydia. She turned and stared.

A man in his midthirties was just tossing his leather overcoat to the attendant at the door, and they were both laughing at something he'd said. Then he strode across the marble floor, his heels echoing with life in the empty dead air, his beautifully tailored suit rippling elegantly as he moved. The thing about him that struck Lydia immediately was his hair. It was thick, springy, and neatly trimmed, but it was an even more fiery shade than her own. As he approached the desk she looked away. One glance at the intense gray eyes with their coppery lashes told her this was a man who would not be easily fooled by her tales. Or by her papers.

Without obvious hurry, she started to back away.

"Comrade Chairman Malofeyev," the desk man said with a respectful nod of his head and a tug at the sleeves of his own ill-fitting jacket. He was standing to stiff attention, chin in the air, clearly an ex-military man, and his face had lost every trace of its earlier bored disdain. In its place emerged an obsequiousness that took Lydia by surprise and made her rethink leaving. For this one brief moment, the desk man was vulnerable.

"*Dobroye utro*, Boris." The man in the immaculate suit spoke in an easy affable tone. "Good morning." But his gaze wandered over Lydia as he asked, "Is the commissioner free yet?"

"No, sir. He asked me to apologize. He has been summoned to the Kremlin."

The newcomer raised one eyebrow. "Has he indeed?"

"*Da*. He asked me to reschedule a meeting tomorrow for you, Comrade Chairman."

A flicker of something that might have been annoyance passed across Chairman Malofeyev's face. It was a distinctive face, too long to be handsome, but it possessed an energy that made it noticeable, and there was unmistakable humor in the tilt of the mouth. Lydia felt uneasy under the scrutiny of the gray eyes, so that when he waved a hand indifferently and said, "What's the point? He may not even still be here tomorrow," for a moment she had no idea who he was talking about. Then it dawned. The commissioner, the faceless apparatchik summoned so abruptly to the Kremlin.

"I wish to put in a request also," she said rapidly, "for a meeting with the commissioner tomorrow."

Both men stared at her in surprise. She felt as though she'd grown two heads.

Boris, the desk man, narrowed his eyes and tapped his pen ferociously. "What is your business with the commissioner?" he demanded.

"I told you, I want to—"

"The commissioner does not deal with requests such as yours." He glanced at Malofeyev, a furtive sideways dance of his eyes that showed Lydia he was nervous.

"But if you're not willing to make the inquiries I've asked for," she said, "I have to apply elsewhere."

Instantly a form appeared on the desk. "Name?" he demanded.

This was for show. She was convinced that as soon as the smart suit was gone from the hall, the form would be in the wastebasket before she could say *spasibo*.

"What is it you want?" Comrade Malofeyev inquired with interest. "What makes a pretty young girl like you so earnest?"

She looked around at him, and it wasn't hard to find a smile for this man with his easy charm who was obviously in some position of authority and who was the first one to show even a glimmer of interest in her problem.

"It's not important," the desk man said quickly.

"It's important to me," she said.

"What is?"

"Comrade Malofeyev," the desk man intervened, "this girl has been pestering this office for weeks, wasting my time, over some petty concern she has about—"

"It's not a petty concern," Lydia said quietly, her eyes on Malofeyev's face. "It's important."

"Ignore her, Comrade Chairman, she's not worth—"

Malofeyev silenced the desk man with an abrupt gesture of his hand.

"Comrade Malofeyev," Lydia said, twirling her hat between her cold fingers, "I am a good Soviet citizen and I have an important message to pass on to a member of the Chinese Communist Party. I am trying to reach him through this International Liaison Office, but—"

"Him?"

"Yes."

"Now why am I not surprised by that?"

She felt her cheeks burn as he gave her a slow speculative smile. Abruptly he turned back to the desk man.

"Telephone," he said, and held out a hand.

The man reached behind to where a heavy black telephone hung on the wall. He detached the mouthpiece, reluctance making his movements slow, and Malofeyev walked around to it, requested a number from the operator, spoke briskly for a moment, then hung up.

"It seems my contact is out to lunch." He flipped open the gold watch case that nestled in the pocket of his trim waistcoat and raised one eyebrow. "A little early perhaps, not yet noon, but"—he looked at Lydia—"I have left a message for him to call my office this afternoon. So don't worry, *good Soviet citizen*, we shall find your Chinese Communist Party member for you if he's findable."

For the first time in all her achingly slow dealings with the impenetrable wall of Russian bureaucracy, here was a man who saw the possible, not the impossible. He made things happen. She wanted to throw her arms around his neck and squeeze the breath out of him with gratitude.

"Thank you."

But something of what she was feeling must have shown on her face because he took her elbow in the palm of his hand and steered her effortlessly back across the marble expanse toward the main door.

"Luncheon now, I think. Then back to my office this afternoon to continue the hunt."

"I'm not hungry."

He laughed, a rich warm sound like one of China's bronze bells. It struck her ears with the same clear ring because it held no fear. In Soviet Russia that was a rare and precious thing.

"My good Soviet citizen," he said with a mocking smile, "a

lovely scarecrow like you must be always hungry. Of course you need lunch."

Lydia allowed herself to be guided through the doors and on to the street, trying to work out whether she'd just been insulted. It didn't matter. The one thing she was sure of was that she wasn't going to let this man out of her sight. It meant missing her noon vigil at the cathedral, but in her heart she knew Alexei wouldn't be there, any more than he was yesterday or the day before or all the days before that. At the curb a chauffeur-driven car was waiting, long, black, and purring, and as she climbed into its leather interior she glanced over her shoulder to where Elena was still standing stiffly on the sidewalk. Her eyes were angry.

Twenty-five

A SAD-EYED PEASANT STARED DOWN AT LYDIA from the wall of the restaurant with dark accusing eyes. The strange, almost strangled face made her nervous. A waiter with a courteous smile and garlic breath pulled out her chair for her and shook out her napkin onto her lap, making her jump. Chairman Malofeyev noticed it and gave her a moment to settle herself while he busied himself with the wine menu.

Lydia had expected a hotel dining room, one of the big impressive but impersonal places like the Hotel Metropol where she'd watched the elite Soviet officials strutting through its doors with chests puffed out like the pigeons that used to whirr overhead in Junchow. But no. She got that wrong.

Instead he took her somewhere that showed exquisite taste, somewhere small and intimate. Immaculate stark white table linen, not stiff or starchy, underlined the sense of elegance without formality. Lydia had never seen anywhere quite like it before and wasn't sure what to make of it. It was modern. Strange and disturbing paintings lined the walls, vivid and demanding, swirls and spikes of color that made no

sense, or bold stylized portrayals of peasants and factory workers.
The chairs were of odd proportions, long backed, the wood painted
an unforgiving black, the seats bright scarlet, and the carpet almost
too dizzying to step on. Geometric shapes in red, black, and white
zigzagged across its surface, so that it seemed to Lydia as though she
were seated in the middle of a bonfire.

She felt ignorant. Acutely aware that this was a different world
she had entered, one where her footing was unsure. The opportunities for making a fool of herself were immense.

"DO YOU LIKE THEM?" HER HOST ASKED, INDICATING THE ART-
works on the wall.

"They're different," she responded guardedly.

He looked at her with amusement, leaning forward, elbows on
the table. "But do you like them?"

She stared around her thoughtfully. "I like that one." She pointed
to one of the baffling explosions of color that she was sure represented something but she couldn't quite work out what. It possessed
an energy that appealed to her.

He nodded approvingly. "It's a copy of a Kandinsky. One of my
favorites."

"But I don't like that one over in the corner."

"The Malevich. Why not?"

"It's depressing. A plain black canvas, all life sucked out of it.
What's it about? It"—the longer she gazed at the painting the more it
made her want to cry—"it hurts. I could do better myself."

"Do you paint?"

"No."

"Do you write?"

"No."

She could feel the ground growing slippery under her feet.

He leaned back in his chair and studied her. "You have an artistic
look about you. I like that."

Chyort! He was making assumptions. She knew absolutely nothing about art. She'd read a bit but that didn't make her a writer. But
her mother *had* been a pianist, so maybe . . .

"I play the piano," she lied modestly.

He was smiling, pleased with himself rather than with her. "I knew I was right. You are a bohemian at heart."

She watched his eyes skim over her thoughtfully. *What?* she wanted to shout. *What are you seeing?*

"So," he said smoothly, "let's start with names. I am Dmitri Malofeyev. I live in Moscow and sit on committees and commissions, hence the Chairman title. I like horse riding and occasional gambling. What about you?"

"Lydia Ivanova."

He inclined his head in a chivalrous little bow that revealed the bone-white line of the parting through the dense waves of his red hair. The skin of his face and hands was winter pale and lightly freckled. "My pleasure, Comrade Ivanova."

"I am from Vladivostok."

"Ah, an interesting place."

She sat dry mouthed. Vladivostok was thousands of miles from Moscow, as far as you could possibly go without falling into the China Sea. *Please, please, let him know absolutely nothing about it.*

"That explains," he said lightly, "your interest in the Chinese Communist Party, just over the border from Russia. Except I'd heard they are active in the south of the country rather than the north."

"They're . . . expanding all the time."

"Ah, good. I'm glad to hear it. So tell me, young comrade, what you are doing here in Moscow?"

"I . . ."

A waiter, tall and thin in black shirt and narrow trousers that made his legs look like sticks, hovered at Malofeyev's shoulder with the bottle of wine he'd ordered, and the moment's delay gave Lydia time to snatch at an answer. As the dark red liquid spilled into her glass and around her the muted meeting of cutlery and bone china hummed softly, politely, throughout the restaurant, she took a wary pace forward. Balanced precariously on the first stepping-stone across a fast-flowing river.

"I've heard things," she said. "About Moscow. I wanted to see them for myself."

She saw interest flare in the gray eyes. She lowered her gaze to the napkin on her lap as though reluctant to say more. Unseen, she wiped her moist palms on the white material.

"What kind of *things*?" His tone was serious, the laughter gone.

"How Stalin is transforming the hearts and minds of Muscovites. Building wonderful new communal housing where everything is shared, even the clothing and the children." She raised her eyes and let regret sneak into her words. "In Vladivostok the people are not so ready for change. Despite the new factories and jobs that Communism is providing, they cling to their old bourgeois ways."

"Is that so?"

"Yes." She noticed that her hands were fidgeting with her cutlery. She stilled them. "I want to be a part of the activist movement. I want to be in the forefront with the Constructivists and the Kinoks who are bringing a whole new kind of cinema and music and design to the people."

Thank you, dear Alexei, for pushing so many books into my hands for me to learn about the new modern Russia. We must be prepared, you said.

"You see, I was right when I said you were artistic." He raised one sandy eyebrow. "But you are remarkably well informed for someone from the backwoods of Vladivostok."

"I read a lot."

"Obviously. So tell me, what is it you want to see?"

"I want to see Eisenstein's films—like *October*. It's wonderful that he uses nonprofessional actors, real people. It's all genuinely about the young proletariat, about their rising up against the capitalist order."

She could hear her voice growing excited.

He nodded. "I admit the cinema is a vital weapon in educating people. To train their minds to grasp socialist concepts." He paused, pulled at his long earlobe. "What else?"

For a moment her mind cast about blankly, and all she could focus on was that this man was her one path to Chang An Lo. *Don't slip.*

"What else?" he asked again.

She thought carefully. "I want to see Tatlin's designs and go to the Kolonny Zal Doma Soyuzov to listen to Shostakovich's music. Did you know he even included the sound of factory whistles in his Second Symphony?"

Her mother had hated that. *Vulgar*, she'd called it.

"No, I didn't know that."

"And," she lowered her voice until it was almost secretive, "there's

talk of an underground railway system to be built beneath Moscow
itself."

He didn't speak. Just stared at her solemnly across the table. *Had
she overdone it?* Was she about to plunge into the churning river's
depths?

"Work," he said at last. "You don't mention work at all."

"Ah, of course I want to work."

"What kind of work?"

What kind? Which should she choose? A teacher? A librarian?
Even a mythical pianist?

She picked up her glass of wine and swirled it around the glass,
aware of the irony of it. "A factory worker, of course. I am applying
for a job in the AMO automobile plant."

"I know the manager there, Likhachev. A good Party member,
though sometimes his words run faster than his brain. He's on the
MGK with me, the Moscow City Committee. I could put in a word
for you."

Despite the wine, her tongue felt dry.

"*Spasibo*," she said. "But I would rather find a job through my
own efforts."

He smiled and raised his glass. "To success."

"*Da*." She breathed again. "To success."

THE MEAL WAS GOOD. SHE EXPECTED NO LESS. BUT SHE BARELY
tasted it, scarcely recalled what she was putting in her mouth. She
encouraged him to talk about himself. At first he was guarded, letting slip no more than that he lived in the Arbat near the Praga restaurant and had only recently returned to Moscow after two years
away from the capital posted out to Siberia, overseeing something
completely different.

"What made you want to leave Moscow in the first place?" she
asked.

Malofeyev ran a hand through his hair, momentarily uncomfortable, and suddenly looked younger than his thirty-something years.
"I was overseeing an import scheme of factory machinery that went
badly wrong." He narrowed his gaze, focusing on the Malevich
painting on the wall, and some of its blackness seemed to seep into

his gray eyes, turning them to soot. "Someone had to pay for the mistake. That person happened to be me, even though . . ." He stopped himself, refusing to complain.

Lydia shifted the subject. "But you're back now. Anyway you probably benefited from what you learned about life outside Moscow."

He pushed aside his coffee cup. "How positive you are. For one so young. But you're right." He drew a silver cigarette case from his jacket, and Lydia eyed it with the professional interest of an ex-pickpocket. Mutely he offered her a cigarette, but she shook her head. He lit one for himself, exhaling an elaborate coil of smoke toward the Malevich painting as if trying to prove something to it. "It's remarkable," he said, "what's going on out there in Siberia. Have you seen it?"

She sidestepped that one. "Tell me."

"Its vast wasteland is being tamed. There are grand new road schemes and railways, factories and mines of all kinds, massive organized timber haulage. Even complete new towns are being built from scratch. It's"—he paused for the right word—"thrilling."

She blinked. That wasn't the word she'd expected from him.

"Thrilling?"

"*Da.*" He abandoned his cigarette in the black onyx ashtray as if it encumbered his thought process. "Everything we dreamed of when we fought the tsar's troops thirteen years ago outside the Winter Palace is coming true. The Communist ideals of equality and justice are being turned into reality right in front of our eyes, and it breaks my heart that Vladimir Ilyich Lenin himself is not alive to see it."

She couldn't look at him. At the belief in his eyes. Instead she concentrated on the slender stem of her glass, as fragile and breakable as Papa's back in that labor camp. A nerve pulsed in her jaw and she placed a hand over it.

"Comrade Malofeyev . . ."

"Call me Dmitri."

"Dmitri." She smiled and flicked a stray lock of hair from her cheek. For a second she was distracted by a smartly dressed man and woman at a table across the room. Both staring at her. She looked away. Was it her clothes? Was she so obviously all wrong in a place like this?

"Dmitri, if I were searching for someone else, as well as for the

Chinese Communist I mentioned earlier, someone in Moscow, would you be willing to help me find this person?"

He studied her carefully, his gaze alighting on each part of her face, even on her throat as she swallowed, and she knew she'd just leapt onto the stepping-stone right in the deepest part of the river.

Twenty-six

✺

FOG ROSE FROM THE MOSKVA RIVER. IT SLUNK IN long tendrils across the road, sneaking up to front doors and unexpectedly swallowing people whole when they emerged from their homes into the street. Sledges slid into it and vanished.

Alexei stood still. He had no desire to move. He felt like a ghost, barely there, a lone figure caught between reality and nonreality. Each time he heard footsteps on the broad steps leading up to where he was propped against the stone pillar of the cathedral's entrance, his breath quickened with expectation. This time it was real, not a figment of his exhausted mind.

A woman drifted out of the white layers of moist air rising toward him. He held out a hand to her, but she veered away abruptly and he realized she thought he was a beggar. The streets were full of them. She had heavy black eyebrows and thick ankles, he registered that much. Not Lydia after all, then. Nor Antonina, whose ankles were slender, the bones beautifully carved. He yearned for her touch now to rid him of this deadness. His eyes closed as the cold crept with sharp fingers through his thin jacket and into his blood, making it sluggish and stubborn, painful as it pushed through his veins.

It was past noon. Long past. He forced his eyelids open in case he missed her. In this fog she might pass three feet from him and not know he was there. He tilted his head back but the golden domes of the Cathedral of Christ the Redeemer had ceased to exist, stolen from sight by the dank moist air, and something fluttered on the edge of his thoughts. Something about this church. He'd read something. That was it. It was going to be blown up. Involuntarily he stepped away from the pillar as if it were about to explode, but immediately felt the loss of its stone solidity at his back. Is that what worshippers would feel, the loss of solidity, of belief?

He walked slowly around the outside of the great towering building till he came to the Moskva River at its back, where the water flowed in ripples of steel; it looked so hard, so substantial. He started to cross the bridge that spanned the river but had to stop halfway because the muscles in his legs were shaking with exhaustion. He leaned on the parapet and was aware that he had disappeared. This close to the river he was wrapped in a cocoon of fog, invisible and unknown.

It didn't matter. Lydia wasn't coming. Had she lied to him? No. He shook his head. She didn't lie to him in the letter, he was certain. Either she had left Moscow—with or without their father—or she was unable to make it to the church. Whatever the truth, he couldn't help either of them now, not Jens Friis, not Lydia. But he missed her, missed her laugh and her stubborn chin, and the way she knew exactly how to get under his skin. And her moments of unexpected gentleness, he missed them more than ever now.

The journey to Moscow had cost him dearly and stripped him of everything, both physical and mental. It had taken all his strength to get here, walking for weeks without end, no food, losing track of time. He leaned his head over the bridge and stared down at the cushion of thick white air that hung just below him. It looked tempting. On that soft pillow of air he could rest at last and dream again of galloping through the autumn woods beside his father.

Twenty-seven

THE GROUP OF PRISONERS STOOD ALONE IN THE central courtyard behind heavy studded doors. Nine men, three women. In the back of a truck, sheltering out of the bitter wind, two soldiers watched over them, unseen in its dark metallic interior with rifles across their knees, cigarette smoke warm in their lungs. Outside, snow fluttered down in spinning spirals, settling on hats and shoulders, burrowing into eyebrows, yet despite the cold and despite the tall gloomy buildings that loomed over them blocking out what little winter light filtered down, each of the prisoners was smiling.

It was always the same. A day free from the rattle of locks. No jangle of keys, no interminable gray corridors that led only to more locks and more keys. Anticipation prickled their skin. It reminded Jens of when he was a young man in St. Petersburg, standing in the stable courtyard waiting for the carriage to arrive to whisk them away to the summer palace for the day. Well, today wasn't an outing to any palace. Far from it. Just to a gigantic hangar in a well-guarded field surrounded by dense forest. Not that he'd ever seen the forest here, but he'd heard the wind in the branches, the sigh of wooden limbs as they flexed and shivered. It was a sound he'd listened to a million times in the forests of Siberia, a sound as familiar as his own breath.

"Jens."

"Olga," he smiled. "No need to be nervous."

"I'm not nervous." She said it breezily. "It's the noise of the wheels I hate, that's all, as they drive over rough ground. Like bones being crushed."

Olga was a skilled chemist, no more than forty but she looked older, the lines around her mouth etched deep after eight years hard labor in a lead mine. Her body was fleshless, stick thin, and she complained of stomach pains whenever she ate her meals. Here in this prison they were decently fed, a world away from the labor camps. They routinely devoured more protein in one week than they'd previously had sight of in a whole year. Stalin was feeding them the way a farmer fattens a pig before slitting its throat. To get the best out of them. Stalin wanted the best out of their brains.

The prison doctor declared that Olga's pains were all in her mind, and he might be right. Guilt, Jens believed, guilt was eating her up each time she pushed a forkful of food past her lips because her daughter was still out there in the lead mine, where bones were regularly crushed under rockfalls.

"I hate going in the truck," Olga muttered.

"Just imagine that you are in a horse carriage," Jens urged, "trotting down the Arbat to take tea at the Arbatskiy Podval café. That would put a smile on your face. Cakes and pastries and sweet strawberry tarts and . . ."

"Mmm," murmured a younger woman nearby, "plum tart with cream and chocolate sauce."

"Annoushka, you never think of anything but food," Olga scolded.

"Food is comforting," Annoushka confessed. "And God knows we all need comfort in this place."

"If you keep eating the way you do, you'll soon be too fat to fit in the truck," Olga teased.

It was true. Annoushka did eat a lot, but so did most of them. They'd been starved for too many years to let even a crumb remain uneaten on a plate. Like squirrels, they hoarded nuts for the winter that was sure to come again one day soon when Stalin and Kaganovich and Colonel Tursenov had finished picking their brains clean. Behind them the truck's engine started up, the noise of it rebounding off the high courtyard walls, and a plume of black exhaust billowed into the chill air. The two soldiers in the back jumped out and held open the rear doors.

"Let's go," Elkin called out from among the huddle of engineers and strode toward the truck. He was eager to be gone.

The others followed at varying speeds.

"Friis, everything had better damn well work today," an elderly unshaven prisoner grumbled as a young mechanic hoisted him up into the back of the vehicle.

"It will, old man. Have faith."

"Faith!" Annoushka said, stamping her feet on the cobbles while she waited her turn. "I've forgotten what that word even means." She beckoned to Jens and Olga. "Come on, you don't want to get left behind. Today's a big day."

Olga shivered as she tightened her scarf around her neck and was helped by Jens to pick her way across the slippery courtyard.

"Close your eyes on the journey and think only of the day your daughter was born," Jens murmured and felt her hand tighten gratefully on his arm.

It wasn't often they were all together like this, though it was happening more frequently now as the project neared completion. Most of the time they worked in isolation in their separate workshops, with messengers passing between them with blueprints and reports. So when they did come together there was always a sense of celebration, but today of all days Jens saw nothing to celebrate.

THERE WERE NO WINDOWS IN THE BACK OF THE TRUCK. THE moment the rear doors clanged shut, the prisoners were plunged into darkness as thick as tar. Jens placed his hands on his knees and closed his eyes. He knew exactly what to expect and braced himself, concentrating on breathing steadily and making no noise. The blackness started to crush him as soon as the truck began to rumble its way into the street. Slowly and relentlessly the blackness descended, squeezing him, pressing down on his skin, slithering under his eyelids however tightly he held them shut. His tongue was wrapped in its sticky coils and his lungs felt as though they would collapse under its weight. He sat still. Shallow breaths. His heart rate battering his ears.

It hadn't always been like this. He used to enjoy the dark, relish the privacy it granted in the overcrowded barrack hut in the Zone in the forest, but too many weeks in the camp's cramped and unlit solitary confinement cell had robbed him of that. Now the darkness was his enemy and he fought his war in silence.

The truck stopped, but it was only an intersection. The streets of Moscow were full of strange unexplained sounds, unfamiliar to him, noises that fifteen years ago when he had last roamed its side-walks had not existed. Engines and klaxons, exhaust pipes and fac-tory sirens. But now out of the surrounding darkness as the truck waited in the street, one noise leapt into his head and brought a faint smile to his lips. It was music. Unmistakably an organ-grinder. The tinkling notes dragged into his head a memory that elbowed its way through the bleak tunnels. Of a time when with his four-year-old daughter he had watched a black-skinned organ-grinder.

He had learned long ago to block out all thoughts of the past, to live moment by moment, but the knowledge that his own daughter was out there searching for him broke down all the rules he'd made for himself. He could feel it now, Lydia's tiny hand tucked warm and safe in his, hear her laughter as she fed peanuts to the organ-grinder's tiny monkey. Its wrinkled little face had enchanted her and she had enchanted him.

The truck jolted over potholes, shaking its passengers as they sat on the metal benches that lined both sides of the black interior. The music faded and a murmur of loss pushed its way out between Jens's lips, hollow and barely audible. A sigh? A groan? A bastard attempt at both. At neither. The precious memory was fading.

Fingers touched his. They brushed along the bones of his hands with light little taps on his wrists as if to waken them, and then the fingers curled around his own, holding them tight. Stayed like that. It was Olga. She was seated opposite him at the back of the truck. He lifted one of her hands to his lips, inhaled the familiar chemical scent of her skin, and kissed it gently.

Twenty-eight

❦

WHEN LYDIA EMERGED FROM THE RESTAURANT, she didn't even notice that it was raining. The fat drainpipes that ran down the fronts of Moscow's buildings but stopped a meter above the level of the sidewalk, as if someone had run out of metal before finishing the job, were spewing water in ferocious fountains over the feet of passing pedestrians. At night the water would freeze. That's when the sidewalks turned to sheet ice. Lydia had learned to tread carefully. An umbrella suddenly materialized above her head, black and shiny, held firmly in a steady hand. Only then did she register the rain.

"*Spasibo,* Dmitri." She smiled up at him. "And thank you for my lunch."

"It was a pleasure. I enjoyed the company."

They stood close, in the enforced intimacy of the umbrella's canopy, so close they could smell each other's wet coats. For a moment their eyes locked and Lydia didn't know what to say next. He seemed totally at ease, unconcerned by either the rain or the silence between them, still that intense look in his eyes as if he could see things she couldn't.

"Well, my office next, I suggest."

She was cautious. "Will your contact call back?"

"He'd better." He laughed and twirled the umbrella.

"He knows someone in the Chinese Communist Party?"

"That's his job."

"Very well, then. I'll come to your office if I may."

"I'd be honored, comrade."

He was laughing at her. Yet she didn't mind, even though he was wearing an astrakhan hat that obscured his red hair, making it harder for her to trust him. The hair color was a kind of bond between them in some strange way.

"And the other man I asked you about?" she reminded him.

"Ah, that's a different matter altogether. Much harder. You must understand, such information is not . . . available. Even to people like myself," he added.

"Of course. Will you inquire though? Please?"

"Yes." He didn't elaborate.

"Thank you."

At that moment his black car drew up at the curb.

THE CAR DOOR WAS OPENED AND SHE SCUTTLED INTO THE BACK, out of the rain. Malofeyev leaned in, and she noticed his face was faintly flushed. "One moment," he said, "I want to buy a paper."

She watched him approach the newspaper kiosk that was set up beside a shoeshine boy touting for business. Malofeyev said a few quick words and returned to the car with a copy of *Rabochaya Moskva*, Moscow's own newspaper, tucked under his arm. He jumped onto the seat next to her, shaking himself like a wet dog, and tossed the umbrella on the floor.

"It's cold in here," he said, lifting a fur rug from beside him and draping it over her knees and his own as the car pulled into the stream of traffic. "Better?"

"*Spasibo*." She tucked her hands into its warm folds.

Malofeyev leaned forward toward the driver, who sat silently in cap and uniform. "My office, comrade."

Then he stretched back comfortably against the leather seat and gave Lydia another quick inspection, as if he thought she might have changed in some way.

"Do you like Moscow?"

His question caught her unawares. She felt her heart beat faster. She continued to stare out at the tall pastel-painted buildings of Tverskaya Street as the tempting display of food in the windows of Eliseevsky Gastronom slid past, while in the small side streets, where children played on sledges, the shops were bleak and empty. Elegant apartments rubbed shoulders with run-down *communalka*. It was a city of separate villages where the elite were pampered and the poor went hungry, where ration cards were designed for the proletariat while men like Malofeyev dined in splendor in smart restaurants and grand hotels.

"Yes," she said. "I like Moscow very much."

"I'm glad. One day Moscow will be more advanced than any other city. The *doma kommuny*, the huge communal blocks of rooms, will teach people how to live their lives collectively and Moscow will become the symbol for future socialist societies."

"Is that so?"

"Yes, it is, I promise you. So tell me why you like this city."

"I love its energy. It's unpredictable. I like its new monumental buildings and"—she smiled as the car swept past a Chinese laundry that had a picture of a shirt on its signboard and two Chinese women with broad faces and smooth skin chattering to each other on the front step—"I like its trams."

He laughed and shook open the newspaper. She liked the way he gave it his full concentration. It meant she could be alone with her own thoughts while he read the *Rabochaya,* so she almost missed it, his sudden intake of breath. Cut off abruptly. Without appearing to hurry, she turned her head to look at him and saw that his attention was focused on an inside page.

"What is it?"

He appeared not to have heard.

"Something important?" she asked.

He raised his gray eyes, and the way he looked at her made her blood pulse beneath her skin. "Important to you, yes."

She withdrew a hand from under the fur rug and rested her fingers on her chin to hold it still. "Tell me," she said quietly.

"It seems your timing is impeccable."

She waited.

"It says here," he rustled the paper, "that a delegation from China has arrived in Moscow."

She could hear her own heart stop. He held out the paper for her to inspect the front page.

"See," he said, "there's a photograph. There's to be a reception for them this evening. In the Hotel Metropol. Take a look to see if you recognize any . . ."

She reached for it and blinked hard. Six blurred figures in a grainy photograph. Her eyes scanned each face hungrily, but the one she was searching for wasn't there. Her heart started up again, sluggish and painful. At first she thought that all the figures in the photograph were men, each one dressed in a heavy cap and bulky padded coat, but as she studied them in detail she realized that two of them were female.

"Do you recognize any of them?" Dmitri asked.

She started to shake her head, but stopped. "Possibly. The one on the end."

"The girl?"

"*Da*." High cheekbones, determined dark eyes, cropped hair. She was sure it was the Chinese girl she'd seen with Chang An Lo last year in Junchow. "I think I saw her at a funeral once."

"Does she also know this Chinese Communist you are trying to contact?"

"Yes."

Something in her voice must have alerted him because his mouth grew solemn, his eyes gentle. "Too well, perhaps?"

Lydia could find no response. *Too well, perhaps*. The words spiked inside her skull.

"Let me see." He took the paper from her hand and studied the names printed under the photograph. "Tang Kuan. Is that her?"

"Yes."

"She would know where he is?"

"She might."

There was another pause. A horse-drawn wagon piled high with barrels lumbered dangerously across their path and the car had to break harshly.

"Don't look so distraught," Dmitri said.

"I'd like to ask her myself tonight."

"Where?"

"At the Metropol."

"NO, LYDIA."

"Don't let's go through this again, Liev. Dmitri Malofeyev has invited me."

"No."

"It's my only way of finding out where Chang is."

"No."

"I don't want to argue with you, Liev."

"No."

"Just saying no over and over isn't going to convince me."

"No. Or I'll break your skinny neck."

"Now that's a much more persuasive argument."

LYDIA STOMPED OFF TO THE COMMUNAL KITCHEN. SHE HEATED up a pot of potato and onion soup that she'd made the day before and returned tight-lipped to their room. Elena was looking out the window and Liev was slumped in the chair knocking back vodka straight from the bottle. She put the bowl of soup on his lap.

"I'm coming with you," Popkov announced.

"No, of course you can't."

"I'm coming."

"No, don't . . ."

Lydia was going to say *No, don't be absurd. Look at you.* But she stopped herself in time. It was the expression trapped in his black eye that silenced her. It was dull with fear and she knew it wasn't for himself.

"No, Liev," she said gently, "you can't. Malofeyev is only obtaining an invitation for himself and me. Anyway, you would be . . . too conspicuous. You'd draw attention to us."

Popkov grunted and turned his back on her in the chair. End of conversation. She wasn't sure who had won.

"What will you wear?" Elena asked to break the silence. Lydia was grateful to her.

"My green skirt and white blouse, I suppose." She shrugged. "It's the best I have, so it'll have to do."

"But the women will be all dressed up in evening gowns and . . ."

"It doesn't matter, Elena. I'm only going there for one reason. To speak to Kuan."

"You'll look out of place."

Lydia stared wretchedly at Liev's uncommunicative back. "Wherever I go, I seem to be out of place," she muttered.

The broad back hunched and his shoulder blades shifted under his coat like tectonic plates.

"I have a silk scarf you can borrow," Elena offered.

"*Spasibo.*"

"And this."

Lydia glanced across at her. She was standing by the dividing curtain now, one hand holding onto it, her bosom heaving slightly as though breathing had suddenly become an effort for some reason. Her other hand was stretched out toward Lydia and on its upturned palm lay a bundle of white ten-rouble notes.

"Enough for a smart new skirt," she said, her tone offhand. "Or at least a blouse from somewhere decent. You can use my *zabornaya knizhka*, my ration card."

Lydia's gaze fixed on the money. She wanted to snatch it, stuff it into her money belt. *Chyort*, it was tempting. Forget skirts or blouses, just concentrate on adding it to the escape fund. She swallowed awkwardly, and out of the corner of her eye she could see Liev move around and stare too. Not at the roubles. At Elena's face. Her cheeks had colored to a vivid pink, but her mouth was pulled in a pale straight defiant line.

"*Spasibo,*" Lydia said again. "Elena, you are too kind to me. I am grateful."

Elena jerked her head, as if rearranging the thoughts inside it.

"But," Lydia continued, "I can't accept it. I'll go to the party in my own skirt and blouse. They'll have to do."

Elena stepped forward and slammed the money down on the table with a force that vibrated the floor.

"It's not dirty," she snapped, and snatched her coat from a hook on the wall. "And neither am I." She pulled open the door and yanked it closed behind her. Her footsteps sounded loud outside as she hurried down the corridor, but inside the room the air felt thick and unbreathable.

"Go after her, Liev," Lydia whispered, her voice tight. "Tell her that's not what I meant."

THEY COMPROMISED.

Lydia agreed to allow Liev to accompany her as far as the hotel steps. She had declined Malofeyev's offer of a car to pick her up because she wanted to keep secret from him where she lived. It was dark outside when they set off, sleeting fitfully, and the Hotel Metropol was some distance away near the Kremlin.

Their own living quarters were situated in Sokolniki. It was one of the smoky industrial districts, squeezed between a tire factory that belched out disgusting smells and a small brick building in which a family manufactured dog leads. The house was divided up into numerous apartments, with a courtyard at its center and a booth at its front that did shoe repairs as well as sharpening knives and scissors. It was run by an Armenian with three gold teeth. Popkov declared he was working for OGPU, the secret police, but Lydia didn't believe a word of it and waved cheerfully to him each morning when she walked past. Popkov claimed everyone was informing for OGPU. But if that were true, it seemed to Lydia that there'd be no one left to inform on.

They traveled across the city by tram. Lydia adored the trams. Muscovites took them for granted, but to Lydia they were exotic and quaint. She would have happily ridden up and down in one all day watching the people, finding out in their faces what it meant to be Russian.

She and Liev hopped on through the rear door and paid the conductress fourteen kopecks each for the fare. Three spools of differently priced tickets hung from the woman's neck, bouncing on her ample bosom, and as she shouted out, "Move on down. Move on down," Lydia saw her give Popkov an unabashed wink. *What is it about this greasy old bear that gets women so heated up?* Everyone shuffled toward the front of the tram. It was cold on board and Lydia stayed close to Liev, tucked in against his bulk, shivering. She was nervous.

It seemed to take forever, the rattling and the bumping, but finally she jumped down from the tram and that was when she felt a nudge on her hip. The sidewalk was still crowded with workers hurrying home from their offices and factories, the yellow lamplight twisting their faces into tired unfamiliar masks in the darkness. Most people would not have noticed the nudge, just one of many brushes with other pedestrians, but Lydia knew exactly what it was. Her hand shot out and clamped over a bony wrist. She swung around and found Elena's silk scarf dangling from a pair of grubby fingers.

"You dirty thief!" she hissed.

She snatched the scarf and thrust it back into her pocket but did not release her grasp on the culprit's wrist. It was a grubby boy.

The thief swore at her. "Fuck you."

She blinked. Milk-white hair and bright blue eyes. A thin bony face with a mouth older than his years. It was the boy from inside the cardboard box. She saw recognition dawn in him as he glared at her.

"Let me go," he muttered.

She was just thinking about unclamping her fingers when the boy's head darted down. Pain shot through the back of her hand and she gasped. He'd bitten her. The filthy little guttersnipe had sunk his rat's teeth into her, slicing through her thin glove and into her skin. Yet when she snatched her hand away, he didn't run. Lydia stepped back in surprise. The boy was suddenly dangling in the air, feet off the ground, struggling and swearing, kicking like a mule. Popkov was scowling as he held the urchin by the scruff at the end of an outstretched arm.

"*Nyet,*" the Cossack growled, and shook the boy so hard his eyes rolled up in his head.

"Stop it, Liev," she said.

Popkov gave the boy another vicious shake. This time his prisoner hung limp and for one sickening moment Lydia thought he was dead, but a car's headlights swept across his face. His eyes were wide open, frightened and furious.

"Let the kid go, Liev. Put him down." She peeled off her torn glove and sucked at the scarlet trickle oozing from the back of her hand. "I'll probably catch rabies."

But Popkov wasn't ready to listen. He searched the boy's pockets and pulled out a pair of ladies' gloves, a handful of coins, and two cigarette lighters. One was inlaid with enamel and gold. He tucked the stolen haul into his own pocket, chuckling, then tore free the canvas bag that was slung across the thief's thin chest. Immediately the boy surged back to life. He thudded his fists into his captor's ribs, so that Popkov gave a deep huff of irritation and cuffed the boy across the head. That silenced him.

The Cossack tossed the bag to Lydia and before she even caught it, she knew what would be inside. Gently she eased open the draw-string at the top and gazed down at two moist brown eyes, enormous with fright. A pink muzzle whimpered.

"Put the boy down," Lydia ordered.

Popkov dumped the kid on the sidewalk, but still the boy didn't run. Just stared at the sack in Lydia's arms.

"Here," she said and held it out to him. "Take Misty."

He took it and hugged it close to his chest, arms wrapped protectively around the canvas bundle. Lydia reached into Popkov's deep pocket and pulled out the enameled lighter, which she admired for a moment before reluctantly flipping it over to the boy.

"Now fuck off," she said with a smile.

He didn't smile back. Just gave Popkov a glare of pure hatred, then raced away down a side alleyway.

"Gutter rats need exterminating," the Cossack growled.

"He's just a kid scrounging a living."

Lydia tucked her arm through Popkov's and steered him toward the bright lights of the Hotel Metropol. Its grand façade stood opposite the Bolshoi Theatre, festive and inviting, but they were only a stone's throw from the Kremlin, a fortress whose walls loomed red as though stained with blood. Even in the darkness Lydia shuddered.

"The trouble with you, Liev," she said sternly, "is that you like to fight all the time."

"The trouble with you, Lydia," he growled back, "is that you have too many ideas in your head."

"Doesn't everyone?"

He frowned at her. "Some more than others."

Twenty-nine

LYDIA WAS DANCING. IT WAS SO LONG SINCE she'd danced that she'd forgotten how intoxicating it could be. The music swayed through the air, soft and lilting in the grand room as a five-piece orchestra picked up a Strauss waltz and Dmitri Malofeyev spun her across the floor. Above her head a domed roof of intricate glass, stained a rich blue and green, gave Lydia the strange feeling that she was moving under the sea. The other dancers were as bright and fluid as fish, their gowns flitting past in purples and golds and rippling reds, their perfumes wafting like waves around her.

The delegation had been delayed. Dmitri didn't say why and she hid her impatience, accepting his hand when he invited her to dance. He looked good in his evening jacket and smelled even better. Where his hand touched her back with no more weight than a feather, her skin grew hot under her white blouse. For some time they danced in silence until Lydia felt the need to offer her host some conversation.

"You dance well, Dmitri."

"Thank you, Lydia. And you look lovely."

"The shoes aren't mine."

He looked down at her feet in Elena's heavy green shoes and raised an amused eyebrow. "Exquisite."

"At least they fit."

He laughed.

"Dmitri, why are you doing this for me? Helping me."

He slid his gaze off the huddle of army officers locked in deep conversation over by one of the tall windows and smiled at her.

"Why do you think?" he asked.

"Out of the goodness of your heart?"

He laughed, that rich sound she liked but didn't quite trust. "Don't tease," he said. For a split second he stopped dancing. "I don't think there's much goodness in my heart, Lydia. I warn you."

They stood still as stone for one more second, and then he laughed and swept her up in his arms once more so that they became just another of the swirling couples. But Lydia's stomach was turning, and turning in a way that had nothing to do with the sway of the music. *He'd warned her.* She couldn't find a smile to give him, to make light of what he'd said. She turned her face aside and let her gaze drift sightlessly over the dazzling chandeliers.

"Lydia."

"Yes?"

"You are too easy to read."

She tossed her head, annoyed. With him. With the Chinese delegation for being late. With the boy for biting her hand. With herself for needing him.

"You're still young," he said quietly. "Your eyes tell everything, however much you disguise it with a smile and a laugh, however enchanting you look."

She turned directly to him. "Don't be so sure."

"Ah, now you have me worried."

He laughed again, and this time she made herself laugh with him. His hand at her back increased its pressure, drawing her a fraction closer as he guided her expertly across the floor.

Kuan, where are you? Come quickly.

"There are a lot of army people here tonight," she commented to distract him.

"Yes, they are keen to talk to the Chinese delegation about Mao Tse-tung's Red Army."

"A lot of power gathered in one room."

"More than you can imagine, Lydia. Be careful. These men would send you off to ten years' hard labor for no more than smiling at the wrong person."

"Would you?"

He spun her past an elegant couple, both attired in raven black, and nodded politely to them. Lydia could feel his shoulder muscles stiffen under her fingers. A rival on the ladder to the Politburo, perhaps?

"Would I what?"

"Send me to a prison camp for smiling at the wrong person?"

His mouth softened and his gray eyes were suddenly sad, changing color like the sea when a fog rolls in. "No, Lydia, I wouldn't."

"But you warned me."

"Yes. I did."

Everything in her wanted to trust him, and yet she couldn't work out why.

"*Spasibo*," she murmured. "For your help."

He tightened his grip on her fingers. "Why am I doing it? I'll tell you why. Because you're not like them." He glanced with scorn at the other dancers. "Fear controls them. Jerks their limbs like puppets. In your neat little white blouse and green skirt and your borrowed shoes you're not like them. There's something still alive in you, something vibrating its wings. At times when I'm this close to you I can hear it."

Lydia inhaled and felt a trickle of sweat on her neck. "I . . ."

"Hello, Dmitri."

Everything changed. It was as though the man she'd just been dancing with slipped from her grasp and another one took his place. This one was smooth and untouchable, the one with effortless charm and an easy smile, the one she'd first seen in the Liaison Office. For a moment Lydia was disconcerted. The man who was becoming her friend had gone.

"Lydia," he said, "let me introduce you . . . to my dear wife, Antonina."

Lydia swung around quickly and felt her cheeks flush red. The woman in front of her was dressed in a stylish beaded gown, her dark hair swept up on her head to emphasize her long pale neck. Her brown eyes were glittering with real amusement, so different from when Lydia had seen them in the hotel bathroom in Selyansk or on the station platform in Trovitsk.

"Well, I do believe it's young Lydia Ivanova," Antonina said. "The girl from the train."

The words came out with a slight mocking edge, but she extended a hand with what looked like genuine warmth. Lydia shook it, aware of the long white evening glove that covered the woman's arm all the way to above her elbow.

"DMITRI, DARLING, WOULD YOU BE AN ANGEL AND FETCH ME A drink? And a glass of something for our young friend here. She looks as though she needs it."

"It would be my pleasure, Antonina," her husband said, taking her hand and kissing the back of the glove. Lydia was aware that something passed between them, but she couldn't make out what.

His tall figure disappeared into the crowd and Antonina drew Lydia aside, settling herself at one of the tables and fitting a cigarette into an ivory cigarette holder. Instantly a passing waiter lit it for her, and she delayed speaking until he had moved away.

"So," she said. Her deep-set eyes had shed their amusement. "My husband has been entertaining you, I see."

"No. He's helping me."

"Oh?"

"To find someone."

"Ah, I see. Your long-lost half-brother, I assume."

"Alexei?"

"Yes." Antonina registered Lydia's expression of surprise. "Isn't that who you mean?"

"How do you know Alexei?"

"I met him in Felanka. After you'd left. He was looking for you."

In Felanka. After you'd left. Looking for you.

Lydia clasped her hands together on her lap to stop them banging in fury on the table. All these weeks she'd believed Alexei had deserted her. When all the time the truth was that she'd walked out on him. She could hear a noise, an odd rasping sound, and it took a moment for her to realize it was her own breathing.

"Are you all right?" Antonina was leaning across the table, one white-gloved hand stretched out, but she cast a wary glance around the room. "Take care." She waited quietly while Lydia struggled for control. "Can I help?"

"I . . . didn't know."

"That he came back for you?"

Lydia ducked her head, her hair falling across her face. She tugged at a lock of it. "How was he?" she whispered.

"Alexei?" Antonina took a long drag on the ivory holder and let smoke coil from her nose like a waking dragon. "Not in good shape, I'm afraid."

"Why?"

"He'd been beaten up." She hesitated and something caught in her throat when she added, "Stabbed."

Lydia refused to cry. "Was he badly hurt?"

"The wound was healing, so don't worry. But it must have been bad at first." Again that catch in her voice.

"Did he receive my letter?"

"What letter? I'm sorry, I know nothing about a letter."

Lydia stared down at her own hands in her lap and shook her head.

"Listen to me, Lydia." Antonina spoke fast, checking that no one was near. "I went to Felanka to find you, but you'd disappeared. I had the information you wanted. I told Alexei that Jens Friis had been transferred to Moscow. But"—she flicked ash thoughtfully into a silver ashtray—"you obviously already know that and that's why you're here, I presume. You must have discovered he'd been moved out of Trovitsk camp."

Lydia nodded.

"Clever of you," Antonina murmured.

"Where is Alexei now?"

"I don't know. I wish to God I did."

It was the way she said it, rather than the words themselves. As if they hurt her. Enough to draw Lydia's attention from her own despair and focus it on her companion. She looked lovely. Cool and elegant with bare fragile shoulders and a single strand of pearls around her long pale neck. Her face looked calm, serene as a doll's, and it seemed to Lydia that this woman had learned to construct a hard shell between herself and the world that her husband was so convinced would one day be the Mecca of mankind's happiness. Her eyes were cool and secretive, but only her full carmine mouth gave her away. One small corner of it trembled beyond her control when she mentioned Lydia's brother.

Lydia lifted her hand and hesitantly placed it on the white-gloved one where it lay on the table. "Tell me what happened," she said in a low voice.

"Nothing much. We met in Felanka . . . we talked. Then he left."

"To come to Moscow?"

"That's what he said. Something about having to go to the Cathedral of Christ the Redeemer."

"I know Alexei. If that's what he said, he will get here even if he has to drag himself by his fingernails."

"Really?"

One word. That's all. But the unguarded eagerness in it told Lydia everything. So that was it, her brother and Antonina. It made her own loneliness even sharper, but she nodded and squeezed the hand under hers. "He'll come. I know he'll come."

"You'll tell me when . . ."

"Yes, of course."

Lydia was aware of Dmitri's tall figure approaching their table. So this was the man who for the last few years had controlled the brutal camp where her father was imprisoned. How could she bring herself to speak to him? How could she bear even to look at him?

"Here you are, my darling," Dmitri said as he placed a glass of red wine in front of his wife. "And for you, young Lydia, a glass of champagne."

"Champagne," she said stiffly.

"Yes. To celebrate."

"What am I celebrating?"

He studied her face for a moment and his expression struck her as sad, as if he knew he'd lost something. "The Chinese delegation has arrived."

Lydia rose to her feet, her legs suddenly clumsy. She looked around the crowded room and made it seem as if it meant nothing to her. "Where are they?"

"Some of them are over there with General Vasiliev. The others are . . ."

Antonina's dark eyes widened as she focused on something over Lydia's right shoulder. Lydia's mouth went dry.

". . . behind you," Dmitri finished.

Lydia spun around expecting Kuan. Her breathing stopped. Her heart split open. All the happiness stored inside it flooded through her veins. She was looking straight into the beautiful dark eyes of Chang An Lo.

THERE ARE TIMES, LYDIA KNEW, WHEN LIFE GIVES YOU MORE than you ask for. Oh yes, this was one. She wanted to shout a thousand *spasibos* to all his gods, to make it echo from the glass roof. Their abundant generosity took her breath away. She'd asked for Kuan tonight, but instead she was given Chang An Lo.

He was real. Not a figment this time. Her eyes feasted greedily on him. His lithe figure was tall and supple as a bamboo tree, his black hair longer than she'd seen it before but just as thick and energetic. And yes, he possessed that same stillness at his core that pulled at her heart. But his eyes . . . the eyes she'd kissed and bathed and even brushed with her own lashes, dark and intent and able to see right inside her soul . . . those black eyes had changed. They were more guarded and aloof. Withdrawn into himself.

He stood in front of her in a black tunic and black trousers, and she wanted to touch him so badly her hands were shaking. She forced them together in front of her and performed a polite bow of greeting.

"It is good to see you again, Chang An Lo."

Good to see him. How did she find such restrained words on her tongue? How did she speak at all when her heart was thundering in her throat? And that was when he presented Kuan to the gathering and Lydia felt something crack inside her. Kuan, dressed in a similar black tunic and trousers, possessed solemn black eyes, hair cropped to jaw level, and a determined capable mouth that made Lydia wary. But worse—far, far worse—she possessed a piece of Chang An Lo. Her arm rested against his as if their flesh were fused.

Thirty

CHANG AN LO THANKED THE GODS. HE WANTED to drop to his knees and touch his forehead to the floor nine times in gratitude to them for granting him the impossible. His fox girl was safe. Alive and safe.

Yet as he observed the two people standing on either side of her, the man with the fox hair and the woman with the wounded eyes, he had a sense that they were gnawing at her, wanting a piece of her. It was in the way their glances kept skimming her, reluctant to leave her, a hunger in their eyes that she seemed unaware of.

He bowed respectfully in Chinese custom to Lydia, but shook hands with the man and the woman in the expected manner. For the first time he understood why Westerners chose to shake hands on meeting instead of the cleaner and more civilized habit of bowing to each other. A handshake reveals the secrets of a man's heart whether he wishes to or not. This man with the fox pelt and the wolf's eyes had a handshake that was firm, too firm. He was trying to prove something to himself. And to warn Chang off, even though his smile of welcome was so genuine Chang couldn't spot where the fake began and the real one ended. This Russian, this Comrade Malofeyev knew well how to control his smiles, but not his handshakes.

The woman was a different matter. Her hand rested so briefly in Chang's it barely touched his skin, as meaningless as the casual look of detachment she gave him. She saw *a Chinese*, nothing more. But as his fingers brushed against her gloved ones, he could feel the tremor in them. Was it revulsion . . . or pain? He couldn't tell. She hid it too well.

"I am honored to be in this great city," Chang said, "and my delegation humbly anticipates learning much from our Soviet comrades."

He didn't look again at Lydia. Wouldn't let himself. Didn't trust himself. Instead he introduced his two companions.

"This is Hu Biao, my assistant."

Hu Biao bowed low. "I am honored."

"And this is Tang Kuan, my invaluable liaison officer."

He heard Lydia's breath. Faint as the beat of a butterfly's wing but so tied to his own he could not mistake it.

Kuan neither bowed nor shook hands. She nodded her head in greeting and said in the perfect Russian he had taught her, "It is a privilege to be here in Moscow. It gives us all hope to see the impressive strides Communism has made in our comrades' great country."

"I would be proud to show you around our city," Wolf Eyes said so smoothly it was as though there were oil on his tongue.

Kuan nodded. "*Spasibo*, comrade, *tovarishch*. I would very much like to inspect some of the new communal housing."

"And the industrial and technological developments," Chang added. "Perhaps a tour of some of your new factories?"

"Of course. I believe that has already been arranged."

"We would all be honored to visit Lenin's Mausoleum in Red Square. To view the greatest man in history, a man whose ideas will change the whole world."

"It would be my pleasure to—"

"Comrade Chang," Lydia interrupted the exchange, forcing him to look at her. Her amber eyes glittered brighter than sunlight as she asked, "Would you do me the honor of dancing with me?"

His chest tightened. What was she doing, trailing her fingers through the fire? The two Russians stared at her in surprise, but she ignored them and smiled at Chang in a way that robbed him of caution.

"My humble apologies," he said, "but I don't know your dances."

"Then I shall teach you. It's not hard."

He bowed. "As our intention in coming to Russia is to learn as much as we can of your ways, I thank you and accept with pleasure." The words sneaked out of his mouth before he could put a chain on them.

At his side Kuan frowned, opened her mouth to say something, but at a look from him shut it again. Under her breath she murmured a few words to Hu Biao, who gave a brief nod. Hu Biao would stay close and watch who talked to whom.

Lydia turned with a determined little flounce and walked onto the dance floor. Chang followed.

HER HAIR SMELLED OF TOBACCO. AS IF SHE'D BEEN BREATHED on by too many men. Chang felt a twist of jealousy in his gut. Other men in the room were looking at her and not just because she was breaking unwritten rules by dancing with a Chinese. He could feel their gaze, yet she seemed unaware of it. She didn't pout or preen or toss her head self-consciously as women so often did when they felt the heat of admiration. She was herself in her green skirt and her plain white blouse.

She floated, weightless as sunlight in his arms as he moved with her in time to the music, fitting herself with ease to his unstructured steps. Neither spoke. If he spoke, the words would never stop. He let his eyes take their time, let them dwell on each precious part of her face. The delicate balance of its bones, the arch of each eyebrow, the full soft sweep of her lips. The nose that was too long for Chinese taste and the chin too strong. A tiny white scar on the angle of her jaw was new and a hollowness under her cheekbones.

These things he absorbed to join those parts of her already living and breathing inside him. Her hair—which he had touched a thousand times in his dreams—was longer and he allowed his fingers to nudge its fiery ends where his hand lay on her back. A small recent wound had not yet healed on the skin of her pale hand where it nestled like a bird in his palm. Yet she was still his fox girl, still Lydia.

But there were changes in her. In her eyes. The loss of her mother, of her home, maybe even of himself, had done something to her. There was a sadness at the back of her eyes that hadn't been there before, and he longed to kiss it away. She moved differently as well, more from her hips like a young woman, not like a girl any more. She had grown up. While they had been apart his fox girl had matured at some deeper level that he had not expected, and it grieved him to know he had not been there to keep the bad spirits from stealing her laughter.

He had deserted her—though he'd sworn it was only for as long as it took to fight for the future of China and for the ideals that were wrapped around his soul. Denying himself. Denying her. Communism had demanded everything of him and he had given it.

But now . . . now things had changed.

"I'VE MISSED YOU."

She breathed the words softly. He inhaled them. Did not let them go.

"I have missed you too, Lydia. Like an eagle misses its wings."

She didn't smile as they drifted around the room. It seemed to him that her smiles were not as easy to find as they used to be in China, but her eyes never left his face.

"Lydia, my love."

He felt her tremble. Saw the pulse at the edge of her delicate jaw.

"Lydia, I am watched every moment. The Soviet wolves circle our delegation day and night, wherever we go, regulating who we speak to and what we see. They will not let our delegation be *contaminated*." His thumb imperceptibly stroked one of her fingers. Her eyes flickered, half-closed. "If we are seen together you will be seized, taken to the Lubyanka for questioning, and not released."

For the first time during the dance she smiled at him. He wanted to touch her face, to feel her skin.

"Don't worry, my love," she said barely above a whisper. "I know what you are saying. I won't put you in danger."

"No, Lydia. Don't put yourself in danger."

"I feel safe now. Like this." For a moment she let her head tip back with pleasure, the way a cat will when stroked on its throat, and her hair danced free and unfettered in the sedate atmosphere of the Hotel Metropol. "Here with you."

Their eyes clung to each other.

"We must stop, my love," he told her.

"I know."

"Others are watching."

"I know."

"Look away."

"I can't."

"Then I must."

"Don't." She blew a gentle puff of air from her lips to his, more intimate than a kiss. "Not yet."

They were locked together in silence as they danced. With a strange unfamiliar movement he guided her across the floor, turning her again and again the way he'd seen others turn, so no eyes other than his own could remain on her face for long.

"Where are you?" he murmured.

"In your arms."

Her eyes were laughing, though her mouth was under control.

"I meant where are you living?"

"I know."

He smiled. To release her would be unthinkable. Unbearable. "Your address?"

"Unit 14, Sidorov Ulitsa 128. In the Sokolniki district." She raised one eyebrow at him. "Near a tire factory."

"It sounds . . ."

"Inviting?"

"Yes."

"And you? Where are you?"

"In the Hotel Triumfal."

Her lips parted, revealing the soft pink tip of her tongue and her strong white teeth. With the appearance of clumsiness he stepped on her foot, withdrew his hands from her, and bowed low.

"My apologies. I am no good at your dancing. I suggest we return to our comrades."

She said nothing. Smiled politely. But he saw her swallow, saw the effort it took. As he escorted her back to the table where the Russians and Kuan were waiting, he could hear her breath. Feel it pulling the air from his chest.

Thirty-one

THE HOSTEL WAS STIFLINGLY HOT. ALEXEI SHIFTED position. He was stretched out on a narrow bed, blanket kicked to the floor. Uncertain whether to feel good that with his last few kopecks he had managed to secure a bed for the night, however seedy the place, or annoyed that the water pipes slung along the side of the wall were always rattling and boiling hot. And the fleas, thousands of the bastard things. How did such minuscule bloodsuckers possess a bite as big as a rat's? And the heat was making the bites worse. He sat up.

"Comrade," he said to the man on the bed right next to him, "does it ever get cooler in here?"

The man didn't look up. He was sitting in just his vest and pants, picking at the hard layers of dead skin on the base of his heels with intense concentration and dirty fingernails. Beside him lay his tattered socks and an open pack of Belomor cigarettes.

"*Nyet,*" he said as he flicked a yellow strip of skin onto the floor. "It gets hotter at night when all the beds are full."

"Full of fleas, you mean."

The man chuckled. "The little fuckers. They drive you insane."

The room was a dormitory of sorts with ten beds pushed close together to squeeze them all in, but no other furniture. Any belongings were thrust under the metal bed frame or tucked under the wafer of a pillow for safekeeping while you slept.

"Comrade," Alexei said, "for four cigarettes I'll trade you one good sock."

The man glanced across and grinned. He patted the Belomors. "I got them off a *tovarishch* for minding his horse and cart for an hour."

Alexei peeled off his own unwashed sock and dangled it in the air at arm's length. "Three cigarettes?"

"Done."

"And a match."

"I'm feeling generous. You can have three of them."

Alexei tossed over the sock. He'd have to find a rag to wrap around his foot in his boot or he'd get frostbite outside in the streets. A sock for three cigarettes? Not a good deal, not sensible. But there were times when sense was no more welcome than fleas.

MOSCOW WAS GREEDY. IT WAS A CITY IN A HURRY, TEARING down old streets, constructing new buildings on a scale that made its inhabitants' heads spin. It had once relied on the textile industry to maintain its growth, but now factories of all kinds were stealing every spare scrap of space and cramming workers inside their walls in three-shift rotations. It was happening at a rate that some warned would empty the fields of Russia and bring food production to a standstill.

Alexei walked its streets in the dark, smoking the first of his cigarettes. He inhaled slowly, relishing the taste of it. It was his first cigarette in more than a month. The stale overheated atmosphere and the fleas at the hostel had eventually driven him out for some clear night air, and despite one cold foot in his galoshes he was enjoying familiarizing himself with the city.

Moscow's street system was made up of a series of concentric circles at the heart of which crouched the Kremlin, like a red spider with a vicious, poisonous bite. The Arbat was the prosperous area where upmarket cafes, well-stocked shops, lice-free cinemas,

and spacious apartments could fool a person into thinking there was
no such thing as rationing or empty shelves or shirts being traded in
street markets for half a loaf of bread. Streetlights gave the main roads
an aura of civilized safety, though the sidewalks were often narrow
and the mounds of ice against the walls so thick that at times Alexei
was forced to pick his way along the road instead. But he would turn
a corner and find himself in what felt more like a village than a great
capital city. In these districts the roads were unpaved and boasted
no streetlamps, just old-fashioned buildings with wooden front steps
and outhouses.

There were still lights in the windows of one or two of the shabby
taverns, but his pockets were empty. He breathed deeply, inhaling
the scent of the city, listening to the murmur of its heart. Somewhere here was Lydia. Somewhere here was Jens Friis. Now all he
had to do was find them.

THE MAN AHEAD OF HIM STUMBLED. ALEXEI WAS THREADING
his way back toward the Krasnoselskaya district and the fleas, the
night air like needles in his lungs it was so cold, when he saw the figure step out of a side street, swaying slightly. A night on the vodka,
that was obvious.

The road was unlit here, but a half moon had climbed sluggishly
into the sky and was shedding just enough of its liquid gleam to
enable Alexei to make out that the drunk was fat and that the dingy
street was otherwise empty. The packed snow and ice crunched like
broken glass under their feet, but the man in front seemed unaware
of Alexei's presence behind him. He stumbled again, let out a groan
loud enough for Alexei to catch it, and sank to his knees. Oh Christ,
drunks were always trouble. And right now Alexei had more than
enough of his own already. But he couldn't leave the poor bastard to
freeze to death on the sidewalk. He covered the distance between
them in a few strides.

"Comrade?"

He rested his hand on the man's shoulder, steadying the swaying
figure, preventing it from collapsing face first onto the ice. His fingers sank into a thick damp pelt and he realized the man's apparent

bulk was caused by an immense fur coat with its broad collar rolled up around his ears.

"Comrade," Alexei said again, "you need to sleep it off somewhere warm."

A muttering, slow and incoherent, slid from unresponsive lips.

Mudak! Shit! Alexei was impatient to get this over with. He put his shoulder under the man's arm and braced himself to take the weight. "Come on, on your feet."

The fur coat's only response was to lean heavily on Alexei, breathing hard, but the legs underneath didn't move. His chin lay on his chest, his eyes tight shut.

"You must move, comrade, or you'll freeze."

Still nothing. Every night a dozen drunks froze to death in the gutters of Moscow. The heavy breathing uncoiled like white silk into the air and his hand gripped Alexei's arm, tightening in spasms. Alexei leaned closer, his face so near that he could smell a sickly odor rising from the fur pelt.

"What is it, comrade? Are you ill?"

A strange noise squeezed from the man's throat like the whistle of a small bird. Shit! This wasn't just a skinful of vodka. That whistle made the hair stand up on the back of Alexei's neck. It was the sound Death makes when it comes calling. He'd heard it before, that high-pitched warning. He crouched quickly beside the man, his own heart beating like a hammer in his chest, peered intently at the puffy face and, taking the weight in his arms, lowered him with care on his back onto the sidewalk. His head was propped against Alexei's own knees to keep it out of reach of the icy claws that were accustomed to wrapping around drunks the moment they hit the ground.

Inside the voluminous coat the man was at least as warm as it was possible to be on a cold Moscow night outdoors, but in the semi-darkness the skin of his face looked grayer than the sidewalk under him. He had a fleshy face, full heavy lips, and a thick mustache that was neatly trimmed to curl down either side of his mouth. About fifty years old, Alexei guessed, but he looked more like a hundred and fifty right now. The ice was turning Alexei's legs numb already and must be doing something similar to this man's, but there was no one in the street to shout to. Yet he couldn't bring himself to leave him and fetch help himself—something about that grip on his arm, the sense of need in it.

Think clearly. What was going on here? A heart attack? A stroke? A fit of some kind?

He checked the man's mouth. The jaw was rigid but the tongue hadn't rolled back, though the skin of his face was cold and clammy to touch. *Oh Christ, don't die on me.* He quickly unfastened the man's coat and rummaged through his jacket pockets. Cigar case, wallet, keys, handkerchief, a clip of papers, and—what he'd been searching for—a small pill box. It was round and warm from contact with its owner's body. He flipped it open to reveal a clutch of white tablets. Damn it, they could be anything. Headache pills or indigestion remedies? He tipped one onto the palm of his hand and closed the box.

"Comrade." He spoke loudly, as though the man were deaf. "Comrade, are these tablets what you need?"

The man made no response, just lay like a log against Alexei's knees, eyes closed. Breath silent. Still the grip, weaker now, on Alexei's sleeve. It was all that indicated he was alive. Alexei put a hand to the man's jaw. Thank God it had gone slack. Gently he opened the thick lips and pushed a tablet under his tongue. The throat spasmed.

"Come on, don't give up on me yet."

Then he found himself doing something he didn't expect. In the bitter cold on this dismal street, hunched on the sidewalk in the dark, he wrapped his arms around this stranger and held him close. As if his own arms were stronger than Death's. He rested his cheek on the fur, felt its warmth trickle into his own flesh, listened to the short gasps as the man struggled to draw in air. He twinned his own breathing to match it, willing the heart to keep beating. And he waited.

"FRIEND?"

The word was a whisper. Barely that.

"So you're not dead yet," Alexei smiled.

"Not yet."

"Can you move?"

"Soon."

"Then we'll wait."

A murmur.

"What did you say? I couldn't hear." Alexei leaned closer, his ear by the man's lips.

"Tablets."

"I gave you one earlier. From your pill box."

The heavy head nodded faintly. "*Spasibo.*"

"Is it your heart?"

"*Da.*"

"You need to get out of the cold. When you're ready I'll get you on your feet."

"Soon." His voice faded in and out. "Not yet."

"I am in the Kalinin Hostel, but it's too far away for you to walk. What you need is a hospital—and fast."

"*Nyet.*"

The hand on his sleeve tightened, the fingers agitated.

"Don't worry, my friend," Alexei said. "Calm down. We'll sit here together like this as long as you want, waiting for the morning sun to shine and melt our bones."

The man smiled, just a slight twitch of the corners of his mouth, but still a smile. For the first time Alexei believed he might live. He felt the body relax, heard the breathing quiet and was just considering whether it would be wise to ease himself away, so that he could bang on one of the doors farther up the street where there was a light in an upstairs window, when he heard the sound of a car engine. It was traveling slowly along the road, so slowly in fact the driver must be very nervous of ice.

"Comrade, a car is coming. I'll stop it and—"

"Don't let me go, friend."

"I'll be gone only a moment, I promise."

"If you let go of me, I'll slide into the pit."

"What pit?"

"That black hole. There at my feet."

"Friend, there's no hole."

"I can see it."

"*Nyet.* Look at me."

The man turned his head. His eyes were just slits in his fleshy face.

"There's no hole," Alexei repeated.

The fingers squeezed. "Swear it."

"I swear it."

The engine stopped. Alexei looked up. At the opposite curb, not one but two old black cars with long bonnets had pulled up. The doors slammed. Six men leapt out and raced across the road toward them. Without a word Alexei tightened one arm around his new comrade, ready to haul him to his feet whether he wanted to or not, but his other hand slid under the man's coat to the holster that lay next to his chest and removed the gun. Quietly he released the safety catch and braced himself.

"*Pakhan*!"

A young man approached and saw the gun. From nowhere a snub-nosed revolver materialized in his own fist. He had thick black hair and the same mustache as the older man.

"*Pakhan*!" he shouted again. He stopped less than two meters away.

"Anatoly," the sick man murmured, and, releasing his grip on Alexei, he stretched out his hand. "Don't, Anatoly. This man helped me."

"Your friend collapsed here in the street." Alexei lowered the gun.

Men dressed in black swarmed around them, lean figures, each with eyes that did not invite familiarity. Between them they lifted the man and had him stowed inside one of the cars before Alexei could even bid him good-bye. He stood on the packed ice in the gutter and watched the cars slide away into the night like sharks. He felt the loss. It took him by surprise.

"Get well, *tovarishch*," Alexei said as he pushed the gun into his waistband and set off back to the fleas.

Thirty-two

✿

"GO TO BED, LYDIA." IT WAS ELENA'S VOICE, SOFT from behind the curtain.

"Not yet."

"There's no point waiting."

"There is."

"He won't come, girl. Not tonight. He can't. He told you that he's watched every moment."

"You don't know him."

A low chuckle. "No, but I know men. Even the most devoted won't walk into a lion's mouth if it means no chance of walking out again. Give him time. You're in too much of a hurry."

"Chang An Lo is not like other men."

"So you say."

"It's true, Elena."

There was a sudden somnolent snort from Liev on the far side of the curtain. Their talk had woken him. "Fuck this. Go to sleep. The pair of you."

"Shut up, you old goat," Elena chuckled fondly, and the bedsprings creaked as she settled down beside her man.

Lydia leaned over from the chair she was sitting in beside the window and blew out the candle on the sill. But she remained there, staring out into darkness.

CHANG SAW THE LIGHT GO OUT. HE WAS IN THE COURTYARD below, a black shadow among black shadows. He had no way of knowing it was her window or her candle, but he was as certain of it as he was of his own heartbeat.

He knew she would be waiting, but he moved no closer. A bitter wind moaned under the roof tiles, the night spirits urging him on, trying to steal his senses, setting fire to his blood. Nevertheless he remained totally immobile on the courtyard cobbles, as bit by bit through the soles of his feet he felt a part of himself sneak away, lift like smoke on the wind and trail across the windowpane seeking cracks to whisper through.

Coming here was a risk, but he could not stay away. It was no hardship for him to slip out the hotel bathroom window, scale the drainpipe, and prowl like one of the city cats over the rooftops. No, that was only a small danger. The big danger was here, on her own doorstep. Did she really think she could become friendly with one of the Party elite, the man with the wolf eyes, and not pay the price? She would be watched. Every moment now. There would be someone to report on who she met, where she went, what she did, and, above all, who came to her living quarters. Day or night. But here in the shadows he was invisible.

My Lydia, my love. Take care.

HE RETURNED TO HIS HOTEL THE SAME WAY HE'D LEFT IT, THE roof tiles lethal in the dark under their coating of ice. As he swung in through the bathroom window once more, he listened but all was quiet. It was four o'clock on a winter's morning and the hotel's clients were slumbering contentedly under their thick quilts.

While still in the bathroom he changed into the nightwear he'd carried in the leather satchel on his back and pushed his shoes and clothes into it instead. He ran water from the tap to indicate to any hidden ears that the bathroom was in use, stilled his heart, and opened the door. The corridor was empty. On bare feet he padded silently to his room, slipped inside, and closed the door behind him.

"So you're back."

In the dark Chang's hand slid to the knife at his waist, as with the other he turned on the light.

"Kuan," he said. "What are you doing in my room?"

She'd been sitting in a chair and had risen to her feet. Her face was flushed and he knew her heart well enough to recognize it as the fire of anger.

"Waiting for you to return."

"I am here now."

"Where have you been?"

"That is my business, Kuan, not yours."

She was wearing a plain blue cotton wrap and he saw her hands sink into its pockets, bunching into fists, but her voice was low and controlled.

"Chang An Lo, you could be arrested for what you've done tonight."

Chang drew in a slow breath. A sadness swam into his blood and he felt it pulse through his veins. It was too late to take back her words.

"We could *all* be arrested for what you've done tonight," she continued in a tense whisper. "Leaving the hotel secretly indicates you are doing something you don't wish the authorities to know about."

"Kuan," he said so softly she had to take several steps closer to hear, "if this room is fitted with listening devices, which is very likely, your words have just condemned us to a labor camp in Siberia."

Her flush deepened. Her dark eyes widened in alarm and darted around the room as if the devices might be visible.

"Chang," she whispered, "I'm sorry."

"Go to your room now. Get some sleep."

"How can I sleep when . . . ?"

He opened the door and held it ajar. "Good night, Tang Kuan."

Without looking at him she bowed, sidled through the gap, and left the room. He turned off the light and sat down on the bed. He closed his eyes, focused his thoughts, and let Lydia come to him. He filled his mind with the image of her dancing in his arms tonight,

the flames of her hair burning away all sense of caution within him,
her amber eyes drawing his spirit to hers once more, tightening the
thread that bound them. He pictured again the way she turned her
head, chin held high, the way her mouth curved up at the corners
even when she wasn't smiling. His thoughts lingered on the feel of
his hand on her back as they moved across the floor, each fragment
of his skin aware of the ripple of her young muscles under his fingers, of her ribs, of her long straight spine.

For the sake of China, for the country he loved, he'd given her
up once already. Not again. Not this time, may the gods forgive
him. He opened his eyes and stared out into the blackness.

THE COLD WAS LIKE A SLAP IN THE FACE AS LYDIA WALKED OUT
into the courtyard. The sky wasn't yet light, that was still several
hours away, so the yardman wasn't in his usual position of leaning on
his snow shovel, puffing on a cigarette stub and complaining about
the carelessness of the women at the pump, spilling water over the
cobbles. It made his job harder, hacking at the sheets of ice. Liev
claimed all yardmen were paid informers for OGPU, keeping a careful watch over the comings and goings of the inhabitants of their
buildings, but whether or not that was true, Lydia was eager to avoid
his lecherous gaze.

She set off at a fast pace, retracing the route she and Elena had
taken to the Housing Office. The night sky had cleared, stars glittering as bright and numerous as the sequins on Antonina's black dress
in the Hotel Metropol yesterday evening. The thought of Antonina
and Alexei together was one she chose not to dwell on, but there was
something about the woman that she liked. She was an individual,
unwilling—or was it unable?—to conform, not yet jammed into the
Soviet mold despite being married to one of Stalin's elite. And now
the certainty that Alexei was heading for Moscow too.

Hurry, brother. I'll be waiting. At the Cathedral today, I promise.

"BOY! WAKE UP."

Lydia kicked at the cardboard shelter. It trembled but didn't fall
down.

"Get up," she called out. "I want to talk to you."

She stood in the opening of the alcove, ready to block any sudden dash for freedom, but nothing moved.

"Get your skinny bones out here and this time keep your rat fangs inside your head," she snapped.

She began to think the shelter was empty. It was too dark to see properly, so she didn't bother peering in but gave it another kick. Inside, a faint whimper was abruptly silenced.

"I've brought a biscuit for Misty."

She waited. Caught the sound of movement. A rustle, then a dark shape stood in front of her.

"What d'you want?" The boy's voice was wary.

"I told you. To talk."

"The biscuit?"

She held it out. He snatched it and didn't even snap it in half, part for himself, part for the dog. He gave it all to the puppy in his arms, who gobbled it down, then licked the boy's chin, eagerly asking for more.

"What's your name?" Lydia asked.

"What's it to you?"

"Nothing. It's easier, that's all. I'm Lydia."

"Fuck off, Lydia."

She spun on her heel and started to march away. Over her shoulder she called, "So you don't want breakfast, or some money in your pocket after all. I see I misjudged you, you stupid little rat-brain."

For a moment she thought she'd lost him. But suddenly there was the sound of scurrying steps and the young boy was in front of her, facing her, but moving backward on his toes as she kept walking forward. A trickle of moonlight brushed his milky hair, giving him a strange elfin appearance, his chin pointed, his blue eyes as reflective as mirrors.

"Breakfast?" he asked.

"*Da.*"

"Money?"

"*Da.*"

"How much?"

"We'll negotiate that over *kasha.*"

"For Misty too?"

"Of course."

"What do I have to do?"

"Deliver a note."

The boy laughed, a sweet clear sound that gave Lydia hope.

THE BOY'S NAME WAS EDIK. HE PERCHED ON THE END OF LYDIA'S bed and spooned porridge into his mouth without a word, while at his feet the puppy was snuffling around its empty bowl, its full stomach distended wider than its flimsy rib cage. Lydia sat in the chair, aware that Liev and Elena, still in their nightshirts, had pulled back the curtain and were sipping cups of *chai*. Through its steam they watched him with suspicion.

Lydia bent down, scooped up the puppy, and placed it on her lap. Instantly a moist pink tongue licked her chin and she laughed, stroking the eager little gray head. The puppy had large yellow-brown eyes and paws two sizes too large.

"Where did you find her?" she asked the boy. "Misty, I mean."

"In a sack." He didn't look up from his porridge and spoke between mouthfuls. "A man was trying to drown her in the river."

"Poor Misty," she smiled, ruffling the wispy ears. "And lucky Misty."

"Lydia."

"Yes?"

"I'm sorry I bit you."

"As long as you don't do it again."

"I was frightened you wouldn't let me go."

"I know. Forget it."

The boy's eyes fixed on hers for a second before returning to the spoon. He didn't look anywhere near Liev. Lydia was just beginning to think this was going surprisingly well, when Liev hauled himself to his feet and lumbered over to where Edik was seated. He seized a hank of his pale hair. The boy dropped the spoon with a yelp.

"Chuck this thieving little bastard back out on the street, Lydia. And his animal with him."

"No, Liev. Leave the kid alone. He's going to help me."

"Lydia." It was Elena this time. "Look at him. He's filthy. He's one of the urchins that live on the streets and will be riddled with lice and fleas. The dog as well. For heaven's sake, do as Liev says."

"Out!" Liev growled at the boy.

The dog bounced up to Liev's foot and started to chew at his bare toes. The big man's hand abandoned the boy and descended on the animal, swinging it up in the air as if to throw it across the room.

"No!" Lydia shouted, as she snatched the puppy from his grasp and smacked the Cossack's great paw. "You are heartless."

Liev's one eye stared at her with an expression of both surprise and hurt. "They're vermin," he muttered, and slammed his way out of the room.

Elena, the boy, and the dog all looked at Lydia.

"Damn it!" she hissed.

She grabbed the boy and the dog by the scruff and hauled them down to the water pump in the courtyard.

"IT'S AN HONOR, CHANG," HU BIAO POINTED OUT.

He was at Chang's side as they came down the steps of the Hotel Triumfal. The rest of the delegation followed behind, with Kuan at the rear. She had not spoken to Chang since last night.

"It is a great honor, Hu Biao," he corrected his young assistant, loudly enough for their Russian escorts to hear. He was speaking in Mandarin, but an interpreter was never more than a pace away from his elbow. "To be invited to the Kremlin to have talks with Josef Stalin himself will enable us to report back to Mao Tse-tung the thoughts in the Great Leader's mind. Mao will be humbly grateful. China needs such guidance in spreading the ideals of Communism among our people."

Biao glanced at him, just a flicker of the eyes. Chang suppressed a smile. Even this young soldier knew there was nothing humble about Mao, not even in the tip of his little finger. But entry to the very heart of the Soviet system, a meeting in the Kremlin, and a talk with the man who grasped the reins of power at the center of it would be of great interest. There was even a ripple of danger about it that made the delegation nervy and uncommunicative this morning. As if they knew they might walk in but never walk out, caught like flies in a web.

The day was bright, the streets drenched in sunlight. Blue skies had replaced the clouds of yesterday, but Chang's heart hung heavy in his chest because it was not to the Kremlin that his feet longed to direct themselves. The frosting of snow on the trees opposite the hotel glittered invitingly and people were strolling under them, young couples openly hand in hand. He looked away.

Wherever he and the Chinese delegation went, soldiers cleared an open space for them, pushing people aside as though to keep the delegates from contamination. Or was it from contaminating? The pavement in front of the steps had been scrupulously swept free of any Muscovites, while three official cars with the hammer and sickle pennant flapping on their hoods purred patiently at the curb. Their chief escort, a brisk woman in uniform, opened one of the doors and treated them to a stiff smile, but just as Chang was about to enter the cushioned interior he heard a shout.

The cause was a boy. No more than ten or twelve years old, thin as a weasel but running fast. He had wormed his way past a soldier and was dodging another's grasp, racing across the empty space in front of the hotel as if his tail were on fire.

Chang's heart opened up in his chest. With two strides he stepped into the boy's path, knocking him off balance and causing him to crash. For no more time than it takes for one of the gods to frown, they stumbled against each other. Then a soldier's gloved hand reached out and seized the urchin by his thin arm, shaking him so hard into submission that the rag wrapped around his head fell off to reveal pale hair that gleamed like pearls in the sunshine. The chief escort hurried over to Chang, stern annoyance on her face. But something more was there as well. It was fear. She was frightened he would report her for incompetence.

"Comrade Chang," she said quickly, "I apologize. The boy will be punished."

"Let him go."

"*Nyet*. The street urchin must be taught a lesson."

"Let him go, comrade."

Chang's tone was quiet. The escort studied him for a second, then readjusted the collar of her military coat.

"Let him go, comrade," he said again. It was unmistakably an order. He turned to the soldier who was twisting the boy's arm behind his back like a brittle twig. "Release him. He did me no harm."

The chief escort gave a sharp nod and the soldier's grip loosened. Instantly the boy was running up the street and disappearing into the crowd faster than a rat down a drainpipe. Without comment Chang took his seat in the car and nodded appreciatively as the escort pointed out the new constructions undertaken along their route, the improved street lighting, the widening of the roads.

"Very good," he murmured.

Only when she and his fellow delegates were engrossed in the appearance of the great Kremlin fortress with its towering red walls and gleaming roofs did Chang slide a hand into his coat pocket. A folded piece of paper lay inside that had not been there before.

Thirty-three

&

"IT'S FASCINATING TO SEE THE CONSTRUCTION of it."

"I agree," Jens Friis responded to Olga, who was standing at his side. They were both gazing upward. "Every time I see it, it takes my breath away."

"It's like a huge pregnant whale floating up there."

Jens laughed, his breath a shimmer of white in the early-morning air. "Ah, Olga, you don't do it justice. It's an airship. Look at it. Sleek and elegant. A gigantic silver bullet waiting for someone to pull the trigger."

He was proud of the design. However much he hated it, he was proud of it. Like a child who goes bad, you still can't stop loving it. Airships had a far greater range than airplanes and this one, with two biplanes attached to it, would provide a weapon that could terrorize whole cities and battlegrounds.

With a shiver Olga looked away from the creation looming above their heads. Instead she stared at young Fillyp struggling with the ropes, at the cement floor meticulously clean, at her own hands, a skilled chemist's hands.

"Olga," Jens said gently, and for a brief second while everyone's attention was elsewhere he touched her shoulder. "It's not your fault. You have no choice. None of us have."

She turned her bleak blue eyes on him. "Is that true, Jens? Is that really true?"

THE AIRSHIP'S HANGAR WAS AS HIGH AND AS INTRICATELY ribbed as the vaulted ceiling of a cathedral. It towered above them like a new kind of sky, but no sun ever shone inside this world. It dwarfed the band of engineers and scientists who set about their work with well-schooled efficiency, dwarfed to the significance of worker ants by the vast structure.

Today it was Jens's task to reconstruct the release triggers on the gas containers and adjust his new design for one of the holding brackets on the underside of the biplanes in the adjoining hangar. The weight of each biplane was crucial to the airship's balance, so he had to calibrate his measurements with minute precision. He was watched carefully. Not only by the guards who shuffled up and down, rifles slung over their shoulders, beating their arms across their chests to keep warm, but by the others. He never knew who they were or what they did. Lean-faced, gray-haired observers, two of them, always dressed in black suits. He called them the Black Widows because they crawled all over the place, poisonous as spiders.

They both wore spectacles and one was constantly unwinding the wire frames from his ears and polishing the glass with his pristine white handkerchief, which seemed to be reserved for that one specific task. They rarely spoke. Just watched. Everything he did. Sometimes when he glanced over his shoulder at them, one of the overhead lamps would be reflected in their lenses and it looked to Jens as if hellfire itself was trapped in their eyes.

OUTSIDE IN THE MIST ELKIN WAS LOLLING ON A BENCH AT THE side of the hangar, smoking a cigarette and picking at a burn on the back of his hand. Smoking of any kind was strictly forbidden inside the hangars or even anywhere near them for that matter, but once out here in the surrounding compound no one bothered much and the massive buildings provided good protection from the biting wind.

Jens lit his own cigarette—one of the bonuses of being part of this unit was free smokes—and took a place next to his colleague on the bench, folding his long legs under the seat.

"Elkin," he said, "you and I have got to have a serious talk about timing. You told Colonel Tursenov that we'll have it fixed in two weeks."

"It's true, we can."

"I think that's very doubtful. We'll have to run a sequence of tests first."

"For Christ's sake, Friis, don't treat me like one of those dimwits over there." He gestured with the tip of his cigarette toward a guard sitting on the top step of a stone storage hut over by the compound's brick wall. Near enough to keep an eye on them but too far for words to carry.

"Elkin, just think about what we're doing here," Jens murmured. "Think about the monster we're creating."

"All I'm thinking about is my release at the end of it. That's what they promised us. Our freedom."

"You're a fool, Elkin."

"What the hell do you mean by that?"

"Use that big brain of yours. What we're involved in here is top secret. Do you honestly believe that when we've completed our work on it, they'll just open the doors and let us walk out?"

"Yes!"

"Like I said, you're a fool."

Elkin jumped to his feet and glared down at Jens, who remained seated, unwilling to attract the guard's attention.

"Friis, I did nine years in the camps in Siberia, including three in the Kolyma gold mine. I'm bloody lucky to be still alive at all. I'm not going to risk this one chance of becoming a free citizen, of returning to my family, just because you have some stupid misplaced notion of noble behavior to protect others."

"We are all lucky to be alive. And every one of us wants our freedom."

Elkin leaned over so that his scarred face was only inches from Jens and whispered fiercely, "Then don't fucking ruin it for the rest of us by causing any more delays." He turned on his heel and strode through the damp air back toward the entrance to the hangar, his figure dissolving in the mist.

Jens didn't move. He let his unfinished cigarette fall to the wet grass and inhaled deeply while he fought off a black wave of sorrow. He was used to depression. It always came and sat at his heels like a faithful dog until he was as accustomed to its rank and fetid breath as he was to his own. But now he had a weapon against it, a bright light he could switch on at will, shine in its dull lifeless eyes and drive it back into the darkness from which it came: the knowledge that his daughter was alive.

He closed his eyes and conjured her up in his head. An elfin dancing creature. He tried to imagine her as she would be now, a young girl of seventeen with hair the color of flames and clear amber eyes that looked at you straight. A face that kept private thoughts hidden behind a slow curious smile. But he couldn't do it. That seventeen-year-old kept sliding away into the mist like Elkin, and in her place skipped a laughing child, one who tossed her head when she ran into a room or creased her smooth forehead into a frown of concentration when helping her father bang a nail into a length of wood or draw a perfect angle of ninety degrees. A heart-shaped face that would tilt up at him, eyes bright, and break into a wide grin when he tapped her little chin and said, "Well done, *maleeshka*."

"I'm glad you've found something to look happy about."

Jens opened his eyes to find Olga standing in front of him. He liked that shy uncertain way she had about her and had an overwhelming urge to take her hand firmly in his and walk away to freedom. Except that the field and the hangars were surrounded by a ten-meter-high wall topped with coils of vicious wire, and guards patrolled its perimeter day and night.

So instead he said for her ears only, "Someone is looking for me."

"Who?"

"My daughter."

Olga's eyes widened, soft blue eyes that were good at spotting his moods. "I didn't know you even had a daughter."

There was something in her voice, something regretful just under the surface, but he was too engrossed in the images in his head to notice it.

"I thought she was dead," he said.

"What happened?"

His ears heard the crack of a gunshot, and he looked around quickly before he realized it was in his mind. "We were on a train." He recalled the temperature in the cattle wagons. So cold it transformed the blood in his veins to agonizing ice and he'd watched the lips of his wife and daughter turn blue, their skin whiter than the snow outside in the wastelands of Siberia.

"The Bolsheviks were everywhere," he said, "stopping all White Russians escaping. They hauled all the men off the train and . . ." He grimaced and lit himself another cigarette to rid his mouth of the taste of death.

"Shot them?" Olga asked.

He nodded. "I was one of the lucky ones. Because I'm Danish, they threw me in a labor camp instead." He drew hard on his cigarette. "Lucky," he repeated bitterly. "It depends what you mean by that word, doesn't it?"

"What about your wife and daughter? What happened to them?"

"I thought they would have been killed as well."

"But now you've heard your daughter is alive?"

"Yes." His broad smile came as a surprise to both of them. "Her name is Lydia."

Thirty-four

ALEXEI SLEPT LATE. HIS LEGS ACHED, HIS SKIN itched. A woman with sores on her face and a broom in her hand prodded him with the bristles.

"Up! *Kozel!* Out now."

Alexei rolled out of bed fully clothed, aware of his own stink, and saw that the dormitory had already emptied of last night's occupants. The rule was that no one was permitted indoors in daylight hours. These were mercifully short in winter. He was heading down a tiled corridor on the ground floor toward the single bathroom when a rush of cold air signaled that the main door had swung open and a voice behind him drew his attention.

"*Tovarishch!*"

He turned. Three men in long coats with fur *shapkas* jammed on their heads were standing just inside the front door, staring at him. The lethargic concierge behind the reception desk eyed them with dislike but made no comment, and Alexei experienced a flicker of alarm. He folded his arms across his chest as though bored by the interruption and remained where he was, his mouth pulled into a tight line.

"*Da?*" he responded.

"We want you to come with us."

Alexei's mind raced. OGPU operatives. They had to be. That's all he could think. The secret police. They come for you when you least expect it, especially when there are few people around to witness it. Somehow they'd traced him. Now the bastards had come to arrest him. Because of his social origins? Just because he was from an aristocratic family? Or was there something else? Immediately his thoughts went to Antonina. Had she betrayed him? A bitter taste stung the back of his tongue because he'd believed he could trust her. How the hell could he help his father when he couldn't even help himself? He forced his shoulders to relax and stuck a smile of sorts on his face.

"Well, *tovarishchi,* why on earth would I want to go with you?" he asked easily. "I'm busy now. Another time maybe."

He took a stride away down the corridor but didn't turn his back on them. To his surprise, instead of snapping at his heels like a pack of wolves eager for the taste of flesh, they just stood there by the main door looking perplexed. Four more steps along the tiles and he pushed open the bathroom door.

"Of course, comrade," the tall coat in the front of the threesome said politely. "When would be convenient?"

Alexei stalled, hand still on the door. *Convenient?* Since when did OGPU do anything at your *convenience?* He released the door, moved back along the corridor, and studied the intruders more closely. They were no older than himself, around midtwenties, one short and plump, the others taller and leaner with identical mustaches. All had eyes that made him nervy.

"Who are you?" he asked.

"We met last night." It was one of the tall figures who spoke.

"Last night?"

"*Da.* Don't you remember me?"

Then it came to him and he cursed his starved brain for its sluggishness. The mustaches. Of course, just like the man they called *pakhan* with the droop around each side of the mouth.

"Of course I do. Tell me, how is he today?"

"Better."

"I'm glad. Send him my good wishes for his recovery."

"He wants to see you."

"Now?"

"Now." The man paused and added reluctantly, "If it is convenient. He asks whether you would come to eat bread with him."

Alexei laughed with relief, a good strong belly laugh that made the threesome shuffle uneasily.

"*Da*," he said. "Tell him yes."

BREAD AND SALT.

Alexei accepted the piece of black bread on the tray that greeted him as he walked into the apartment and dipped it in the bowl of salt. In Russia bread and salt represented much more than mere bread and salt. They meant hospitality. They meant welcome. On bread and salt you could live. Beside them on the tray stood a shot glass filled to the brim with vodka. He picked it up, knocked it back in one, and felt it burn the cobwebs from his stomach.

His mind kicked into gear and he looked around with interest. The apartment was an odd mixture of old and new. On the walls hung hefty oil paintings in elaborate frames, all portraits of different men. Sharp observant eyes gazed out at him from each one. Family portraits? Could be. For a moment Alexei recalled the severe paintings of his own ancestors that used to line the grand staircase in the villa in St. Petersburg and frighten him as a child. At least some of these looked as if they knew how to smile. The furniture, in contrast, was new and utilitarian, a plain bleached pine that looked at odds with the paintings, but everything was clean and there was no curtain dividing the large living room into separate quarters.

"This way, *pozhalusta*."

Alexei followed the plump one of the trio into a corridor and to a heavy door with an ancient brass handle that looked as though it might have come from somewhere else. Somewhere like a church. The soft-looking knuckles knocked.

"*Da?*"

"*Pakhan*, I have the comrade from last night."

"Come in, damn you."

They entered a room that belonged to a man with a passion. Though the curtains were half-closed, a strip of sunlight lay dim and dusty in the air, exposing the contents of the room. Wings seemed to flutter, feathers flashed scarlet, eyes gleamed corn yellow. The place was full of birds. Alexei blinked but the birds didn't move. They were all stuffed. Exquisite masters of the air trapped under glass domes and doomed to pose on mossy branches until their feathers blackened and turned to dust. With a jolt Alexei pictured his own father, Jens Friis, trapped, penned, ensnared for so many years, unable to fly.

"Welcome, friend."

The words were a deep rumble. They issued from a large four-poster bed that was adorned with mulberry-red drapes and long white bolster pillows piled up like snowdrifts. Sunk deep in the middle of them was the pale puffy face of last night.

"Good morning, comrade. *Dobroye utro*," Alexei greeted him cheerfully. "I hope you're feeling better."

"I feel like I've been kicked by a bloody camel," his host grimaced, causing his mustache to writhe like something alive.

"Have you seen a doctor?"

"*Pakhan* has his usual pills," the young man at Alexei's elbow volunteered, "but he is too stubborn to let us call a doctor."

"Go away, Igor. You're annoying me." But it was said with a fond smile that belied the words.

"*Pakhan*, I don't think . . ."

"Go."

Igor glanced at Alexei.

"Don't worry," the older man insisted, "this person has not come here to do me harm. Have you, comrade?"

"*Nyet*. Of course not."

"Good. Leave us then, Igor."

The plump face creased with concern, and Alexei had the feeling the young man did not much appreciate being dismissed as if he were a schoolboy. Nevertheless he left with no further objection, just shut the door a shade harder than was necessary.

"Come over here, my friend."

Alexei approached the bed. It struck him as a strangely intimate act in the presence of a stranger and he became aware of the smell of the bedsheets, the blue veins bunched at the base of the aging throat. A closer look disclosed a man considerably frailer than the voice he chose to use. Strands of gray hair were scraped severely back from his face, which despite being fleshy had sunk in on itself, falling into crevices, crowding around the dark eyes.

"I'm not dying," the sick man announced gruffly.

"I'm glad to hear it. But it's your friends on the other side of that door you need to convince, not me. They're out there whittling your coffin right now."

The man laughed, a great guffaw that had him rubbing his hand on his chest, as if it pained him under his nightshirt. "What's your name, comrade?"

"Alexei Serov."

"Well, Alexei Serov, you don't look much like a guardian angel to me but I thank God for putting you in that street last night, especially when I had dismissed my companions for the evening." His mouth twisted in a grimace. "This experience will teach me to avoid brothels in future."

Alexei sat down on the chair beside the bed and smiled. "Our paths crossed, friend. I was there at the right time. Now you're safe with your friends, so get well again."

"I intend to." He held out his hand to Alexei. "Accept the sincere thanks of Maksim Voshchinsky."

Alexei shook the hand. It felt surprisingly firm in his, and he respected the strength of will that made it so. But his eyes were drawn to where the sleeve of the nightshirt had ridden up and the muscular forearm lay briefly on view. What he saw there slowed his heartbeat. A fleeting glimpse, that was all, before Voshchinsky withdrew his hand once more, but it was enough to tell Alexei this was someone to keep far away from.

Voshchinsky's hooded eyes conducted a slow inspection of Alexei's appearance. "Most people as dirty and ragged as you, Comrade Serov, if you don't mind my saying, would have had my watch in their pocket, my wallet in their hand, and left me to die alone on the ice."

Alexei rose to his feet. "Not everyone is like that," he said with a polite bow. "But you must rest now. Don't tire yourself. I am happy to see you are recovering well. Comrade Voshchinsky, I wish you good day."

He walked to the door, eager to be out of this room with its winter light glinting off a multitude of glazed staring eyes. The sound of the man's shallow breathing followed him.

"Wait."

Alexei paused.

"Comrade Serov, are you in such a rush to be elsewhere?"

"Nothing stands still in life, my friend."

The gray head nodded again, lolling slightly on its neck as though it were too heavy. "I know." He smiled, a brief forgiving twitch of his lips. "Especially when you are young." Sadness rustled like dry leaves in his words, and the fingers of one hand slowly opened and flexed on the sheet, an unconscious movement as if trying to grasp at Alexei. Or maybe at life. "But I am not ready to see you go yet."

"You have your friends."

"Yes, that's true. They are good friends. I can't complain. They do what I say."

With a quiet click Alexei opened the door. Outside on the polished boards stood the three men, and at the sight of him in the doorway all three took a step forward. They wanted to know what had been said in there, but in that moment when he could have walked away, back to the fleas and the prospect of never seeing his own father again, he felt a shift within himself. Through his own arrogance on the bridge in Felanka he had lost everything that would open the doors to set Jens Friis free. But now he couldn't allow himself to walk away from the strange room with the dead birds and the sick man. This time he must swallow the arrogance. Bend the knee. Take the risk.

"He's resting," Alexei announced. Then he entered the bedroom once more and softly shut the door behind him.

"So?" It came from the bed.

"You say your friends do what you say. Because I saved your life, would they do what I say? Would they owe me that?"

Voshchinsky frowned, a wary pucker of his heavy eyebrows. Alexei returned to the chair and sat down.

"Maksim," he said, "you have many friends."

He lifted the man's hand in his own, touched the veins that ran like serpents under the skin, and slid the nightshirt sleeve up the forearm. Underneath it writhed more serpents, black ones. Two of them slithered around the base of the slender skeleton of a birch tree, their eyes red, their fangs sharp as knife blades. Beneath them written in elaborate italic script were the three names: *Alisa, Leonid, Stepan.*

"A fine tattoo," Alexei commented.

Maksim Voshchinsky touched the trunk of the tree lovingly with the finger of his other hand. "That was my Alisa, the mother of my sons, God rest her soul."

"Maksim, we must talk. About the *vory.*"

The sick man's eyes narrowed and his voice grew rough. "What do you know about the *vory*?"

"They are the criminals of Moscow."

"So?"

"And they wear tattoos."

Thirty-five

LYDIA STOOD ON THE STEPS OF THE CATHEDRAL of Christ the Redeemer in the thin sunshine. The Moskva River slid past, boats bobbing on the molten silver of its surface, and she'd counted twenty-two of them in the hour she'd been waiting.

"Alexei," she murmured, "I can't wait any longer."

She'd really believed it today. That he would come. When she said to Liev, "My brother will be there," for once she hadn't been annoyed by his big laugh because now she knew for certain that Alexei had received the letter she'd left in Felanka and that he wanted to see her again. It had lifted a dead weight that lay in her stomach as solid and cold as the tombstones in the cathedral's crypt. She was alone on its wide steps. No one loitering in the street or slowing their pace as they walked along the sidewalk. Everyone seemed to be going about their own business as normal: an elderly man with a fat dog in tow, a young woman with a net bag and a child hanging off each hand. Lydia studied the street intently. It was hard to shake the chill of being observed.

After twenty minutes she had convinced herself that no one was watching her, but even so she intended to take a circuitous route across Moscow. First in one of the horse-drawn carriages, an *izvoz-chik* with the horse still wearing its summertime hat, its ears peeking up through the plaited straw like curious weasels, then a tram, an intricate weaving through shops, in and out of side doors, another tram, another shop, a final quick desperate dash on foot. Then the park. She had it all planned.

LYDIA HAD RUN THE LAST STRETCH AND HER HEART WAS SOME-where in her throat. She made her way along the path, everything around her so piercingly bright that she had to narrow her eyes against the sunlight. On each side of the path stretched pristine lawns dressed up in lacy layers of snow. Ragged edges marked the boundaries between paths and lawns as if the black earth were peeking out from under its white blanket like a sleepy mole to test the temperature outside. Lydia hurried her pace. She couldn't see him.

She had entered the park from the Krymsky bridge end, but Chang An Lo might easily approach from a different direction. She kept turning her head, searching. Years earlier the site was just one big scrap heap for old metal where scavengers used to prowl at night and stray packs of dogs scraped out dens, but the site had been cleared and flattened first for the Agricultural Exhibition and then in 1928 turned into the Central Park of Culture and Leisure.

She couldn't see any sign of culture, but people were certainly taking advantage of the leisure. The sun had tempted them out into the crisp cold air, well-swaddled figures strolling arm in arm and children scampering like kittens, released from the confines of their cramped living quarters. One athletic-looking man was kicking a ball to five young boys, all dressed in Young Pioneer uniforms with Communist-red scarves, flashing bright as robins on the snow. Such an ordinary sight, a father playing with his children, yet Lydia felt a sharp tug of envy and hated herself for it, for that weakness she couldn't seem to free herself from.

She moved on through the park, past the lily-of-the-valley electric lights, losing confidence with each step. This was all wrong. The park wasn't at all what she'd anticipated when she put it forward as a meeting place. She cursed her own ignorance. She'd imagined there would be trees and tangled undergrowth, offering privacy and shadowy nooks where two people could speak without being observed, but the Central Park of Culture and Leisure was still new, with wide empty stretches of grassland and flowerbeds barren under the snow, the trees freshly planted and no taller than herself. It didn't take her long to see that Chang An Lo was not here.

The realization slid as sharp as ice into her skull. She closed her eyes, the fingers of sunlight almost warm on her lashes. *Think, think.*

Where are you, my love?

She breathed quietly. Letting loose her thoughts. When something in her mind unknotted, she knew she'd been looking for the wrong thing. Slowly she retraced her steps, scanning the ground this time instead of the Muscovites at leisure, and she saw the sign when she was back where she'd started. She smiled and felt a whisper of wind ruffle a strand of her hair. The sign was a tiny pile of stones, so small it was barely noticeable. But Lydia knew. Knew without doubt. When she and Chang had been separated in China, they had left messages for each other in a place called Lizard Creek, and those messages had been buried in a jar beneath a cairn of stones. This, she realized, was her new Lizard Creek.

She crouched down and scrabbled at the stones. The miniature cairn had been placed in a corner of one of the flowerbeds where the soil was not so compacted under its skin of ice. It broke up quickly under her fingers and she found a small fold of leather. Inside it lay a slip of paper. In delicate black script were written the six words: *At the end of Semenov Ulitsa.* Six words that altered her world.

She glanced around quickly, but nothing had changed. A young woman wheeling her bicycle, an elderly couple throwing crumbs like confetti for a flock of starlings whose wings fluttered an oily black in the sunlight. Lydia piled the small cairn back together, rose to her feet, brushing her fingers on her coat, and slipped the paper deep in her pocket. Her hand wouldn't release its grasp on it but lay there, curled around it. She started to walk at a steady pace along the path once more but her feet wouldn't wait. They picked up speed, lengthening their stride, and before she could stop them, they were running.

* * *

SEMENOV STREET WAS NEAR THE RIVER. SET IN THE SOUTH-
ern part of the city, it might have been transplanted straight out of
one of the villages Lydia had viewed from the train on her journey
across Russia. The houses were simple, a jumble of wooden one-story
buildings tilting at different angles under patched and mossy roofs.

The road was nothing more than a mix of potholes and dirt, but
today it was bustling with people. A street market filled up most of
the walkway, goods displayed on mats thrown on the ground. One
stall boasted neat rows of secondhand boots, each one molded to the
shape of the previous owner's life, jostling between displays of paper
flowers and buckets of rusty metal clamps and washers. None of the
traders had licenses. If the police turned up to check on them they
would melt away faster than ice on the tongue. Lydia was thankful
for all the activity. She slid unnoticed along the street.

"Apples? Good clean apples?"

"*Nyet.*"

A woman had thrust a shriveled yellow apple under her nose. She
was tempted, as she'd not eaten since a mouthful of the *kasha* she'd
cooked for the boy this morning. The woman looked thin and tired
under her headscarf, but then so did everyone else. It was the way
things were. Two woven baskets stood at her side, apples in one, nuts
in the other, both protected from the cold by a woolen shawl draped
over them. A handful of the better samples lay on top to tempt passing trade.

On impulse Lydia snatched up two of the apples and handed over
ten kopecks from the dwindling supply in her pocket, before she
darted off down the road to where it came to a dead end. Beyond it
lay a wild bushy stretch of commonland that nestled in a lazy loop
of the Moskva River. It looked as though it would be marshy in the
spring, which was probably why it hadn't been built on, but right
now the ground was hard as iron and covered with brown spiky
grass that pushed up like fingers through the glistening snow.

Lydia set off across it. She was startled by the unexpected sight of
a dirty-white circus tent over to one side, flags flapping halfheart-
edly from its topmost ridge, while down toward the river was a stand
of birch and alder trees and a maze of bushes that even in winter

created a dense screen of cover. She couldn't see Chang An Lo. Not yet. But she knew he was here as surely as she knew her next breath would whiten the air in front of her.

There were no paths, so she walked in a straight line across the snow and brittle grass, crunching it beneath her feet as she headed toward the birch trees. Their naked branches reached out like pale spiders' legs against the startling blue of the sky, and she felt something trembling inside her. What if he'd changed? What if nothing was the same? What if he'd traveled too far for her to reach him this time? The back of her throat tasted coppery, yet her lips were smiling broadly without her knowledge, her cheeks flushed despite the cold.

She stepped in among the slender tree trunks and though the temperature abruptly dropped a few degrees in the shadows, she felt the heat of her body rise. She unbuttoned her coat. Her eyes scanned the undergrowth, but the only living creature she saw was a gray-faced jackdaw that bobbed its head up and down at her. She pushed farther into the strip of woodland, picking her way deep into the gloomiest spots where concealment would be easiest. Every few steps she stood still, listening intently. But all she could hear was the distant murmur of water and the fretting of the wind in the branches.

Yet suddenly he was there, directly in front of her. Tall and slender, graceful as the mottled trunks of the birches. That same intent stillness in the way he looked at her. She'd caught no sound of footfalls, no rustle of bushes, but now she could hear his breath, see its white trail from his lips, and it came as fast as her own.

"Lydia," he said in a whisper.

She didn't speak. She was gazing at his face again, at his full mouth, his beautiful almond eyes. At the long strong throat and the line of his hair brushed back from his forehead, silky and black. It stole from her tongue all the words she had prepared. She reached out. He could be a phantom and this could be another of the dreams that tormented and tantalized her each night. She could be asleep in her bed, with Liev Popkov yawning like a hippopotamus on the other side of the curtain.

He touched her cheek. His fingers rested there and she leaned against them, the weight of her head in his palm. A murmur escaped her lips, a wordless sigh that shuddered up from deep within her and without warning his arms curled around her. He held her so tight against his chest that neither could breathe. His hand pulled off her hat, dropped it to the ground, and cradled the back of her head, fingers moving in the dense waves of her hair. A low moan rose from his lungs and brushed the skin of her temple.

They stood like that. No words. No kisses. No greeting. Unaware of where they were, and when they'd been still so long that a vole scuttled past their feet, pattering over the black loam, Chang An Lo tipped back his head and smiled at her.

"Lydia," he said again, "you have brought my soul back to me."

She kissed him. Breathed in his breath, tasted his tongue. Grew aware of his hunger for her. She felt her skin come alive again, though until this moment she hadn't even realized it was dead.

THEY WALKED, ARMS CLOSE AROUND EACH OTHER'S WAIST, HIPS touching, feeling their bones and muscles relearning how to be one instead of two. Back across the patchy grass and over the trodden snow toward the circus tent where people were milling round.

A moment earlier when they had sat down on Chang's coat in a buttery patch of sunlight slanting through the trees, a man in leather trousers with four children, all twig-thin, had come barging through the undergrowth gathering firewood. He was bundling it up with the help of the swarthy urchins into a stack on his back, held there by a leather strap. From their colorful garb and bright neckerchiefs Lydia guessed they were part of the circus. Chang had put a finger to Lydia's lips. It smelled clean and fresh, and she'd kissed the knot of scarred flesh where his little finger used to be. The man didn't even see them but his presence was enough to dispel the sense of privacy, so they'd risen to their feet, picked up her hat, and reluctantly emerged from the shelter of the trees.

"You look well, Lydia. It pleases my heart to see it."

"You look alive." She glanced sideways at him. "It pleases me to see that."

He smiled, that slow inward smile she had not forgotten.

"How is the war in China?" she asked.

"There is much to tell and much to ask," he said without answering her directly, his arm holding her close against his side as they walked. He shortened his stride to hers; she lengthened hers to his.

"Questions like how did you become part of the Chinese delegation?"

"And what happened on your journey across the Russian steppes?"

"Nothing much."

"Lydia, I can see it in your eyes. That things happened."

As their footsteps faltered on a patch of snow, their gaze fixed on each other.

"And Kuan?" Lydia asked quietly. "Is she part of your delegation? Or part of your life?"

"And the Soviet officer with the wolf eyes? Is he an element in your *nothing much*?"

They smiled at each other and let it go. She thought she had remembered everything about him, but she was wrong. She had forgotten the way she felt herself change when she was with him, slowing the blood in her veins and the thoughts in her head. She became more like the person she wanted to be.

"No questions," he said.

She nodded. "Later."

He kissed her hair. "There will be a later."

They strolled on toward the circus tent, their movements in rhythm with each other's, but the fact that he'd felt the need to reassure her there would be a *later* for them instantly raised doubts in her mind. Her throat grew tight and she fought back sudden tears. What was going wrong? She was here with Chang An Lo, his arm around her waist, his ribs rising and falling in time with her own, the long muscles of his thigh stretching and shortening next to hers as they walked, and they were speaking in English. This was everything she had longed for day after day, month after month. So . . . what was wrong?

It was the words. They felt like burs between them. As if their bodies remembered but their tongues had forgotten, no longer able to find the words to share. She leaned her head on his shoulder, her ear on the strong line of his collarbone. *Ignore the words. Ignore the questions. Listen to his heartbeat instead.*

One side of the tent slapped noisily in the wind as they approached it, harsh as a whip crack, and a man in a short padded jacket and torn rubber boots came out with a wooden mallet and a handful of iron pegs. He knelt on the ground and started to hammer one of the rope loops attached to the canvas into the ice-bound earth.

"Are there any animals?" Chang asked in Russian.

"Around the back." The circus man didn't look up.

"*Spasibo.*"

The question surprised Lydia. She didn't know he had an interest in animals. Back home in China when she showed him her pet rabbit, he'd wanted to eat it. That memory made her smile. They stepped over the guy ropes and followed a well-trodden mud path that skirted the tent and led to a row of wagons at the back. The vehicles were painted in great splashes of color with designs of circus acts—a lion tamer curling a whip, a ballerina upside down on horseback, and though most of the trucks were closed up, several had their sides pinned back to reveal cages within. A rope fence stretched several feet in front of the cage bars to deter the public from approaching too close.

Lydia could see why. "Look," she said, "lions."

In one of the cages lazed two lionesses, their big square heads resting on their front paws, their tawny eyes half-closed, their coats shaggy to keep out the cold. An interested group of people had gathered in front of them, but a small boy was trying to drag his father over to the next cage. Lydia glanced at Chang. His attention was also on the next cage and his black eyes possessed something that hadn't been there before, a kind of focusing of himself in the moment. She looked across at the cage; behind the bars a massive male tiger was standing with muscles tensed, defiantly glaring with yellow eyes at the puny spectators. He was utterly magnificent. He snarled silently to reveal fangs that turned Lydia's stomach. She noticed Chang take a step closer to the cage.

"You are drawn to danger," she said.

His body stilled. She saw it. As if he'd slowed his heartbeat at will. He spun around to look at her, turning his back on the wild creature behind the bars, and reached out to lift a lock of her hair and let it trail through his fingers like flames.

"I only put my hand in the fire when I have to, my love."

"Coming to Moscow"—she gestured toward the scrubby patch of wasteland where they were standing and the tired-looking tent—"and coming here today, that's putting your head as well as your hand in the flames, it seems to me."

He shook his head, saying nothing at first, but his black eyes drifted back to the tiger and stayed there. Lydia was jealous of the animal.

"I came," he said softly, "because I had to."

"Because Mao Tse-tung ordered you to?"

Ignore the words.

His gaze flicked abruptly back to her face. It brushed against her with a touch that was almost physical, over her hair, the planes of her face, the neat curve of her ear, the fullness of her mouth.

"I came," he said again, "because I had to."

She didn't ask for more.

Instead she looped her fingers around his. "How did you know I was in Moscow?"

"I didn't. I knew you were in Russia. That was enough."

"Russia is a big country, Chang An Lo," she laughed. "I could have been anywhere."

"But you weren't. You were here in Moscow, just as I am here."

"Yes."

She felt his hand tighten on hers. "The gods look after those they love."

She smiled. "Well, they've certainly looked after me." She raised an eyebrow at him. "So what did you promise them in exchange?"

"Hah! My Lydia," he smiled, "you know me too well. You are right. I did in fact promise them the earth."

They both laughed. The separate sounds of it rolled between them, hers light and teasing, his low but full of pleasure, merging into one single breath that hung in the air. They relaxed. She felt some of the tension, the uncertainty that lay like a shadow at their feet, fade to a shapeless blur, and into its place slid a brighter shade of something else. It might have been the sunlight, bright and sparkling. But to Lydia it felt like something solid. It felt like happiness.

THEY WALKED OUT OF THE CIRCUS FIELD AND BACK THROUGH the street market, arm in arm like any normal couple, eating the apples she had bought.

"Now please tell me, Lydia," Chang asked, "have you discovered news of your father?"

"We said no questions."

"I know."

He felt her shiver, just a flicker through her fingers that lay curled on his arm. Nothing more. But he waited patiently.

"We traveled to the prison camp," she said in a low voice, "the one near Felanka where he'd been held, but . . ."

"*We?*"

"Yes, Liev Popkov came with me, the Cossack." She glanced up at him with that little twist of amusement on her lips that always tugged at something deep in him. "You remember him, I'm sure."

"Of course. Is he here in Moscow?"

"Yes. He and a woman friend of his are sharing a room with me." She laughed. "All very cozy."

He studied her. Listening to the words behind her words. "Soviet Russia," he said, "has its own problems. Please give my greetings to Comrade Popkov. I hope his back is still as broad and as strong as the Peiho River."

She laughed again. "Yes," she said, "Liev is as strong as ever."

Chang had met the big Cossack only once, though *met* was hardly the right word. In China Popkov had hauled Chang's sick body through the streets of Junchow for Lydia to nurse back to health. The memory was still a dark stain in his mind; it filled him with a sense of shame. That he had needed another man's legs to carry him to safety.

"But my father was no longer in that camp," Lydia continued. "He'd been moved to Moscow. Alexei and I parted company in Felanka."

"Alexei Serov?"

"My brother," she pointed out quickly and bit into her apple.

He knew he'd spoken too fast.

"Alexei Serov, is he here?"

"He came with me to Russia to help in the search." She stepped deliberately on a pristine patch of snow and left a clear footprint in it, as if she would stamp her imprint on the world. "Jens Friis is his father as well as mine, remember."

She let her hair swing forward, concealing the side of her face from him and he wanted to lift it aside, to see the sadness behind it. What was it she felt for her father? Instead he stopped walking.

He stood still, one hand holding hers, and immediately she turned toward him, her lips parted in a small breath of surprise at the sudden change. He drew her to him. In a tired back street in this faceless city he centered them both on this sunlit patch of dirt and encircled her fragile waist easily with one arm. He drew her so close that she was pressed hard against him, their bodies molding to each other, her breasts under her coat firm against his chest. She didn't resist in any way, though people in the street stared for a moment; she just took to herself the shape of him as if it belonged to her.

He tapped a finger on the pale center of her forehead. It made a startlingly loud sound, and her eyes widened.

"My dearest love," he murmured, "in here"—he tapped again—"you are alone. In here we are all alone. You cannot cram into your head a father you do not know and a brother who until recently you weren't aware existed. Or into your heart. A family is more than just blood, it is also made of those you trust. In China I have people who are my family even though we share no bond of blood."

He saw her throat constrict, the delicate bones rise and fall, and his heart grieved for her.

"I am your family," he promised her softly.

A sound came from her lips, a low wordless utterance that spilled from somewhere deep within her. Her eyes darkened till they were the color of winter's rain as she leaned forward, nestling her head in the hollow of his neck. He stroked her hair, smelled its familiar fragrance, its strands alive under his fingers.

"But you left me," she whispered.

He had no answer to that.

Thirty-six

LYDIA SPOTTED THE BOY IMMEDIATELY. SKULKING on the edge of a cluster of residents. The courtyard lay in deep shadow and as she hurried under its archway her eyes took a moment to adjust to the gloom after the brightness of the street. She had zigzagged her way home across the city, waiting her turn with impatience in the tram lines that snaked through the dying shafts of afternoon sun. The surrounding buildings seemed to lean forward, casting their black shapes possessively over the yard's cobbles, but she didn't miss the thin figure of Edik.

What struck her as odd as she entered was the sound of music and laughter. It was coming from the heart of the small crowd gathered there, a scratchy plonking sound that made her smile it was so comical. She knew it at once. An organ-grinder. The last time she'd seen an organ-grinder was as a child in St. Petersburg with her hand tucked safely into her father's, but the memory was hazy and before she could prod it into life, a sudden squawk from what sounded like a parrot caused ripples of laughter in the courtyard. People pressed closer and she saw the boy's pale hair move in, smooth as buttermilk. A light brush against the man at the back of the crowd as though eager to see more.

Lydia stepped forward, seized a handful of Edik's filthy jacket sleeve, and yanked hard. His feet scrabbled on the ice.

"Get off my . . ." He swung around, wide-eyed, realized who it was, and grinned. "*Privet*. Hello."

"Put it back."

The grin fell off his face.

"Put it back," she said again.

For a moment there was a wordless battle, and then his boneless shoulders slumped. He shuffled back to the man and easily replaced whatever it was he'd stolen. The boy refused to look at Lydia, but she took hold of his sleeve again and dragged him back to their doorway.

"That's better," she said.

"For you?"

"No, stupid, for you."

As they climbed the stairs, neither mentioned that his sleeve had torn and was hanging in tatters between her fingers.

"HERE, GIVE HER THIS."

Lydia handed a piece of *kolbasa* sausage to the boy, and though he accepted it, he still wouldn't look at her. He had sidled into their room and found a spot for himself on the floor, his back propped against the wall where even the ecstatic greetings of Misty didn't bring a smile to his sallow face. He broke off a snippet of the sausage and popped it onto the dog's moist little tongue, then one on his own. Elena was seated in the chair, hands busy with needle and thread, a navy garment of some kind spread on her broad lap.

"Sausage is too good for that animal," she grumbled.

Lydia wasn't sure whether she meant the boy or the dog.

"And what are you grinning at?" Elena aimed the question at Lydia.

"Me?"

"Yes, you."

"Nothing."

"The kind of nothing that puts a smile the width of the moon on your face and a purr in that voice of yours?"

"I don't know what you mean."

"Come on, girl, you look like a cat that's landed in a bucket of cream."

The boy laughed and stared up at Lydia, suddenly interested. Despite herself, Lydia felt her cheeks start to burn.

"Is it your brother?" Elena pressed her. "Did Alexei turn up today?"

"No."

"Then what happened?"

"I waited at the cathedral, but—"

"I mean what *else* happened?"

Lydia looked at the boy. He and the dog were both watching her with bright eyes.

"Nothing," she said, and added a convincing shrug. "Nothing else, Elena. But today I'm hoping to hear from the Party member I was with at the reception. His name is Dmitri Malofeyev. I had no idea until I met his wife that he used to be the commandant at Trovitsk camp where my father was held. It means he knows the right people to ask."

"You think he'll help you?"

"I hope so."

"Why should he?"

"Because . . ." Lydia glanced awkwardly at the boy and back to Elena. "I think he likes me."

Elena tied off her stitch, calmly bit through the thread, and asked, "What then? When he gives you the information you want. What will you give this important Soviet official in return?"

Silence spread like oil in the room, smooth and thick and cloying. It seeped into Lydia's nostrils, making it hard for her to breathe. The only sounds were the little gray dog panting and the churning of the organ outside.

"Elena." She spoke quickly, as if the words would do less harm all squashed together. "I have no choice. I can't just sit here any more. Don't you see? Liev goes out night after night searching for a slip from someone's tongue or a loose piece of grumbling from a cook or a guard who's had one vodka too many. He's trying. *Chyort*, I know he's trying—to find out more about the whereabouts of this secret prison, number 1908. He's asking dangerous questions in bars and taverns throughout Moscow. And it frightens me, Elena. It frightens me so much I . . ." She stopped. Took a deep breath and forced the words to slow down. "I'm frightened that one night the stupid Cossack will ask the wrong person the wrong question and end up in a labor camp himself."

Elena sat very still, hands in her lap. She said nothing, but her colorless eyes forgot to blink and her mouth grew slack.

"That fear haunts me, Elena. Every time the big bear goes out. Like now. Where is he? What is he doing? Who is he talking with? What bloody rifle barrel is he staring into?" She looked down at her fingers knotted together and asked in a whisper, "How much should a person risk for love?"

Elena lifted a hand and ran it down her face, over her eyes and her mouth until her fleshy chin sat cradled in her palm. The action seemed to bring her back to life, and she stabbed her needle into the reel of thread with a shake of her head. "It's his choice. No one is making him do it."

"But I want him to stop. Now. It's too dangerous. But he won't, I know he won't."

"And this Soviet official, your Dmitri Malofeyev. Is he not dangerous?"

"I can handle him."

Elena burst out laughing, a girlish sound that made the puppy bark. She rose heavily to her feet and shook out the garment she'd been stitching, revealing it to be an old but thick wool coat, which she tossed carelessly to the boy.

"Here, Edik. Shut your ears, wear this, and get out of here, you and that fleabag of yours." She hesitated for a second in the middle of the floor and placed her hands on her ample hips, glancing around the room with a sudden tension that made the veins of her neck stand out. "I have enough to take care of here, I don't need more."

She walked over in the direction of the door, and as she passed she did an unexpected thing. She ran a hand down Lydia's hair, something she'd never done before. Her touch took Lydia by surprise and was far gentler than she would ever have imagined.

"*Maleeshka,* little one," Elena said softly, "that man eats girls like you for breakfast."

Then she took down her coat from the hook behind the door and pulled on her galoshes, ran a comb through her dead-straw hair, wound a scarf around her head, and left.

The boy stared at the door as it closed behind her. A sound came from him, a subdued kind of whimper that at first Lydia thought came from the dog.

"She doesn't like me," he said.

Lydia went over and knelt on the hard floor in front of him, stroking the puppy's fur as if it were a part of the boy. "Don't be foolish. If she didn't like you, why would she go to all the trouble of finding and patching up a coat for you?"

"I don't know."

She ruffled his milk-white hair and let Misty lick her wrist. Reluctantly the boy dragged his gaze from the door, as though finally accepting that Elena wasn't coming back for a while, and turned to look at Lydia.

After a moment he said, "I still don't think she likes me."

"I think the trouble is that she likes you too much."

The bones of his face seemed to hunch together, as if that thought were too hard to squeeze in between them. "What d'you mean?"

"Edik," Lydia said gently, "I think you remind her of her dead son."

THE ORGAN-GRINDER HAD CEASED HIS MUSIC, AND THE ROOM felt empty without it. The light was growing smoky, as gray as Misty's coat. Edik had fallen asleep curled up on the floor with his dog, and though the puppy was awake it lay still, one yellow eye on Lydia. When she stood up and moved over to the window to watch the square patch of sky above the courtyard turn from blue to a lilac before it merged with the roofs, the puppy gave a low growl in the back of its throat. Although no more than a skinful of wobbly bones and milk teeth, already it was guarding its master. That reassured Lydia. She wasn't sure why she cared so much, but she did.

She wanted to be alone with her thoughts. They were hammering on her skull to be let out. *I'll find a way.* That's what Chang had

said as they parted: *I'll find a way,* and she believed him. If Chang An
Lo promised he would find a way for them to be together—really
be together, rather than the few snatched kisses of today—then he
would. It was as simple as that.

She shivered, not that she was cold, quite the reverse in fact. The
blood in her veins was hot and in a hurry, but her body wouldn't
keep still. It was restless. Her skin felt hungry. It wanted his touch
the way it used to long for the balm of ice on a hot summer's day
in Junchow market. It wanted to be beside him. To see his face.
To watch his slow smile spread up into his eyes. She'd thought the
kisses today would be enough, but they weren't. She was greedy. She
wanted more.

She dropped her head against the windowpane and sighed. She'd
been in a state of waiting for so long, she had forgotten how exhila-
rating it was to live in the here and now. To have what you want. To
want what you have.

"Chang An Lo," she whispered, as if he could hear her.

She touched the glass where her breath had clouded it and wrote
his name in the mist. She smiled and studied the flow of the letters
intently as if it could magically conjure up Chang himself, her heart
banging on her ribs. As she stared at it, her own reflection took shape
around it, merging the two, and she shifted focus to examine its features. What did he see when he looked at it? The hair, the eyes, the
facial bones, all seemed the same to her. But is that what he saw? The
girl he'd fallen in love with back in China? Or someone else?

And Kuan? There like a spider at his side with every step he took,
a living breathing invitation in each hotel room he stayed in. *No, not
that. Don't think like that.*

Send me the boy. That's what he'd said. She turned away from the
window and noticed it was almost dark in the room.

"YOU EAT TOO FAST. THE PAIR OF YOU."

Lydia was seated in the chair. The boy was still on the floor, stuffing bread into his mouth, and beside him the dog had its muzzle in
a bowl of *kasha,* neither coming up for air. She'd heated Edik some
soup and warmed the porridge for Misty, then prodded the sleeping
boy in the ribs and plonked the bowls in front of them. Edik had

gone from deep sleep to eating in less than a blink of an eye. He held the bowl close to his chest, hunched over it, guarding it as he swallowed, and the sight had disturbed Lydia.

"Edik," she asked, "what happened to your parents?"

He gulped down two more mouthfuls of soup. "Shot." He crammed in more bread.

"I'm so sorry."

"Four years ago."

"Why?"

She waited again. Didn't push.

"They read a book," he said between mouthfuls. "A book that was banned because it was anti-Soviet."

"What book?"

"Can't remember."

She left it at that. His hair hung in a pale limp curtain around his face as he started to lick the bowl.

"Have you lived on the streets ever since?"

"*Da.*"

"That's tough."

"It's not so bad. Winter is hardest."

"Thieving is dangerous."

He lifted his head for the first time and his muddy blue eyes brightened. "I'm good at it. One of the best."

I'm good at it. She'd said the same words herself not so long ago. Her stomach knotted when she thought of the risks.

"Where do you sell the stuff you steal?"

"I don't." He gave her a scornful look as though she were stupid. "The *vory* does."

"Who is the *vory*?"

He rolled his eyes in his head in exaggerated disgust, wiped his mouth on the back of his hand, and gave it to the dog to lick.

"There's this man," he explained as slowly as if talking to a simpleton, "he runs a gang of us street kids. We steal and hand it over to him. He pays us." The boy thought about what he'd just said and scowled. He made as if to spit on the floor, but stopped himself just in time. "Not much though, the bastard. Just a few measly kopecks. Some of the other *vory* bastards pay better, but I got to take what I can get."

Lydia leaned forward. "Are there many boys like you on the streets of Moscow?"

"Yeah. Thousands."

"And are they all run in gangs by *vory* men?"

"Most of them."

"Who are these *vory*?"

"Criminals, of course." He grinned and ruffled the pup's ears. "Like me."

"Edik, what you're doing is dangerous."

"And what you're doing isn't?" He laughed, an open childish laugh that made her smile.

She wanted to go over and wrap an arm around his skinny shoulders, to give this tough young kid the kind of hug his small frame was crying out for, but she didn't. She had a feeling he would bite her again if she did. She scraped her hair back from her forehead as if she could scrape from her mind the doubts about what she was about to ask.

"Edik."

"Yeah?"

She reached into her pocket, pulled out a ten-rouble note, and waved it in the air. His eyes followed the white note hungrily, the way Misty's followed a biscuit.

"Here," she said, screwed it up into a ball, and tossed it to him.

It was in his pocket before she could blink.

He grinned. "What now?"

"I need you to go to the Hotel Triumfal again and watch out for the same Chinese man. He will pass you a note for me."

"Is that all? For all this money?"

"Take care, Edik."

He jumped to his feet, grabbing his new coat under one arm and his dog under the other. "The trouble with you, Lydia"—this time his smile was shy and yet it leapt the gap between them effortlessly—"you're too easy to please."

She laughed and felt the guilt shift a fraction under her ribs. "Don't—"

A sharp knock on the door silenced her.

★　★　★

IT WAS DMITRI MALOFEYEV. HE WAS STANDING IN THE DOORWAY of the shabby room in his elegantly tailored leather coat, a white silk scarf at his neck. In one hand he carried a large brown paper bag, in the other a bunch of flowers that looked to Lydia as if they might be lilies. Where the hell he'd got them in the middle of winter, she couldn't imagine.

"Hello, Lydia."

"Comrade Malofeyev, this is a surprise."

"May I come in?"

"Of course."

But she hesitated. To let this man with his shiny shoes and polished white teeth into her home was like inviting a crocodile into her bed.

She smiled at him, matching him tooth for tooth. "Come in."

He walked in, his male presence filling every corner of the drab room. "So this is where you hide."

Hide? Why did he use that word?

"It's where I live, yes. How did you find me?"

"Not hard."

"No, I bet it wasn't. For a member of the Party elite, nothing comes hard." She said it with a smile.

He returned the smile and with a gallant bow presented her with the flowers. As she accepted them she bent her head to inhale their fragrance and realized they were made of silk. Stupidly, she felt cheated.

"Thank you."

Her guest looked around the room with interest. His gaze settled on Edik and registered surprise. Whatever he'd gleaned from the concierge's tittle-tattle, a boy and a dog were clearly not part of the picture. He nodded a greeting of sorts, then reached into the paper bag under his arm, pulled out a pack of biscuits, and tossed it across the room to him.

"Here, young man," he said, "take this. And get out."

It was said so politely that it was impossible to judge how serious he was.

The boy didn't put out a hand to the biscuits. He just let them spin through the air and fall to the floor with a crunch. He didn't even give Malofeyev the courtesy of looking at him. Instead he focused on Lydia.

"Do you want me to stay?" he muttered.

She loved him for it, and at that moment he seemed to become part of her family. As Chang had said, you don't need the bond of blood.

"No," she answered and gave him a grateful smile. "You can go. I believe you have an errand to run."

Edik put down the dog, shrugged into the coat that was far too big for his slight frame, and, without a glance at the visitor, slouched out the door. The dog snatched up the biscuits between its tiny teeth and trotted after him.

SHE MADE HIM TEA. IT WAS THE LEAST SHE COULD DO. ON HER bed was spread an array of food the likes of which she hadn't set eyes on since she'd entered Russia. Not even in the shops did they have such riches. Tins of glossy caviar from the Caspian Sea. Almond biscuits and ginger cake. Bars of Swiss chocolate and silvered boxes of glacé fruits from Paris. A leg of smoked ham that made the room smell wonderful, and numerous kinds of fat spicy sausage. She had laid it all out on the bed with care, the way a woman would lay out her gowns and stand back to admire them. When she lifted out from the bottom of the bag a bottle of vodka and a metal case of five fat cigars, she had looked at Malofeyev and raised one eyebrow.

"You think I'm a secret smoker?" she laughed, then hesitated and added a little stiffly, "Or are these meant for your own use?"

"No." He was sitting on the windowsill, legs crossed, swinging one foot and watching her. "They're for you to use. As trade for whatever else you need. Kerosene perhaps."

"Ah." Lydia placed the cigars between a jar of Greek olives and a packet of roast coffee, patted them affectionately like long-lost children, and imagined what a guard might be persuaded to do in exchange for such a gift. "*Spasibo.*" She smiled, not sure whether it was at him or at the food, and tried not to feel bought. Her feet wouldn't move away from the bed, and she was frightened that if she looked away it might all disappear in a puff of smoke.

"You're welcome, Lydia."

She waited for more words, but none came.

"Comrade Malofeyev, what do I owe you for this?"

"Nothing. Don't worry"—he smiled at her—"there's no price tag."

She picked up the olives, succulent and tangy, and recalled how her mother would have slit her own throat for such a jar.

"No price tag on the food?" She made herself replace the olives. "Or on the information I asked for?"

"Not much success there, I'm afraid."

A small silence tumbled into the ragged gap between them, but he didn't seem to notice it. It made her uncomfortable.

"You've not found where Jens Friis is?" she asked at last.

"No."

Another silence. He swung his leg carelessly, and she wanted to seize it and wrap it around his neck.

"But I thought . . . ," she started. The words trailed off. What was the point of them?

"So did I."

"Is that why you brought the food? In place of any information."

Abruptly the leg stilled its movement. "Lydia, I am no longer involved with prisons or labor camps."

"Do you remember him at Trovitsk camp? Jens Friis. Tall and red-haired."

"Of course not. There were hundreds of prisoners there, and I had little to do with them myself. I was just there to ensure that the work norms were fulfilled and the timber shipped south. I didn't sit and hold a prisoner's hand and tell him bedtime stories, if that's what you mean."

She stared at him.

He didn't smile, just looked back at her, a patient expression on his face. It goaded her further.

"But I told you," she said. "I gave you the exact number of the prison that he's supposed to be held in—number 1908. Surely you can find out from your contacts where it is in Moscow." She shifted impatiently from one foot to the other. "Even if you can't find out whether he's in there."

"Lydia, my dear girl, I would if I could, I promise you. But you must understand, some secrets are secret even from me." His forehead was furrowed, and she wasn't sure whether it was concern or annoyance. "I'm sorry I can't help you more." As an afterthought, he added, "I wish I could."

Lydia stooped and picked up the large brown paper bag on the floor. One by one she started to place the food items back inside it. Malofeyev made no comment.

"I don't believe you," she said quietly, her back to him.

She left the cigars till last, then positioned them neatly on the top. They made her think of Alexei and how he would have enjoyed them. She turned to face Malofeyev.

"Dmitri, why are you doing this? Helping me, I mean. Bringing me such lavish gifts when you barely know me and certainly owe me nothing. You know as well as I do that just one of those cans of caviar would buy you any girl of your choice here in Moscow." She studied his face. Saw it soften and heard a sigh start to escape before it was cut off.

"Ah, Lydia, I'm not here to buy you."

"Aren't you?"

"No."

"Then why are you here?"

He observed her thoughtfully. "Because one day I want you to look at me just the way you looked at your Chinese friend at the Metropol the other evening."

Something hot flared in Lydia's chest. "We danced, that's all. Rather badly."

"No. That wasn't all."

"What do you mean?"

"You know exactly what I mean."

"No, I don't. Anyway, Dmitri, you seem to be forgetting that you have a beautiful wife at home."

"Ah yes, my Antonina. But you're wrong, Lydia, not for one second do I ever forget my beautiful wife." There was a sadness, gray and soft as a shadow in his voice. "In fact, it was she who suggested that as I couldn't help you in any other way, I should come over with these gifts."

"How convenient."

He smiled politely.

Lydia tried to ignore the elegance that hung on him as effortlessly as his leather coat and the fiery red hair that triggered all sorts of memories of her father. They ran like ripples under her skin. For some reason she couldn't understand, when she was in the presence of this man, her life in China seemed oddly opaque and far away. That annoyed her more than she cared to admit.

"Comrade," she said with an abrupt change of tone, "thank you for your generosity, but I cannot accept these gifts." Yet her hand was treacherous. It hovered there, touching the bulges of the brown paper bag with the same caress it used to fondle Misty's ears. She snatched it away.

"I'm trying to help you, Lydia. Remember that."

"In which case, tell me, Dmitri, please, which street is prison 1908 on."

"Oh, Lydia, I would if I knew."

"Maybe you don't want to know."

"Maybe."

If she was going to find her father, she needed him, needed his knowledge and contacts and familiarity with the prison system. It unnerved her to think that someone on the next rung above him on the Soviet ladder was stamping on his fingers.

"Who knows you're here?" she asked.

He didn't answer the question but picked up the tea that was growing cold on the sill beside him, sipped it with a quiet delicacy as if lost in his thoughts, and replaced it. Only then did he focus on Lydia, and immediately she could see a change in him. His gaze was fixed and fierce and reminded her that he'd very recently been the commandant of a prison camp.

"Lydia, listen to me. Soviet Russia is still just a child. It is growing and learning. Every day we are drawing closer to our goal of a just and well-balanced society where equality is so taken for granted that we will be astonished at what our fathers and grandfathers were stupid enough to put up with."

She didn't react, didn't look away. The pulse in her wrist was racing, and the dying light from the window behind him seemed to be setting fire to his hair.

"And the prison camps?" she asked. "Is that how you teach this growing child of Soviet Russia to behave?"

He nodded.

"Through fear?" she demanded. "Through informers?"

"Yes." He rose from the sill, a slow casual movement that nevertheless made Lydia watchful. He'd grown taller and suddenly darker as he stepped away from the window. "The people of Russia have to be taught to rethink themselves."

He came closer.

Her heart thumped. "Jens Friis is not even a Soviet citizen," she pointed out. "He's Danish. What good can teaching him to *rethink* possibly achieve?"

"As an example to others. It demonstrates that no one is safe if they indulge in anti-Soviet activities. No one, Lydia. Not one single person is more important than the Soviet State. Not me." He paused, his words suddenly soft. "And not you."

She tried to slow her breathing but couldn't. Abruptly he seized both her wrists and shook her hard. Wordlessly she fought to break free, but his fingers held her with ease, so she ceased her struggles.

"Let me go," she hissed at him.

"You see, Lydia," he said calmly, "how fear changes people. Look at yourself now, wide-eyed with fear, a little lion cub eager to claw my throat out. But when I release you, you will have learned something. You will have learned to fear what I might do—to you, to your friends, to Jens Friis, even to that damn Chinese lover of yours—and it will hold you in check. That's how Stalin's penal system works."

He smiled, an uneven twist of his mouth that offered no threat, just a warning. She stared straight into his gray eyes. With a cautious nod of his head, he uncurled his fingers. She didn't move. With no hesitation he leaned forward and kissed her mouth, hard and hungry, and his hand touched her breast. She took a step backward, away from him, and he didn't stop her.

"Fear," he said, "is something you have to learn how to use. Remember that, Lydia." He gave her a playful tilt of his head, the easy charm back in place. "I meant you no harm. I just wanted you to know."

She was too angry to speak. But her eyes never left his.

"You can slap my face if it would make you feel any better," he offered with a light laugh.

She turned her face rigidly to one side, no longer able to look at him. Without another word he walked out, shutting the door quietly behind him. She started to shake. Anger raged inside her, hot and painful, burning her throat. She hurried to the window and watched the tall figure of Dmitri Malofeyev stride through the gloom of the courtyard, his back toward her and one hand raised in farewell. Without even turning around, he'd known she'd be there, watching.

As he disappeared under the archway she sank her forehead against the glass and tried to freeze out the thoughts in her head. But not the anger. She needed that. Because it was not anger at Dmitri Malofeyev, it was at herself. She groaned long and loud and thumped her forehead against the pane as if she could force the images from inside her skull. The feel of his lips. The spicy scent of his cologne. The hot flutter of his breath on her face. His fingers gentle on her breast.

Where did it come from, this treacherous pleasure she'd felt? She hated him. But worse, she hated herself.

THE BATHROOM WAS COLD, SO COLD LYDIA COULD SEE HER breath. A naked lightbulb hung from the ceiling like a dull yellow eye and a finger of damp was creeping down one wall blistering the paint, as if something were living under it. It wasn't Lydia's evening for a bath, the use of which was on a strict rotation, so she stood on her towel to keep her feet warm and stripped off her clothes.

Her skirt. Her cardigan. Her blouse. Her undergarments. She dropped them in a haphazard pile on the floor and stood naked in front of the washbasin. Her eyes meticulously avoided the small square of mirror above it because she couldn't bear to see up close what betrayal looked like. What color it was. What shape it took. What holes it chiseled in a person's face. She ran the cold water and started to wash herself.

At the end of ten minutes her skin was sore and she was shivering, but her hands finally stilled. She'd realized it wasn't the dirt on the outside that mattered, it was the dirt on the inside, and she didn't know how to get at it.

Thirty-seven

THE BATHROOM WAS WARM. THE HOTEL TRIUMFAL looked after its privileged guests well, and Chang An Lo heard Biao's intake of breath when he walked in and set eyes on the gold taps and the chrome and marble fittings. Biao's own accommodation in the hotel was somewhat humbler, down on the second floor, a small room above a noisy bar. Chang shut the door behind them and turned on both taps in the washbasin and then in the bath. Water flooded out in a rush, spurting around the shining porcelain, gurgling down the plug holes, filling the small space with the sound of swirling and splashing and water pipes juddering.

"Now, my friend, let us talk," Chang said in an undertone.

"Is it safe?"

"Half the time I think the listeners are asleep."

Biao still looked wary. His long arms moved restlessly at his side like bamboo leaves in the wind, his dark eyes roaming the tiled walls. Chang was thankful that he'd brought this young companion with him to Russia, and not just because it removed him from the battlefields of China and allowed his father to sleep at night. Biao was the shield at his back. He needed him.

"Don't disturb your thoughts with concern about the listeners, my brother," Chang said. He brought his lips close to Biao's ear. "In this waterfall they are deaf anyway. But when Kuan said words that were ill-chosen yesterday, neither she nor I were questioned about them, so I am certain the bearded ones find our Mandarin words as hard and unruly on the ear as we find their Russian ones."

Biao nodded.

Chang spoke quickly. "There is a way out through the bathroom window, across the roofs. I need you to go out into Moscow unobserved. You must go now, before it is time for the dinner they have planned for us tonight."

Biao nodded again, black eyes bright. "The bearded ones have wits as slow as a worm. It will be no problem."

"Thank you, my friend. *Xie xie.*"

For a moment they listened to the water.

"Is this for the *fanqui* girl?" Biao asked at last. "The one you danced with."

Chang was surprised that Biao would question him, but he nodded. His young companion rearranged his face, sucking in the walls of his cheeks.

"Comrade Chang," he muttered, "I offer my humble opinion that it is not wise to take such risks for a Foreign Devil, a *fanqui*. She is clearly not worth . . ."

Chang stiffened, a lengthening of his muscles, no more. But it was enough.

Biao bowed his head low. "Forgive my worthless tongue. It does not know when to be silent."

"It was always so," Chang laughed. "You have not changed."

"Of course it is my pleasure to perform whatever task will be of assistance to the friend of my heart."

"Thank you, Hu Biao."

"It's just that I . . ." He stopped, his head still bowed, so that the tendons at the back of his strong neck were pulled taut.

"What is it?" Chang asked.

"My tongue has no ears to listen or to learn."

"Finish what you wish to say."

Hu Biao lifted his eyes, and with their upturned tips and hooded lids they reminded Chang sharply of his father, Hu Tai-wai, the man to whom he owed so much, the man who was his father in all but name. He felt a rush of affection for his young companion.

"Spit out the words, Biao, or I shall be tempted to push my fist down your throat and drag them out myself, the way your mother pulls pups from a bitch."

He laughed and saw Biao take a breath, followed by a faint shiver of relief, and for the first time it occurred to Chang that his childhood friend viewed him with fear as much as with love. That saddened him. Had the war turned him into someone he no longer recognized? Had he left the best of himself on the killing fields of China?

"Biao, let me listen to your words of advice."

"The gods have taken good care of you, Chang An Lo. Don't tempt them to forsake you because you have swapped their attention for that of a long-nosed Foreign Devil."

"I have promised them much already. I have sworn it in the proud name of my ancestors."

"No, my comrade. The gods are fickle. Stay with your own kind. Come back to China and marry my sister, Si-qi. You know how much she loves you."

Chang smiled. "The beautiful Si-qi already has my worthless heart and that of many others too. I will always love her sweet face and her wise mind."

"Then marry her."

"I can't."

"It's what my father and mother would wish with their dying breaths."

"Ah, Biao, that is cruel. You know I can refuse them nothing."

For a long time the two men looked into each other's eyes with only the sound of the running water between them. It was Hu Biao who finally looked away.

"What is it you need, Chang An Lo?"

"I need a room."

EDIK RETURNED LATE IN THE EVENING LOOKING PLEASED WITH himself, puffing out his bony chest, and Lydia gave him a hug before he could object. He handed over a note in a hurry as though he had somewhere else to be, and then he and the pup disappeared.

The note contained an address and a street map of how to find it. The map was drawn by hand and she imagined Chang sitting in his hotel room, carefully sketching the lines for her so that she'd make no mistake. There was no *Dearest Lydia* and no signature on it. Nothing that could be traced to them.

Just four brief words at the bottom. *You are my life.*

LYDIA WAITED UNTIL SHE HEARD THE SNORES OF LIEV AND Elena, thickened by Malofeyev's bottle of vodka, and only then did she slide out of bed.

The room was black, the window blacker. Outside, the night sky had disappeared, no moon, no stars, just an emptiness that looked as if it had swallowed the city. Quickly Lydia pulled a bundle from under her bed and dressed herself in several layers of Elena's sweaters and skirts, one squeezed on top of the other, until she was fat and bulky. Only then was she satisfied.

She couldn't fit into her own coat anymore but didn't want to take Elena's, as it might be recognized by prying eyes. So instead she took her own blanket and folded it around herself like a long shawl pulled up over her hair and cheeks, padding them out. On top of it she tied a scarf, knotted under her chin. Now she would be unrecognizable in the dark. It made her feel, just for the moment, free from herself. Holding her breath, she opened the door and slipped out of the room. No one would know her.

Not even Chang An Lo.

SHE SCUTTLED ALONG THE STREET, HEAD DOWN AGAINST THE wind. Most houses were shrouded in darkness, so she could concentrate on where she was going rather than on her fear of being stopped and questioned. It was an uneven dirt road with a cemetery on one side and rows of wooden buildings propping each other up on the other. A strong odor of damp earth and pigs combined with wood smoke to make it smell like a Chinese village, and she tried to smile at the memory but couldn't. Her palms were moist and clammy inside her gloves despite the cold, and the skin at the nape of her neck prickled as though spiders were trapped under the blanket. Her pace slowed and stuttered to a halt. What was the matter with her?

Why so nervous? Why the reluctant feet?

She closed her eyes. The heavy night air weighed down on her, yet as she stood there, breathing fast, she felt the truth rise to the surface of her mind. She was frightened. Frightened they would be polite to each other.

HOW LONG SHE STOOD LIKE THAT SHE DIDN'T KNOW. THE sound of footsteps in the street roused her, and for one moment she thought Chang An Lo had come to find her. But then she saw the flashlight bobbing a yellow path toward her over the snow. No, not Chang An Lo, he wouldn't use a flashlight. She was just about to cross the road to avoid the newcomer when the beam of light swung up into her face, blinding her. She lifted a hand to shield her eyes and heard running feet, and then suddenly she was slammed against a wall, her head rebounding off something hard. Hands tore off her blanket and scrabbled roughly at her clothes. Only the numerous layers of Elena's bulky garments saved her from her attacker's intruding fingers. She lashed out with her fist at his head and heard him yelp. His skull hurt her knuckles.

"Get off me," she screamed.

"Shut up, *suka,* bitch."

"Go to hell, you bastard." She kicked out hard and found his shinbone.

A hand struck her across her mouth, flat and hard. She tasted blood. A mouth stinking of beer closed on hers. She kicked out again but couldn't breathe. His arm was pressed down on her windpipe, the weight of his body pinning her to the wall. She tried to scream. Felt her brain screech to a halt.

And suddenly it was over. With no sound her attacker released her as if he'd had enough of the fight and sat down on a pile of snow. He seemed exhausted. She dragged air into her starved throat.

"Bastard!" she gasped, and thumped his back where he sat.

Slowly, almost thoughtfully, he toppled over onto his face and lay sprawled across the snow beside the torch, his neck at an odd angle. Only then did she see the other figure, a face of hollows and shadows, a ghost risen from the churchyard opposite.

"Chang An Lo," she breathed.

"Come."

He gripped her wrist and led her away from the broken figure on the ground, striding ahead of her along the dark road so that she had to hurry to keep up. She glanced behind her, but the body hadn't moved. The night seemed to gather into something thick and solid. When they reached a paneled door on the street, he withdrew a key and inserted it into the lock. The door opened with a whine from its hinge and then they were inside. The hallway was in total blackness but she could hear his breathing. She was sure he could hear hers, labored and uneven.

He moved with no hesitation, as though he could see in the darkness, and drew her with him up a flight of stairs to a door on the first landing. He opened it, guided her into the room, and closed it behind them.

"Wait here," he whispered, placing her against a wall.

He disappeared and a moment later a match flared. His face leapt out of the night. He was lighting a gas lamp that hung from the ceiling, adjusting the slender chains that regulated the flow. She heard it hiss into life and an amber glow nudged into the room. She released her breath. The place was small with a bed, an armchair, and a bedside table. Surprisingly, a crucifix hung on the wall. But this space was all they needed.

He came to her and stood in front of her, his eyes dark and alive. Yet she knew him too well. In the uneasy set of his jaw and in the soft line of his mouth she could see the reflection of her own uncertainty. She took a breath and moved forward till her arms were entwined around his neck and his hands were on her back, holding her, caressing her, finding the reality of her under all the layers.

"My own love," she murmured and lifted her mouth to his.

As his lips found hers, hard and possessive, she felt the fragile barriers between them shift. Heard the crack as they broke into a thousand pieces, and she knew there would be no politeness.

Thirty-eight

❦

THE BLINDFOLD WAS REMOVED FROM ALEXEI'S eyes. He blinked fiercely as his vision adjusted to the sudden light and he examined his surroundings. It was an underground wine store. The stone walls were lined with racks of bottles of all shapes and sizes, the air so dusty it caught in his throat.

"Who is this?"

"Why have you brought him to us, Igor?"

The questions came from the group of about twenty young men gathered in the room, each with his shirt open to the waist. Tattoos covered their naked chests, distinctive blue messages to the outside world, and above them were lean faces and sharp suspicious eyes. None of them smiled a welcome. Shit, this looked like a bad mistake.

"Good evening, comrades," he said amiably. He nodded a greeting and tried to steer his gaze away from the tattoos, which wasn't easy. "My name is Alexei Serov."

He placed the sack he was carrying on the floor in front of them, where dust and cobwebs coated the black tiles. One of the men, with a whispery voice and his hair oiled on either side of a neat parting, stepped forward and untwisted the neck of the sack. He lifted out its contents. Immediately the tension in the air eased.

It had been an easy steal. Yet it had disgusted Alexei. Revolted him. But it was what Maksim Voshchinsky demanded, a show of his fidelity, a demonstration of his courage. A gift for the *vory*. He'd said yes immediately and gave himself no time to change his mind. That same evening he went out on the streets of Moscow to prove he was worthy of their trust, that he was as much a thief as they were and had no fear of State authority. He'd spent two hours roaming the back roads, searching out an opportunity with the same precision with which he used to reconnoiter military maneuvers. When the chance came, he took it without hesitation.

He'd moved out of the darkness of a narrow lane into a rectangle of light thrown from an open door and slipped silently through into a stranger's hallway. That's all it took to turn him into a thief, to make that jump that crossed the boundaries of decent conduct and plunged him into the wrong side of the world. His hands had reached out as though they had been performing such acts for years and removed the carved clock from the wall, as well as a small pewter vase from a table. In and out of the house in less than a minute. Less time than it took to slit your own throat.

The man who lived in the house saw nothing. He was outside in the dark street roping pieces of furniture on a cart, a horse dozing between the shafts, and he had no idea he'd just been robbed. Why someone would be shifting furniture at this hour of the night Alexei chose not to inquire, but it served his purpose well. The eagerness with which he wrapped his spoils under his coat appalled him.

He wasn't seen. Except by the short dogged figure of Igor, who hovered somewhere hidden by the darkness. He had seen. He knew.

"IT'S A GOOD CLOCK," THE MAN WITH THE HAIR OIL ANNOUNCED, and held it up for the gathering to inspect.

It was a beautiful timepiece, old and beloved, judging by the patina of polish on its case, and Alexei felt guilt, raw and spiteful, take a great bite out of his sense of self.

"It's for the *vory v zakone*, the brotherhood of the thieves-in-law,"

Alexei stated. "I offer it to this *kodla* for your *obshchak,* your communal fund."

They nodded, pleased.

"Was there a witness?" one asked.

"I bear witness," Igor said. He stood up in front of everybody, his eyes challenging any dissenters. "He stole like a professional."

"Good."

"But has he been in prison?"

"Or in one of the labor camps? Has he been in Kolyma?"

"Or worked the Belomorsko-Baltiiskii Canal?"

"Who else speaks for him?"

Alexei spoke for himself. "Brotherhood of *vory v zakone,* I am a *vor,* a thief, like you, and I am here because Maksim Voshchinsky ordered me to be brought to this place tonight. He is sick and in bed, but it is his word that speaks for me."

"There must be two who speak."

"I, Igor, speak for him. My word stands side by side with that of Maksim, our *pakhan.*"

So this was it. Dear God, he had become a *vor.* He still had much to prove before they fully accepted him as one of their own, but with Maksim behind him, he'd pushed open the door. He'd learned from his talk with Maksim that cells of *vory* criminals exactly like this one ranged throughout the length and breadth of Russia, especially in the prisons, all with the same strict code of allegiance and system of punishments. Some called them the Russian Mafia. But in reality they were very different from that Italian organization because they were not supposed to have a boss; the status of each member was meant to be equal, and family connections were rejected. The brotherhood was the only family that mattered. Decisions were made and disputes settled by the *skhodka,* the *vory* court that was as all-powerful as it was ruthless. But the *pakhan* was nevertheless in a senior position and his word counted. Maksim was the *pakhan.*

Alexei prayed to God that Maksim's name, even on his sickbed, was enough. Oddly, he felt no fear. He knew he should. He'd lied to them about his past and their punishments were harsh. But these men reminded him too much of the young recruits he'd commanded in the army training camps in Japan, except that here they had banded into a criminal fraternity rather than a military one.

They drew courage from each other as eagerly as the owner of this storeroom drew wine from the bottles. It flowed red and intoxicating. But as he studied their faces and their disfigured chests, he had a sense that these were damaged men. Both inside and out.

"So where are the older men of the *vory* brotherhood?" he'd asked Maksim.

"In prison, of course. In the labor camps. That's what the *obshchak* fund is for."

"Do you use it to get them out?"

"Sometimes. But more often to supply our brothers with food or clothes and with roubles for bribes. You see, Alexei, a prison is a *vor*'s natural home, it's where he rules. Most of our brotherhood lie behind bars because each prison sentence is a badge of pride and is marked by a new tattoo."

"That's incomprehensible."

Maksim had smiled, his eyes secretive. "To you, maybe. Not to me."

Alexei wondered what the hell was going on here. What was this man's history and what crimes had he committed? As if Maksim could read his younger friend's doubts, he rolled onto his side in the wide bed and carefully undid the buttons of his pajama jacket. He peeled it back to reveal his chest. It was broad and powerful, ribs like a bull's, with hairless tired skin.

Alexei had drawn in a breath. "Impressive."

In the center of Maksim's chest was a lavish blue tattoo of a large and elaborate crucifix.

"You see this?" The older man had prodded a stern finger at the decoration that curved above it, hanging between his collarbones. "You see this crown? That's to indicate I am the *pakhan*. The boss of our *vory* cell. Without me, they'd be nothing. What I say goes."

He yanked up his other sleeve and Alexei leaned closer, fascinated. From shoulder to wrist, tattoos crowded over every scrap of skin. An onion-domed cathedral and gentle-faced Madonna tumbled disturbingly into a tangle of barbed wire and a row of prison bars. On his bicep a death skull grinned, and on his elbow a spider's web had entangled an eagle by its wings.

Maksim watched Alexei, saw the fire rising within him. "Each one has a meaning," he said in a soft seductive whisper. "Look at my tattoos and you look at my life. God placed a mark on the world's first murderer before sending him into exile. The mark of Cain." He pulled down his sleeve and covered up his chest. "It branded its bearer as a criminal and a social outcast. Tell me, is that what you are, Alexei Serov? An outcast?"

THE PAIN WAS NOT BAD. BUT BAD ENOUGH. THE TATTOOIST turned out to be a bald man with a smooth hairless face and a teardrop tattooed at the outer corner of one eye. He was an artist who enjoyed his job, smiling to himself as he prepared to work on Alexei's chest, humming the same snatch of Beethoven's Fifth over and over again.

Alexei lit a cigarette and hoped to God he wouldn't get blood poisoning.

"It happens sometimes," the tattooist grinned. "Some even die."

Alexei blew smoke at him. "Not this time," he said as he unbuttoned his shirt.

"No smoking, please."

"I'll smoke if I choose."

"*Nyet.* Your chest must remain still as stone."

"Fuck!" Alexei said and stubbed it out.

The men in the wine store laughed as they watched, enjoying his discomfort. One thief, a wiry twenty-year-old with a rash of pock craters on his cheeks, walked over to one of the wine racks and extracted a bottle. He wiped the dust off it with his shirt sleeve and used the corkscrew on a chain by the door to remove the cork. He pushed the bottle at Alexei.

"Here, *malyutka,* drink."

"*Spasibo*, it might make you lot look a bit prettier."

The young man laughed. "What could be prettier than this, friend?" He unlaced his boot, kicked it off, and removed his sock. "Look, *tovarishch.* Is that pretty enough for you?"

It was a cat. Covering the surface of his foot, a laughing cat's face with striped fur and a large blue bow under its chin, a wide-brimmed hat on its head.

Alexei laughed. "And what does that one mean? That your feet smell like cat's piss?"

The *vor* nudged the tattooist's elbow and the needle cut deeper. Alexei didn't wince but accepted the wine.

"It means I'm sly." The *vor* narrowed his eyes. "Sly as a cat. I smell out rats."

"Hah, comrade, smell *like* a rat is what you—"

"No talking!" The needle was buzzing and stinging, busy as a wasp. "Keep still."

The tattooist had tattoos on his knuckles, a mix of letters and numbers that meant nothing unless you knew the code. His breath smelled of beer strongly enough to make Alexei turn his face away. He let his eyes close, and unexpected images came to him. It was the sharp burning point of the needle that brought them, its stinging pain on his chest. He remembered another day with a similar pain, his final day in Leningrad when he was twelve. His mother, the Countess Serova, was whisking him away to China, away from the Bolshevik troubles, and Jens had come to say good-bye. He had shaken Alexei's hand as if he were a grown man and asked him to take care of his mother. "I'm proud of you," Jens had said, and Alexei recalled now the sorrow in his green eyes, the sun burnishing his hair as he rode away on his horse and the crippling pain in his own chest. Not on the skin like this, but deep inside his flesh and his bones.

Lydia had once said to him, "The trouble with you, Alexei, is that you're too damn arrogant."

Look at me now, Lydia. No arrogance left, is there? Here I am in rags, at the mercy of a gang of thieves, my skin massacred in the midst of filth and unclean needles. Humble enough for you now? And if they find I'm lying about having been a prisoner at Trovitsk camp they will remove this brand of membership with acid. Or worse, with a knife.

"Look at him." It was the whispery voice of the one with the hair oil. "He's fallen asleep."

"Trying to show how tough he is."

"Too bored to stay awake."

"He's an arrogant bastard. What the fuck does Maksim want with him?"

Alexei opened his eyes, stared directly at the faces, and lifted the bottle to his lips. He took a long drowning drink.

★ ★ ★

CHANG WAS GENTLE WITH HER. GENTLER THAN LYDIA REMEM-bered from before. As if he feared she would break. Or was it that he'd grown used to delicate Chinese orchids who had to be handled carefully? She heard herself whimpering. She tried to silence the sound but couldn't because she wanted him to tear her apart and put her back together in such a way that she was fused with him, body and soul.

But as he caressed her, stroked her, kissed her breasts, explored her naked body as if it were familiar territory he was committing to memory once more, she felt something inside her break loose. She started to shake. Her bones seemed to be emptying, releasing some-thing bad from within, all the pain and the fear and the anger and the yearning. It came flooding out of her.

He held her. He rocked her in his arms, murmuring, soothing, locking her so tight against his heart that she lost all sense of boundar-ies and mistook its strong beat for her own. She clung to him, breathed him in, felt him slowly, breath by breath, become a part of her again.

And when the flow of his hand on her skin had quieted the trem-ors within her and the sounds in her head, he kissed her mouth with a harsh hunger that made her ache. She realized he'd known she wasn't ready before. How was it that he could know her better than she knew herself? Her limbs entwined with his and she kept her eyes fixed on his as they found each other all over again.

HER SKIN STILL SMELLED THE SAME. IT GLISTENED WITH SWEAT and soothed Chang's fear that his fox girl might have traveled too far from him. Until she trembled in his arms, he thought he'd lost her to the Russian with the wolf eyes. He brushed his lips along the soft hollow at the base of her throat and heard a moan, though he didn't know if it was from his own lips or hers.

He lay on his side and gazed at her. At her arms, at her chin, at the scar on her breast. At the intense moist mound of red curls between her legs, a fire inside and out. She was beautiful. Not in a Chinese way. For Oriental taste, her hands and her feet and even her knees were too big and her nose too long, but he loved those parts of her.

Her skin was pale and shimmered like river water in the dim golden light, yet when he touched the flat plain of her stomach or the tight muscles of her thigh he could sense a fine steel mesh under the flesh. Had that been there before?

No, that was new.

In Junchow she had shown a determination he had never before found in a female, a courage he'd thought belonged only to men. She had opened his eyes and taught him otherwise. But this new inner strength of hers, this was something different. It made his pulse miss a beat. This had been forged by her journey through Russia, and he felt a stab of guilt that he had not been there at her side. It stole a part of her from his soul. As if the greedy gods had decided to keep his fox girl for themselves after all instead of giving her to him.

"Lydia."

The night was passing too quickly.

"Lydia, tell me where your father is."

She tucked her face into his chest and said nothing.

"Have you discovered yet where he is?" he persisted.

"He's here," she muttered against his skin.

"In Moscow?"

She nodded.

"That's good news."

She shrugged in the crook of his arm and he remembered it, that gesture of her thin shoulders. A small gesture of defiance. He'd forgotten how each little movement of hers had the power to creep into his heart.

He stroked her back, waiting.

"I can't find him," she murmured in a flat tone.

"Tell me. Tell me what you do know."

He felt her ribs quiver.

"I discovered that he's been moved from Trovitsk labor camp to a secret prison in Moscow. But I don't know where it is." She raised her head, amber eyes questioning. "Why would they do that?"

"He was an engineer, wasn't he?"

"Yes."

"Perhaps they are using his skills to work on something."

"I thought the bastards had moved him for"—the word seemed to stick in her throat—"experiments."

He frowned. "What kind of experiments?"

"Medical ones. I've heard rumors that this kind of thing goes on, and I thought the secret prison in Moscow could be for that."

"Human guinea pigs?"

"Yes."

"Oh, Lydia, you really believe that's what's happened to him?"

She rubbed her face against his skin. "I don't know."

"Let's believe it is his engineering ability that they want. You said he was one of the best."

"He was one of the chief advisers to the tsar before . . . all this." She balanced her chin on his chest and looked up at him.

"You know nothing more? Just that he was moved to Moscow?"

"I have the prison number."

"What is it?"

"Number 1908."

He narrowed his eyes, contemplating the possibilities and the impossibilities, while she laid her cheek on his naked chest again and remained quiet. He looked down at the glorious tangle of hair and the clean line of her forehead. How could he tell her? How could he make her see that maybe her father wouldn't welcome her interference. That perhaps it could put at risk a life he was building for himself now.

LYDIA SLIPPED INTO HER ROOM, HER *VALENKI* BOOTS DANGLING in one hand so as to make no noise in her stocking feet. It was snowing outside, the night suddenly alive with huge damp flakes. As Chang had walked her through the damp streets of Moscow, she'd asked him about China. He talked of his travels in Canton and of city life in Shanghai, but she knew his voice better than she knew her own. She could sense the secrets hiding like shadows behind his words. She didn't push or pry. But what he didn't say frightened her. Her hand tucked into his and she held him safe.

At the corner of her road he kissed her good-bye and she rested her forehead against his cold cheekbone.

"Tomorrow?" he asked.

"Tomorrow."

She didn't turn on the light in the room but threw off the wet blanket and knew she wouldn't sleep.

"So you're back."

Lydia froze. "You're up early, Elena."

"And you're up late."

"I was restless. I went for a walk."

They were both talking in whispers, and Lydia realized with relief that Liev must be still asleep. She could just make out Elena's bulk in the chair. How long had she been sitting like that?

"You went for a walk?"

"Yes."

Elena gave a low laugh. "*Maleeshka*, little one, it's me you're talking to, not the Cossack. I am a whore and I know the smell of men and the smell of sex. You stink of both."

The night hid the flush that rose to Lydia's cheeks. She started to undress, to peel off the clothes that belonged to Elena, unconsciously smelling them, searching for Chang.

"Elena, it's kind of you to sit up for me but you don't need to worry so much. I can take care of myself."

"Can you?"

"Yes."

Elena gave a little snort. "Come here, *maleeshka*."

Lydia tugged her nightdress down over her head, went over to the chair, and knelt down beside it, so that their heads were close. In the unlit room eyes were just dark holes in paler moons. Elena's hand found Lydia's shoulder.

"Leave him, Lydia. Let the Chinese go."

It hurt. Even the thought of it hurt.

"Why do you say such a thing, Elena?"

"Because he's no good for you. No, don't look away, listen to what I'm saying. Why would a Chinese Communist be so interested in a little Russian chit of a girl?"

Lydia wanted to shout, *Because he loves me, of course,* but the question made her nervous. It was one she had asked herself a thousand times.

"Why do you think, Elena?" she asked softly.

"He wants to get between your sheets, that goes without saying, a Western girl notch on his bedpost."

"Don't."

"But that isn't the main reason, is it?"

"No." Now she would hear the words she wanted: *It's because he loves you.*

"It's because he's using you, girl. Simple as that."

"Using me?"

"Yes."

"How?"

"That's for you to find out. You're not stupid. Maybe the Chinese have ordered him to find out through your friendship with that Russian officer what is going on behind the smiles at the Kremlin. Who knows?"

"No, you're wrong. Wrong, I tell you." She couldn't swallow.

"Hush, *maleeshka*. You'll wake Liev." Suddenly her hand touched Lydia's cheek, a brief caress in the dark room. "What is it? Is he keeping secrets from you, little one? Can you trust him?"

Lydia pulled away angrily, remembering the shadows behind Chang's words. "More to the point, can I trust you?"

"Hah, a good question. But think about this, girl. What future is there in it for him? Or for you?"

"Elena," she said, flat and firm, so that Elena would know. "I trust him. I trust him with my life."

"More fool you, girl." She leaned closer, her nightclothes musty. "I don't want to see you hurt."

"I won't be. Not by him."

A silence trickled into the room, a small stream of it between them, and they both waited to see who would be first to cross it.

"Picture this," Elena whispered in a rush. "That your Soviet admirer, this Malofeyev, knows about you and your Chinese friend. And that is why he brought you just food today instead of the information you want on Jens Friis. He is jealous. He doesn't like you being with another man and so will not be as obliging as he might. It seems you can't have both, little one. Your Chinese or your father. You must choose."

Lydia rose from her knees. She uttered no sound, but curled up on her bed and pulled the damp blanket over her head. The ache inside her throat was strangling her. She thrust Elena's words away into somewhere dark and unreachable, and instead she flooded her mind with the hours spent in the room with the crucifix on the wall, holding those moments up to the light. Polishing them. Making them shine.

Thirty-nine

JENS FOUND HIS MIND DISTRACTED. THE NIGHT-mares visited more often. They broke his routine, chipped his night's sleep into pieces. He was restless, pacing the workroom for hours on end, aware that the work he had so relished over the past months had turned sour in his mouth as it came closer to completion.

Not like when he first came to this unit. Then it had been a dream come true. This was work, real work, the kind of engineering he had been bred to. It was what he'd craved, the way a drowning man craves air. He used to wake up each morning convinced that he had finally died, slumped over his shovel on the icy wastes of the labor camp, and been transported up to heaven. Ahead of him stretched a day of handling pens and papers and brass calipers instead of skin freezing to axes and shovels and his guts weeping with hunger. Even now every day he opened his eyes and couldn't believe his good fortune.

The prison camp had been bad. That's as far as he ever allowed his mind to go, no further. Twelve years of bad, but now it had ended. He didn't let it into his

head any more, not into his conscious mind anyway. But he didn't
pretend to himself. He knew it was in there somewhere, hiding deep
in the darkest coils of his brain, where it only slithered out at night.
So he had dreams. Nightmares. So what? He shrugged them off as a
minor inconvenience. If people regarded a few unpleasant dreams as
bad, they hadn't been in a camp.

Since he'd learned of his daughter's search for him, thoughts of
Valentina and Lydia were distracting him, stirring up emotions he
had long ago forgotten how to handle. Especially as now there was
Olga. He ceased his pacing. Here in this safe and cozy haven he had
rediscovered things. Things he valued. Work. Warmth. Food. And
love? Yes, even that. A kind of love, very different from what he'd
known before but still love. He'd thought it had vanished from his
heart forever, but it had sneaked in through hairline cracks in the
shell he'd constructed around himself. He smiled because he knew
now from Olga, a scientist, that a smile sent certain chemicals racing to the brain, chemicals that magically make you feel better. And
God knows, he needed to feel better. She'd taught him that the more
you smile, the more you want to smile. So he practiced it each day,
and the muscles around his mouth that had grown stiff and gritty
with disuse started to soften and come to life.

Olga had taught him much. Not just as a chemist but as a person;
she taught him to become a member of the human race again, and it
pained him that there was nothing he could do in return to fill the
black agony inside her that was caused by her daughter being left
behind in the lead mine.

"I pray each night, Jens," she'd told him one day when they were
working together on realigning a gas cylinder, "that my Valerya will
be killed in a cave-in. They happen often, tons of rock collapsing
with a roar like a train in a tunnel. *Whoosh* and it's over. It would be
quick. But then I hate myself. What kind of mother would wish such
a thing on her daughter?"

He'd brushed her hand for a brief moment. "One who loves
her."

Her tear had dropped on the blueprint in front of them and
before one of the sharp-eyed watchers noticed it, he had swept it
aside, smudging the ink. The tiny drop of salty fluid had felt warm
and intimate on his skin and he hadn't wiped it away, instead letting

it dry on his skin. At first his and Olga's paths crossed only rarely, though they inevitably saw each other in the exercise courtyard each morning and evening during the enforced parade of prisoners for half an hour in rain, wind, or snow. But as the project progressed they worked together more often, sometimes three or four times a month, and now that the visits to the hangars were occurring every few days, he found himself doing something he hadn't done for many years: anticipating.

In the camps he'd lived from moment to moment because it was the only way to survive. Never think about tomorrow and all the other tomorrows. Never. It was a cardinal rule. But now he found himself taking that risk, looking at the future from behind laced fingers. It was so new to him. He thought he'd forgotten how. To anticipate something, anything, took a ridiculous amount of courage. Just to look forward to something as small as a meeting with a friend in a black truck felt good.

But now his distracted mind had run away from him. It was anticipating all on its own and it made him nervous.

SO WHEN THE DOOR TO HIS WORKROOM SWUNG OPEN WITH a bang as it slammed into the wall behind, it came as a relief.

"Ah, Comrade Babitsky, do join me."

The guard walked over to the table, his boots squeaking on the linoleum floor. He placed a roll of engineering drawings on it, treating them with respect. He was a large lumbering man, good-looking with thick fair hair, but he had the faintly bemused look in his eyes of someone who is not quite sure where he's going. He'd joined the team of guards only recently, and Jens was interested to see that he had not yet managed to overcome his awe at such a gathering of impressive brains.

"Who is it from this time, Comrade Babitsky?"

"Unit four."

"Ah, the squabblers."

"Prisoner Elkin and Prisoner Titov. They're not speaking to each other."

Jens rested his elbows on his desk and chewed on the end of his pen. It gave him such intense pleasure to hold a pen after all those years without that he was reluctant to put it down even for a moment. He'd even been known to sleep with one wrapped up in his tight fist, a talisman against the nightmares.

"You have to understand," he said, "that scientists and engineers like to argue. It's how they sharpen their minds."

"Then Prisoner Elkin and Prisoner Titov should have bloody sharp minds."

Jens laughed. "They do."

He remembered in the camp, the starvation of the mind. Starvation of the body he'd learned to live with, but a blank nothing in the mind was a form of death. Twelve long years of dying.

"Tell me, Babitsky, are you married?"

"I was," the guard said gruffly.

"What happened?"

"The usual. She got her tail tied up with my neighbor, a metal-worker from Omsk, and left."

"Any children?"

His big face grew soft and he chuckled. "My son, Georgi. He's five."

"Do you still see him?"

"*Da*. Once a month I take the train to Leningrad. That's where my boy is living. It's better now I'm here in Moscow. When I was stationed in Siberia I only saw him at Easter time."

Siberia. Jens studied his guard and was astonished at the way he could look at this man without anger. Maybe that was a necessary part of the process, the way of returning to the human race. It was ironic. Babitsky didn't recognize him. Now that Jens was well fed and clean shaven and wore a pair of rimless spectacles for close work, the guard didn't remember him. But Jens remembered Babitsky, oh yes, he remembered him well. In Trovitsk camp Babitsky wasn't nearly so polite. He possessed a liking for jabbing his rifle butt between fragile shoulder blades.

"Friis." Babitsky leaned closer. "I like the way you don't look at me like I'm some piece of shit on the bottom of your boot, the way some of the scientists here do."

Jens looked at him, startled.

Babitsky lowered his voice to a whisper. "I heard something the other day, something I thought you might want to know."

"What's that?" Jens slid the end of the pen into his mouth.

"They're thinking of bringing in a new team to finish this project. I don't know what the fuck it is that you do, but someone up the ladder obviously does know and thinks you all aren't doing the job you were brought here for. So you're out."

"No."

"Oh yes, so just watch your step."

Jens froze. His face hurt where his teeth were clamped like a vise around the pen. "Who said?"

"Colonel Tursenov."

"No," Jens said again. "He can't do that."

"Don't be stupid, Friis. Of course he can."

"But it's our design, it's the result of all this team's hard work, our careful calculations and efforts, our successes and, yes, our errors too. He can't take it away, it's"—his voice was growing agitated but he was unable to stop it—"it's *my* project."

The words were out. He couldn't take them back.

Babitsky gave him a look that placed them firmly back in the roles of guard and prisoner. "Friis, whatever the hell it is you and the team do here, sure as fuck it isn't yours. It's the Soviet State's project. It's Stalin's project. So don't think just because you're using your brain that you have suddenly got any rights here. You don't. You're still a nobody, a nonperson. A prisoner. Don't ever forget that."

The big guard walked out of the workroom and slammed the door behind him with relish. The key grated as it turned in the lock.

Forty

LYDIA LEFT THE HOUSE EARLY WHILE LIEV AND
Elena still slept. She wanted time to herself, needed
room to breathe, space to think about Chang. But
she could no more think straight than she could walk
straight on the city's sidewalks, which were still thick
with mounds of ice at this hour. She was not thinking of him, but being him. There was no other word
for it. Being a part of him, as he was a part of her.
Already she missed the physical weight of him and
the feel of his skin next to hers. Her feet moved faster,
stretching her stride.

"No, Elena, you're wrong," she whispered as she
walked. "I trust Chang with my life ten times over."

"Talking to yourself?"

It was Edik. He'd sneaked up on her as she crossed
the street and fell into step beside her. He carried his
usual pack on his chest, and the little dog's domed
head rose out of it with golden eyes as round and
watchful as an owl's.

"Do you need me to take another message?" he
asked.

"No, not today. Thanks anyway."

He looked disappointed. "So where are you going?"

"To stand in line for bread."

"Can I come?"

"Of course."

She wasn't sure whether it was her company he wanted or the bread. Either was fine with her. They walked together past a row of shops, enjoying the bright morning sunshine despite the snow thick on the ground. She noticed he was up on his toes again, bouncing with energy, eyes darting everywhere. It was, she decided, his eyes that betrayed him. He had thief's eyes. She must warn him of that, but not now.

"Are you warmer in your new coat?" she asked.

He grinned. "It's all right."

"You must thank Elena."

"If I thank her nicely, do you think she'll boil me some more *pelmeni*? And cook a sausage for Misty?" He winked one of his blue eyes slyly at her. "I needn't bother with thanks if she won't."

Lydia laughed, putting an arm across his thin shoulders as they walked down the street, and to her surprise he didn't shrug it off.

ALEXEI FELT THE SUNLIGHT SETTLE ON HIS SKIN. HE WAS standing on the steps of the Cathedral of Christ the Redeemer and relished this moment of stillness. The last twenty-four hours had been anything but still. Hell, his head felt heavy from last night. Too much wine and too many cigarettes. He closed his eyes. Minutes passed. He thought about Jens Friis and offered up a small prayer to the God he didn't believe in. *Let him be alive.* On the steps of God's glorious house, surely he would listen if he was in there.

"Hello, Alexei. So you got here at last."

He didn't bother opening his eyes. He was sure the voice was coming from inside his own head, but it was so real he smiled and conjured up the teasing stare that would go with the words.

"Alexei?"

A hand touched his arm. Dimly something jarred. He realized he was falling asleep standing up, like a lazy old horse, and he opened

his eyes with an effort. She was here, right in front of him, her hand
on his arm holding him upright, and it occurred to him that she was
swaying. Or was it him?

"Alexei," she said softly, and kissed his cheek.

HE FELT THE WARMTH OF HER SMALL ARM TUCK THROUGH HIS,
and she led him onto a tram. It was crowded, full of bodies wrapped
in *fufaikas* and headscarves and battered old cloth caps, but Lydia
pushed her way to a seat for him and sat him down in it. She stood
over him, hanging onto a strap, and he had the odd sensation that
she was guarding him.

The windows had steamed up, boxing him in, so he had little
idea of where they were heading. Each time the doors clanked open
he caught a glimpse of streets he didn't know as people piled on and
off, but he was more disconcerted by the care with which Lydia was
keeping anyone from jostling against him and the frequent glances
she directed at him. They were so attentive, full of a gentleness he'd
not seen in his sister before. Where had that come from? Where
were the sparks and the fire and the impatience? Her concern worried him. Did he really look that bad? Did he need to be treated like
a sick kitten?

"Time to get off, Alexei."

"Right," he said, but continued to sit there.

She didn't yell or shout or tell him he was a lazy bastard, which is
what he half expected. Instead she bent down, smiled into his eyes
as she positioned her arms under his armpits, and straightened up,
scooping him up with her. He was embarrassed. He had a feeling he
probably smelled.

"I didn't sleep at all last night," he explained.

"And how many days ago did you last eat?"

"I don't know."

It made him sound stupid. She held his hand and led him off the
tram. The air outside was crisp and bright and it startled him.

"Alexei," Lydia said, "how did you get in such a mess?"

"I'm not sure. I got lost."

"Well, let's see if we can find our way home, brother. Without
getting separated this time."

She laughed as she threaded his arm through hers. It gave him hope.

HE ROLLED INTO BED WITH ONE THOUGHT FLICKERING THROUGH his head. He hadn't told her about the *vory*. But before he could open his mouth to let her know, the flickering died out and he had no idea what the thought had been. His eyelids sank as if dragged down by lead weights. It was black inside his head and he liked it that way.

He slept. His dreams were so busy it seemed that he was dead to the world for a whole month, but each time his eyelids lifted a crack, Lydia was sitting by his bed wearing the same brown cardigan. It had to be all the same day. At one point he heard raised voices, but he had no interest in them and drifted back into the blackness, unsure whether the sounds were in his head. Then a door slammed. That was real.

He dreamed that a tattooist's vibrating needle plunged right through his chest wall, penetrating his lungs, and he began to drown in his own blood. He choked violently. A hand stroked his forehead and he slept again. But there was something he needed to say. It was sticking spikes in his brain.

LYDIA SAT AND WATCHED HER BROTHER. HE'D SLEPT FOR HOURS, though she could scarcely call it sleep. More like running a race with eyes tightly shut. His body was never still, eyelids twitching, legs scrabbling, arms flailing. His teeth clenching and unclenching, releasing sounds that belonged to a dog. She learned to place a hand on his cheeks and whisper words to drive out whatever demon had dug a hole for itself inside his head. When the door opened and Liev Popkov stumbled into the room, she knew he would not be best pleased.

"Hello, Liev," she smiled up at him. "Look who's here."

"*Dermo!* Shit!"

"He was on the steps of the cathedral. I told you he'd be there one day soon."

"Shit!" he said again and walked over to her bed, scowling down at Alexei with his one black eye.

"Let him sleep," she said.

"Skin and fucking bone, that's all there is to him. And he stinks like a horse's arse."

"It doesn't matter."

"I was sure the bastard was dead in Felanka somewhere."

Lydia looked up at him, shocked. "You never said."

He grunted.

"I've said he can stay here."

Popkov snorted. "No, he can't."

"Damn you, I say he can."

"*Nyet.*"

"What do you expect me to do? Throw my brother out on the street?"

"Yes. He can't stay."

"Why not?"

"He doesn't have a resident's permit, so he'll bring the police down on our necks."

She forced down the hard lump in her throat. "We can get him one on the black market."

Slowly Popkov turned his shaggy head, beard first, and glowered at Lydia in the chair. "You would use the few good roubles we have left? The ones we need to spend on finding Jens Friis? You'd use them on this worthless piece of shit?"

"Yes."

"Ha! Then you are not your father's daughter."

Lydia leapt to her feet. "Take that back, you dumb Cossack."

He stood immobile in front of her, and she knew he would take back nothing. She slapped his stubborn chest hard with the flat of her hand and he caught her wrist, held her until she was quiet. His big scarred face leaned down to hers and she could see the creases in it deepen.

"Lydia, my little friend, you must decide what it is you want. Use that clever mind of yours. Who is it you have come here to find?"

He released her wrist, lumbered out of the room without a glance at Alexei and slammed the door behind him.

LYDIA SAT QUIETLY AGAIN IN THE CHAIR. BUT THIS TIME SHE didn't sip her tea, even though her throat was burning. Instead she forced herself to handle the words Liev had thrown in her lap, to turn them endlessly around and around the way a potter turns his wheel. *Who is it you've come to find?*

Who is it? Who?

My father. It's my father I've come to find, Jens Friis. The words sounded faint inside her head, so she repeated them out loud.

"I've come to find my father, Jens Friis."

But voices dragged at her mind. Sharp as fingernails on a windowpane. She sank her head into her hands, burying her fingers in her hair as if she could tease out the lies from the truth among the tangle of its strands. She heard a low whimper. She looked around, surprised, expecting Misty to crawl out from under one of the beds, and she was horrified when it dawned on her that it had come from herself.

A hand touched her knee. For a moment it startled her. With an effort she came back into herself, into the room, into the present, and realized it was her brother's hand she was staring at. Strong fingers, blue veins snaking deep under the skin, a scar on one knuckle, a long crimson scab down the thumb. But dirty nails, grimy skin. Not the hand she remembered.

"Alexei," she smiled at him. "I'm sorry if I woke you."

"Are you all right?"

She widened her smile. "More importantly, are you all right?"

He nodded. "I'm fine."

"You don't look fine."

"I just need something to eat."

"You've certainly slept a long time." She patted his hand and rose to her feet. "I'll go and heat some soup."

She was aware of his eyes on her as she left the room, but when she returned with a tray of soup, a chunk of black bread, and a slice of Malofeyev's smoked ham, he said little, just a polite "*Spasibo.*" He sat on the edge of the bed and she let him eat in peace, but when he'd finished she rose from her chair and sat beside him.

"Take care," he said with a crooked sort of smile, "I probably have fleas."

"Looking at the state of you, I think they're more in danger from you than you are from them."

He smiled, and she caught a glimpse of the old Alexei in it.

"Tell me what happened to you, Alexei. I waited for you in Felanka for weeks, but you didn't come and I thought you'd left me behind. Gone off on your own."

He frowned. "You are my sister, Lydia. How could you think I would do such a thing?"

Guilt, thick and sticky, rose in her chest. She picked up his hand and held it between her own, resting them on her knee. "Because I'm stupid." She shrugged and was relieved when he smiled. "So where did you go?" she asked.

He took a breath. She waited, watching the tension in the tendons of his neck, and after a long silence he told her. About the attack on him by prison guards in Felanka, the drowning in the black choking waters of the river, and then finding himself on a boat.

"I lost our money, Lydia. Every bloody rouble of it."

"Even what was hidden in your boots?"

"Even those."

She forced herself not to react. Willed her hands not to tremble. "You should have let me look after half of it, Alexei. You should have trusted me."

"I know. You're right, I'm sorry." He shook his head and his hair sent out a smell of something bad. "But what good is *sorry* to us now?"

"None."

"Lydia, I can't get that money back, but I'm doing everything in my power to make up for . . ." He exhaled sharply. It was an angry disappointed sound that joined Lydia's own anger and own disappointment. "For my hubris," he finished.

"Your hubris?"

"My pride. My arrogance, my blind belief in my invincibility. Look at me. Nothing to be proud of now, is there?"

"You're wrong. I am still proud to have you as my brother."

He threw back his head and barked a noise that unnerved her until she realized it was meant as a laugh. "God knows why!"

She studied the gaunt face. The eyes sunken in their sockets, mulberry patches like bruises on his skin. It had changed. Some crucial part of who he was had been stolen from it, something far more important than the money.

"Was it so hideous, Alexei? Your journey to Moscow."

"Oh, Lydia, you wouldn't believe what I saw. The suffering and the greed, the anger and the enmity. Brother against brother, father against son, all so convinced they have the right answer. In one village I saw the *Komsomols* burning a man's possessions in the street because he couldn't pay his taxes. His wife threw herself and her baby on the bonfire and had to be dragged off it."

"Oh, Alexei."

"I understand at last what Communism is about. I know they spout about justice and equality, but it's much more than that. It's about changing the whole way mankind is made. Turning them away from being people and making them into a new and improved mass creation that allows for none of the weaknesses inherent in mankind. To do that, the State must become a god and at the same time a monster."

"That is a bleak future you see for Russia."

"How else can we make this unwieldy and godforsaken country work?"

"You sound like Chang An Lo."

For the first time he looked at her hard, a fierce stare that felt as though he were using a shovel to dig around inside her.

"He's here?"

"Yes. He is part of a Chinese Communist delegation to Moscow."

"I see."

He said no more, just the two flat words. But he looked around the room, taking in its stained wallpaper and shabby curtains, and she could see him thinking what a disgusting little room it was.

"It's all we can afford," she explained. "Popkov and Elena are living here with me. We were lucky to get it at all. Rooms are like gold dust in Moscow. It's not easy, Alexei. Nothing here is easy. It's the way life is."

He lowered his chin to his chest. "And Jens? What news of him?"

"Not good. We've been searching to find the prison he's in, but people are too frightened. They won't talk."

"I see," he said again.

She wondered if he did. She pressed his hand to make him look directly at her again, and when he did she wanted to tell him that she was just as frightened as everyone else and she didn't blame any of them for keeping their mouths firmly shut. She wanted to say that having Chang An Lo here in Moscow made her come alive again, but at the same time she was seething with rage at the Soviet watchers for making it so hard for them to be together. She wanted to tell Alexei that having her brother here in her room made her feel safe, even though he was in a worse state than she was. But what about their father? What kind of world was he in? Was he surviving? How in this twisted and secretive city would they ever be able to find him? *Tell me how. How?* Yet when she looked into Alexei's eyes, which used to be green but now were the color of mud, she said none of it.

Instead she smiled at him. "I'm so pleased you're here, as safe and as handsome as ever under all that filth."

"Thank you, Lydia. You know I wouldn't abandon you to do this alone."

She felt two hot tears trickle down her cheeks. Alexei brushed a thumb lightly along her cheekbones, wiping the tears away with an affection that she knew she didn't deserve after all the times she'd sworn at him behind his back.

"I'm happy," he said, "to see you happy."

She was just working out whether he meant it or was just trying to please her when a heavy fist banged on the door. Twice. They froze, his thumb still on her skin, her fingers still clasping his other hand on her knee.

"No," she whispered. "No."

Quickly she bundled her brother back into bed, pulled the blanket up to his ears, and tucked it tightly around him.

"Don't move," she hissed.

Then she opened the door.

OUTSIDE ON THE LANDING STOOD THREE MEN. LYDIA TOOK one look at them and slammed the door in their face.

"Who is it?" Alexei was struggling up in the bed.

"It's bad news."

"Police?"

"No."

"Who, Lydia? Tell me."

She had her back pressed to the door, breathing hard. "They look like killers."

Alexei tumbled out of bed and moved close to the door, listening. The fist slammed on the door again, three bangs this time.

"Alexei Serov," a rough voice called out. "Open this fucking door or I'll kick it down."

Lydia stared in horror at Alexei. "They know you. Who are they?"

Alexei leaned around her, took hold of the doorknob, and clicked the door open. "My dear sister," he said with a smile so crooked it made him look like a stranger, "I'd like you to meet my new friends."

Forty-one

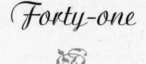

"THEY TOOK HIM AWAY. IN A CAR."

"They're welcome to the bastard."

"Liev," Lydia snapped, "shut that foul mouth of yours."

The big man laughed. Elena smacked him. "So who the hell were these people?" she asked. She was more agitated than Lydia expected.

"I don't know," she moaned. "They were rough. Shabby but wore good boots."

"You noticed their boots?"

Lydia shrugged. Yes, she noticed boots. They told you more about what lay in a man's wallet than any amount of furs on his back.

"They had hard cold eyes and hard cold smiles."

"But were they his friends?" Elena asked. "He told you they were his new friends."

"They were no more his friends than rats are friends to day-old chicks."

"Did they give any idea where they were taking him?"

"No."

"Did he look frightened?"

"Alexei would never let it show if he were." Lydia thought back to it, pictured for the hundredth time Alexei's expression as he walked out the door. His back was straight, his stride stiff-legged, and he reminded her of the dogs that circle each other, bristling, before hurling themselves at each other's throats. She shivered.

"Elena, I can't lose him again."

Liev's teeth flashed somewhere in the depths of his black beard. "Don't fret, little Lydia. It'll take more than a rat or two to kill off that bastard brother of yours."

"There's something else."

"What?"

"I remember that one of them wasn't wearing gloves. He was standing in the doorway with hands stuck in his coat pockets, watching the corridor."

"So?"

"So I was scared he'd have a gun in there. But just as the other two were walking out with Alexei between them, this man took his hands out of his pockets and they were empty. But I saw that right across his middle fingers he had dark tattoos."

Nobody moved. Nobody spoke. It was as if the room had splintered.

"What?" Lydia demanded. "What is it? What have I said?"

"Tattoos," Popkov growled.

"Yes." Lydia seized his massive arm and shook it hard. "What does it mean?"

Elena and Popkov exchanged a look. Lydia's pulse was suddenly pounding, a noise like water rushing through her brain, flushing away her control.

"Who are they? Who are these rats?"

Elena's face changed. Her concern was replaced by disgust, and her fleshy mouth twitched with distaste. "It's the *vory v zakone*," she muttered. "He's in with the *vory*."

"Those words—*vory v zakone*—Lydia had heard them before, from the girl on the train."

The Cossack sank down on Lydia's narrow bed, making its metal frame yowl like a tomcat. "The *vory*," he muttered, sighing out a great rush of stale air. "He's a dead man."

Lydia thought she'd heard wrong. She could feel the spaces in her chest shaking, and it seemed to shake the whole house.

"Tell me, Liev, who these *vory* are."

"Criminals."

"A criminal brotherhood," Elena explained.

Lydia sat herself down beside Popkov on the bed. "Tell me more."

"They use tattoos all over their bodies to show allegiance. The *vory v zakone*, thieves-in-law, is what they call themselves. I've come across them before. It started in the prisons and labor camps, but now they're all over the cities of Russia like a fucking plague."

"Why would they want Alexei? He's not a thief."

Popkov grunted and offered no answer. Lydia leaned against his arm as though it were a wall. "Why the tattoos?"

"Apparently each tattoo means something," Elena said. "It's like a secret language within the brotherhood. And just the sight of the tattoos warns people off."

"Are they dangerous?"

They hesitated. It was slight, but she didn't miss it. Then Popkov clapped her on the back with his great bear's paw, which made her teeth sink into her tongue. She sucked the blood off it.

"Come on, little Lydia," Popkov frowned at her, "you don't need him. We manage well enough without this brother of yours."

His eyebrows, black horny beetles, descended above the broad bridge of his nose, and he raised his arm only just in time to ward off her punch to his face. With a growl he wrapped both his arms around her slight frame so that she couldn't move. She sat with the weight of her head on his chest and started at last to think clearly.

"If he's with these criminals, these *vory*," she said into his stinking coat, "the boy will know. Edik will have an idea where to find them." She wriggled free and jumped to her feet. "Elena, I'm going to need some sausage for the dog."

EDIK, WHERE ARE YOU?

Lydia was running down the stairs when the front door opened. The concierge had scuttled across the hallway with the movements of an arthritic mouse to do her duty at the door. She made a note of the visitor's name and scuttled out of sight back to her mouse hole at the rear of the house with a speed that should have alerted Lydia. But she was preoccupied, working out where to start her search for the boy.

"Good evening, Lydia. *Dobroi nochi.*"

In the drab hallway with its brown walls and its halfhearted lamp, Lydia had not even given the visitor a glance. She did so now and her feet came to a halt.

"Antonina. I didn't expect to see you here."

The elegant woman smiled. "I found your address in Dmitri's diary. I hope you don't mind."

"Of course not. You're always welcome."

"I've come to talk to you, but it seems you're on your way out."

Lydia hesitated. She was in a hurry. But just the sight of this woman, with her long dark hair loose on her shoulders and her fur coat collar turned high up around her small ears like a fortress against the world, made her want to stay.

"Walk with me," Lydia said and headed for the door.

In the street Antonina's soft gray boots struggled to keep up and Lydia made herself slow down, though it hurt to do so. The sky was a sooty gray, sinking down onto the city roofs, nearly dark now, and even at this hour there were lines outside the butcher's, women shuffling in sawdust in the hope that more meat might arrive. A scrap of belly pork. A fistful of bones for soup.

"You're looking well," Lydia commented, and steered them across the road, picking a path around a pile of frozen horse dung.

Antonina smiled again, a small twist of her wide mouth, and flicked her hair from her collar. Lydia wished she wouldn't do that. Her mother used to use the exact same gesture.

"You're the one looking well, Lydia," Antonina said. "Quite different, in fact. You seem"—she tipped her head to one side and inspected Lydia—"happy."

"I like Moscow. It suits me."

"Obviously. But take care, Lydia. There are many whisperers."

For a moment as they walked step for step alongside each other, their gaze held on each other, and then they looked away and concentrated on avoiding the patches of ice.

"What have you come for?" Lydia asked eventually when

it seemed Antonina was going to trot at her side forever with no explanation.

"Dmitri tells me things sometimes, you know. Particularly when he's had a few brandies."

"What things?"

"Things like where your father is."

Lydia almost fell flat on her face as she walked straight into a heap of soiled snow.

"Tell me," she said, her lips dry.

"He's in a prison here in Moscow, a secret prison."

More? Please let there be more. "I know that much already, but where?"

"He's working on some development project for the military."

Not medical experiments. Not a guinea pig.

"He's well, apparently."

Not injured. Not sick.

Lydia walked faster. As if she could reach him if she moved quickly enough. But Antonina slowed and she was forced to turn and wait for the pale gray boots to catch up.

"Don't rush off," Antonina complained. "I haven't finished."

Lydia stood still on the sidewalk and faced her. Her cheeks felt stiff. "Where is the prison and why are you telling me this?"

Antonina's carefully guarded face softened as she tilted her head apologetically and gripped her gloved hands together. "I'm sorry, Lydia, I don't know where it is. Dmitri didn't say."

"Did you ask?"

"No."

"Will you ask him?"

"If you want."

"Of course I want."

"He's being very attentive at the moment, so maybe I can try. Look what he gave me." She slipped back the wide cuff of the silver fox coat and revealed a slender wrist encased in a gray leather glove, so pale it was almost white. Around it was clasped a wide gold bracelet inlaid with amethysts and ivory.

"What do you think?"

"It's obviously very old and very lovely."

Antonina inspected it quizzically for a second and then slid it off her wrist and pushed it deep into her coat pocket.

"I hate it," she said.

"Why?"

"I fear it might be a blood gift. That it might have been given to Dmitri by some old tsarist countess as a bribe. To let her husband live. In the camp, I mean. Some old White Russian general with a big white mustache and proud eyes, but too weak to work in the mines or forests anymore." She turned her head and spat in the gutter. "That's what I fear."

"Antonina, why are you telling me all this?"

"Because I want you to trust me."

"Why on earth would you care whether I trust you?"

The woman's gloves started to fret against each other, making a soft fluttering sound. Like birds' wings. "If I tell you that your father leaves the guarded prison every few days and travels through the streets of Moscow in the back of a truck, taken to work in a less well-guarded place . . . will you trust me then?"

Lydia put out a hand and gently held the nervous gloves, preventing their movement. "What is it you want, Antonina? Tell me."

"I want to know where your brother Alexei is."

"He's gone missing again."

"What?"

"We don't know where he is."

"*Chyort!*" Antonina's face was stricken with dismay. "Lydia, you lost him once already. What's the matter with you? Can't you keep anyone safe? You seem to lose everyone, even your own father. For heaven's sake, I . . ." She shook her dark hair so that it swung around her like a cloud of unhappiness and strode on along the sidewalk.

Lydia wasn't certain what made her do what she did next. Was it anger? Despair? Guilt? She wasn't sure. All three churned inside her. Or just that she was stung by Antonina's rebuke and needed to strike back. Whichever it was, she didn't care. But when she hurried to catch up with her companion, brushing against her as she touched her arm to turn her around, it was the work of less than a second to slide the bracelet from the fur pocket into her own.

"I'll find him," Lydia told her. The conviction in it sounded genuine even to her own ears.

A car drove past, wheels hissing, and sprayed them with oily
chips of ice, but neither noticed. Lydia's attention fixed on Antonina,
on the dark deep-set eyes with the long lashes and the look of secret
despair. In that second Lydia saw an outsider like herself, a woman
struggling to find where she was going.

"I'll help you," Lydia said urgently, "and you help me. Find out
from Dmitri where the prison is."

"I'll try."

"Do more than try."

"I think he might prefer to tell you himself."

"I've already asked. He said no."

"And what will you do for me in return?" Antonina asked it
faintly, as if she didn't expect kindness for its own sake.

"I'll find Alexei. I promise. And I'll tell you where he is as soon
as I know."

They smiled at each other, a little ripple of relief. Neither knew
quite why, but they were both aware of an odd connection of sorts
between them. Lydia could feel the bracelet breathing hot against
her hip. Yet when Antonina opened her pale leather purse, pulled
out a bunch of rouble coins and notes, and thrust it into Lydia's hand,
she took it without hesitation.

AFTER THAT, SHE RAN. TO MAKE UP THE LOST TIME AND TO
keep ahead of the thoughts that pursued her like a swarm of mosqui-
toes. She scoured the streets, searched doorways, walked the glossy
district of the Arbat, and dredged the scruffy areas where drunks
were already sprawled in the gutters wrapped in newspapers and
death's icy shadow.

"Do you know a boy called Edik?"

She asked every street urchin she found. The dirty ones selling single cigarettes on street corners or bottles of watered-down
vodka outside the bars. The cleaner delivery lads running errands for
shopkeepers and even the pretty ones who wore lipstick and paraded
their tiny hips behind the Bolshoi. A thousand times: "Do you know
a boy called Edik?"

It started to snow. The streets grew darker as the shops closed their doors and rattled their shutters. She no longer knew where she was, her feet hurt, and she didn't know if it was the cold or the holes in her *valenki*. She should go home. Perhaps Alexei had already returned. Liev would be growling and pacing their poky little room. Probably Elena was scolding him, telling him Lydia was quite capable of looking after herself. Yet instead her feet kept walking and as the night and the snow descended, she had a sense that Moscow was swallowing her. She spotted another boy across the street pulling something bulky behind him on a length of string. Pale hair and a long dark coat, shoulders iced with snowflakes.

"Edik!" she shouted.

The boy turned his head nervously. In the spill of yellow light from a gas streetlamp she realized her mistake. It wasn't him. He started to run.

"Wait!"

She raced across the empty street. He would have been too fast for her but whatever he was dragging along slowed him down, and she caught him with ease. The something on a string, she discovered, was a plump piglet. It was trussed, front and back legs, its snout tied shut with a filthy rag, and lying on its side on a small ramshackle sledge that was steadily disappearing under a blanket of snow. The animal looked paralyzed with fear, its pink eye rolling wildly in its socket. The boy was no more than eight or nine years old and squinted at her with the eyes of a feral creature.

"Where on earth did you get this from?"

"It's my grandfather's," the boy lied and trotted off again, dragging the sledge over the ruts in the ice, jerking it in fits and starts.

"Wait!"

Lydia pulled out one of Antonina's roubles. Instantly the boy became more alert. Even though he had his back to her, he could smell the money.

"I'm searching for—"

"I know. A boy called Edik."

"How do you know that?"

He gazed at her as if she were stupid. "Because you've been going around all evening asking for him."

"Who told you?"

"Everybody." But the answer didn't come from the boy; it came from behind her.

She swung around. A man was standing right at her shoulder, a large looming shadow. How he'd come so close without making a sound, even over the ice, she couldn't imagine. He must possess the feet of a cat. Though he had heavy burly shoulders, his hair was brown and curly and gave the impression of boyish friendliness. In the dark she couldn't make out his expression properly, but she had the distinct feeling that, unlike his curls, it wasn't friendly. She backed off a step.

"*Dobroi nochi*," she said. "Good evening."

That was when she saw the tattoo on his forehead.

"YOU ARE MY SON, ALEXEI."

"You are my father, Maksim."

"I hold you to my heart."

"It is an honor for me."

Maksim Voshchinsky hugged Alexei to his chest and drummed his satisfaction on Alexei's back with the flat of his hands, so that their meaning vibrated through his ribs.

"You are my son," he said again, and held Alexei away at arm's length, studying his young captive with pride. "You wear my shirt, you use my bath and my razor, just as a son should."

"Thank you, Maksim. *Spasibo*."

"You look much better now, clean and fresh. A good-looking Russian was hiding under all that shit and stubble."

"I feel better."

"*Da*. That's good."

Alexei helped lower Maksim back into the big black armchair beside the bed and tucked a blanket around him. It was made of the softest green velvet with exquisite embroidery around the border. Was it bought? Or stolen? As Alexei glanced around the bedroom at the stuffed birds in cages, he found himself wondering the same thing. Bought or stolen? Did it matter?

Oh, fuck these people. Already they'd gotten inside his head. *It matters. Of course it matters. Don't forget that.*

If this was the price he had to pay, all right, he'd pay it. *But don't be fooled. Don't be fucking stupid.* He had listened to Maksim tell stories all evening, extraordinary tales of his exploits in prisons and camps, refusing to acknowledge the authority of the guards, the beatings he took, the money he won at cards or stole from mattresses. The power he gained within the prisons and now on the streets of Moscow by sheer force of will. He might be ruthless but, damn him, he was a likable man. He made Alexei laugh as they relaxed together over cigarettes and French brandy.

But don't forget. Don't ever forget.

"SO," ALEXEI SAID, EXHALING A SERIES OF SMOKE RINGS THAT spread out like ripples in a duck pond and drifted up into the haze that hovered just below the ceiling. He made it casual. Unimportant almost. "You have made me a *vor,* one of yours. Not a full member of the *vory v zakone,* the thieves-in-law, I understand that. That will take time, and you say I have more to prove before I can be accepted. But you've marked me. Your stamp is on me."

"It will protect you, Alexei. Keep you safe in this city."

"I am grateful, father."

Maksim beamed at him, wide fleshy cheeks turning pink with pleasure. "I had a family once upon a time, two sons. But when a criminal joins the *vory v zakone,* all family must be renounced because the thieves-in-law become a man's only family."

"Where are they now, your sons?"

He shrugged. "They used to be in Leningrad, but now . . . who knows? I haven't seen or heard of them for more than twenty years. I wouldn't even recognize them now if I passed them in the street, nor they me."

Great meaty tears rolled unchecked down his face. Alexei leaned forward.

"I am your new son, *pakhan.*" The words scorched his tongue. Yet he repeated them. "I am your new son, *pakhan.*"

"Then pour me another brandy and we'll drink to it."

When he had refilled their glasses, Alexei returned to blowing smoke rings and inspected this new father through half-closed eyes. Now he had to ask.

"So, Maksim, will you order your *vory* to help me?"

"Ah, my son, that's a big request. You are not yet a real member of the brotherhood and they may think you unworthy."

"I ask you not as a *vor* but as a son."

A pause grew between them, as green and solid as the rug. It seemed to suck the air from the room.

"You saved my life," Maksim stated. But still he didn't say yes.

Alexei reached down into his own tattered boot and drew from it the fine-bladed knife he had taken from Konstantin on the boat. The older man froze for one fleeting second, but Alexei yanked up his own right sleeve, revealing the pale vulnerable flesh under his forearm. With careful consideration he pressed the point of the blade into his skin and saw blood spurt. In one rapid stroke he sliced down to his wrist, and the movement was chased by a ribbon of crimson.

He looked up at Maksim. "Is the answer yes?"

In the smoke-filled silence that followed, it was as though he could hear Lydia breathing. Then the man opposite him nodded and proffered his arm. Alexei took it and thrust back the sleeve of his robe. As he lifted the knife he asked himself, what price was the nod of a criminal? He dragged the blade down the loose hairy flesh of Maksim's right arm, parting the surface skin cleanly, skimming through the grinning jawbone of a tattooed skull, the sign of a killer. But not deep. He didn't want to hurt this man.

"Now," said Alexei. He wiped the blade on his thigh, took hold of Maksim's heavy arm, and pressed it against his own where it was dripping onto his lap. Flesh to flesh. Life to life.

"Now," he said again, "now, father, we are blood."

A RESPECTFUL KNOCK ON THE BEDROOM DOOR MADE MAKsim swear.

"*Yob tvoyu mat!* Fuck you!" He and Alexei were playing cards. Maksim played fiercely and was winning with ease. "What do you want?"

The door opened tentatively and the shape of Igor filled the narrow gap. The short young man looked nervous.

"I'm sorry to disturb you, *pakhan*, but Nikolai is here. He wishes to speak with you."

"Doesn't he know I'm fucking sick?" Voshchinsky bellowed.

Spittle flecked his lips and he flicked an irritated tongue over them. "Tell him to go away."

"*Pakhan,* I . . ."

The door was shunted fully open from the other side, but it wasn't Nikolai who stood there in the doorway to report to his boss. It was a beautiful thin girl with large passionate eyes and skin like fine ivory. It took Alexei the blink of an eye to realize it was Lydia. How the hell had she found him? A grubby urchin with a shock of pale hair hovered behind her. Her ugly hat was clutched in her hand, and her fiery mane shone bright as a new coin in the dim room full of dead things. She ignored everyone else, just focused on her brother.

"Alexei," she said firmly, and held out a slender hand to him. "I've come to take you home."

Forty-two

✿

THE NOISE. THE HEAT. THE SLAM OF SHEET METAL, the grinding of machinery. The bang and rattle of the overhead hoist chains. All crashed into Chang's mind. Like the gods stamping their feet in anger, blasting their fiery breath into his skull till it was scorched to a cinder.

How could any man work in this?

The gaping mouth of the blast furnace blistered the skin and turned the workers' faces into scarlet sweating masks of fiends, as white-hot sheets of metal were maneuvered into position. Tongs and drills and steam hammers beat out a deafening roar inside the steel factory, an infernal sound that Chang knew was needed all over China if his country was ever to progress. Stalin was turning Russia into a powerful force in the world. This surge of industrial development was what China cried out for; mechanization was the future. But was Mao Tse-tung the leader to enforce it? He was still at war and still absorbed in his own private pleasures. So it meant China must wait, and if there was one thing the people of China excelled at, it was patience. Their day would come. But until then, they knew how to wait. It was their strength.

The delegation moved on through the factory behind their Russian guide. Chang could see that his compatriots were over-awed by the scale of its metal production. As they were meant to be. They stood in a group and watched a man operate a hole punch, a massive steam-driven fist that slammed down and punched out a wide circle in sheet after sheet of steel. What its purpose might be, Chang had no idea, and the sound of it was too deafening to allow him to ask. The Russian worker, aware of being watched, kept his eyes lowered submissively and his hands in constant motion. Over and over the same movement, the same pull of a lever, turn of a winch, rattle of a sheet of steel on rollers, then *bang* and on to the next.

The delegation moved on, but Chang remained. Watching and waiting for the moment the man would look up. Because Chang knew he would; eventually he would be unable to resist. Then Chang would see what a Russian worker was made of. It was the same in China, the peasant mentality, hiding all behind sub-missive downturned eyes. It angered Chang, their refusal to lift the head and stand out in a crowd. It was one of the things he'd loved from the start about Lydia, that willingness to look the world straight in the eye. He smiled at the image in his head and touched a finger to his throat, laying it on the exact spot where her lips had lain.

That was the moment the metalworker chose to raise his eyes. It looked to Chang a very Russian face with its broad cheekbones, long nose, jaw hidden in a fringe of beard. But the eyes told him every-thing he needed to know. Pale gray and exhausted, the steam ham-mer pounding its reflection in them from dawn to dusk. These were not the eyes of the contented proletariat they had been led to believe worked in these factories.

For a second their gaze fixed on each other, and gradually Chang felt the heat. Not from the furnace this time, but coming from the worker himself. It was the kind of heat that was pinpoint sharp. Like a blade that has rested in flames. Chang recognized it at once. It was hate.

★ ★ ★

"KUAN."

She stopped and waited for him. Chang moved closer as they crossed the factory yard. The snow had turned to rain, but it was the kind of rain that was like ice picks in the face. They were due to be taken to a meeting now, and he would have no other moment for his words to curl in private into her ear. She didn't ask what he wanted but inspected him, eyes black and bright. He could see the fire in them despite the gloom.

"The factory was impressive," he said.

"Did you see the number of people employed there?"

"Yes. Communism in action. It works. Here in Stalin's Russia we see how Lenin's ideas function as a practical reality. They are forging a successful future for this country. It is what China weeps for, that same strong hand."

"A father's firm hand."

"But one that will caress as well as rebuke. One that will give as well as take."

"Chang An Lo," Kuan said in her usual quiet way, but Chang could hear the unease in her voice, "I am concerned."

"Concerned for China?"

"No, concerned for you, my comrade."

"There is no need for concern."

"I think maybe there is."

In her thick padded blue coat, with her short black hair framing a wide-boned face, she could have been a rice grower's daughter from any stretch of rural China, one of millions like her condemned to a life of servitude on a tenant plot of land or in the family home. But her eyes told a different story. They were thoughtful and intelligent. She possessed a university degree in law and a mind that could recognize problems and decide how to deal with them effectively. Chang had no intention of being one of those problems.

"Kuan," he said, "do not let yourself be distracted from what we have come here to achieve. Focus your attention. Our leader, Mao Tse-tung, needs us to be sharp. We have come to Moscow to learn."

"You are right, of course." She brushed the rain from her face.

"It is what we are all concentrating on. Each of us in the delegation writes a report late into the night." She looked at him speculatively. "But I am not certain that you are as dedicated as usual to the affairs of Communism. As if your thoughts are elsewhere."

The soles of Chang's feet felt as though he'd just slipped on ice. "That is not the case, comrade. I have been focusing on how we can take greater advantage of the opportunities here, and I think it is time we put in a request to inspect something different. Something more . . . challenging."

He smiled at her and observed the suspicion slip away from her mouth as her eyes widened with anticipation.

"What do you have in mind, Comrade Chang?"

He walked forward through the rain and she moved quickly to his side. *People are like the fish in the Peiho River,* he reminded himself. *All you need to do is dangle the right bait.*

"SHOW ME YOUR TATTOO."

"It's of no interest, Lydia."

"It is to me."

She was determined to see what they'd done to him, so that she'd know. Know what she owed him. He was seated on the edge of her bed, smarter now, cleaner in his new white shirt and smelling of an unfamiliar cologne. But more like the old Alexei she remembered, legs crossed at the ankles in a pose of indifference. It was a relief to see him back in his old skin, but at the same time he was different. Something had changed. She could see it in his eyes and in the softer angle of his neck, and she didn't know whether to be glad or sorry. She watched as he started to unbutton his shirt. Behind her Popkov and Elena stood stiff and silent. She could feel their disapproval as sharply as she could feel the hole in her shoe. Alexei's fingers worked fast, and she could detect no hint of the shame she was certain he must feel.

"There," he said and flung back his shirt.

She felt sick. It was larger than she'd expected. A cathedral covering the whole expanse of his skin. It seemed to crush the bones of his chest, its one elegant onion dome tattooed just under the point of his collarbones.

"It's beautiful," she said.

Lydia heard a grunt behind her but ignored it.

Alexei raised one eyebrow at her. "Its beauty or lack of it is not the point."

"So what is the point?"

"I'm marked as one of their own. For life."

"Oh, Alexei, I'm sorry."

"Don't be."

She gave him a smile. "You won't be able to go swimming so often, that's all."

"I never did like getting wet and cold anyway."

He smiled back at her, and it made her want to cry.

"So now you're one of the *vory*; what will they do for you?"

"I have yet to find out."

He started to button up his shirt. He didn't hurry. For the first time it occurred to her to wonder whether belonging to this brotherhood meant more to him than she realized.

"I have a new father," he said in a quiet voice. "One who will help me."

The shock of it caught her across her throat. She coughed and stared down at her hands because they seemed to be strangling each other, but she needed badly to talk about something else. Anything else.

"Antonina wants to speak to you," she said.

Instantly his head came up, the green eyes alert and interested. "You've seen her?"

"Yes. I'll take you to her tomorrow."

"Thank you."

That was all. They'd both said enough. Lydia walked over to the peg on the door and pulled on her coat.

"Sleep well, brother," she murmured, opened the door and walked out onto the dim landing.

Before she reached the black courtyard outside, a burly shadow merged with her own, so that it turned into a two-headed monster on the prowl through the night. It was Liev Popkov. They didn't speak. He loped beside her and she lengthened her stride to his as they disappeared into the dark streets of Moscow. Only when he'd seen her safely to her destination would he return to the warmth of Elena and his own bed.

THE CRUCIFIX STILL HUNG ON THE WALL, BUT IT DIDN'T MATTER to Lydia. Nothing mattered. Not now. Chang had lit the gas lamp.

"So that I can look at you," he'd said.

When she'd entered the room he'd taken her face gently between his hands, his fingers feeling the bones under her skin as if they could tell him something. His eyes studied hers intently for a long moment, and then he had kissed her forehead and folded her into his arms.

That was when suddenly nothing else mattered.

SHE LAY WITH HER CHEEK ON HIS NAKED CHEST, HER LIMBS spread lazily over his, and let her fingers trail over his skin. With intense pleasure she smoothed out the slick sheen of sweat that made it glow in the yellow light as if it had been oiled. Each time she touched one of the ridged scars on his chest, she lifted her head and brushed it with her lips, tasting his saltiness. Those old scars, like the ones where his little fingers had once been, she could bear. They were surface damage. But what lay under his fine precious skin? What new damage had been inflicted while he was away from her, scars she couldn't see?

She pressed her ear even closer to his chest to listen for what lay underneath, but caught only the steady drumbeat of his heart and the soft sigh of air entering and leaving the secret cavities within him. His hand was buried in the tangle of her hair, moving among its strands, fingering them, burrowing deeper.

Their first lovemaking had been intense, hungry for each other as starved creatures are for food, but this time they allowed themselves a slower pace as if they could start to believe they were not going to be snatched apart again at any moment. Their bodies began to relax. To trust. They found each other's rhythm with ease, and Lydia experienced again that familiar ache for him that no amount of feeling him hard inside her, becoming a physical part of her, ever banished completely.

She stroked the long taut muscle of his thigh, saw it twitch with pleasure. "Tell me," she said softly, "what it is that is hurting so much inside you."

"Now that I am here with you, all pain has vanished." He was smiling; she could hear it in his voice even though she couldn't see his face.

"You lie well, my love."

With his hand still entwined in her hair, he raised her head a fraction and turned it so that her chin was balanced on his ribs and he could see her face. His black almond-shaped eyes were smiling at her.

"It's the truth, Lydia. The rest of the world does not exist when we are together. What's out there"—he glanced at the black window and for a second the smile slipped—"with all its hardships, it ceases to be." He smoothed a lock of fiery hair back from her forehead and touched her mouth with a fingertip. She parted her lips and he touched her teeth. "But it's waiting for us."

His other hand strayed to her breast, stroking it with a slow aching caress. Abruptly she rolled herself on top of him, laying her own body along the length of him. Their bones and their flesh molded together, her ankles slotted between his, her thighs on his, her stomach flat against his, her ribs joined to his. She could feel the heat at his groin and needed to merge it with her own. She rested her elbows on either side of his head and stared down into his solemn gaze.

"Tell me about China," she ordered.

The flicker was slight. A tiny black shutter somewhere deep in the darkness behind his eyes. But enough. She knew now she'd been right. She kissed his beautiful straight nose.

"Tell me," she said in a gentler tone, "what has happened in China that causes you such grief."

His smile came slowly. It started with a faint curve of one corner of his lips, and she watched it rise through the muscles of his cheeks to his eyes.

"You know me too well, my Lydia."

"Don't hide from me."

"I'm not hiding. Just careful of you." His hand lifted and settled on the small of her back as if it had a will and a desire of its own. "You have enough to think of here in Moscow. Enough . . . complications."

"So tell me now." She bounced her chin on his. "Or I'll lie here all night and all day until you do."

He laughed. "That's an excellent reason," he said, "for not telling you anything."

"I'm waiting."

He breathed quietly and she matched the rhythm of her own breath to his. The silence in the small room lay like a blanket around them, warm and intimate. His nostrils flared, and she knew he would tell her.

"Mao Tse-tung is still battling it out, at war with Chang Kai-shek's Nationalist Kuomintang forces." He spoke quietly, but the very softness of his words made Lydia nervous. "I believe that Mao and our Communist Red Army will win. One day they will take control. Maybe not soon, but eventually the people of China will realize that their only chance of a future of freedom is through Communism. It is the only way forward for a country like China. We've seen it here in Russia, we've viewed the advances that will come."

"But what about . . . ?" She stopped.

"About what?"

"About the mistakes?" She waved an impatient hand in the direction of the window and whispered, "What about the fear out there?"

Chang wrapped both arms around her naked back and pulled her tight against his chest. "It is the leader who is wrong, Lydia, not the Communist system. Stalin is the wrong leader for Russia."

"And Mao Tse-tung?"

"I have fought for him. Endangered my life for him. And risked the lives of my friends and colleagues."

"I thought you worked in their head office in Shanghai. Decoding encrypted messages, that's what you told me."

He gave her an apologetic smile. "I do. Some of the time."

She let it pass. *Endangered my life*, he'd said.

His fingers stroked her spine, soothing her. "But like Stalin," he continued, "Mao is the wrong leader. He is a corrupt man and will cripple China if he gets his hands on her."

She let her mouth rest on the hollow of his throat, aware of his
pulse.

"Chang An Lo, if that is so, you must stop fighting for him."

He tightened his grip on her till she could barely breathe. "I
know," he said bleakly. "But where does that leave China? And
where does that leave me?"

Forty-three

THE PRISON WAS COLD TODAY. IT HAPPENED regularly, the air turning white in front of your face when you breathed out. Jens wasn't certain why it should be so cold. Plumbing incompetence? Perhaps. But he had an unpleasant suspicion that it was done intentionally by Colonel Tursenov to keep his charges on their toes. To jog their memories of what it was like to spend winters in the forests or the mines or on canal construction. Such hints sharpened the mind.

Jens was seated at his broad desk in his workroom, blueprints spread out in front of him like great rectangular lakes into which he could plunge and shut off his mind to all else. He was proud of them. He couldn't help it. And certainly he wasn't ready to hand them over to someone else. They represented many hours of hard scrupulous work, a well-designed, carefully thought out and expertly calibrated piece of engineering. Even after all those years of mind-numbing servitude in the timber forests of Siberia, he could still think. Still draw. Still plan.

Still desire to live.

Especially now. Now that there was Lydia.

"STAND."

The door banged open. Babitsky, the big greasy guard who was always sweating whatever the temperature, sprang to attention and Jens could almost smell his fear from across the room. It set the hairs on his own neck bristling.

The senior group of engineers and scientists had been herded out of their individual workshops into the meeting hall. It was a fine elegant room with a high ceiling and good proportions. In the days before the Revolution when the villa used to be an aristocrat's mansion rather than a dismal prison with bars at the windows, this had been the dining room, and still it contained a massive mahogany table on which blueprints and technical drawings were stacked. No silver candlesticks, no crystal goblets, no murmur of laughter. Practicality and utility were the new gods of Soviet Russia. Well, that suited Jens just fine. He had learned to be a practical man.

They stood in a straight line, hands neatly behind their backs, eyes front, chins to chests, no talking. Exactly the way they'd been taught in the camps. A row of highly educated and intelligent brains acting like trained seals. Beside him Olga gave a barely audible snort of disgust and he noticed a small hole in the hem of her skirt as he directed his eyes downward.

"Comrades." It was Colonel Tursenov himself. "Today we have brought some visitors for you."

Jens's heart jumped in his chest. Lydia? For one foolish moment he thought it could be his daughter come to see him. He glanced up quickly and found himself staring straight at the colonel, flanked by a nervous Babitsky and an only slightly less nervous Poliakov. Visitors of importance, then. Behind them, instead of the red-haired young woman he'd stupidly hoped for, stood a row of six hard-eyed Orientals, four men, two women, though it was not easy to tell the difference the way they dressed. A red band branded the arm of their blue coats. Communists. Chinese Communists? He had no idea they existed. The world out there must be changing fast. And why on earth would they bring these Chinese to a top-secret project?

"Comrades," Colonel Tursenov said again. He didn't usually address them with such a proletarian term. *Tovarishchi.* Normally it was their surname or number. Nothing as respectful as *tovarishch.* "Today we are honored by a visit from our comrades in the Chinese Communist Party." He gave a courteous nod to the older figure at the front of the group, a man with iron-gray cropped hair and a deeply lined face that revealed nothing. But Jens noticed Tursenov's eyes shift quickly to the tall young Chinese behind him and linger there. As though that was where the power—or maybe the trouble—lay.

"Comrade Li Min, these are our senior workers," he announced to the older Chinese, and gestured toward the docile row, the way a farmer might indicate ownership of pigs. "Top brains."

"You have done well to gather such skills together." It was the older visitor who spoke in fluent Russian. "They must be deeply honored to work for the State and for your great leader, Stalin."

"I'm sure they are."

Honored? That was a question none of the prisoners cared to answer.

"We will now inspect the workrooms downstairs," Tursenov announced.

No, stay out of my workroom.

The colonel knew perfectly well they all hated the ignorant fingers rearranging and even removing their papers. But he insisted on it. To remind them what they were.

"First, I wish to speak to them."

Everyone looked toward the tall young Chinese who had spoken, and General Tursenov's face creased into an uneasy frown. To be polite he must say yes. But to be safe he must say no. Jens observed the struggle and was not surprised when the Chinese stepped away from the group of armbands and took long strides over to the line of workers, as if the colonel had already given permission. The determination of it made Jens want to smile at what must be going on in Tursenov's head right now. The visitor stood at one end of the line and studied them.

"They are all prisoners, are they not?"

"*Da.* But no names, please."

The colonel started to draw the rest of the delegation toward the door in the hope that the renegade would follow. But the young Chinese took no notice. His dark eyes took in the face of each of the five male prisoners; the two women he ignored completely. When his gaze settled on Jens, there was a question in it but Jens couldn't work out what it was. This young man disturbed him but at the same time excited him. With a jolt he realized he was being confronted by an independent mind, one that had not been sucked dry of all its inner intricacies by a blunt State system. Jens had almost forgotten what that felt like, and the unexpected challenge brought a smile to his lips. The Chinese approached but stopped first in front of Ivanovich, who stood next to Jens, a man nearly as tall as himself.

"You," he said, eyes fixed on Ivanovich's face. "What is it you do?"

"Comrade Chang," Tursenov burst out, "such details are not—"

"I do not ask what he is working on. Only what his field of work is." The black eyes centered on the colonel, and there was a pause.

"Very well," Tursenov said with ill grace, and nodded at Ivanovich.

"I am an explosives expert," the prisoner said in an undertone.

Jens saw the interest slide out of the black eyes, the way the tide ebbs off a beach and leaves nothing behind.

"And you? What is your job?"

Jens glanced at Tursenov. Received a nod.

"I am an engineer."

The Chinese made no comment, just drew breath quietly and studied Jens, inspected his face, his hair, his clothes, as though committing them to memory. Suddenly the lengthy inspection by this foreigner irritated Jens. He looked away.

"I am an engineer," he said in a curt voice, "not a zoo animal."

"Are you good?"

"I'm the best. That's why I'm here."

Despite himself, he was drawn to look back at the Chinese, and something in the black eyes had changed. Somewhere deep inside them lay laughter. Whoever this man was, he'd brought a breath of the outside world into this stifling airless cage.

"And you, Comrade Chang," Jens said with a half-smile, "are you the best at whatever the hell it is you do?"

"Silence, prisoner," Tursenov snapped from across the room.

"You will see," the Chinese answered.

He surprised Jens by reaching out and touching Jens's chest. A brief pat, nothing more. But the physical contact came as a shock. Abruptly the tall slender figure was gone. Yet as he walked through the door, he glanced back over his shoulder, as Jens had known he would. Their eyes held, then it was over. The door closed, and the prisoners relaxed and started to complain that their workroom space was being invaded yet again.

"Are you all right, Jens?" Olga asked. Her large blue eyes were concerned. "You look pale."

"In this hole, we're all pale," he said angrily. "So pale we're invisible."

"Don't be upset, Jens. They may treat us like zoo animals but we're still here. Still alive."

"Is this alive?"

"As long as your heart is beating, you are alive."

He touched his hand to his chest and smiled at her. "Then I must still be alive because it's pounding like a blacksmith's hammer."

"I'm glad. Make sure you keep it that way."

She gave him an affectionate look and turned away in response to a query from one of the others. Jens immediately slid his fingers inside the front of his jacket to retrieve the note that he knew he'd find there.

Jens Friis.

I am a friend of your daughter, Lydia. She is here in Moscow. Now that I know where you are, I will inform her. Be alert for communication.

Jens was sitting on the end of his bed, hunched over the note to protect it from prying eyes. He read it once more, for the thousandth time, before tearing it into minute shreds that lay on his lap like confetti. When he was satisfied he could make the scraps no smaller, he started to sprinkle them on his tongue and swallow them. His hands were shaking.

Lydia's face felt stiff. It was smiling and the muscles of her cheeks still moved when she spoke, but only just. She had to force them.

Her gaze kept straying back to the strong lines of Dmitri Malofeyev's face as he sat next to her sipping his coffee, and she wondered how she was managing to keep her own coffee in her cup instead of in his face. He knew where her father was locked up. He'd admitted as much to his wife. But he refused to reveal it.

"Lydia, may I offer you another one?"

It was Alexei who spoke. He was sitting opposite her at the table.

"Of course, *spasibo*. They're so good."

Her brother passed her the gilt-edged plate of tiny iced cakes, each topped with a cherry curled inside a sugary case. She nodded her thanks, but it wasn't for the cakes. He was alerting her. Dmitri had noticed her scrutiny of him, and his response was sharp curiosity.

"Eat up, my dear girl," Dmitri encouraged easily. "Put more flesh on those lovely bones of yours."

"Thank you."

She took another cake in her fingers and smiled at him, but left the delicacy untouched. Right now it would choke her. This whole thing was Dmitri's idea. To bring them all to this elite hotel for morning coffee, instead of to his apartment as Antonina had intended. His hand rested lightly on his wife's on the table, pinning down the white glove, and his eyes darted continually from Lydia to Alexei and back again. It was the kind of place Lydia had spent her childhood gazing at from outside, yearning to be allowed in: all white linen napery, bone china, and carpets so thick they felt like cats under her feet. But now that she was here, she was not so sure. She didn't like the way the waiters never met her eye or the sense that somehow there seemed to be the smell of dead bones under the tables.

Conversation was stilted. Lydia didn't much care, but Dmitri appeared amused and she couldn't imagine why. Antonina and Alexei said little, drinking their coffee and smoking their cigarettes. Antonina was dressed in black and using a neat ebony cigarette holder that Lydia loved. There was an air of anticipation. Everyone waiting for something to happen. No one quite sure what.

"Have you made good use of the food I brought you?" Dmitri asked, eyeing her over the rim of his feather-fine coffee cup.

"The puppy has been enjoying the ham."

Now why did she say that? Just to annoy him?

"It was meant for you, Lydia."

She leaned forward, elbows on the pristine white cloth as she met his gaze and gave it one more go. "Tell me, Dmitri, please, have you managed to find out yet where Jens Friis is being held?"

"I'll say this for you, my dear. You don't give up."

"So?"

"So no, I'm sorry. I'm afraid not."

She frowned at him. "You're a useless liar."

He threw back his head and released a great rush of laughter. "Listen to the girl, Antonina. She thinks I'm a bad liar."

His wife tipped her head to one side, considering the point for a moment, like a bright-eyed blackbird. "She doesn't know you as well as I do, does she?"

He laughed again. "The trouble with women," he said to Alexei, "is that they think they know you better than you know yourself. Don't you agree?"

"In my experience," Alexei said a little stiffly but with every appearance of courtesy, "they usually know more than we think they do."

A silence so brief it was barely noticeable scuttled across the table. Lydia fiddled with her spoon, rattling its silver edge against the saucer to fill the gap, and flicked a glance at her brother. Ever since she'd returned to their room in the gray light of early morning he had been aloof and uncommunicative. He made no secret of the fact that he disapproved of Chang, regarded him as an unwelcome distraction. Well, she disapproved of his disapproval.

"Your brother appears to be a connoisseur of women," Dmitri teased. "Don't you agree, Antonina?"

His wife turned her head and studied the silent figure of Alexei sitting beside her. "I think he looks tired," she murmured gently, and smiled, first at Alexei, then at Dmitri.

"How long do you intend to stay in Moscow, Comrade Serov?" Malofeyev asked.

"As long as it takes to get my business completed."

Malofeyev inclined his head. "If I can be of assistance, don't hesitate to ask. I have contacts in this city."

"So have I," Alexei responded curtly.

Under the table Lydia stepped on his toe.

"I don't doubt that for a moment," Malofeyev said, his tone cooler. He regarded his guest in silence for the time it took his wife to fit a new cigarette into her holder. "I'm only offering help. If you should need it," he added.

"Like you offered help to my sister. Is this a habit of yours? Helping strangers?"

Chyort! Lydia cursed under her breath. She glanced across at Antonina and found her smiling, a big broad smile, eyes bright with amusement. She looked ten years younger, and for once the white gloves were free from fretting fingernails.

"Lydia," she said, "don't you think this place is charming?" She gestured at the crystal chandeliers and the silk water lilies that floated in a fountain of fragrant water in the center of the room. "It's so civilized."

"So civilized," Lydia repeated softly. A needle point of anger pricked under her ribs. She snapped her head around to face Dmitri. "Unlike the place you were stationed in before, I believe."

He didn't move. She wondered if he was even breathing, he was so still. It was Antonina who laughed delightedly and tapped her husband's arm with the tip of her cigarette holder.

"What do you think, my darling? Is Moscow more civilized than Trovitsk camp? Or less? I can think of arguments for both."

Her husband ignored her. Just as he ignored Lydia.

"It seems to me, Comrade Serov, for a brother and sister, you are not at all alike."

"That, comrade, is where you are mistaken. Lydia and I are very similar."

"Is that so? In what way?"

"In the way we view the world."

"What, from under a pile of rules and regulations like everyone else?"

"Perhaps. But nevertheless we do believe we can influence what happens to us."

"Ah, I see. The cult of the individual. Surely Marx and Lenin and Stalin have firmly established that it is the forward progress of the collective whole that counts, not the cogs in the wheels. They are . . . dispensable."

Lydia and Antonina exchanged a glance.

"Dmitri," Antonina interrupted with an anxious flick of her hair, "let our guests enjoy their coffee in peace. You are so provocative."

"I believe your husband is right," Alexei pointed out. "Certain cogs are dispensable. It's a matter of choosing the right ones." He leaned back in his chair, his face set hard.

"Dmitri," Lydia said quickly, and jumped to her feet. A nudge of coffee spoiled the whiteness of the cloth. "Come with me, please. I want a word."

DMITRI MALOFEYEV AND LYDIA WALKED TOWARD THE LARGE revolving front door of the hotel, but before they reached it she spotted a heavy oak door off to the left marked CARD ROOM. She pushed it open, entered, and held the door ajar to admit Dmitri after her.

"You in the mood for a game of poker?" He smiled.

"I'm willing to gamble, if that's what you mean."

The room was unused at this hour of the morning. Small square green baize tables were dotted around, and an impressive aspidistra plant blocked most of the light from the window so that the air had a strange greenish shimmer to it. As if they were underwater. Lydia turned to face her companion. She placed her hands on her hips to keep them still and she spoke seriously.

"Dmitri, help me. We both know you can. Please."

He didn't smile or laugh or raise a mocking eyebrow this time. He regarded her with a solemn expression. "What is it you want?"

"The same as before. Where Jens Friis is held."

Slowly he shook his head, his red hair closer to purple in this strange light. She knew her own must look the same. "That's not possible, Lydia. I've told you already. Now you must stop asking me."

"It is possible. All you have to do is tell me. No one need know."

"But I would know."

"Does that matter?"

"Yes, I rather think it does."

The gap between them was about three paces. Very deliberately, her mouth as dry as the green baize, she reduced it to two.

"What would persuade you to say yes?" she whispered.

To her astonishment his eyes grew sad and he murmured, "I'm not worth it, Lydia. Take your beautiful wares elsewhere before I spoil them."

"I'm staying right here."

"Ah, I see. This is where you fall into my arms and I whisper sweet prison names in your ear in return."

"Something like that."

"It's what I should have expected."

"You make me feel cheap."

"No, lovely Lydia, you'll never come cheap, of that I'm certain. The price will always be high."

She swallowed, beating down a sense of being out of her depth. Of drowning in this strange watery light.

"It's not a high price," she insisted. "One prison name and address. Easy for you."

He let his eyes inspect her carefully, from her scruffy shoes to her thin hips, up to her breasts, her throat, and finally her face, as though judging her worth. Her cheeks started to burn.

He smiled, an odd crooked smile. "You are particularly desirable when you blush like that, Lydia. Do you know that?"

"Are you in the mood to gamble, Dmitri?"

Again he surprised her. Each time she tried to take control he seemed to sidestep her. He pulled his silver cigarette case from inside his jacket, removed one cigarette, and tossed the case to her. She caught it.

"Use that, Lydia. Go and buy yourself your information with that. I have no intention of destroying my future career in the Kremlin just because I can't say no to a beautiful girl. Not even one with the face of an angel and the eyes of a tiger ready to rip my heart out of my chest if I don't do what she asks."

Lydia was stunned. She wanted to drop the silver case to the floor, but her fingers wouldn't let it go. She watched him light his cigarette with a steady hand.

"So," he said when he had exhaled a gray plume of smoke from his nostrils, "what would you do if you knew the address of this prison? Write to Jens Friis? *Hello, how are you? I'm having a good time in Moscow.* Is that what you plan to do?"

"Of course not."

"Then what?"

"That's my business."

They stared at each other. Suddenly hostile.

"They aren't allowed letters or contact of any sort," he said. "You must know that."

"I'm not thinking of sending a postcard."

"No." He nodded thoughtfully. "I dare say you aren't."

This was it. Her heart banged on her ribs. She took another step forward. They were close now, so close she could smell the spicy fragrance of his hair oil, see the tiny pockmark on his jaw. He stood immobile, the cigarette dangling from his fingers at his side, but his gray eyes watched her.

She reached out, took the cigarette from him, and stubbed it out in an ashtray on the nearest table. She lifted his hand and placed it over her racing heart. His mouth softened instantly. She stretched up on her toes, encircled his neck with her arms, and pulled his head down to hers till her lips were pressed hard against his. At first he didn't respond. Unyielding and reluctant. She feared she'd gotten it all wrong. But as soon as she leaned her weight against him, letting the heat of her body sweep over his, he changed abruptly. His tongue darted into her mouth, his hands started to pull at her blouse, and a sound like a drunken moan escaped his lips. He had her now. Exactly what he wanted.

Lydia kept her eyes open. Forced herself to look at him as his hand slid under the waistband of her skirt.

"Well, what a pretty party this is. Can anyone join in or is it private?"

Lydia froze. Dmitri unwound himself. He breathed out heavily.

"Hello, Antonina," he said with an untroubled smile. "Lydia was just teaching me the skills of gambling."

"Bidding high, were you?"

"Extremely."

Antonina's fingernails began to trace a path up and down her long white gloves. "Lydia, your brother wishes to speak with you."

Lydia felt a tremor moving like a snake in her gut. Without a word and without a glance at the Russian husband and wife, she

walked out of the room. The snake shifted its coils inside her, sliding up from her stomach to her throat till she thought she would
be sick.

"LYDIA IVANOVA, YOU'RE UNDER ARREST."

Lydia spun around to face the speaker, heart racing, legs tensed to
run. A scruffy mop of milk-white hair and a boy's wide grin greeted
her. Even the dog in its sack on his chest had its pink tongue lolling
out, laughing.

"You bastard," she moaned, and tried to clip Edik on the ear but
he ducked away with ease and pranced up on his toes beside her.

"What are you doing here?" he asked.

"I needed some air. So I've come to take a look at the Kremlin."

"Why?"

"I want to see where all the decisions are made. Where it is that
someone can just scribble his name on a piece of paper and decide
my future." She shrugged in the bitter wind that rose off the water.
"Whether I live or die."

They were walking along a rough path on the edge of the Moskva
River at the rear of the Kremlin, the massive red walls towering over
them, its shadow heavy and cumbersome, its crenellations like teeth
eager to bite. Lydia tipped her head back and studied it thoughtfully.
"Do you know what I think, Edik? I think this fortress is a poisonous spider hunched at the center of the web that is Moscow, and I
feel as though I'm caught inside its sticky mesh. If I move, I know
the spider will come for me."

The boy stared at her for a second, then burst out laughing and
swept a hand through the air with a rapid slicing movement. "That's
what I do to spiders' webs. Tear them apart. It's easy."

Lydia laughed. "I envy you, Edik."

"Why?"

"Because you see life in black and white. No grays."

"Is that wrong?"

"No. I remember when not long ago I saw it like that too."

"So?"

She ruffled his hair and he danced out from under her hand, skip-
ping along in front of her but backward, so that he was facing her. She

noticed for the first time that the gray tinge of his skin was gone and that his cheekbones bore less of a resemblance to knives. The sausage and the ham and the warm coat were getting to work on him.

"So hang on to your blacks and whites. They make life simpler."

The boy pulled a face. He didn't understand. Why should he? She wasn't sure she did herself. But he had all the rest of his life to find out what she meant. She pulled a face back at him. He made her, at only seventeen, feel old. She removed from her coat pocket the dainty cake with the sugary cherry that had accompanied her coffee earlier.

"Look, Misty, I've brought something for you."

It was meant as a treat for Edik, but the dog came first with him. The puppy yapped and scrabbled to jump free, so the boy tipped his pup onto the path, its gray ears instantly buffeted into wings by the strong wind.

"Half each," she insisted as she handed the cake over to Edik.

He knelt down, nibbled a small bite, and dangled the rest above the little animal's head until it danced up on its spindly hind legs.

"I'm teaching her tricks, see. To earn money."

"Good idea."

Tricks. For money. Just like she used to do. In China she'd believed that was the key. But now? She shrugged again, aware of the Kremlin walls. Now she saw more clearly despite the black shadows.

"So what are you and Misty hanging around here for?"

He was concentrating on keeping the dog wobbling on two legs. "Looking for you."

"Why me?"

"I got a message for you."

She grabbed one of Edik's ears hard, so that he squealed. "And when exactly did you intend to pass on this message?"

The puppy leapt up, trying to nip at her fingers.

"Now," he said with a surly scowl. She released him.

"Well?"

The boy narrowed his eyes at her speculatively. "Any more cakes?"

"You thief," she complained and handed over the one she'd been saving to slide onto Chang's tongue tonight. "You *vor*."

He grinned. Popped the cake into Misty's mouth. "He wants to see you. Right now."

Before he'd finished speaking, she'd spun on her heel and was running over the wet grass.

Forty-four

CHANG AN LO WAS NAKED. AS LYDIA BURST INTO the room, the sight of him stopped her in her tracks and stole her breath. He was standing by the window looking out, a blade of pearly light painting the long lines of his body, defining the muscles of his chest and the strong tendons that ran from his hip to his thigh. He was beautiful.

He must have been watching for her approach, checking that no one had followed her. And when she entered he turned his head, looking at her over one shoulder. She didn't breathe. Didn't move.

His eyes were as naked as his body. Dark, complex, a battleground of emotion. The center of him, that stillness she so loved, was plunged into turmoil. His gods must be laughing at him. Yet one corner of his mouth started to curl into a smile.

It was an image she knew she would not forget.

WHEN LYDIA OPENED HER EYES, CHANG WAS leaning on his elbow on the pillow watching her. She wondered whether he'd seen her dreams.

"Hello," she said and smiled up at him.

He kissed her forehead and the tip of her nose, but avoided the temptation of her lips. That was when she knew he was ready to talk. Outside the wind was fierce, scratching at the window, sliding through the gaps, and the sound of it made her nervous. It was the sound of things falling apart.

He stroked her face. "Are you ready to listen?" he asked.

Her pulse set up a beat in her ears. "Yes."

"I've found him."

"Jens?"

"Yes."

She couldn't speak.

"I've been to the prison. I've inspected his workroom." Chang gazed down at her, his black eyes gentle and watchful. "I've seen him. I've spoken with Jens Friis himself."

She started to shake.

"Don't cry, my love."

"Tell me," she whispered.

"He's well. Tall and strong."

"How?" It was all she could say.

"I requested a visit by our delegation to prison 1908. Of course the Russians refused at first. They were shocked by the fact I even knew the place existed, and it made them nervous of what else our Chinese secret agents might know."

She watched his mouth move but had to listen hard to hear the words. There was too much noise in her head. He stroked her forehead, softening the sharp edges of her brain.

"I asked our delegation leader, Li Min, to point out to them," he said, "that we don't wish to know what it is their prisoners are working on, but rather how they construct an institution like that. So many fields of expertise assembled from different camps and all working on one project. Still they said no." His finger twined around a lock of her hair. "So I reminded them of their food shortages and of China's abundance of rice." His dark eyes gleamed briefly with satisfaction. "They quickly understood."

"Jens?"

"The building he's in is strong. Impregnable, I would say. Three stories high with an extensive basement. A walled courtyard at the front with massive reinforced iron gates."

"And Jens?"

"He looks like you."

The tears ran silent and warm onto her skin. "You spoke to him?"

"Yes. But not in private. I wasn't able to talk of you."

She shut her eyes. Imagined her father.

"He was lined up with the other chiefs working on the project. As you said"—his thumb traced along her wet eyelashes—"he is one of the best in engineering."

She opened her eyes. "How did he seem?"

"The way you described him. A tall man, strong features, and— this will please you—still a proud man. The years have not destroyed that. His Viking spirit has survived."

"Oh Chang, thank you."

He said no more for a while, letting his words settle in her mind. Slowly she stopped the tears. The tremors shuddered through her bones one last time, then subsided. Only the pain in her chest remained, and that she could live with.

"Papa," she whispered, the word so soft it barely stirred the air. She heard her father's laugh. Remembered again feeling his whiskers tickle her ribs. She sat up and studied Chang's careful expression.

"What aren't you telling me?"

"Nothing of importance."

"The truth, my love. I want the truth."

"Ah Lydia, be patient. Give yourself time."

"I don't have patience. I don't have time. Tell me the rest."

Chang moved off the bed.

"What is it?" she asked.

He stood with his back to the window, facing her squarely. "The man I saw today is still your father, Lydia. He has the same fire in his eyes as yourself, the same lift of the chin, and"—she heard him hesitate and wondered what was coming—"the identical way of challenging you with just a look."

She put her hands in her naked lap and made them stay there.

"But Lydia, a man with that kind of determination and pride is bound to suffer hardest in the labor camps. They would try to break him. He would represent a threat to the system."

She nodded.

"His hair is white, though he's only in his early forties. Pure white. Like the snows of Siberia."

She nodded again. Her teeth clenched on her tongue.

"His nose is crooked. Where it has been broken more than once. Several of his teeth are missing."

The pain in her chest sharpened.

"His hands are badly scarred. After more than ten years in the Siberian timber forests, he is lucky to have hands at all. But they must work well even so, or he would not have been selected for the project here in Moscow."

She said nothing, but tucked her knees tight under her chin and wrapped her arms around her shins, binding herself together. He allowed her to think. Let the images build in her mind.

"Is there more?" she asked finally.

"Isn't that enough?"

She attempted a smile. "More than enough."

There must have been something in her voice, something she was unaware of, because Chang returned to the bed, sat down on the rumpled cover, and put his arms around her. Gently he rocked her. He kissed the top of her head and rocked her.

"He knows you're here."

"IT'S THE NEXT STREET, ALEXEI."

Maksim Voshchinsky gestured to the right, and the car slowed to take the corner. A horse-drawn wagon lumbered past them and somewhere a horn hooted with impatience. It was midafternoon and the roads were busy, the pavements crowded, the sky gray and life-less. But in the long black saloon car nerves were taut. Three of them were seated along the backseat: Alexei in the middle, Maksim on his right, Lydia on his left. In front Igor was skewed sideways, his eyes constantly darting into the back toward Lydia, uneasy and dis-dainful. Females were not part of the *vory* pack, except to tend and support their men when needed, so both Maksim and Igor treated Lydia as an unwelcome intruder. Nevertheless, she had insisted on coming.

"I'm the person who gave you the location of the prison," she pointed out flatly. "So I have a right to see it too."

"*Nyet,*" Maksim had laughed with a dismissive wave of his hand. Like brushing aside a fly. "You wait here."

"No, I'm coming." She'd opened the car door and climbed inside.

"Alexei, do something about your sister!"

"Let her come."

"Remember what I told you, Alexei. A *vor* has no family except the *vory v zakone.*"

"I remember, *pakhan*. But let her come."

So now she was hunched beside him on the green leather seat, her face glued to the side window, watching as intently as a cat watches a butterfly. Her fingers tapped the glass in rapid disjointed movements.

IT TOOK AN HOUR. THEY DROVE PAST THE PRISON FOUR TIMES but spread out at fifteen-minute intervals, so as to rouse no suspicions. After the shock of the first time Alexei found it easier, the thought of his father inside there. He knew what to expect. Massive gray walls. Barbed wire on top. Metal doors large enough to swallow a truck. All protecting the three-story building behind. Bars on the windows. On the street, armed guards with dogs.

Not good.

"Are you certain, Lydia? That this is where Jens is being held, I mean?"

She nodded. Ever since the car had started to whisk them northward toward the grander houses with the horseshoe of factories and warehouses that had sprung up around them, his sister had barely spoken. Maksim leaned back in the seat and lit a cigar, satisfied that the girl was overawed. Alexei was not so sure.

The driver was unknown to him, someone who drove in silence and acknowledged instructions with a subdued "*Da, pakhan.*" The back of his neck was blue where the tip of a tattooed sword blade emerged from his collar and ran up into his hairline. After the fourth pass in front of the prison they took no more chances and turned the car south.

"So?" Alexei asked Maksim. "What about the truck that we're told takes the prisoners out to their project center?"

"Don't worry, my son. The place will be watched by our people now. We will trace it wherever it goes." He thumped a fist down on Alexei's knee. "Trust me. The OGPU bastard secret police will be like a dog with a bone, unaware of the fleas jumping on their backs. You shall soon know."

"*Spasibo*, father."

Beside him Lydia stirred. Her eyes stared at her brother's face. He gazed straight ahead through the windscreen, cutting her out. As they traveled back toward the city, skirting Izmailovski Park, the streets grew broader and a forest of concrete monster apartment blocks for communal living sprang up around them.

"We could do more."

"What do you mean, little girl?" Maksim gave Lydia a patronizing smile.

Alexei could see how much it annoyed her, but she kept herself in check.

"I mean we should try to get someone inside the prison."

The men all looked at her as if she'd suggested taking her clothes off. A slight shiver of disgust.

"You've seen it," Alexei pointed out patiently. "It's too well guarded."

"I don't think so."

"Please, Lydia, don't . . ."

"Other people must go in and out," she continued reasonably. "Coalmen, butchers, bakers, secretaries, vets, window cleaners, cooks . . .

"All right, that's enough."

"Couldn't we pass a note to Jens through one of the civilian workers?"

Maksim wound down the window as though to clear the air of her words, and tossed out the remains of his cigar along with them.

"Shut her up, Alexei. What she says is impossible."

"Why?"

"Lydia, please, just listen for a second. What you suggest is far too dangerous. Impossible to do without raising suspicion and maybe losing everything by alerting OGPU to what we're doing. People talk. You know that. If you start asking workers to pass notes, they would tell someone who would tell someone else who would inform the police to gain favor with them. Whispers flare quickly here. It would put not just us in danger, but also Jens himself."

"No, I don't agree because—"

"Forget it, Lydia."

"But—"

"No."

Alexei saw her dart a glance across at Maksim, but she found no ally there. His fleshy face was looking puffy, veins showing like crimson threads over his cheeks, but his expression was intractable. Alexei noticed a whiteness around his lips and felt a flash of concern.

"Home," he ordered the driver.

Lydia leaned forward, reaching out across Alexei and touched Maksim's fur-coated arm. "Please, *pakhan*."

"*Nyet*. Alexei is right. Only a fool would take that risk. Leave it to us."

Alexei felt her shiver. She retreated into her corner. But at the first road junction when the car slowed to a halt to allow a tram to pass, she pushed down the chrome handle, swung the door open and slipped out of the car. She didn't say good-bye. Or *Thank you, pakhan*. That annoyed Alexei.

MIRRORED TILES. SILK ROBE. THE FRAGRANCE OF PARISIAN perfume. A peacock's tail feather heavy with steam. Alexei sank into the bath and struggled not to close his eyes. Behind his eyelids lay worlds that frightened him, and he was not used to being frightened.

A soft white-gloved hand stroked his damp forehead and trailed through his hair.

"I missed you," Antonina murmured and gently tipped the silver edge of a champagne glass to his lips.

Her slender figure was perched on the side of the bath, naked except for the gloves that reached her elbows. The length of her dark hair hung down her back like a glossy curtain shimmering with moisture, and her face was washed free of makeup and lipstick, the way he liked her best. They were alone in the Malofeyev apartment. It was a risk, they both knew it, but neither cared right now. Alexei swallowed the chill liquid but it was not to his taste, and he wished for a shot of Maksim's French brandy.

"That was a strange little scene over coffee this morning," Antonina murmured, and dipped her tongue in the champagne bubbles.

"Whose bright idea was it to get us together in the first place?"

"Dmitri's, of course. When I mentioned that Lydia was coming here with you, he insisted on staging a cozy little foursome instead and chose a suitably grand setting. He likes to remind everyone who is the one with the power at his fingertips."

Alexei raised one dark eyebrow. "Maybe he was just planning on keeping me out of his apartment."

She sipped her champagne. "Well, he didn't succeed, did he?"

"Is that why I'm here? To annoy Dmitri?"

The shadows under her eyes darkened as she leaned forward and trailed her tongue down the side of his cheek, forming a line through the beads of steam. "You're here because I want you here."

He regarded her face intently. What was it about this woman that drew him? Not her handsome looks or her elegance or even her position among the elite of Communist society. All those things got in the way. It was something about her vulnerability under all that polish, something that crept under his skin and lodged there like a bur that he couldn't shift. Didn't want to shift. He sat up suddenly with a *whoosh* of water, twined an arm around her naked waist, and tumbled her down into the bubbles on top of him.

She squealed and scooped water into the champagne glass to pour over his head.

"You'll drown me," she laughed.

Very deliberately he lifted one of the white gloves, dripping with scented bubbles, and kissed the delicate skin in the crook of her elbow.

"I'm going to teach you to swim," he said, and started to peel down the sodden fabric. Inch by inch the damaged skin came into view.

Forty-five

THEY WALKED SIDE BY SIDE. TOGETHER BUT NOT touching. Heads ducked against the wind. Chang was tense, Lydia could sense it. In the way he placed each foot on the ground, like a cat taking care on ice, and in the fact that his hand hovered close to his thigh, where she knew a knife was strapped. Yet when she glanced across at his face, it looked calm and his eyes focused.

The street they were on was gray. Gray walls, fat gray drainpipes tipped with slivers of gray ice, gray air gusting toward them. Gray balconies clinging by a hair to the cracked walls.

"It isn't wise, Lydia," Chang had warned her.

"Please, my love."

"You would tweak the dragon's tail yet again."

"The dragon is snoring like a New Year drunk in his lair. He won't even know I'm there." But when she'd seen the shadows gather in his eyes, she said simply, "I need this, Chang An Lo. I need to look for myself."

He had nodded. "Then you shall."

The prison was two blocks ahead. They walked in

silence, aware of the dogs alert on chains as they approached, of the guards in gray coats, of the rifles on their backs. Chang and Lydia kept to the far side of the road, tucked in close to the buildings opposite. It was obvious this had once been an avenue of gracious villas and shady trees, but nothing remained of them now. Blocks of government offices now lined the pavement, and only the moss-covered stumps at the curb sheltered the ghosts of what once had been.

Lydia forced herself not to stare. She walked quickly, though her feet begged to stop. Out here on the street, it was different from when she was caged in the comfort of Maksim Voshchinsky's car. Here it was raw. The pain sharper. The walls higher, the gates grimmer. But here she could listen for Jens Friis. For the ticking of his mind. His breath, his sigh, his voice.

His voice. She hadn't asked Chang to tell her about the sound of his voice. How could she have overlooked something so intimate?

Papa, can you hear me? Can you feel me here?

She allowed herself one look, a slight turn of the eyes, one rapid glance, that's all. Then she ducked her head again and hurried on past. But a part of her remained there on the gray sidewalk among the ice and the tree stumps, watching and waiting.

CHANG WAS BRAIDING STRANDS OF HER HAIR, WEAVING THEM in and out of fine silk ribbons. He could sense the rhythmic movement soothing her, helping to still the vibrations his fingertips could feel through the fragile bones of her skull. He breathed out deeply and saw a lock of her hair rise, flutter, and settle once more.

"Lydia, what is it that you want from Jens Friis? Want so badly you take risks that could swamp us all?"

"He's my father," she said.

He wove another ribbon into the flames. "But what are you doing here in Russia? Running toward Jens? Or away from China?"

"What do you mean, away from China? Why should I want to run away from China?"

"Because your mother died there."

She said nothing. Her hands lay unmoving at her sides. He wondered at what cost.

"Your mother died there, violently, and I went off to fight the

Kuomintang, leaving you there. You were treated cruelly by my Chinese enemies." He kissed the back of her neck. "You had every reason to run away. But your father disappeared from your life when you were just five years old, so you scarcely know him. What is it that makes you cling so hard?"

"He's my father," she said again. Her voice came out as a whisper.

He stroked her naked shoulders, fine elegant shapes.

"I let my mother die," she said. "I can't let my father die too."

"Your mother's death was no fault of yours. It was the work of the gods, a random moment when an act of revenge went wrong. You were not responsible in any way."

"I know."

"And your father is not dying."

"Nor is he living."

"You can't know that."

"What? Is that place we passed today somewhere worth living? It's more like a tomb."

"So what are you planning to do?"

"To contact him. Somehow. At first, that's all."

"And then?"

But she had gone from him, deep within herself where he couldn't reach her. His fingers continued to braid her hair, and into his mind came an image of her standing on a small beach in China staring out at sunlit water, every inch of her straining to rush forward with the current toward her future. What had happened to her? He lowered his head until it was almost touching the neat triangle of her shoulder blade and inhaled the scent of her skin. She smelled the same, that intoxicating mix of delicate jasmine and the musk of a wild animal. But where had his fox girl gone? Gently he wound his arms around her, drawing her back against his bare chest, the heat of her body surprising him.

"Chang," she said, and her sadness came at him like a slap in the face, "what are we going to do, you and I?"

"My love, you cannot avoid the future by chasing after the past."

She swiveled around within the circle of his arms, so that her tawny eyes were fixed on his. "Is that what you think this is about?"

"I think that you are frightened of what the future might hold for you, for us, so you are trying to build a future out of the past."

"So Jens Friis is my past?"

"Yes."

Slowly she shook her head, the ends of the ribbons whispering against his cheek. "You don't understand," she said. "You don't understand at all."

Her words hurt, chipped a small hole in his chest. He lifted his hands and cradled her face between them.

"I understand that we are together. That is enough." He smiled at her. "Look at what you are wearing in your hair. Look at the ribbons."

It took a moment. But the smile came. "Red ribbons," she said.

"Red is for happiness."

IT WAS RAINING AND DARK. FLURRIES OF ICE LIKE NEEDLE points stabbed at the neck. Jens pulled his cap lower over his face and his collar higher over his ears. Exercise at six thirty on a dark miserable morning brought out the worst in people. They grumbled at each other, at the guards, at the weather, but most of all at Colonel Tursenov.

"Sadistic shit."

"Still with his arse tucked up in bed."

"Enjoying his breakfast ham and eggs. Warm white rolls and hot chocolate."

"Hope it chokes the miserable bastard."

It was Tursenov who insisted on half an hour of exercise for his prisoners, trudging around and around the courtyard every morning before the working day started and again at the end of the day before the evening meal was handed out. Rain, wind, or snow, it made no difference. Floodlights, dogs, and armed guards watched over them as they shuffled in a wide circle behind a chain-link metal fence, single file, four paces behind each other. In silence.

Today was unpleasant. But there had been worse days, much worse, when marching out to work in the Siberian timber forests. Hours of stumbling through snow and whiteouts to reach the Work

Zone. So Jens was not tempted to complain or voice hostility, but
he did worry about Olga out here in the rain. He glanced across at
her wet huddled figure farther along the circle. She was moving as
though her shoes were packed full of the lead she used to dig out of
the mine. Legs thin as pins. And she was coughing. The sound of
her rasping breath made him nervous. He'd seen too many die, too
many coughs tear lungs to shreds and shudder to an end in a death
rattle. If only she would eat more.

Was Lydia eating?

The thought slipped into his head. Time and again it happened.
When he was pushing a spoonful of good hot stew into his mouth he
would freeze for a second and ask himself, was she pushing scraps of
dry black bread into hers? Curled up himself under warm blankets at
night, he imagined her cold and shivering. When it rained on him
like now, was she wet too? And did she dream of him the way he
dreamed of her?

He ached to know more. The Chinese had said nothing in the
note of his wife, Valentina. His beloved Valentina. Did she also
escape from the Bolsheviks? *Please God, let her be still alive, somewhere
safe and warm where she could grow fat and lazy if she pleased.* Or was she
here in Moscow with Lydia? In this cold and wet courtyard his mind
filled with a shimmer of dark velvety hair that he loved to brush for
her each evening before bed and a face so beautiful no man could
turn his eyes from her. *Are you here, Valentina? Have you come home to
Russia?* He couldn't imagine anyone so vibrant and colorful existing
in this drab new world of the Soviets.

A sound like hell cracking open broke up his thoughts. It was the
noise of the metal gates. Instantly Jens was attentive.

Be alert for communication.

That's what the note had said. But the heavy grating sound of the
hinges was followed by nothing more than the usual horse and cart
of the baker rolling into the yard. It arrived every morning around
this hour packed with trays of bread and rolls but carefully separated
from the prisoners by the metal fence that marched down the center
of the courtyard and divided off the exercise compound. No one
took much notice of the cart, not even the guards. Only the dogs
on their leashes were interested, sniffing the scent of freshly baked
dough on the air, tongues drooling.

Be alert.

Jens pushed his feet over the rain-slicked cobbles, fighting the urge to stop, but under his cap he threw a sideways glance at the old horse, swaybacked and somnolent. At the boy standing by its head, holding the nag's rein. He felt a little click behind his eyes. Like a shutter sliding up. Letting in light. The boy was new.

The baker was the same as usual. No change there, in his white apron and floury canvas coat. From the back of the covered cart he shouldered a wide tray of bread loaves that was draped with sheets of greaseproof paper against the rain. In his deep bass voice he greeted the prisoners through the wire fence with his customary *"Dobroye utro"* and disappeared through a side doorway into the building. The boy started to whistle, a bright cheery sound. What was it, that tune? Jens kept moving forward but at the same time watched the boy in the navy coat that was too big for his skinny frame. A dark hat with a brim hid most of his face, so that all Jens could make out under the glare of the floodlights were the hollow cheeks, and the lips pursed as he whistled.

Jens whistled back.

"Silence!" The order came from one of the guards.

Jens ceased whistling. When he glanced back at the baker's cart, the boy was hauling a large tray of bread rolls from the back and hoisted it up to carry on his head, flattening his hat, hands spread wide to reach the sides. Jens was at the point of the circle within the compound that meant he was just approaching the chain fence and he slowed.

"Get going," the man behind grumbled.

The boy was fast. Before the baker emerged, he tottered unsteadily over the wet uneven ground, stumbled suddenly, caught himself, twisted to save the tray, and let his legs go flying from under him. As he hit the ground hard he seemed to fling the tray in the direction of the fence. Dozens of white bread rolls cannoned toward the prisoners. Locusts could not have been quicker. Fingers shot through the gaps and the rolls vanished.

"You bastards, fucking thieves, give me back my rolls," the boy yelled.

He kicked out at the fence, making it rattle, and the men inside grinned back at him. Even the guards laughed at his antics.

"I'll report you all," he shouted, "I'll get you shot." The furious young boy hurled his hat at the fence, where it slithered down into a puddle. His pale hair was plastered to his thin face by the rain, and what looked like tears started to run down his face.

"I'll lose my job," he sobbed.

"Here, boy." Jens approached the fence. "You can take mine." He pushed the roll he'd picked up back through the wire and the boy seized it eagerly.

"*Spasibo.*"

"Watch out, here comes your boss."

The boy glanced fearfully over his shoulder, then rapidly back at Jens. "*Spasibo,*" he said again. "You can eat this instead." From his pocket he yanked a thick slice of black bread. "It's my breakfast." He folded it up and pushed it through the fence into Jens's hand.

"Just a fucking minute," one of the guards called out, lifting his rifle to his shoulder. "No fucking gifts!" But Jens bit into the bread with relish.

"You don't begrudge me a mouthful of *khleb*, do you? I think your General Tursenov might have something to say about that."

"What the hell is going on here?" The baker was lumbering over through the shadows. "Get over here, you stupid piece of dog shit. Where are my rolls?"

The boy had scuttled around and bundled those that had lain out of the prisoners' reach back onto the tray, but even in the dark they looked wet and gritty. The baker snatched the tray away and lashed out at the boy with his fist, sending him flying back on his heels, his head slamming onto the cobbles. He curled in a ball, hid his face in his hands, and let out a long wretched wail, his shoulders shaking.

"Leave the kid alone," Jens shouted.

"Fuck off, prisoner. It's none of your business. The bloody little fool has cost me trade." The baker strode back to his cart to remove another tray.

A guard stepped forward. "Get moving. The entertainment is over."

Ill at ease because of what their greed had caused, the prisoners sank back into the monotony of the exercise circle. Jens was the last to move from the fence.

"Boy," he called. "You all right?"

"Me? Yeah." One bright eye winked at Jens from behind his fingers.

"See that seat over there?"

"Yeah."

"If you're feeling dizzy, sit there for a minute." Jens's gaze fixed hard on the boy. "That's where we sit sometimes when we're waiting for the truck to arrive."

A slow sly grin greeted him.

"Get over here"—the baker's voice ripped through the silence of the early morning air—"and carry those trays properly, you useless dog turd."

The boy bounced to his feet, grabbed his hat, and scampered to work without a backward glance.

Dearest Papa.

Jens could read no further. His eyes filled with tears.

Dearest Papa.

So many years since he'd heard those words. He lay down on his bed and pictured his daughter and her bright hair ablaze in the sunlight of a St. Petersburg garden.

He tried again.

Dearest Papa,

A short note squashed in a slice of bread. No way to say hello after twelve long years. So I'll write about what matters most. I've missed you and never stopped thinking of you. Mama always said I reminded her of you each time she looked at me. I'm sorry, Papa, but I have to tell you that Mama died last year in an accident in China . . .

The piece of paper shook in his hand, the words blurred. *No, Valentina, no. Why didn't you wait for me? However many lies I told myself, I always believed I would see you again one day despite . . .* Rage tore through his chest, ripping vital tubes and airways so that he couldn't breathe. Rage at the system that had imprisoned him for no reason, at the desolate wasted years, at whoever caused the accident that robbed him of his wife.

He rested his forehead on the note as if it could pass its words into his mind without use of his eyes. For a long while he remained like that. Images crowding in, images he'd not dared to let loose before for fear they might shatter the fragile scaffolding that held up his world. The overhead light in a prisoner's cell was never switched off, even at night, to make surveillance by a passing guard a simple task, so when an hour had passed and then another, he rose from the bed, splashed his burning cheeks with water from the bowl in the corner, and tried once more.

Dearest Papa,

A short note squashed in a slice of bread. No way to say hello after twelve long years. So I'll write about what matters most. I've missed you and never stopped thinking of you. Mama always said I reminded her of you each time she looked at me. I'm sorry, Papa, but I have to tell you that Mama died last year in an accident in China. She left me a letter that said you are alive. I left China and traced you to Trovitsk camp and now Moscow. Alexei Serov and Liev Popkov are with me. I know that to communicate like this is dangerous and I fear for you. But if you can write something—somehow—the boy will be back tomorrow.

Ever your loving daughter,
Lydia

Jens read it again. And again and again. He paced his cell, reading her words, studying the bold slant of her script until he knew each comma and each letter by heart. Then he tore it into confetti and fed it to his tongue.

"HAVE YOU TOLD ALEXEI?" POPKOV ASKED.
Lydia shook her head. "No."
"Hah!"

It was warm as summertime in the bakery, the heat from the ovens misting the window so that Lydia had to struggle to see out. She shifted impatiently from foot to foot, watching the road for the cart, nerves brittle as ice. Behind her Liev was lounging against a wall, a loaf of thick black bread tucked under his arm, casually tearing off great chunks and stuffing them into his mouth. *Chyort!* How could he eat? Her own stomach churned.

At last the lazy sound of a horse's hooves carried through the dark street, and seconds later the boy burst into the shop, a wide grin and a livid bruise spread across his face. She seized his bony shoulders and hugged him so hard he squealed and wriggled free. Even Popkov cuffed the mop of milky hair in a gesture of relief.

Lydia walked over to the counter where the baker was waiting, and she placed Antonina's gold bracelet down on it.

"You did well," she said.

"WHAT PRICE A FATHER, ALEXEI?" LYDIA ASKED.

They were walking side by side down Granovsky Street near the university, the way they had once strolled the streets of Felanka together not so many months ago. But nothing was as simple between them as it had seemed then. Alexei was insisting on finding himself a room of his own in Moscow, and though the rain had eased, they were moving fast, as if they could outpace the dark shadows they threw behind them.

"What do you mean?" Alexei asked.

"I mean are you so ready to buy yourself a new father? One who provides false identity papers as soon as you ask and in return tells you what you can and can't do. Is that the kind of father you want?"

Alexei didn't slow his pace, but he turned his head to look at her for a moment. "This isn't about fathers, is it?" he said quietly. "It's about sisters."

Lydia lowered her eyes. She refused to say yes.

"You must understand, Lydia, that Maksim Voshchinsky is my way of reaching Jens. It's not a question of changing fathers. Or"— he paused and the wind snatched at his coat, flapping it around his legs—"or sisters."

"But you like this Maksim."

"Yes, I like him. He's clever, he's complicated." He shrugged as he walked. "And he's amusing."

"He doesn't like me."

"What does that matter? I like you."

She looked straight at him. "That's all right, then."

Forty-six

❦

THE MOON HAD RISEN AND FOUGHT ITS WAY OUT
from behind the clouds that had sat stubbornly over
the city all day. It drenched the small silent room in
a silvery light that made it hard for Lydia to hold on
to what was real and what was shadow. She sat very
still.

Chang An Lo lay on his side, breathing softly, his
head on her lap, the weight of his cheek warm on the
skin of her naked thigh. His eyes were closed, and
Lydia was studying his face with the same intensity
she used to study a snowflake as a child. As if by looking hard enough and long enough she could learn to
unravel what it was that held such miraculous beauty
and so know how to put it back together again when
it melted.

She studied his features minutely. The fine bone
under his eyebrow that swept up in such an expressive
arch when he was amused, the thick fringe of black
lashes. The long smooth eyelids. Were there images,
she wondered, that never left the inside surface of
them? In the translucent gleam of the moon the flesh
of his lips looked metallic. Was that what his gods

did? Forge him for themselves? And for China? Were they gathering unseen around her head even now, laughing at her presumption?

She listened carefully. No sound. No whispers, no sneers hidden behind hands. No invisible presences floating through the cracks in the window or crawling in thin trails under the door. The night was godless. Just Chang's breath, soft as the moonlight itself. How long could she keep him isolated? Steal him like this from his gods and his companions, and slide him right from under the nose of danger? She knew it couldn't last forever. Her fear for him was like a knot inside her, tightening each day, and her fear frightened her.

"Does Kuan know you leave the hotel at night?"

Chang opened his eyes, his black lashes heavy, and Lydia regretted speaking. His gaze was unfocused. She hadn't realized he was on the edge of sleep. He'd told her earlier that she needed more rest, that if she was tired she'd make mistakes, but the same applied to him. Now she'd woken him.

"Do you mean," he said with a slow smile, "is Kuan jealous that I leave the hotel at night?"

"Of course not."

He laughed, and she bent her head and kissed his open mouth.

"Does she know?" she asked again.

"She says nothing, but I'm sure she suspects."

"Is it safe?"

"Nothing is safe."

"Do the Russian watchdogs know?"

"I think not. I am quiet. I leave through the bathroom window and over the roofs."

"Take care."

"I do."

"Promise me."

"I promise."

She laid a hand on his silky black hair, fanning out her fingers to keep him safe. "Sleep now," she whispered. "You need rest."

"I need you."

"You have me."

She could feel his breath stirring the fiery curls at the base of her stomach. At times like this she had taught herself to stop thinking, to disconnect from all the wires in her brain and just be. To feel the musky warmth of his body and the bone of his shoulder embedded in her own flesh, as comfortable as though it were part of herself.

"Chang An Lo," she said. Because it was time.

His lips lazily brushed her thigh in response. "What are you hatching now?"

"Chang An Lo, if I asked you to come to America with me, would you come?"

IT WAS SO EASY JENS ALMOST LAUGHED OUT LOUD. NO RAIN this time, just a mass of pinpricks of stars lurking somewhere above the floodlights. The baker drove into the courtyard, the boy in the wide brimmed hat scurried back and forth with trays and woven baskets, his limbs shooting off in different directions as he juggled his loads, scuffling his feet. Jens was impressed. His timing was immaculate.

The boy emerged with an empty tray just as his boss plunged into the building with another full one, which meant the boy had about one minute. But he didn't appear to rush. With a moan of irritation he dumped his tray against the wall, flopped down on the mildewed stone bench that remained where it was in the yard because it was too heavy to move away, and started fiddling with the fastening on his boot. It seemed to have come undone.

Jens was watching through the compound fence the whole time and knew exactly where to look, but still he didn't spot the moment the letter vanished. He had slotted it inside a square fold of thin metal that he had fashioned specially for it, like a rusty old flake that had dropped off the guttering above. It was behind one foot of the bench, no more than a scrap of shadow on the cobbles.

Jens didn't see when it disappeared. It was there. Then it wasn't there. Behind his back he clasped his hands together to stop them from shaking and when the horse clopped its way safely out into the street, he started breathing again.

THIS MOMENT HAD TO COME. CHANG KNEW IT. LIKE HE KNEW the sun would rise and the stonechats would fly south in the winter. But not yet. There was no need for it yet. He didn't lift his head from

Lydia's lap. Instead he raised a hand and touched the strong tip of her chin and felt a quiver so faint she would have sworn it wasn't there.

"America?" he smiled up at her, keeping everything the same. "Why America?"

"But would you? When this is over."

"Would I come?"

"Yes."

"Would you ask me?"

She swallowed. He saw the struggle of it. For a brief second her hand clenched in his hair, then released its grasp on him and withdrew, and the loss of it made him feel suddenly naked. The moment slowed his heart.

"They say it's the land of opportunity," she said, her voice growing animated. "Wide open spaces. There's room for everyone. We could start a whole new life together without all the old rules. In America we would be free."

He reached up and tapped the side of her forehead. "This is the only place a person can be free. In the mind."

She smiled. "According to you, my love, everything is in the mind."

"And this? Is this in my mind?"

He pulled her head down to his and kissed her soft mouth because her lips had said enough. But with her eyes shining silver, she astonished him by murmuring, "Chang An Lo, it seems to me it is you who are running from the future. Away from what is real. I am the one preparing us."

"Preparing us for what?"

"For whatever is to come."

"Preparing us in what way?"

The silver gleam of her wide eyes flared bright and seemed to arc deep into his own mind. "By loving you," she whispered.

My precious daughter,

How can I tell you what it meant to me to receive your note? It was as if I'd been living in a black and rancid hole in the ground for the last twelve years and had suddenly come up for air. It filled me with joy.

Even my companions here questioned my unaccustomed good tem-

per! I fear I have become cold and difficult, turned in on my miserable self and my endless thoughts, but that is the way I have learned to survive. Not letting the outside world take bites out of me. Everything in me was focused on self because without self there is no hope of survival in the brutal and barbaric Soviet zoo out there in the Siberian wilderness. It was how I held myself together. Stripped of humanity. Just the hard core of self. I am not nice to know.

Now you are here. My daughter. Lydia, you are blood of my blood. You are all that was best in me, while I retain the worst. In you I can laugh and sing and love and be the person I yearn to be once more but know I can no longer be inside myself. You are my life, Lydia. Live it well.

I grieve deeply for the loss of your mother. It is terrible that we have both left you, unguarded and alone. Forgive us, my daughter. Give my fondest thoughts and gratitude to Alexei and that old reprobate Popkov.

I love you.
Your joyful Papa

Lydia stood by the window, gazing out but seeing nothing, her back to Popkov and Elena and the boy. For a long time she made no sound and would not relinquish her hold on the sheet of paper in her hand. Any more than she would relinquish her hold on life. They made her tea, which she didn't drink, and draped a coat over her shoulders as the sun escaped behind the roofs and the courtyard below was plunged into black shadow.

That was when she turned to Popkov and handed him the letter.

"Liev," she said, "we have to get him out."

"NO."

"Alexei, please."

"No, Lydia, no more letters."

"But why?"

"I've already warned you. The risk is too great. It will alert the authorities and end up with Jens Friis being packed off to one of the mines as punishment. Can't you see? You're making things worse for him, not better. Is that what you want?"

She shook her head.

"Then you have to stop at once."

They were in Maksim Voshchinsky's living room. Lydia hated having this argument in the first place, but to have it in front of the thief made her sick. Nevertheless she had no choice. Until he succeeded in finding a room of his own, Alexei had abandoned her empty bed at night in the room with Popkov and Elena and was sleeping in Maksim's apartment. But by the look of him he hadn't slept at all well. Damn him. She couldn't help hoping it was an excess of brandy and late-night cards and too many cigarettes, rather than anything more sinister. The thought of her brother crawling through windows and stuffing someone else's clocks and candlesticks into sacks sent the soles of her feet into spasms of fear. She didn't trust this Maksim. Any more than he trusted her.

"Alexei," she said with a patience that astonished even herself, "I am grateful that you and Maksim are working out a—"

"No need for you to be grateful, my dear," Maksim said with a smile so smooth and empty she wanted to knock it off his face.

"Of course I'm grateful to you, *pakhan*. Alexei is my dear brother, so—"

"Brothers and sisters don't exist in the *vory v zakone*," Maksim pointed out.

He leaned toward her in his chair, gathering the soft folds of his liver-colored dressing gown around his fleshy body, and he let her see into his eyes. Let her peer at the sharpened daggers in there. He wanted her to know. To make no mistake. She blinked but didn't look away.

"Lydia, my dear," he said in a tone as pleasant as though about to offer her more tea, "go away. Alexei and I are busy."

She remained seated. "I'd like to hear, if I may, the plans you have for—"

"When we are ready, you will know."

She didn't argue, but neither did she believe him.

"The truck?" she asked instead.

"Alexei," Maksim addressed his new *vor*, "is this necessary?"

"Yes."

At least that was something. She smiled at her brother, but he gave nothing in return. She wanted to seize his hand and drag him out of here.

Maksim applied his empty smile to her with a sigh that rumpled his mustache and wobbled his chins. "We've tracked the truck."

"To where?"

"To a location well outside Moscow."

"I'd like to see it."

"*Nyet.*"

"I assume it's well guarded."

"Of course."

"I need to see it, Maksim. Please."

"*Nyet.*"

She thought fast. It was that or scratch the bastard's empty eyes out.

"My brother will not want me to make a nuisance of myself, any more than you do. He knows how difficult I can be. After this," she smiled sweetly, "I shall not bother either of you any more."

His small eyes didn't even flicker. "Agreed."

It all happened so quickly. "Thank you."

"Now go," the thief said politely.

"May I have the letter back?" she asked Alexei, and held out her hand. She was frightened he would destroy it if she left it with him. He'd been so annoyed. Even now she wasn't sure he wouldn't tear it up in front of her just to make his point.

"No more letters," he reiterated as he passed it to her.

Lydia took it and tried to hide her relief. She nodded stiffly to Alexei, rose to her feet and moved over to the door. She made herself smile at Maksim before leaving.

"Thank you, *pakhan. Spasibo.* I look forward to hearing from you soon."

A cool stare was the only response. Alexei had the courtesy to join her at the door, but his manner was still withdrawn. She knew what the real problem was, where the hurt and the anger came from. *I love you,* their father had written to her in the letter. But only scrawled *Give my fondest thoughts and gratitude to Alexei.* A world of difference. She didn't want that gap to open up at their feet. She might tumble into the void.

She said quietly, "Walk with me to the corner of the street, Alexei."

IN HIS COAT ALEXEI LOOKED MORE LIKE HIS OLD SELF. SHE was pleased to see it was the one with the tear in the collar, the one against which she'd slept on the train with her head rolling around on its itchy shoulder. At least Maksim Voshchinsky had not replaced that. Not yet. Outside, the street was almost deserted instead of the usual bustle and rush of workers, and the chill air smelled of burned rubber. It settled like stinging black bees in the nostrils.

Alexei frowned. "Damn it, another factory burnt down. Poor bloody fools. That means jobs gone. No jobs means no food, and this winter is far from over yet. It's the second fire this month. Industrial fires happen all the time because of lack of safety regulations. Just carelessness. The workers smoke cigarettes where they shouldn't, hanging around chemicals and gas cylinders. No one stops them."

"What about the unions? Don't they enforce rules?"

"They try, but no one takes a blind bit of notice. It's the old working habits. They die hard."

"Unlike old family habits, it seems."

"What's that supposed to mean?"

"It means that you seem to have forgotten we're brother and sister."

"That's absurd."

"Is it?"

"Yes."

"Please, Alexei, don't forget about Jens too."

He seized her arm, drew her across the road to a baker's shop, and made her look at the queue outside. A line of women with gaunt faces and old men with eyes hard as iron. He headed to the front of the line and into the shop. Through the window Lydia watched the woman behind the counter smile at him, a cautious twitch of the mouth, remove a gray paper bag from a back shelf, and present it to Alexei. There was no exchange of kopecks.

Alexei rejoined Lydia on the pavement. With a solemn face he removed two *pirozhki* from the bag and presented her with one.

"That," he said, "is why your implications are absurd." She could hear the quiver of anger in his words.

"The advantages of a *vor*?"

"Exactly."

He was breathing hard. Lydia wanted to throw the *pirozhok* on the ground and tread on it. She was the first to look away.

"Alexei, there are disadvantages, as well as advantages. Don't forget that."

To her surprise Alexei laughed. He put an arm around her shoulders and drew her close, steering her past the dismal line. She slipped the *pirozhok* into the hand of a pockmarked child hiding in its mother's skirts and concentrated on enjoying the unexpected warmth of her brother's attention.

"Now what is it," he asked as he marched her to the corner of the street, "that you wanted to say to me in private?"

"Don't trust Maksim."

He stopped. Faced her. The anger there once more at the back of his eyes.

"Be careful," she added. "I don't want you to be . . ."

The word wouldn't come.

"You don't want me to be what?" he demanded.

"To be . . . damaged."

She didn't look at him. The silence that ballooned between them was pricked by the sound of a cart rumbling past. Alexei kissed Lydia's cheek, a quick touch of his lips to her cold skin and then away. As though ashamed of the gesture. When she looked up he was off striding back down the street, arms swinging as though to drive him even faster away from her.

Without turning around he shouted, "No more letters, Lydia."

Damn you, Alexei Serov. Damn you to hell.

ELENA WAS IN A BAD MOOD WHEN POPKOV CAME HOME WITH a nasty gash on his cheek and one leg of his trousers slashed up to the knee. A bruise the color of split damsons had hatched along the length of his shin. He slunk into the room, making low rumbling noises, and collapsed facedown on his bed, inert.

Lydia leapt past the dividing curtain and perched on the edge of the quilt, gently patting his back.

"Liev," she murmured, "are you all right?"

No answer. Just the rumbling sound seeping out of him. Elena rose from where she was sewing in the chair and came over to examine him. A quick firm finger to the pulse below his ear and a slap on the back of his head.

"He's drunk," she grumbled. "Drunk and bested in a fight. Stupid fool. If he's going to fight a gang of dolts, I've told him again and again, make sure it's a number he can flatten." She slapped him again, on his buttocks this time, and returned her bulk to the chair, where she scowled at the needle in her hand and jabbed it into the fabric as though it were into somebody's eyes.

Lydia waited for peace to settle, then fetched a bowl of cold water and bathed Liev's cheek as best she could without moving him. The white enamel bowl turned pink. Did he need stitches? She wasn't sure. The gash was deep. It reminded her of when she'd sewn up Chang's foot by the river in Junchow, and suddenly the ache for him that was always there inside her hit so sharply that her hand shook and she spilled crimson liquid over Liev's broad back.

"You trying to drown me, girl?"

The water flowed downhill to his neck and under his ear.

"Yes, but I'm not doing a very good job of it."

"Men bigger than you have failed."

"Don't talk. It makes it bleed worse."

"Shit!"

Lydia held a cloth pressed hard to his cheek and sat beside him without moving as time trickled past in silence. The rumbling had drifted off somewhere until it was no more than a cat's purr. But his breathing was labored. When abruptly all noise ceased, Lydia leaned close, heart thumping, listening hard. She prodded him in the ribs. Nothing happened. She jabbed an elbow into the ridge of his neck and only breathed again when he jerked back into life. He slammed a hand out at her in a reflex action that nearly knocked her head off, and the rumbling started up again at a lower volume.

"Feel like talking?" she whispered. Afraid he'd die in his sleep.

"Hah!"

"I bet the others are in worse shape. The ones who did this to you."

"Hah!"

"What was the fight about?"

"The bastard motherfuckers."

"What did they do?"

"They were waiting outside."

"Outside where?"

"Outside that place of yours."

Her heart stopped. She leaned down. Whispered in his ear. "The one on Raikov Ulitsa?"

"*Da.*"

Suddenly she was cold. Teeth chattering.

"How did they know? Chang and I are so careful. We double back again and again, so no one can follow."

"Hah!"

"How many of them?"

"*Chetyre.* Four."

"But now they'll inform on us and . . ."

"*Nyet.*" He twisted his head around and the black eye patch was wrenched upward, revealing the deformed empty socket. "*Nyet*, little Lydia, they're dead." A crooked grimace stretched his cheek and set the blood oozing once more. "So smile," he growled, "because you and me, Lydia, we're alive."

She rested her cheek on his, the stink of him warm and familiar, the feel of his shoulder like a sun-baked rock next to hers.

"The trouble with you, Liev Popkov, is that you're just too nice to people. Try being tougher next time."

He chuckled, his rib cage rattling like iron bars. "I need a drink."

Lydia sat up. "I'm going out to buy you the biggest bloody bottle of vodka in the whole of Moscow."

He grinned at her. One of his teeth was missing.

"Elena," Lydia said, "get over here, please. Keep him warm. Watch him while I'm gone."

The woman put down her needle and gave Lydia a long look. In that single moment Lydia felt Elena take a step back from her, as clearly as if she'd picked up the scissors on her lap and snipped at the thread that held them together. Their friendship had suddenly come unraveled in some way, and yet Lydia couldn't be angry. She knew it was her own fault. She trailed danger around with her the way other girls trailed ribbons. She watched sadly as the woman left her chair and clambered fully dressed onto the bed, where she wrapped herself around the big man, one arm tight around his neck, almost throttling him. Within seconds he was snoring.

As Lydia pulled on her coat, Elena tucked her face into his greasy black hair and muttered, "One of these days, Lydia Ivanova, you'll be the death of him."

Forty-seven

EDIK WAS OUT STALKING. LYDIA SPOTTED HIS PREY immediately, a man carrying parcels. He had just emerged from a tobacconist's store where smoking pipes of all shapes and sizes were displayed in the window, and he was far too preoccupied with relighting the fat cigar he was rolling between his equally fat lips to notice the skinny bag of bones tagging along behind him.

Lydia touched the boy's shoulder. "Bite me and I'll keep Misty's chunk of *kolbasa* sausage for myself."

Edik stopped and narrowed his eyes at her. "Piss off, I'm working."

"Don't let me stop you."

He regarded her with suspicion, recalling the time she'd made him replace his spoils in the pocket he'd stolen it from. With a shrug he darted forward, tucking in behind two women busy discussing the merits of their hats. Lydia admired the way he glided up to people and hovered briefly at their elbows, close enough so that he looked to others as though he might be with them, but not close enough to alarm them. Lone youths were always suspect.

"Mind if I tag along?" she asked.

"You'll get me spotted."

"No, I won't. I'll give you cover."

He thought for two seconds, saw the sense of it, and let her come alongside.

"I have a job for you," she murmured under her breath.

"Another letter?"

"Yes."

"No."

The speed of the *no* rattled her. "I thought . . ."

"No. No more letters."

"Is this about wanting more money? Because . . ."

His blue eyes skimmed her face scornfully. "Of course not. I just can't do it anymore."

"Why not?"

"I can't. That's all."

"Frightened of the prison?"

He didn't even deign to answer that one. They had worked their way nearer to the man with the cigar and the parcels, and Edik was up on his toes, hands loose at his sides, ready.

"I'll get you a good snatch," Lydia promised, "if you'll deliver one more letter."

"Yeah?"

"Watch me."

Lydia moved in close. She swung to one side of the man, the boy to the other. As if hurrying past the unsuspecting mark, she banged her hip on his bundle of parcels, winced, stumbled, and clutched at him for support. Instantly the man was all solicitude. She smiled her most charming smile, thanked him, and moved on rapidly. By the time Edik caught up with her in the next side street, he was laughing.

"You're good. For a girl."

"You're not bad yourself. For a kid. What did you get?"

He held out a heavy silver cigar case inlaid with diagonal stripes of jet. "It'll do, I suppose." He said it in an offhand manner, but both knew it was a valuable snatch. "You?"

She hoisted a calfskin wallet from her pocket. It felt well stocked. She tossed it to him.

"Mine?"

"I promised, didn't I?" she said. "Now the letter." On her palm lay the square metal folder. She proffered it to him.

"No." The sallow cheeks flushed a dull pink and made him look very young.

"Edik! What the . . .?" And that was when it dawned on her. *Chyort!* She should have seen it coming. "It's the *vory v zakone*, isn't it? They've ordered you to stop."

He nodded. Angry and ashamed.

Then something else clicked into place in her head. "Misty? Where's Misty?"

He looked away. Wouldn't let her see his face. His fingers were counting out the rouble notes in the wallet, but his whole body drooped with an inner misery that seeped out at the mention of the pup's name.

"They've got her, haven't they?" Lydia exclaimed. "The *vory* have taken your dog to make sure you obey."

Edik stuffed the wallet into his oversized pocket. "Bastards," he whispered.

"Bastards," Lydia echoed.

But she knew it was Alexei. Controlling her the only way he knew how.

"Bastard," she said again and squeezed the boy's arm. "I'll get her back for you, don't worry."

Edik kicked out at a mound of ice that shattered in the sunshine, creating a thousand shimmering rainbows. "I'll kill them if they hurt her."

Lydia slipped the metal folder into her pocket next to where the cigar man's gold watch was ticking discreetly, and she started to run, slipping and sliding on the snow.

"KUAN."

The Chinese girl looked surprised at first, then nervous. She was coming down the wide steps of the Hotel Triumfal and hadn't noticed the slight figure in the shadows across the road. It was her habit to walk in the park opposite the hotel before it grew dark. She hesitated.

"Kuan," Lydia called again.

She was thankful when the Chinese girl moved toward her. She didn't want to have to chase her up the steps of the hotel. The blue coat and the bulky hat with the ugly gray rabbit fur trimming made Kuan satisfyingly shapeless, not a figure of allure for her fellow delegates. Nevertheless, Lydia's palms were sweating. There was something about the Chinese girl's smooth face, something you wouldn't want to cross. Determination was chiseled into its features, commitment luminous in the eyes. Chang would admire it.

Kuan placed her small palms together and bowed politely over them. Lydia ignored the courtesy.

"Kuan," she said, her voice bordering on rude. "Will you please tell Chang An Lo that my aunt is ill, so I must leave." It was the wording they had agreed on should she ever need to warn him to stay away.

The girl studied her, black eyes carefully featureless. Lydia wondered how much Russian she understood.

"You will tell him?" Lydia prompted.

"*Da.*"

"Thank you."

They stood there in the twilight, their shadows merging on the scrubby grass, and Lydia stepped to one side to separate them. The naked silhouettes of the trees jabbed fingers at them in the wind.

"Kuan, why did you betray Chang to the Soviet police? You told them about the room on Raikov Ulitsa, didn't you?"

The black eyes revealed nothing. "I do not know the meaning of the word *betray.*"

"It's what you do to your enemies. Not to your friends."

"Comrade Chang is my friend."

"Then treat him like one."

The blank eyes suddenly came alive, the stolid body unexpectedly fluid and mobile as it swung to face Lydia. "Leave him in peace, *fanqui.*"

Lydia knew the word, she'd heard it a thousand times in Junchow. *Fanqui.* It meant *Foreign Devil.*

But Kuan hadn't finished. "You have no need of him," she said. "There are many Russian men you can take instead. Choose your Soviet officer, the one with the fox-colored hair. One of your own.

But leave Chang An Lo alone." She was close enough for Lydia to see the faint tremble in the corner of her eyelid. "Give him back to China," Kuan hissed.

JENS WOKE WITH A SENSE OF SHARP HUNGER. NOT IN HIS stomach. It was centered somewhere in his brain, gnawing its way along the coils, devouring parts of him. He tried desperately to recall what he'd been dreaming about, but it had drifted out of reach already, leaving him with just the hunger and a waft of perfume more real in his nostrils than the dank odor of the basement cell.

Today would bring another letter.

Jens rolled onto his front to avoid the constant light of the dim overhead bulb and buried his face in the grubby pillow, so thin he could feel the bed slats through it. Today another letter. From his daughter.

That one word—*daughter. Dochka.* It altered him. Changed his perception and made a different person of him. It made it harder to bear what he had done and what he was still doing on the project. He groaned into the flimsy pillow. He wanted to sit Lydia down in front of him and explain. *Don't judge harshly, maleeshka. A man on his own with no one and nothing in an inhuman wasteland is one thing. He hardens like the shell of a walnut and over time the soft kernel inside slowly shrivels and dies. But a man with a daughter is quite another.*

A man with a daughter has a hold on the future.

"PRISONER FRIIS, DO YOU AGREE WITH PRISONER ELKIN? THAT everything is ready?"

"Yes, Comrade Colonel."

"You surprise me."

"We have worked hard, Comrade Colonel."

They were in Colonel Tursenov's office, strung out in a nervous line. The chief scientists and engineers on the project stood uneasily in front of his leather-topped desk, eyes fixed on the faded Turkish carpet under their feet. When spoken to directly, their gaze crept up to Tursenov's collar with its red flashes. No higher.

"I expect to be impressed," the colonel said. "There will be

guests, high-level military observers. So no mistakes. You understand me?"

"Yes, Colonel."

Tursenov strutted along the line, his spectacles glinting with satisfaction. "I have selected the location for a full test."

"A full test?" Elkin exclaimed. "I thought . . ." He looked suddenly pale.

"What you thought, prisoner, is irrelevant." Tursenov turned his
head and scrutinized Jens. "A full test," he snapped. "No mistake of
any kind."

Jens stared straight at him, right to the back of the hard gray eyes,
and what he saw there wasn't satisfaction. It was fear. Failure was
not an option for a man like Tursenov because failure would mean a
sentence of twenty years in a prison labor camp, and long before the
first year was up he'd be torn limb from limb when the guards' backs
were turned. Jens had seen it happen. Had heard the screams.

"No mistakes," Jens assured him.

"Good."

"May I ask the location of the test?"

"This will amuse you, Prisoner Friis. It is to be in Surkov
camp."

"But Colonel, there are hundreds of prisoners there."

"So?"

"You can't kill all—"

"It's not me doing the killing, Prisoner Friis. It's you."

"But there's no need to."

"Of course there is, Prisoner Friis. We need to ascertain how low
the planes must fly and the exact concentration of the gas. The test
will be conducted at Surkov camp. The decision is made."

Surkov camp. A flash of memories arced through Jens's head,
jolting it on his shoulders. Barbed wire tied around his wrists, beatings with an iron pipe till it buckled, solitary confinement in a cell
smaller than a coffin, a robin fluttering bright as a ruby on his finger
until a guard broke both the bird and his finger with his rifle butt.

"It's the place where you started your life as a prisoner, I
believe."

"Started my death as a prisoner," Jens corrected.

Tursenov laughed. "That's good. I like that." The laughter trickled away as he studied Jens's face. "Well now, it looks like you'll be starting the death of other prisoners too. But I wouldn't let that worry you. You're alive, aren't you? You've survived."

"Yes, Comrade Colonel. I have survived."

THE LIGHT IN THE COURTYARD WAS YELLOW. IT TUMBLED through the darkness and spilled like oil onto the figures hunched in the cold morning air. Today it seemed to Jens that it made everyone look sick, but maybe that was because they all felt sick after yesterday's meeting with Tursenov.

A full test. At Surkov camp. Dear God, he hadn't expected that. There were people he knew there, men he'd eaten with, worked with, prisoners who had cared for him when he was sick.

He walked, limbs stiff and heavy, around the circle behind the compound's metal fence, pleased not to talk, not to think. His gaze was fixed on the massive iron gate, his ears tuned for the screech of its hinges, and he didn't even notice that Olga was limping. He didn't see her distress because he was too blinded by his own.

"GET OUT HERE, YOU BIG OAF!"

The baker was throwing open the back of the cart but the horse was jittery, tossing its head from side to side, picking up each feathery foot in turn, and all the time Jens watched out of the corner of his eye for the boy. Why wasn't the thin figure there? He should be grabbing the reins.

"Keep moving," a guard yelled.

It was Babitsky, his temper fraying at the edges this morning because he had woken with a thumping cold and the last thing he wanted was to be stuck on exercise duty. Jens moved his feet. He hadn't even realized they'd stopped. Other prisoners muttered impatiently, their combined breath a white fog in the compound, so it took a moment before he could glance again at the cart, a quick glimpse over his shoulder as he followed the trail of footprints that stirred up the ice underfoot.

What he saw slammed into his mind. Either his eyes or his brain surely had got it wrong. It had to be a mistake. He looked away, concentrating on keeping his limbs functioning, and three seconds later when he again turned his head, he was convinced the scene would be rearranged.

It wasn't.

He had to clamp his teeth viciously on his tongue to stop himself shouting out. His mind froze. He rounded the bottom of the exercise circle, unaware that he had speeded up until he crashed into the man in front.

"Watch yourself," the man snapped.

Jens didn't even hear. He was staring at the bread cart. At the horse. At the big man who had come from the far side and was now facing in Jens's direction, holding the reins and running a massive hand down the animal's sweating neck. Jens recognized him at once even after all these years. It was Popkov, Liev Popkov. Older and dirtier, but Jens would know that damn Cossack anywhere. The black eye patch, the saber scar across the forehead that Jens remembered being inflicted as if it were yesterday.

"What's up with you?" The man behind jabbed him.

"Silence!" Babitsky yelled.

Jens noticed Olga watching him, but her face was a blur. He kept walking. How long had he been out here in the yellow-stained darkness? Fifteen minutes? Twenty? Twenty-five? He might have only a few minutes left. He drew a deep breath, the air scouring his lungs, but it calmed him. His mind started to tick.

Hadn't Lydia mentioned in her note that the Cossack was with her here in Moscow? Popkov and Alexei, she'd said. Without seeming to rush, he glanced again through the wire fence and across the thirty or so meters that separated him from the baker's cart.

An involuntary flicker of the eyes skipped over to the stone seat against the wall. Jens had made another small flat folder of metal, so that the boy could pick up the new one at the same time that he returned with a note from Lydia. But the boy wasn't here. Popkov was. The big man was carrying a tray of *pelmeni* that wafted a mouth-watering meaty smell over to the prisoners, and Jens saw him glance casually at the seat, at the cobbles under the seat, as he lumbered past it into the building. All smooth so far.

It was as Popkov emerged that everything went wrong. As if by accident their eyes met and the Cossack gave what could have been a nod or just a nervous twitch of the thick neck. Jens lifted a hand and adjusted his hat. A wave of sorts. The baker was in a hurry. To Jens's watchful eyes he seemed even more nervous today, tetchier, his feet scampering over the cobbles as though walking on coals.

"You!' The roar came from Babitsky. "I know you, you fucking bastard."

Everyone turned and stared at the hefty guard. Babitsky's rifle was aimed straight at Popkov's chest.

"Grab that big bastard," Babitsky shouted. Even in the predawn cold, his face had turned vermilion. He was pounding across the courtyard, his rifle stuck out in front of him. "You," he bellowed, "I'm going to kill you."

Jens hurled himself at the fence. "Run," he screamed.

But there was nowhere to run and the Cossack knew it. The gate was barred, the courtyard ringed with uniforms edging closer, rifle muzzles tracking every move he made. He gave Jens a flash of teeth in the black beard, flexed his massive shoulders, and prepared to fight with bare hands.

"*Nyet*," Jens shouted. "Don't . . ."

Babitsky exploded onto Popkov, rifle thrust hard at his stomach. The guard was big, but Popkov was bigger and faster. He stepped neatly to one side, pivoted on his heel, and snapped the edge of one hand across Babitsky's throat so that his knees buckled like bent straws. He clawed for air as he crashed to the ground. The other guards moved forward warily, surrounding the Cossack, who had snatched Babitsky's rifle from the ground and started to swing it around the circle like a club, cracking elbows and jabbing at jaws.

Jens clutched the wire. Everyone knew what was coming.

A shot rang out. The sound of it was deafening in the enclosed yard as it ricocheted off the walls. The prisoners groaned in unison, all pressing their faces against the fence, the exercise circle forgotten. Popkov fell, his hand groping under the stone seat. Blood flowed onto the cobbles.

Forty-eight

LYDIA POUNDED HER FIST ON THE DOOR TILL it shook on its hinges and rattled in its frame. Still it didn't open. She thumped it harder, again and again. Until the skin on her knuckles split. At long last there was the turning of a lock and the door jerked open.

"What the bloody hell . . .?" A pause. "Well now, if it isn't little Lydia. What on earth are you doing here making such a row at this unseemly hour of the morning?"

"I need your help, Dmitri."

The Soviet officer smiled, a quiet steady smile that seemed to bob to the surface from somewhere deep down as if he'd been expecting this moment, just not certain where among all the other moments it was hiding. He stepped back into the hallway, pulling the door wide open for her, and waved her inside.

"What was wrong with the doorbell?" he asked mildly.

"It was too . . . easy."

"Too easy? What crazy place does that idea come from?"

"I needed to hit something."

★ ★ ★

THEY SAT IN THE DINING ROOM FACING EACH OTHER ACROSS the middle of a long oak table. It was a beautiful piece of furniture, but so ornate with heavily carved feet that it jarred with the modernism of its owner. It occurred to Lydia that, like Antonina's bracelet, it may have been acquired from someone needing help. Someone like herself.

"So," he said with an easy smile, "what has got young Lydia so worked up this morning?"

"I'm not worked up." She picked up her coffee and sipped it with a show of calm, but she couldn't swallow, couldn't shift the pulse of pain.

His gray eyes creased with amusement, and she realized she wasn't fooling him. He had sat her down, insisting that she join him for breakfast, poured her coffee and offered warm croissants from a French bakery, bottled peaches, and wafer-thin slices of smoked pork. She stuck to just the coffee. She would choke if she tried to eat. He was wearing embroidered slippers and a Japanese silk robe with a white linen napkin tucked into its front. With surgical precision he was slicing one of the peaches.

Lydia took a deep breath and let out the words she'd come to say. "Dmitri, today a friend of mine was shot."

He raised one eyebrow. "The Chinese?"

"No." The word jumped out of her mouth. "No, it was a Cossack friend of mine called Liev Popkov."

"A Cossack? He probably deserved to be shot then."

In a low voice she said, "Dmitri, I will stick this knife in your throat if you say that about Liev Popkov."

He placed a sliver of fruit in his mouth, dabbed the napkin to his lips, and sat back with a serious expression. "Tell me what happened," he said.

"I wasn't there."

I wasn't there, I wasn't there. Chyort! I wasn't there to help him when he needed me. Guilt jammed in her throat like a pebble from the Moskva River.

"So someone told you what happened?"

"Yes." She leaned forward on the table. "My friend had just

started work for a baker and they were making a delivery to a prison here in Moscow."

"A prison?" The Russian smiled. "What a coincidence."

Lydia hurried on. "The baker said that suddenly one of the guards came charging at Popkov, and he just defended himself. One of the other guards shot him."

"Understandably if he was creating trouble."

Lydia made herself ignore the comment. "The baker was ordered to leave immediately and has no idea whether my friend lived or died."

"Ah!" He inclined his head. "Distressing for you."

There was an awkward little silence. Lydia put her hands on her lap and made them stay there. "The baker says the guard claimed to recognize Popkov. It seems they had a fight some time ago in Felanka." She watched his pupils dilate with a sudden spike of interest at the mention of Felanka, though he maintained an attitude of quiet detachment. "In Felanka," she explained, "Popkov beat the hell out of the guard and he wanted revenge."

"I've seen too many of them, Lydia, these people who think with their fists. The prison camps are full of them. They live by their fists and more often than not they die by them too."

"Popkov may not be dead," she insisted.

"So." Malofeyev raised his coffee cup and studied her over the gilt-edged rim. "You want to know what state this oaf is in and where he is."

"No."

"What then?"

"I want you to get him returned to me."

"Dead?"

"Dead or alive."

"And why would I do that?"

"Dmitri, this isn't like my request for the name of the prison. That was secret information, this isn't. It's just a misunderstanding. A stupid fight that flared up for no reason." She lifted her hands from her lap, placed them on the polished surface of the table, and let them fall apart to reveal a heavy gold watch, its casing exquisitely wrought, its face intricately engraved. It was the one she'd stolen from the cigar man's pocket. She looked at Dmitri and exhaled carefully. "I'm sure it's something you could sort out with just a couple of telephone calls."

His eyes had fixed on the watch. "Well, Lydia, you do surprise me. Is this all your friendship is worth?"

Lydia wasn't sure what he meant, and it angered her. Friendship with him or friendship with the Cossack? But something in the way he looked at the watch made her blood slow and stumble in her veins. It wasn't enough. Already she knew it wasn't going to be enough.

"What is it you want instead?" she asked.

He put down his cup and leaned forward, elbows on the table, eyes intent on hers. She became aware that the room was unbearably overhot. "I told you once before, Lydia, I want you to look at me the way you looked at your Chinese the night at the Metropol."

"That will never happen."

"Never say never, my dear. It could."

Abruptly he rose to his feet, threw his napkin onto his plate, and moved around the length of the table until he was standing directly behind her. The whisper of his slippers on the polished parquet floor made her skin prickle as though she'd brushed against nettles. He touched the back of her hair. She didn't flinch. His fingers burrowed into her dense mane as if they had a right to be there.

"You are very lovely, Lydia, and very young."

"I'm old enough."

He bent down behind her until his lips were soft on her ear. "Old enough to know what you want?"

She nodded.

He kissed her earlobe. She didn't move. Just smelled the clean scent of him and felt his hair mingle with her own.

"And is this what you want?" He lifted a loop of her hair aside, twining its strands around his fist so that she was attached to him, and kissed the pale skin of her neck.

She nodded. It was the least she owed Popkov.

"Then I think I can help you," he murmured, sliding a hand around to the front of her neck. "So sweetly delicate." His fingers started to explore, to caress the fragile stem of her collarbone, to insinuate themselves deeper into the opening of her blouse until they found the soft rise of her breast and she could feel his breath coming hot and moist on the skin of her cheek.

"Your wife, Antonina?" she asked. "Is she here? In the apartment?"
The fingers froze. "She's still in bed."

"Even so. Not ideal, is it?"

"I didn't think you were an idealist, Lydia. More of a realist, it seemed to me." He kissed the top of her head and his other hand came around the side of her chair to encircle her waist, pinning her there.

"Dmitri," she said in a firm voice, "let me go." She heard his exhalation of air. "But I give you my word," she added, "you can pick your time and place—as soon as Liev Popkov is safely home."

"Dead or alive?"

"Dead or alive."

With reluctance he withdrew his arm, uncoiling it slowly. She rose to her feet. She'd bought a breathing space. "Thank you, Dmitri."

"Oh damn it, Lydia, will you ever make life easy for me?" He was still breathing hard.

"I doubt it." She forced a smile of sorts.

"But I have your word?"

"Yes, you have my word. Just find me Liev Popkov." For a moment she stepped nearer. Her face close to his. "Find him," she said harshly, and saw him recoil in surprise.

She moved away to the dining room door and swung it open, only to discover Antonina on the other side. She was wearing an oyster-pink negligée, her sharp painted nails held out in front of her like claws. How long she'd been standing there it was impossible to tell.

"Lydia, my friend, I had no idea you were here," she said brightly. "Dmitri, you should have told me and I'd have joined you both for coffee."

Her smile was as brittle as the stem of a wineglass.

"Another time, Antonina," she said quickly, and walked out of the overheated apartment.

CHANG FOUND HER. HOW ON EARTH HE FOUND HER SHE HAD no idea. All that mattered was that he was here and she could feel his heart beating as hard as if he'd been running. He steered her through a maze of side streets till they came to a shabby stretch of houses where two strangers would be ignored because no one wanted trouble. They already had enough of their own. Chang lifted her chin and kissed her, and she felt sick with shame. He didn't ask her what she was doing running the streets at this early hour of the morning and she wondered if he could smell Dmitri on her.

"Lydia, Kuan gave me your message."

She leaned her face into the collar of his coat.

"Here is a new key to a new room." He pressed a small metal object into her palm and a scrap of paper bearing an address. "Be calm," he murmured. "Tell me what it is that has disturbed you."

She shook her head, mute. He waited until she was able to speak.

"It's Popkov. He's been shot," she whispered. "Because of me he might be dead." Her lips felt numb. "I don't know whether he's alive or dead."

His hand soothed the crumpled line of her spine, and she felt a rush of memory of another man's fingers on her skin. She shivered fiercely and when Chang drew back to look at her face, she knew he would know there was more.

"I'm worried for Elena," she said quickly. "She'll be frantic about Liev."

He leaned forward again and kissed each of her eyelids in turn.

"Close your eyes, Lydia. Rest them. There is nothing you can do to help your Cossack friend."

Her forehead sank onto his collar once more. Her limbs were trembling and she couldn't stop them. Any more than she could stop hating herself.

My dearest Papa,

To talk to my father is wonderful. I never thought I would hear your voice—even if it is only on paper. As I grew up I spoke to you many times and told you many things, but I was always whispering to the empty darkness. How could it be otherwise? I believed you were dead. But now I grow greedy. I want more of you, Papa. I want to know you and I want you to know me.

So what shall I tell you? That I have your hair, you already know. What else? I lack Mama's skill at the piano, but my fingers

*are quick in other ways and my mind is struggling with the concepts
of this new system that is sweeping through Russia and China. This
Communism. I admire its ideals but I despise its inhumanity. Stalin
says you cannot make a revolution with silk gloves, but surely the
individual still matters. You matter. I matter.*

*What else matters in my life? I once owned a white rabbit called
Sun Yat-sen. He mattered. I have a friend called Chang An Lo—
you spoke to him. He means more to me than my own breath. Liev
Popkov is my good friend, more than a friend. And Alexei is the
brother I always wanted. So now you know me, Papa. I wear a horrible brown hat and I like sugary apricot dumplings and have discovered Kandinsky paintings.*

*Tell me about yourself. Tell me what you think. How you spend
your days. Describe for me what you are working on. I long to know.
I send you my love.*

Lydia

Jens kissed the letter. He kissed each word. He would have kissed
Liev Popkov if he could. The big man had delivered it as he died.
Jens had retrieved the flake of metal from under the seat, stooping
to tie his bootlaces as he was led out to the truck. *Oh Popkov, my old
friend.* Dragged away in a roll of canvas. Anger scraped like grit in his
gut as he paced his cell in the semidark, but his rage was as much for
himself as for the Cossack.

"Babitsky," he growled to the dead walls, "I hope you burn."

ALEXEI LOVED THE STREETS OF MOSCOW. IN PLACES WHOLE
roads were being demolished, great new thoroughfares emerging.
Rows of individual houses and shops were swept away at the stroke
of an architect's pen and vast multistory buildings were clawing their
way up out of the soil like a new kind of gigantic urban mushroom.
Seated on the backseat of the car in the moody gray light of a winter's afternoon, he was swept past the sprawl of construction sites and
knew he was witnessing the world changing. It stirred him. Stalin
was throwing everything into redesigning and broadening the Russian streets but also the Russian mind.

"Maksim," he said to the man swaddled in rugs beside him, "one of the *vory* rules is that we mustn't collaborate with authority in any way."

"Of course not. Those in authority destroy every hope of a freedom of mind. The *vory* bow the knee to no man outside the brotherhood. That's why we have stars tattooed on our knees to remind us."

"So if the OGPU secret police turn up at your door at two o'clock in the morning, demanding to know information about one of your members of the thieves-in-law, what then?"

"I spit on their boots."

"And end up in one of the labor camps?"

Maksim laughed. "I've been there before."

"But now you're older."

"Sicker is what you mean."

"All right, sicker." The older man's flesh hung gray and doughy from the bones of his face. "You should have stayed at home. You're tired."

They were riding in an old bone-shaker of a car, which didn't help, but the silky smooth limousine that Alexei had grown accustomed to using when in Maksim Voshchinsky's company had remained in its garage today to avoid any risk of identification. This vehicle was anonymous; it belonged to no one. It was stolen.

"How far now?" Maksim Voshchinsky asked.

"Another few miles," Igor offered from the front seat. There were beads of sweat on the back of his neck. He was nervous.

Alexei gave Lydia a nod. "The route we're taking will take longer. But it's safer."

She said nothing. She'd been silent since they'd set off, hunched into her corner, unresponsive and mute. It annoyed Alexei. He'd had to stand his ground with Maksim to win her this place in the car, and a little politeness wouldn't have come amiss. Sometimes, like today, he couldn't work her out. Shouldn't she be pleased, maybe even impressed, and certainly grateful, at the prospect of where he was taking her this afternoon? But no. Silent and sullen. Tawny eyes refusing to meet his. All she did was cling to the side window with a fixed stare as though memorizing the route. Maybe she was. That thought worried him.

Or was it fear? It surprised him that it hadn't occurred to him before. Was his sister frightened? He felt an odd rush of tenderness toward her despite her withdrawn manner because he knew fear was something Lydia would never admit to. She'd rather bite her tongue off first.

"Lydia," he said in an attempt to draw her out of her isolation, "the truck took the prisoners to the hangars early this morning. It hasn't returned yet, so we believe Jens is actually there right now."

She dragged her face from the window and frowned at Maksim. "Did your *vory* men follow it?"

"*Da*, of course."

"What if they were spotted?"

"Hah! They were not spotted."

"But if they were, there will be soldiers and police waiting for us."

He laughed, a rich amused sound that warmed the chill interior of the car. "My men are *vory*. Thieves. Harder to trace than shadows in snow. You understand?"

She nodded. But Alexei was not sure she did. She didn't realize exactly how these men functioned or that they were outside the normal margins of society. To her they were just criminals. It was clear she didn't trust them, and he was surprised she hadn't insisted on dragging that oaf Popkov along too. When it came to watching her back, that filthy Cossack was the one she relied on, God only knows why.

"No action today," he reminded her. He was wary of what she might do. "We're going out there to observe. Nothing more."

"I know."

"Just don't expect too much."

"I expect nothing."

"That's a good place to start," Maksim chuckled.

She turned her attention back to the window. They had left the streets of the city behind, passing the foul-smelling Red Hercules rubber factory some time back and were driving north of Moscow. Huddles of wooden *izbas,* peasant cottages with a cow tethered at the front and dense rows of vegetables at the rear, popped up at intervals and broke the monotony of the flat and featureless landscape. The road ran straight as a prison bar across it. At one point a group of women were washing their bedsheets in the river and looked up with a moment's interest. Otherwise there was nothing, not even other traffic, just the spiny edge of the pine forest that blocked out the horizon on both sides.

The car stopped.

"Out," Igor ordered.

They all climbed out onto the empty windswept landscape, except the driver, and the car swerved off the deserted road onto a patch of rough ground, where the driver promptly began to remove a wheel.

"Now what?" Maksim demanded.

"Over there." Alexei indicated a darker shadow tucked among the trees. It was a small covered army truck.

This was a point where the pines looped close to the road and a single track dirt trail cut through the tall willowy trunks. The track was obviously well used, and heavy wheels had gouged deep ruts into its frozen surface.

Maksim's eyes narrowed into slits. "This is as far as I go."

Alexei nodded and draped a rug over the older man's shoulders, then climbed into the Soviet army vehicle he had stolen the previous night and tried the engine. It started on the first time. Satisfied, he gunned it to full throttle.

"You can wait here if you prefer," he called out to Lydia.

"No."

"Then get in."

She scrambled up beside him on the front bench and Igor jumped up after her. Alexei kicked the truck into gear.

Forty-nine

"RELAX, LYDIA, ENJOY THE RIDE." HE GRIPPED THE steering wheel as it was almost jolted out of his hands and the truck bounced its way across a narrow ditch.

"Don't they have guards on patrol?" she demanded. "Snipers in the trees?"

"Of course. That's why we're in an army truck. No one will take any notice of it."

"And what happens when we get there?"

"We're not driving up to the front door and knocking on it politely, if that's what you mean. Don't worry."

"I am worried."

Alexei glanced at his sister's face. This wasn't the Lydia he'd traveled halfway across Russia with. That Lydia would have been brimming with excitement.

"What's the matter with you?" he asked quietly.

"*Chyort!* What do you think is the matter with me?" She blinked hard and stared ahead through the windshield. "It's this insane driving."

"You said you wanted to see the layout of where Jens Friis is working?"

"Yes."

"Then hold on tight."

At that moment he swung the heavy wheel, both arms working hard, and abandoned the graveled track.

"This way." Igor indicated off to the right.

The side window was caught by a low branch, and Lydia flinched violently at the crack it made. She was jumpy as hell. For half a mile he concentrated on nothing but wrestling the damn truck through the trees, avoiding gullies and mounds of packed snow that formed traps that wouldn't melt till spring.

"What's the matter, Lydia?" he asked again when he struck a stretch where the terrain grew smoother.

Her hands were huddled like little corpses in her lap, unmoving and stiff. "Let's focus on our father," she murmured in a low voice. "And this crazy ride."

"If that's what you want."

"It is."

"Are you all right? Has something happened?"

"I'm fine."

One of her gloved hands crept off her lap and settled in the valley between his thigh and hers. It curled up there as if needing warmth. He stamped on the brake pedal to avoid a jagged stump and jinked the truck so that its wheels slid into a sideways skid. One fender brushed along the length of a bough that was draped in icicles and gave off a noise like the rattle of buckshot.

"Alexei, do you have any idea where the hell we're going?"

For a split second their eyes met, and he knew she wasn't talking about the forest.

"How about to the top of the tree?"

She smiled.

He looked away quickly and just missed crunching into a blackened pine trunk.

"IS THIS IT?"

"Yes. This is as far as we go. The rest is on foot." Alexei was pushing to move on fast.

They clambered out of the truck, the air bone-white with a mist that twisted in and out of the trees like beckoning fingers. Igor threw a canvas pack on his back.

"It's just up ahead," he said.

They moved off in single file, keeping close to the dark trunks. In this mist it would be easy to lose touch. The remnants of the snow were heaped into hunched shapes by the wind, and underfoot the cracking of brittle pine needles betrayed their movements. Alexei slipped the gun out of his pocket.

"Sentries?" Lydia whispered.

He nodded. "They patrol the forest in pairs. But the guards are cold and bored, and after months of tedium they expect to find nothing, so they pay scant attention to what is in the forest. They spend more time patrolling the complex itself."

"Alexei, why did Maksim come? It's a bitterly cold day and he looks ill. Even back there in the car it could be dangerous for him if he's found and questioned. It wasn't necessary."

"Yes, it was. To remind his *vory* who is their *pakhan*."

"To remind the thieves? Or to remind you?"

"Does it matter?"

"Yes."

It wasn't a question he chose to answer. Instead he silenced her by placing a finger to his lips, so that they crept forward more cautiously, Lydia right on his heel. Igor watched the rear. The forest ended abruptly, switching within the space of ten paces from its own private twilight to an open expanse of slippery white sky. An area the size of a village had been flattened within the heart of the forest, an efficient clearing of timber to carve out a rectangle that was hidden from view by a brick wall erected around its perimeter. Ten meters high and topped with razor wire, while around its base more strands coiled like a sleeping spiny serpent.

"Not very welcoming," Lydia whispered in Alexei's ear.

He grimaced. "It's not meant to be."

"So how do we get in?"

"We don't."

"I thought we were here to observe the complex they've built. That's what you said."

"That's right."

"But the wall hides it all from view. I can't see anything."

He leaned back against one of the pine trunks, merging his silhouette with its rough bark. "You will," he promised.

"TIME TO GO, LYDIA."

Alexei looked up. His sister was still peering intently through Zeiss binoculars high up in one of the pine trees, a good fifteen meters off the ground. She looked small up there in the shadows of the canopy, and he could tell by the concentration on her face how much she wanted to stay.

"Lydia," he said quietly, aware of how sound carried in the heavy damp air.

She removed the binoculars with reluctance. "Bring me down."

Igor played out the rope and dropped her down from her perch so fast that Alexei was surprised her legs didn't break as she hit the ground. She handed the binoculars back to Igor.

"*Spasibo*," was all she said.

She'd been surprised by Igor. By the way he'd looped a strap of leather between his ankles and around one of the narrow trees that was set back from the forest's edge. Using the foot strap and another one between his wrists, he shinned up the trunk as fast as a polecat, his plump stocky legs pumping away with unexpected muscles. Lydia had watched, mouth open, astonished. Alexei had smiled. He'd seen it before in the streets of Moscow at night. That's how Igor scaled the drainpipes of apartment houses. Once up in the canopy he'd hooked a rope from his backpack over a branch and rigged up a sling on a simple pulley. So now Lydia had seen over the wall, exactly as he'd promised.

"It's a hangar," she said, keeping her voice low.

"A massive one."

"What's in it?" Her eyes were huge, shining with the excitement he'd expected to find earlier. This was more like Lydia. "And what do you think all the sheds are for?"

"The sheds are for storage of equipment. We've watched them haul machinery on carts over to the hangar."

"There are some big containers outside it. What are they?"

"They look like gasoline tanks to me. And the brick shed over to the right is the guardhouse."

She nodded, her hat tumbling off. She jammed it back on. "I spotted that, the soldiers, coming and going in and out of it. Dogs as well."

"It's an interesting complex they've constructed here. A vast expanse of open space sliced out of a forest and walled in for secrecy. What the hell are they up to in there?"

"A new kind of airplane?"

"Maybe. But Jens is not—"

Her fingers gripped his wrist, so hard they seemed to drill into the nerves, but he barely noticed. Her face was as white as the mist that draped itself over her shoulders.

"I saw him," she whispered.

"What?"

"I saw Papa."

"No, Lydia, Jens would be inside working. They wouldn't be allowed to wander around at will, and anyway"—he gave a small snort of impatience—"you'd be unlikely to recognize him after all these years."

"I tell you I saw him."

"Where?"

"Through the binoculars. He was sitting on a bench beside the big hangar."

"You're imagining things."

"It was him. I know it was."

Alexei left it there. Why argue the point? If she wanted so badly to believe she'd seen her father, then let her believe it.

"Come on," he said in a brisk voice, and removed his wrist from her grasp. "Let's get moving. Igor has finished packing away the rope."

The wind was picking up, snatching at the branches, stealing through the mist. As they set off in single file once more, keeping close, Lydia cast one last glance back at the perimeter wall and whispered, "He had a woman sitting next to him, Alexei. Her hand was in his."

★ ★ ★

THEY ALMOST STUMBLED OVER THE BODIES.

"Alexei!"

Lydia had seized the back of his coat with a force that almost choked him. As he swung around he was astonished to see a knife in her hand. Where the hell had that come from?

She'd stepped on an arm.

"Down!" he breathed.

He yanked her into a crouch at the base of a tree. Igor had flattened to the ground. The lack of undergrowth in the pine forest made movement easier but was no damn use when you needed cover. He held her down, and under his palm on her back he could feel her heart racing. He waited ten minutes, gun in hand. Then another ten. No sign of any movement, no flicker of branches or flutter of birds. No sound, just a raw silence. They didn't speak, not even a whisper, but Alexei made hand signals to Igor, then crawled away on his belly and elbows.

He found tracks, a number of them. And he found bodies, four of them. All in Red Army uniforms. Covered in blood. He scoured the area minutely, weaving between trunks, studying the high branches, but could spot no one. No one alive, that is, no one whose breath shuddered white trails into the mist. When he returned to Lydia she hadn't moved a muscle, as if the icy air around her had frozen and trapped her there. But as soon as he nodded at her, she sprang to her feet in a low crouch.

"Look," she whispered.

Her gaze was fixed on one of the dead soldiers. He was young and slumped in a sitting position against a pine, legs stiff in front of him, his eyes wide open and staring directly at her. Glassy, useless, sky-blue eyes. His throat had been cut from ear to ear like an extra-wide smile under his chin, and his life had spilled out over his army greatcoat by mistake, except this had been no mistake.

"There are others," Alexei murmured in her ear, and held up four fingers.

She slid a hand across the white skin of her own throat and raised an eyebrow. He nodded. All with smiles under their chins. He saw her flinch and feared she would freeze, her body go rigid. He'd seen it happen. Shock did strange things to a person. He was prepared to throw her over his shoulder if necessary, but when he started to move off, she tucked in behind him like a shadow. Once again Igor brought up the rear, small eyes darting from tree to tree.

It was only when they reached the army truck that Lydia asked quietly, "Who did it? Who killed them?"

Alexei was certain he knew, but something in him was reluctant to tell his sister.

"Alexei," she insisted.

"It'll be Maksim. Watching our backs. That's what a good *pakhan* does for his men."

"But you said the army patrols worked in pairs. And were not thorough in checking the forest. So why were there four soldiers?"

Alexei stamped the snow off his boots and swung up into the truck. "Isn't it obvious?" he scowled.

"Not to me."

"We were betrayed."

"Betrayed? But who knew we were coming here today?"

"Only us."

THE OLD BLACK BONE-SHAKER WAS STILL THERE ON THE TRACK. Relief hit Alexei like a slap in the face, and until that moment he hadn't realized that a part of him had been doubting Maksim Voshchinsky. Fearing that he'd gone. But why would he do that when he'd just proved himself ruthless and thorough in protecting their backs? Alexei and Lydia resumed their earlier positions on the back-seat, and Alexei greeted Maksim with a grateful bear hug. The older man smelled of brandy but his skin felt brittle and cold, as though he'd been out in the wind.

"Good to see you safe, my son," Maksim smiled.

"Thank you, father."

Lydia reached across Alexei and picked up one of Maksim's hands. She removed the glove and lifted the plump hand to her lips, pressing a kiss on its veined flesh.

"*Spasibo, pakhan,*" she murmured.

The leader of the *vory v zakone* withdrew his hand with a chilly smile that went nowhere near his eyes.

"Alexei," he said, "control your sister."

* * *

THE ROOM SMELLED OF BLOOD. METALLIC AND SALTY AND sticky as tar in the nostrils. Alexei stood just inside the door, heart pumping, seeking the source of the smell. He had accompanied Lydia into her house and up the narrow stairs. Something was wrong and he was determined to find out what. But on the top landing waited a thin man with suspicious eyes and a receding hairline, wearing a red armband that declared him to be the head of the Housing Committee. He blocked their path.

The man puffed out his weedy chest. "Comrade, there's a stain on the floor outside your room. Please clean it up."

Lydia blinked as though she hadn't heard properly at first, then let out a gasp and pushed past, rushing to her door.

The man bit his lip, annoyed. "It looks like blood," he shouted after her.

It *was* blood. And in the room there was more. The big woman, the one from the train—what was her name? Elizaveta?—was standing by the bed. She'd lifted her head to see who had burst in without knocking first and her pale eyes were hard and angry. Beside him Lydia was quivering like a small animal.

"Liev," she whispered. "Liev."

On the bed sprawled the big man. His barrel chest was naked and exposed, except for a bandage that looked as though a large crimson dinner plate had been placed on top of it. A vivid strident red. Every inch of his skin was covered in blood, sweat, or bruises, while his one black eye had sunk into an equally blackened socket. But his mouth, though split and scabbed, was twisted into a lopsided attempt at a grin.

"Lydia," he bellowed.

She flew across the room. Smears of blood rubbed off on her as she leaned over and kissed his hairy cheek, wrapping her arms around his bull neck.

"You're not dead," she said. It was an accusation.

"*Nyet.* I thought about it. But changed my mind."

"I'm glad." She was beaming at him, her hands gripping chunks of his beard. "I thought you were dead, you big idiot."

Alexei wondered if she'd act toward himself with quite that

desperate energy if he came back from the dead one day. He doubted it.

"They threw you out, did they?" she laughed. "Didn't want your smelly carcass in their prison."

The Cossack grunted.

She patted the bandage on his granite chest. "Making a bit of a fuss over nothing as usual, aren't you?"

He grunted again, and from somewhere under the bandage rose a bubbling sound. It might have been a laugh.

"Shut up," Elena snapped. "Don't talk, Popkov."

She was standing in the same spot still, staring at Lydia with barely controlled anger. In one hand Elena held a white enamel basin piled high with scarlet swabs of cotton and stained bandages. In the other, which was turned palm upward, lay a blood-streaked rifle bullet.

"Did you take it out of him?" Alexei asked.

"Someone had to."

"Anesthetic?"

She glanced at the empty vodka bottle on the floor and gave it a kick that sent it spinning under the bed.

"Elena," Lydia said, her voice thick with unshed tears. "Thank you."

"I didn't do it for you, girl."

"I know."

"I didn't think you'd be back here."

"Why not?"

"Because without the Cossack, there is nothing here for you to come back for."

"There's you. And Edik with his dog." Her tone was bemused.

"Like I said. Nothing for you to come back for."

"Elena," Lydia said solemnly, "I thought you and I were friends."

"Then you thought wrong."

The woman dumped the bullet on Liev's chest, where it sat like a miniature gravestone on top of the bandage. A heavy stillness settled in the metal-tasting air.

"Lydia," Alexei said quickly, "come with me. We'll buy medicines for him." He wanted her out of this room.

She didn't move. Her huge eyes were lost in shadows, but her gaze was fixed unwaveringly on the Russian woman.

"Why did I think wrong, Elena?"

The woman's expression softened. But that made it worse, as if she saw no hope for the young girl in front of her.

"Because," Elena said, "you damage everything you touch."

Fifty

LYDIA RANG THE DOORBELL THIS TIME. SHE closed her eyes while she waited. To shut herself off from this moment as if it could belong to someone else. She had rattled halfway across Moscow in the trams as the bleached and pungent city air at last grew dark and a moon as yellow as a melon skimmed up into the evening sky.

She'd watched a lamplighter pedal down the street whistling, with his long wooden pole over his shoulder, stop under a streetlamp, and without dismounting turn its gas jet on with the tip of his pole. She wished she was him. She'd seen how the conductor on the tram, a woman with tired eyes, had handed out tickets with due attention to each passenger. Lydia had wanted to be her. Or the girl with the baby with the birthmark. Or the couple in the street with their arms looped together.

Anybody but herself.

The door opened. "Ah, Lydia. How charming of you to call."

"Good evening, Dmitri."

"I can't say I wasn't expecting you. You see how much faith I have in your word."

He was wearing a silk maroon robe over black trousers and a smile so courteous that for one thin sliver of time she let it give her hope. He threw back the door and she walked into the hallway. Music was drifting out from one of the rooms and she recognized it at once. Her mother used to play the piece, one of Chopin's nocturnes.

"You're looking tired, Lydia, distinctly pale. Let me take your coat and pour you a glass of wine. You'll feel better." He held out his hands to help her off with her coat.

She didn't move. Just stood there in his warm apartment with her hat and coat firmly in place. She tried to find him behind his smile, but he was too well hidden.

"Dmitri, don't do this."

His gray eyes widened. "My dearest Lydia, you surprise me. We made a deal."

"I know."

"Your Cossack is back home?"

"Yes."

"Not even dead."

"No."

"So"—he spread his hands as if confused—"what's the problem?"

"I don't want to do this."

He gave her a slow sad look and gently removed her hat, so that her flaming hair tumbled over her shoulders.

"I really don't think," he said softly, "that what you want is relevant. We agreed. A bargain is a bargain. I have fulfilled my half of it and now it's time for your part." His voice was sounding different, as though his mouth were dry and his tongue heavy.

"Dmitri, please. You are a decent man and we can still be friends despite—"

"Friends! I don't want to be friends!"

Anger flared for a second and he bared his teeth at her. And then it was gone, the attentive smile smothering it. That was when she knew nothing would change his mind and that was when she started to hate him. She glanced behind her at the door.

His hand closed over her wrist. "No, my little Lydia, *nyet*." He spoke soothingly, the way he would to a nervous colt. "Don't think of leaving. And don't glare at me like that. Such contempt." He laughed, and the sound of it made her skin crawl. "If you try to leave, my dear, I shall have Comrade Popkov rearrested." His eyes grew brittle as glass. "Understand?"

"Yes."

"Good. Now that we understand each other, let me take your coat."

She didn't move, but he carefully unbuttoned it for her and started to slide it from her stiff shoulders.

"Dmitri," she said without looking at him, "what is to stop you threatening to arrest Popkov in the future every time you want me to come over here?"

He beamed at her, delighted. "Ah, now I see we really do understand each other."

"Answer me. What is to stop you?"

"Nothing. *Neechevo*. Absolutely nothing."

THE ROOM WITH THE MUSIC TURNED OUT TO BE HIS STUDY. IT was an intimate room despite the hard lines of the desk and the shelves of leather-bound books. Well chosen for seduction, it seemed to Lydia. Soft lighting, a gramophone playing, the rich colors of an Afghan rug on the floor, a pot of coffee and a bottle of burgundy on a small delicate table next to a chaise longue. It was the chaise longue that her eyes fixed on, with its elegant curves and dense green velvet. Silk cushions of amber and russet, as inviting as a forest floor in springtime.

"Wine?" he offered.

"No."

"Do sit down."

She remained standing.

He removed the gramophone needle from the record, poured out two glasses of wine, and paused for a moment with one in each hand while he inspected her, head cocked to one side. He seemed to like what he saw. She wanted to slap the smile off his face. The room was overhot. Or was it her? The aroma of coffee seemed to clog up her lungs and she felt suddenly sick. *I can handle him,* she'd boasted to Elena. How naïve could she be? She'd stupidly believed she could flutter her eyelids and toss her hair at this man, extract what she wanted from him, and escape without having to pay the price. *That man eats girls like you for breakfast,* Elena had warned. She should have listened to her.

Yet without Dmitri's help Popkov would still be in prison, or worse, dead by now. Dmitri had waited with the patience of a spider until she blundered into his web, and she had no right to feel surprised when the sticky threads tightened around her.

"Here, this will calm you down." He proffered a glass.

"Do I need calming?"

Again he inspected her. "I rather think you do."

She took the wine and drank it down in one go. He approached, standing close enough for her to smell the pomade on his hair, and the lines of his face seemed to harden as he bent his head and kissed her lips. She could taste whisky on him. So he'd started without her. She let his lips linger on hers but made no response.

"Lydia," he murmured, "so cold? So stony?" He ran a hand up her throat and into her hair, then dropped it down to her breast. "Loosen up, my sweet angel."

She stepped back from him, replaced her glass on the table, and turned to face him. They had laughed together, danced together; surely he wouldn't force her. "Dmitri, release me from this bargain? I'm begging you." She dropped to her knees in front of him. "Please."

He smiled slowly, and for a moment she thought he was going to agree, but he unbuttoned his fly and reached for her head.

"You disgust me, comrade," she said coldly, and rose to her feet. "So let's get it over with."

With no hesitation she undid her blouse buttons, stepped out of her skirt, and removed her underwear. In the time it took for Dmitri to realize she was doing his job for him, Lydia stood stark naked in the study.

His gaze roamed over her body. Her face burned but her eyes remained fixed on his, as if by willpower alone she could force him back from the brink and make this enough. This display for him. She couldn't believe now that she'd been blind enough to find him attractive. He yanked down his trousers and kicked them away, moving closer to her. He touched the smooth milky skin of her stomach, her thigh, the fiery curls in between. He was breathing hard.

"Why me, Dmitri? You could have a thousand others who are willing, so why me?"

He started to move slowly around her, trailing his fingers over her buttocks, along her spine, feeling the bone of her hip, the silky cushion of her breast.

"Because you are a rare creature, Lydia Ivanova."

"There are many more beautiful. Including your own wife."

Still he circled her, again and again as if he were spinning his web. "The world is full of ordinary people, Lydia. You are not one of them."

She drew a breath and said softly, "Then don't crush me. Let me go."

In answer he reached for her, his hands rough on her shoulders, gripping her hard. "Don't be foolish," he whispered as his lips came down fiercely on hers.

She didn't fight him. But she remained rigid and unyielding until he abruptly tired of the game, threw off his robe so that he was totally naked, and pushed her impatiently onto the chaise longue. He was strong and held her down, but as he pressed himself on top of her she squirmed her hips away. With no warning he pulled back and slapped her face.

"No, Dmitri, don't—"

He slapped her again, harder. She tasted blood on her teeth.

"Fuck you," she yelled.

The hand was coming again. "Don't you—"

The study door crashed open. Dmitri didn't even look around. "Get out, Antonina," he growled, and smacked Lydia in the mouth.

"Let her go," Antonina said.

Lydia couldn't see her because Dmitri's body was blocking everything from her view, but she could see his eyes clearly. They were no longer gray and controlled.

"Piss off, Antonina," he shouted. "I'm busy."

Abruptly Lydia felt his whole body give a sudden jerk as though her flailing knee had caught his groin. Only when he slumped down on her with a groan, clutching the back of his head, did it occur to her that his wife had hit him with something. His full weight was crushing her. She could barely breathe, so she grabbed a fistful of his red hair and yanked up his head, freeing her airway. His eyes were black with rage and she could feel the heat of it scorch her face. A fine thread of red was trickling from his ear down to her lips, and she spat it back at him. Over his shoulder she could now make out Antonina, wide-eyed as a deer, a huge studded Bible clutched in her hands.

"You stupid fucking bitch," Dmitri roared at her, and dragged himself off the chaise longue, one hand still gripping his head.

Antonina backed off fast.

Lydia leapt to her feet and seized his arm from behind. He turned, swinging a fist at her, but she was too quick and he missed.

"Dmitri, don't—"

"Shut your mouth."

"Leave your wife alone."

But he lunged for Antonina once more, and this time his fist connected with the side of her head. The crack of it was loud in the room, and she went sprawling backward onto the desk. Her fingers released the Bible and her mouth hung open in a scream that produced no sound.

"I'm going to teach you, you stupid faithless bitch."

He hit her again full in the face, just as Lydia slammed her fist into his kidneys. He grunted with pain, cursing, but seized Antonina's slender neck, squeezing it brutally between his strong hands. Lydia hooked an arm around his throat to twist him off his wife, but she was too late. In panic Antonina lifted a dagger-shaped paper knife from beside her head and rammed it with all her strength into her husband. It slid neatly up to the hilt between his ribs.

A high-pitched whistle issued from his throat before he keeled over sideways, one hand clawing at the silver cross that was sticking out of his chest. He slumped to the floor. Antonina leapt to her feet, her face a mask of blood, and stared down in horror at her husband's inert figure. Her fingernails started to claw fiercely at her arm.

LYDIA WORKED FAST. FIRST SHE FELT FOR A PULSE BUT KNEW before she even pressed her fingers to Dmitri's neck that she'd find none. She had seen dead eyes before. She sat Antonina down with a cloth for her face in one hand and a wineglass full of brandy in the other. She removed the knife from Dmitri's ribs, washed it thoroughly, and replaced it on the desk, then rolled his body up in the Afghan rug before the blood spread farther. Only then did she think to put her clothes back on.

She took a seat beside Antonina on the chaise longue and wrapped her arms around the trembling woman, holding her tight, rocking her, murmuring soft sounds of comfort. She kept pouring brandy into Antonina's glass until finally it took its toll and the tremors ceased, the limbs and the dark hair hung loose. The woman's head lolled on Lydia's shoulder and silent tears streamed down her cheeks.

"I didn't mean to kill him."

"I know."

"I'll go to prison," she whispered.

"Maybe not."

"Yes, I will. The Soviet police will condemn me."

"Is that what you intend to do? Go to the police?"

"Oh Lydia, I've just killed my husband. What else am I supposed to do?"

Lydia stroked the damp hair away from her face. "There is an alternative."

The wretched dark eyes, sunk deep in their sockets, turned to her, and Lydia thought about what Elena had said. This woman was damaged enough. And now this.

"Tell me, Lydia. What do you mean?"

"We can go to the police right now and describe what happened, and after months of prison cells and questioning and a trial if you're lucky, you would end up a prisoner doing hard labor in a coal mine in Siberia somewhere." She wiped away Antonina's tears with her sleeve. "It wouldn't be pleasant."

"Or what?" the woman sobbed.

"Or." Lydia hesitated. "We can bury him. And get on with our lives."

Antonina looked aghast. "Where? In one of the parks? Alexander Gardens maybe? You're crazy."

"No. Think about it. Dmitri is dead." She felt a brief wave of nausea and disbelief. *Dmitri Malofeyev dead*. The words frightened her. "Nothing we can do will bring your husband back. If you go to prison it won't help him where he is now. And I am witness to the fact that it was self-defense. I saw him trying to kill you."

Antonina lifted her head and stared at Lydia, her eyes purple smudges in her bruised face. "You're serious?"

Lydia nodded.

"Oh, you're crazy. Haven't you learned yet? This is Soviet Russia. There's no escape. We're all caught in the Communist net, for good or for bad. I've committed a serious crime and will have to . . ."

"Don't give up. Not yet."

With a sad twist of her lips, Antonina touched Lydia's hand. "That's why he wanted you so much. For that light inside you. He knew you were just using him but he couldn't stay away."

Lydia shuddered. She looked at the rolled-up rug and mourned for the loss of the man Dmitri Malofeyev might have been.

"Antonina," she said, "do you own a car?"

CHANG AN LO KNEW SHE WAS THERE THE MOMENT HE STEPPED into the room even though she had not lit the lamp. In the darkness he could sense her. No sound, no movement, just the feel of her there. Of her mind, of her thoughts, of herself.

"Lydia," he breathed.

Without lighting the lamp he crossed the bare boards. She was standing in a corner of the room with a stillness and a patience that told him she'd been there for a long time, and he cursed that he'd been delayed by an official dinner that had seemed endless. He had not told her yet that the delegation's time here was soon to end. She curled her arms around his neck and he inhaled the familiar scent of her, knew again that sense of completeness that she created within him whenever he touched his fox girl. He held her, but not so close as to crush the thoughts that hovered around her like fireflies in the dark. He gave them space to fly.

"What is it, my love?"

"Do I damage you?"

He felt the evil night spirits flit past his head, rustling in the darkness, trying to burrow into her thoughts. He brushed a hand through the air to disperse them, and she leaned her head back to study his face.

"Do I?"

"No, Lydia, you don't damage me. You make me whole. Who has been pouring such vile oil in your ear?"

"Elena."

"Tell Elena that—"

"Popkov was shot and almost killed today. Because he was helping me."

Chang's breath stilled.

"And"—she whispered the words as if they were fragile— "Dmitri Malofeyev died tonight because of me. Now I'm asking you to help me and it frightens me."

He released his hold on her and lit the gas lamp. In the shadowy light the lines of her mouth were tense and there was a bruise on her face. But in her amber eyes there was something new, as if this day had changed her, and he recognized it at once. It was what he had seen in a soldier's eyes after battle, a self-reliance, an independence of mind, and it chilled his heart. Nevertheless, he smiled tenderly at her and opened his arms to welcome whatever it was she wanted of him.

"Ask me," he said.

SO WOLF EYES WAS DEAD. CHANG FELT NOT A SCRAP OF SORROW for his greedy soul, and when he looked at the wife he saw no depth of sorrow in her bruised eyes either, despite her tears. But it unsettled him to see the concern on Lydia's face when he unrolled the carpet to remove the Russian's watch and wedding ring. The ring was too tight to slide off over the flesh, so Chang used his knife to whittle the finger to the bone.

"Is that necessary?" she asked.

"Yes. There must be nothing on him that will identify the body."

She nodded, tugging uncomfortably at her hair. He looked away because he couldn't bear to see her do that for this man who had hit her face. He rolled up the rug once more and sent the wife for the car while Lydia scrubbed the floor to remove the stains.

"Lydia, his own people will come looking for him."

She was still on her knees. "I know."

"How will the wife explain away his disappearance?"

"She's going to inform them tomorrow that he has traveled to visit his sick uncle in Kazan. He really does have an uncle there, so when she tells them he was taken ill suddenly they will believe her. It will at least buy her time to decide what to do next."

He didn't point out that they might check the travel permits issued. Let her take one step at a time.

"Good," he murmured, and crouched down beside her. He placed one hand over hers on the floor. "Why do you care for this woman? Why not let her go to prison? She is nothing to you."

"She reminds me of someone," she said softly. "Someone equally damaged, equally in need of help."

"Your mother?"

She shrugged. "Anyway," she added with a change of tone, "I've been through Dmitri's desk and found a box of his official stamps. We can use them on any forms we need." She looked at him. "They'll be useful when we need to leave."

"I always said you were my fox." He lifted a lock of her red hair and let it trail through his fingers. "Rummaging in bins and drawers, making use of whatever you can find. Sharp teeth, sharp mind, and dark holes to run to."

For a long moment her stare fixed on him. "I love you, Chang An Lo," she said simply.

It was only later, after he'd carried the rug through the darkness to the trunk of the car and he was driving all three of them through the black streets of Moscow, that he had time to think again about that *someone* Lydia had spoken of. The someone who was damaged and in need of help. For the first time it occurred to him that she wasn't talking about her mother. She was talking about herself.

THE WOMAN WAS NERVOUS IN THE FOREST. CHANG COULD hear her breath next to him, shallow and ragged. She jumped as shadows swayed toward her in the moonlight and picked her footing as delicately as a deer. When an owl screeched above her head, she froze. The sophisticated creature with the scarlet lips that had smiled so indifferently at him in the salon of the Hotel Metropol was now out of place, away from the chandeliers and the cigars. She tucked herself close to his elbow, uttering small gasps and murmurs. But on the other side of him Lydia moved in sure-footed silence, padding over the snow-covered ruts beneath the black arc of pine trees with her eyes wide and watchful, her face lifting at intervals as though scenting the night air with the caution of a fox.

The body was heavy. It lay across his shoulder still shrouded in the rug, weighing down his step and causing him to stumble over unseen branches. The woman tried to help, seizing his arm or holding on to a piece of the fabric, but all she did was drag at him and twist him further off balance. Lydia did not touch the bulk of Wolf Eyes, and even in the darkness he could sense her distaste. That satisfied him. That she didn't wish to touch this man.

"Here will do." Lydia said it quickly, eager to rid Chang of the burden.

But the wife spoke up, her voice brittle in the icy silence of the forest. "Not here, not yet, it's not deep enough in."

"Antonina," Lydia said so softly that the wind almost stole her words, "we are far from the road. No one will come here."

With the wife's help, Chang lay the body on the ground and she immediately crouched down beside it, her hand resting on the rug as if reluctant to release ownership of its contents. No one spoke. Chang flexed his shoulders to ease the muscles of his back and looked around. This was as good a place as any. The moon's pale light barely filtered through the spread of branches, but where it did it transformed the snow-packed ground into a harsh blue sea and the trees into silver sentinels. He took the shovel Lydia had carried and started to dig.

He worked to a steady rhythm, but once through the snow it was like trying to dig into rock. The earth was frozen solid. He could feel his tendons tearing but didn't stop. This was not the first time he had buried a body in a forest or carried a fallen comrade from a battlefield; wherever he turned, in whatever country, death seemed to stalk him. And sadness seemed to rise out of the earth as he dug, with the stink of death on every shovel of soil. It crouched there and he breathed it in till his lungs ached.

"Enough," Lydia murmured.

He looked up, surprised. He had almost forgotten that he was not alone. She was standing off to one side among the trees, watching his movements, her face in shadow, hidden from him.

"Enough," she said again. "No more."

Was it the grave she meant? Or was it death itself she was speaking of?

The wife was still crouched on her knees by the rug, her head bowed, her hair a curtain across her face. In the darkness she looked as though she had settled forever on the forest floor, and he wondered if she felt she was the one who should be lying in the rug, the one who should remain alone in the cold earth. He threw down the shovel and reached for the rug, but at that moment a sudden blundering noise in the forest startled the woman and she leapt to her feet, eyes wide and drained of color by the moonlight.

"A moose," he said and heard her gasp of relief.

With respect for the dead, even if it was Wolf Eyes, he rolled the rug carefully to the edge of the grave, but when he started to remove the body from the folds, the wife stepped forward.

"Let me," she said.

He stepped back while she unwrapped her husband's corpse with slow hesitant movements and slid it into the shallow grave as gently as if it were a sleeping child.

"Good night, Dmitri," she whispered softly. "May God bring peace to your soul." Silver tears were flowing down her cheeks.

Chang bowed his head and commended the Russian's spirit to his ancestors, but when he looked around for Lydia she was standing stiffly beside a tree, arms folded tightly across her chest. She didn't move. Just stared at the black trench he'd dug. What was she seeing? The terrible waste of death? Or the similar hole that had swallowed her mother only months earlier? He breathed slowly, calming the race of his blood as it burned through his veins. Or did she foresee her father's end, as her fears stared straight into the eyes of death? Out here in the forest, life was fragile. Its thread a fine silver filament in the moonlight.

He picked up the shovel and started to cover the body of Dmitri Malofeyev with black Russian soil. He did not mention that wolves would claw open the grave before dawn marked it with the light of day.

* ★ *

THEY WASHED EACH OTHER. CHANG LOVED THE TOUCH OF HER hands on his skin and the sight of her flaming mane spilling over her naked shoulder blades. Together they soaped away the dregs of the day's dirt from their minds and from their bodies, and afterward they made love. They didn't hurry, exploring and caressing each other, teasing tender places and tasting the curve of a neck, the hollow at the top of a thigh, the arch of a foot, the hardness of a nipple.

It was as though they were discovering each other all over again at the end of a day that had changed something between them. He relearned the exact sound of her moan when he was inside her and the way she whimpered when he slowed to long rhythmic strokes, her fingers digging at his back as if they would scoop out his heart. When finally he lay with his cheek flat on her stomach, sweat salty on his tongue, he must have fallen asleep because he woke suddenly and sensed that Lydia had moved. She was kneeling beside him on the bed, moonlight painting her hair silver. Lying across her palms was his knife. She had removed it from his boot.

"It was you, wasn't it, Chang An Lo?"

He felt a rush of blood through his veins, but he lay totally still.

"What was me?"

"In the forest today."

"Of course it was. We were there together. I helped you bury your—"

"No." She turned the blade over and over in her hand, the way she was turning over her thoughts, touching a finger to the unicorn carved into the ivory handle. "You know what I mean."

Her hair hung around her face, shrouding it in silvery secretive shadows.

"Yes, Lydia, I know what you mean."

"In the forest with the soldiers. Four of them dead."

He listened to her breathing. It was fast and shallow.

"I could not bear to let you die," he answered.

"So it wasn't Maksim Voshchinsky watching our backs?"

"No."

"How did you know where I was?"

"It wasn't hard; you are part of my heart. How could I not know where it was beating?"

But she would not be put off. "Tell me how."

"You mentioned to me that you were going out in Voshchinsky's car. It was not hard to guess where you would be heading."

"So you knew? Already knew where the complex is that my father works in?"

"I have a companion who is as capable of tracking trucks as any Muscovite *vor.*"

"Kuan?"

"No. A good friend of my heart named Biao." He removed the knife from her grasp and placed it to one side. "You must take care, my love. Beware of betrayal. Too many people know what you are doing."

"Except my father." He heard her pause and release a long low sigh. "Jens Friis doesn't know."

With an abrupt movement Chang sat up and brushed Lydia's hair from her face. Her pupils were huge as she looked at him, her mouth alive and mobile. Firmly she pressed him back on the bed and moved on top of his body, her hands flat on his chest.

"My love," she murmured, "how do I thank you for my life?"

"By keeping it safe."

As her hips started to move, he yearned to take her away from Moscow. From her father, from her brother, from the woman with the dead husband. From herself.

Fifty-one

SNOW HAD FALLEN OVERNIGHT AND TRANS-
formed the prison into a creature of beauty. Its roofs
and windowsills, its courtyard, and even its stone seat
all glittered under the early-morning floodlights like
pearls on a wedding dress. Jens hated it. Such hypoc-
risy. How could something so ugly inside look so
exquisite outside? He trudged the circle, single file,
head down, no talking. Snowflakes settled on his
eyelashes and melted down his cheeks like tears. In
front of him Olga's small figure stumbled, and for half
a second he held her elbow to support her. It felt as
fragile as a sparrow's wing.

"No touching," Babitsky yelled.

Jens muttered under his breath, "One day soon,
Babitsky, I swear I'll come and touch you."

"Jens," Olga whispered behind her glove without
turning around, "don't. The brute isn't worth it."

"He is to me."

He hadn't told her that the big man shot dead in
the courtyard the day before was his friend. That in
the golden days of the tsar they had sat up all night

playing cards together in the stables of the Winter Palace, that they'd fought each other over a girl, arm wrestled for a horse. That they'd bound each other's wounds and saved each other's lives. No, he hadn't told her any of that. He picked up his feet on the white carpet that was smothering the tramp of their boots, as if they were no longer real. Transparent and soundless. Ghosts of a past that was gone. How could he have imagined that they would ever fit into this real Soviet world again? He must have been mad.

He lifted his face to the falling snow and squinted up past the yellow prison lights to the black clouds beyond, where the moon and the stars lay buried. Out of reach. He thought about his daughter forever out of reach and again felt that dull ache in his chest that, until the letters started arriving, he'd learned to strangle at birth with a simple click of the mind. But now it wouldn't go away. It was stuck there, as though someone had hammered a nail into his heart and left it there to rust.

So engrossed was he in his thoughts that when the iron gate to the courtyard swung open, growling on its massive hinges and letting in the rumble of early traffic noise, he didn't look up. There would be no more letters. He was certain of that. Dimly he was aware of the horse jingling its bridle, of the baker grumbling about the cold, of the rattle of metal trays and the enticing aroma of freshly baked bread. But still he couldn't bear to look beyond their compound.

"Jens." It was Olga. A quick whisper. "Look."

He glanced at her and then through the fence, and saw a girl. She was holding a tray of *pirozhki* on her head, walking into the building. All he caught was a glimpse of her long straight back, of the way she picked her feet up in the snow as daintily as a cat. A dismal brown hat. A flash of flaming hair at her collar.

"Lydia!"

"Lydia!"

"Lydia!"

"Keep walking, Prisoner Friis," a guard growled.

Only then did Jens realize how twelve years in labor camps had trained his tongue. His screams of his daughter's name had been silent, exploding only inside his skull.

"Move, Friis!"

He moved, one foot in front of the other, making it look easy. In front of him Olga glanced over her shoulder at him, eyes worried. "Look," she whispered again and nodded quickly.

He needed no telling this time. Across the whole width of the courtyard, a distance of more than forty meters, the small door into the side of the prison stood open. His attention fixed on it. Suddenly she was there again, swinging the tray in one hand as if she hadn't a care in the world, slender and supple in the way she moved. He recognized her even after all these years. A delicate heart-shaped face that made him want to cry. It was pale except for a livid bruise near her mouth, with her mother's full sensual lips. She was good. No hint of a glance in his direction.

Instead she gave a guard a half-smile, patted the horse, cast a look at the stone seat, walked over to the back of the cart, and only then let her gaze drift toward the prisoners and to Jens. Their eyes met. For a heartbeat she froze. As he looked at her, something cracked inside him and he almost hurled himself at the mesh fence and howled her name. He wanted to feel the touch of his daughter's fingers on his own, to kiss her young cheek, to discover the mind behind the large luminous eyes.

Her lips moved, almost a smile.

"Friis," Babitsky yelled, "how many times do I have to say it? Keep moving!"

Jens had stopped again. With an effort of will he shuffled forward and watched his daughter turn back to the baker's cart, swap the empty tray for a full one, and traipse once more in through the door. He tried to think straight, but couldn't even see straight. Tears had filled his eyes and his chest was about to explode. Or implode. It made no difference. He ached with happiness.

"Jens."

His ears struggled to work out where the voice had come from.

"Jens, it's me, Olga."

He wrenched his gaze from the doorway. Olga was half-looking at him over her shoulder.

"Is it her?" she mouthed in a whisper. "Is it Lydia?"

His mind jammed. Had he told her about his daughter? He couldn't remember. He didn't dare nod. If he did anything wrong this moment might vanish and Lydia might never appear again in the dim hole in the stone wall. He let the snowflakes settle on his eyelids and clamped his tongue between his teeth. His feet moved obediently in the circle, though every second that passed they threatened to race over to the wire.

He waited forever. Another lifetime. Heart kicking his ribs in, and fear for Lydia sharp as acid in his mouth. Yet when she did emerge it all vanished and he felt only a rush of happiness, hot and liquid under his skin. As she neared the seat, the metal tray tumbled from her hand and with an apologetic smile she crouched in the snow to retrieve it.

Her hand was faster than any snake.

Dearest Papa,

Today I will see you. You cannot imagine how happy that makes me. Happy and overwhelmed. I've missed you. Since I was five years old I've missed you and the thought of seeing you today, my dear father, made the night hours slow and cumbersome.

How will I not run to you? I learned from the boy that you will be behind a fence, but what if my feet will not listen to my head? I will want to fling my arms around you, Papa, but that will not be possible., so you must imagine it in your mind, your daughter returning to you.

There is something else I must say. Alexei and I traveled to the forest around the secret clearing where you work, and I have seen the wall. Seen the hangars. I believe I saw you, but my brother says I imagined it because I wanted the person to be you. Today there will be no imagining. Soon everything will change. We are coming for you. Be ready. Alexei has friends here in Moscow who are willing to help us; he has given much to gather these allies to our side. I can't tell you more. I am nervous of putting words to paper.

I cannot come into the prison again as I have nothing more to use to bribe the baker. Fortunately he has a greedy heart, but my pockets are empty now. So this is good-bye for the moment. Au revoir. Till I see you again. I am nervous. What if I am not the daughter you hoped for? I love you, Papa.

Your Lydia

Jens's hand shook. He knew already that he would not be the father she was hoping for. But for one day with her, just one day, he would bargain his miserable soul. *Oh Lydia, my own sweet daughter, how much are you risking?*

"ALEXEI, THIS MAKES ME PROUD."

"That pleases me, Maksim."

"He's done a fine job. He is a true artist."

Alexei lifted his arm and studied the new tattoo. It was of a large spider climbing up his bicep, an indication that the bearer is active in the criminal life. A second mark of Cain.

"Is everything arranged?" he asked.

"My men are ready. The final meeting is today."

"Lydia has asked to be included."

"No."

"*Pakhan,* she and I have traveled a long way for this." He raised his eyes from the spider to Maksim's face. "Let her come."

"My son, you are bewitched by this girl. She is no longer your sister, remember that. A *vor* has no sister." He sipped his brandy, eyes stern.

Alexei pulled on his clean white shirt and buttoned it thoughtfully. "Maksim, I am grateful for all you have done." He lifted his own brandy to his lips, though the morning had only just started and his stomach was still empty. "When this is over, you can ask of me any favor you choose."

"When this is over you may be dead."

Alexei laughed, a loose easy sound that took Voshchinsky by surprise. "In which case I shall hold the door open for you, my friend."

Maksim didn't smile.

My Lydia,

To hear of your Chang An Lo, your white rabbit, and your taste for an artist I have never heard of puts flesh on your bones. You have become real. I also am greedy. I want to know all of your life till now, each day, each success and each stumble, each thought that grows in your young head.

You ask me to tell you about myself and what I think but, Lydia, there is nothing to tell. I barely exist. I don't smile and I don't laugh and I try not to think. Somewhere in the prison camp my laughter died and I no longer mourn for it. What kind of person am I? A nonperson. So instead I shall do as you ask and tell you about my work. It is the one thing left in me that is good and fine and worthwhile. But even that facet of me is one I am corrupting. Nevertheless here it is.

You have probably never heard of the Italian General Nobile. Why should you? He is a brilliantly skilled designer of semi-rigid airships. I was told about him by a young Ukrainian who used to be his assistant but who ended up in the bunk below mine in Trovitsk prison camp. The poor bastard had made a minor error, so that his calculations proved to be inaccurate. "Sabotage!" they screamed and threw the Ukrainian in prison.

He died in the harsh winter of the timber forest, but first he told me things. About Nobile's plans. He intends a massive expansion of the use of airships for military purposes. Lydia, you wouldn't believe how exciting this is. It is the future. Nobile has even enthused Stalin himself. So what will happen now? Stalin is going to order a Red Airship Program to be set up and demand a public subscription of millions of roubles for it. Josef Stalin may be brutal, he may be an egocentric tyrant, but he isn't stupid. He knows another war is coming and he is determined that Russia will be prepared.

He needed engineers, so that's why I was brought back from the dead. There is an airship project at Dolgoprudnaya near Moscow that is public knowledge, but the one I'm working on in the forest is secret. We are constructing a . . . what shall I call it? A monster. A vast silver thin-skinned monster with lethal breath. A killing machine.

Oh Lydia, is that what God felt when He created man? That he had created a beautiful killing machine?

For that is what my project is. Airships can fly long distances, well beyond any airplane's range. So—this is the part I can barely let loose in my brain, let alone set down on paper—we have slung two biplanes under the envelope of the airship, both of which will be equipped with—not bombs—but gas canisters. Equipped with a poisonous gas. Yes, you read it right. Poison gas. Phosgene. When the airship has flown unsuspected, deep into enemy territory, the planes

will drop from a height and skim low over a city or an army barracks.
They will spray their lethal gas and pass on like the Angel of Death.

Stalin intends to build a fleet of these. With my help. My help.
What kind of man am I, Lydia, who can construct such a creature?
This week we carry out the first full test—that means with real phos-
gene instead of soda crystals, and real people instead of rubber dum-
mies. My beautiful killing machine will go to work.

Pray for my soul, Lydia, if you have any faith and if I have any
soul. And for Liev Popkov's.

Your father who loves you with what is left of his heart,
Papa

Chang An Lo watched Alexei fold the letter neatly along the creases in the thin tissue paper with its tiny penmanship and hand it back to Lydia. Saw him struggle to keep the anger out of his voice.

"You went into the prison? You risked your life for a letter?" Alexei demanded of his sister.

"No, there was little risk involved."

They all knew she was lying.

"Let me remind you," Alexei said stiffly, "that Popkov was shot for doing the same."

"No, that's not right. A guard recognized him and Liev was shot for resisting arrest. No one was going to recognize me."

To Chang's eyes it was obvious that Alexei couldn't decide which enraged him more, his sister's disobedience or his own disappointment in his father. And the letter hadn't even mentioned him. As if bastards don't count for anything. But Alexei was clearly shocked by the horror of what Jens Friis had described, far more than it seemed to shock Lydia. To Chang the confession in the letter made little difference because he was not doing any of this for Jens Friis, but it angered his heart that Lydia's father had let her down. He could see it in her eyes, the confusion.

"So," Chang said quietly, "do we drop the plan?"

Four pairs of eyes focused on him, all but one was hostile.

"No."

"Yes."

"Yes."

"No."

The first and loudest *No* was Lydia's, the last was Alexei's. In between came Maksim and Igor's *Yes*. The meeting was taking place in the Russian thief's apartment, and Chang liked neither the place nor its owner but let none of it show on his face. He was here because he had requested it and he took no offense when the fat man with the mottled skin said, "Not a bloody Chink as well as the girl." Chang had seen the *fanqui*'s expression harden in the silence, the way molten iron hardens in water, and he took it as a good sign. A scheme as risky as theirs needed a heart of iron at its center.

"They won't like you coming," Lydia had warned him.

"I'm not here to be liked."

She'd laughed but there was no life in it, and that had saddened him. Now as he regarded their faces and noted the tension in their necks and in their hands, he knew Alexei would prevail. His voice would be the last. The fat man with the cheeks like dough would not say no to Lydia's brother.

Voshchinsky banged his fist down on his broad knee. "Very well, my comrades"—he grinned at them with his jaw jutting in a display of aggression—"let's talk about tomorrow."

CHANG LED HER AWAY FROM THEM. HE WANTED TO RID LYDIA'S skin of the stink of them, to draw her away from their cigars and their words of violence. He walked her across the city to Arbat, to a small Chinese tearoom and it pleased him when her eyes brightened at the sight of it.

"I had no idea it was here."

"There's one in every capital city in the world," he smiled. "We Chinese are like rats; we get everywhere."

She tugged off her hat, shook down her hair, and inhaled the familiar scents of spices and jasmine and incense that rose from the jade fretwork on its façade.

"I had forgotten," he murmured, "how much my spirit misses the colors that bring life and energy. Here in Soviet Russia the streets are gray as death. Even the sky above us is flat and colorless."

He drew Lydia into its fragrant interior. They sat at a low bamboo table and were served steaming red tea by a young Chinese girl in a cheongsam the colors of a ripe watermelon—dark greens, crimson, and black. She bowed low with respect, and Lydia watched Chang with a soft smile on her lips.

"My love," she said when the girl had gone, "do you miss your native country so badly?"

"It is part of me, Lydia; its yellow earth is in my blood."

Her tawny eyes held his. "What are we to do?"

He leaned forward and took one of her hands, curled it in a ball, and wrapped his own around it.

"Let's talk about your father."

She gave a nod, a barely perceptible dip of the chin. "He was a man of power. A man with a family, a guest in the palaces of counts and princes. Under the tsar he had a good life, but under the Bolsheviks he lost everything, stripped to nothing."

"That's what he was trying to explain in the letters, how he had to cling to the hard core of self to survive. You and I, Lydia, we understand that."

"Yes." The sadness in her one word was as heavy as the golden Buddha in the window.

"There's something I haven't told you, something I learned the day I was in your father's prison."

She said nothing, waiting.

"I was told by Colonel Tursenov, who runs the prison, that the whole idea for this project came from Jens Friis himself. It was all out of his brain. He wasn't just an engineer recruited to work on it. While in the labor camp it was he who thought up the birth of this *monster,* as he calls it."

Her lips tightened. "Are you saying you believe he is a monster too? One not worth saving?"

"No, that is not my point. He asked for his freedom in exchange, and that's what the whole team has been promised when the project is completed. Their freedom."

The tension left her face and she smiled. "That's wonderful. Why didn't you tell me this before? He's going to be released."

"That's what they said."

The tone of his voice warned her. The smile faded.

"No, Chang, don't."

"I'm sorry, my love."

"You don't believe them."

"No, I don't. Can you imagine that the military authorities will allow prisoners with top-secret information to wander loose?"

Lydia shook her head. "Would they send them back into the labor camps?"

He made no comment.

Her mouth crumpled and she hid it behind the little porcelain cup. "You mean they'd be shot."

"I believe so."

Her hand quivered inside his.

"He's going to die," she whispered.

"Unless we get him out."

"Don't judge my father harshly, Chang. We can't know what horrors he endured, day after day for twelve years. This was a way to make them stop."

Chang opened his hands and released her. "I know. Either of us would have done the same."

They both knew he was lying.

"Thank you," she murmured and smiled at him.

THE BOY WAS PERCHED ON THE END OF POPKOV'S BED, PLAYING cards and arguing with the big man. The two of them were gambling ferociously for dried beans and by the look of the pile at his elbow, Edik was winning. Misty, who had reappeared at the door last night, was curled up on Elena's lap. The woman was chuckling as the pup licked her fingers as greedily as if they were sausages, but the moment Lydia walked in, the playing and the laughing ceased. She was tempted to walk out again.

"So you're all better now, Liev," she teased. "I knew you were just faking it."

Popkov gave her a crooked smile. "So I wanted a day in bed."

"You lazy Cossack," Lydia frowned. "Why do I bother scurrying around in the snow buying you medicine?"

She tossed him a half-bottle of vodka and the dog galloped over to her, all paws and tongue. She pulled a brown paper bag from her pocket and gave Misty a fried *pirozhok*, one to Edik, and one to Elena.

"What are these?" Elena asked with ill grace. "Good-bye presents?"

"Maybe."

"Is it all arranged then?" Popkov demanded at once, between great swigs from the bottle.

"Yes."

"Tomorrow?"

"Yes."

"I'll be there."

"No you won't!" Lydia and Elena both said it in unison.

"Anyway," Lydia added quickly, "you won't be needed. Alexei is arranging everything, and you know he'd rather have a rabid dog at his side than you."

Popkov scowled, screwed the top back on the vodka bottle, and hurled it across the room at Lydia. It banged against her hip and tumbled unbroken to the floor. "I'm coming, damn you, girl. Jens Friis was my friend."

Elena's pale eyes glared at Lydia, who promptly picked up the bottle, marched over to the bed, and smacked it against the bruise on Popkov's cheek. "You just wait here, you brainless bear, and I'll bring him to you."

"ALEXEI, I HAVE A PRESENT FOR YOU."

"The only present I need is right here."

He lifted Antonina's hand and kissed the pale back of it. It was gloveless. She was still in shock at what she'd done, still prey to shivers and sobs, and the anguish in her dark eyes had not yet abated. Alexei knew only too well that the first time you kill is a moment seared into your brain. It never leaves you, but lingers, fretting at you until you learn to put it safe in a box and close the lid on it, as quietly as a coffin.

"Don't stare at me," she said self-consciously, "I look hideous."

"No, you look lovely."

He meant it, despite the swollen nose and the bruises. Since her husband's death, there was something about her, something real and solid that hadn't been there before. As if she were tentatively removing some of the fragile layers.

"Show me what it is," he said, "this present of yours."

Antonina led him through the apartment to a closet at the far end of the hallway and threw open its doors with a flourish. He frowned at what was inside, surprised at first, and then slowly he started to smile. On a brass rail hung a Red Army officer's uniform.

Fifty-two

THE FOREST WAS A DIFFERENT WORLD IN THE dark. Lydia expected her eyes to adjust to it but they didn't. Still she could see nothing. But she could hear things. Night sounds. They made the hairs on her arms stand on end and the back of her throat grow dry. It was a world of creeping and rustling and great gusts of dank breath, so that she had to force herself to keep still. Her hands wanted to flail around her, feeling for approaching shadows. Her feet just wanted to run.

"All right?" Chang whispered next to her.

"Fine."

She heard his breath inhale slowly and wondered how much her one word had betrayed. How long had they been crouched beside the tree trunk? One hour? Two? She'd lost track of time. There was no moon, no sky, just a black blanket above her head interspersed with even blacker shapes as the trees swayed in the wind, their branches making needy feral whines. It reminded her of wild creatures in a snare. She didn't speak, didn't move. Tried to find stillness. The cold ate into her bones. Warmth from Chang's body seeped through her coat into her arm and she concentrated on that. If she thought too hard about what was about to happen, her limbs started to spasm.

"Frightened?" Chang's breath was moist on her ear.

"Not for me."

"For your father?"

She nodded. He couldn't see it, but she knew he would feel the movement in the darkness.

"He will die for certain if we do nothing."

"I know."

"I will protect him all I can."

"I know."

"But first I will protect you."

He stiffened beside her suddenly, and she realized his sharp senses had picked up something she'd missed. Fifteen seconds later she saw it, the faintest blur of light, far off, coming and going between the trees. It was a good distance away, too far to hear any noise yet, but they both knew immediately what it was. The truck convoy. Lydia's heart thudded in her chest, pumping hot blood and adrenaline into her chilled limbs. She was ready to move, but Chang's hand descended on her thigh, pinning her there.

TODAY WOULD BE HARD. INSIDE THE TRUCK JENS SAT ON THE bench with his eyes closed and his back braced against the metal side panel. That way he shut out the darkness. The truck rattled and roared, its engine straining on the rutted road, its wheels skidding over patches of snow and ice, stabbing into his thoughts. He braced his mind as firmly as he braced his back.

Today would be hard, he was under no illusions about that, but he was used to *hard*. He'd forgotten what *easy* tasted like. And that thought saddened him. He filled his mind instead with the glorious image of the airship, gleaming silver in a cloudless sky, its intricate internal structure of girders that he had so painstakingly created like a spider's web inside the soft outer envelope. He let himself risk a smile. The last months had been good, better than he could ever have imagined, and now his daughter had reentered his life. He'd seen her. He'd actually seen Lydia. Yet even that brought its own sorrow, a sharp stabbing pain at the sight of his daughter because she reminded him so shockingly of the loss of his wife, his Valentina.

He must have shivered because Olga took his hand. Her body next to his on the bench seemed so slight, she felt more like a shadow than a person, and at times in the darkness of the truck he even wondered whether he was imagining her. The way he imagined designs in his head. He squeezed her fingers to convince himself she was real, or was it to convince himself that *he* was real? Sometimes he wasn't sure.

But Colonel Tursenov had made it clear that the test would be real enough, to be carried out with a full load of phosgene in its tanks to be sprayed over the prison camp so that they could study what number of people it would affect. *Affect?* No. What number of people it would *kill*. And Babitsky had warned that other specialists would take over from Jens's team when the first test run was completed, so what then? More tests over more camps? Where did it end?

The truck jolted and somewhere in the dark a head or an elbow cracked against the metal side. Prisoner Elkin swore. Today would be hard.

ALEXEI SLID OUT OF THE HOLLOW HE'D SCRAPED IN THE SOIL and moved closer to the road. Around him others did the same, invisible ripples in the night air. When the yellow headlights drew near, any movement would be spotted, so the *vory* had to be in position and as still as the tree trunks themselves.

The vehicles were approaching, he could hear them now, their engines harsh in the silent forest, three pairs of headlamps cutting tunnels through the darkness. Not what he'd expected. Usually it was just one car in the lead, followed by the truck, but this was a convoy with the truck at its center, a support car in front and another behind. Four soldiers in each of the cars, two in the cab of the truck. Ten men in all. Obviously the colonel had tightened security, but not by much. Who in their right mind would want to ambush a truck full of engineers and scientists?

The tree trunk was in place. A thin pine skewed across the road as if blown down by the previous night's wind, and it brought the lead car to a juddering halt. In the headlamps Alexei could see it was a two-door NAMI-1 with a canvas top, and that behind it the truck and the second NAMI-1 bunched up tight as though seeking safety in numbers. The passenger door of the first car burst open and a tall soldier, with the lights from the truck bouncing off his bald head, descended onto the forest floor.

"Shit! A tree down."

"Shift it," the driver called out.

"Fuck you, I'm not shifting that on my own, it's too heavy. Get out here, you lazy scum."

Two soldiers wrapped in thick greatcoats clambered out from the back, rifles slung carelessly over their shoulders. The driver climbed down reluctantly, but he was much more cautious. He remained tight against the car, his rifle ready in his hands, eyes scanning the forest, trying to probe the shadows beyond the headlamps. He was the danger. Alexei took aim with his Mauser revolver, exhaled slowly to lower his heart rate, and tightened his finger on the trigger. First he saw the eruption of blood from the man's throat, and then the noise hit him, raw and violent in the silence of the forest.

A spray of bullets thudded out of the darkness before the other three soldiers had time to raise their rifles. They jerked like puppets, heads arching back as they were hit, bodies crumpled to the ground. Those in the rear car were better prepared and came out with rifles blazing. A hail of bullets roared into the trees, tearing off branches, ricocheting off trunks, mutilating the forest. One ripped past Alexei's shoulder as he sheltered behind a pine, almost snagging his army uniform, but one of the *vor* farther down the line let out a guttural grunt. Not so lucky.

Alexei felt a hot rush of anger and crouched low, moving forward at a run. He blasted out the truck's headlights. One of the soldiers was climbing back into the rear car and Alexei fired at point-blank range. A huge crimson flower blossomed on the back of the soldier's greatcoat and he slumped into the passenger seat, clawing to shut the door to protect himself. A bullet from somewhere close took his eye out and he stopped moving.

"LET ME GO."

"No, Lydia. No."

"I must see what is—"

"No."

Chang would not release her. His grip on her was too strong. They were hunched behind a tree far back from the road and she could smell the tang of its bark above her own fear, but the gunfire and the shouts in the darkness were unbearable for her. She needed to be there.

"Please, Chang An Lo, let me—"

He clamped a hand over her mouth, listening hard to the sounds from the road. "The guns are growing fewer."

That's when she bit him.

JENS FELT PANIC LIKE SOMETHING SOLID INSIDE THE TRUCK. IT writhed in the blackness and threatened to choke him. People were screaming in here, raging. They hammered on the metal doors, begged to be let out. The noise of the guns outside was loud enough to deafen, reverberating as bullet after bullet thudded into the side of the truck. One hit a tire and they felt the truck lurch as though drunk. Out in the forest, lives were ending. Explosions of glass and shrieks of pain, death trampling over hearts and lungs.

Jens sat on the bench, his face clutched in his hands, and tried to think, but the darkness, the noise and the panic, they knotted the coils of his brain. *Don't do this, Lydia. Don't. Not today of all days, my daughter. This day was to be my redemption.*

We are coming for you. That's what she'd said in her letter.

Suddenly Olga was beside him and she lifted his face, kissed his closed eyes. "This is good-bye," she whispered.

He knew she was right. "I hope you find your daughter again, Olga." He kissed her cheek.

Elkin was bellowing at the doors when suddenly the guns ceased and there was a collective intake of breath, all ears straining, all pulses racing.

"Get out here," someone yelled outside and the truck's rear doors were thrown open.

ALEXEI STOOD AT THE EDGE OF THE TREES, SOMETHING IN HIM unwilling to approach closer. The dirt road was littered with nine bodies, plus one sprawled in the second NAMI-1, but he kept a watch on the forest as though not trusting it to remain silent. He had chosen this spot for the ambush because it was too far from the hangar complex for gunfire to be heard, but still he hung back. He was uncertain about approaching Jens, and for the first time he wished Lydia were there.

The prisoners inside the truck were tumbling out, blinking hard in the rear car's headlights and clutching each other as if they feared they would be snatched away. Some were crying; one was shouting abuse at their rescuers. The *vory* had no interest in them but prodded them into a group the way someone would herd diseased cattle in an abattoir. Alexei spotted Jens Friis easily. He was taller than the rest and stood apart, ignoring the men in black who had stopped the convoy, scanning the darkness, searching the cars, the road, and the dense mass of trees for something. Or someone.

Lydia. Jens wanted Lydia.

His appearance came as a shock to Alexei. The red hair was gone and in its place was a thick white mane. Even though Lydia had told him about it, it still jarred, and his face was gaunt and weathered, his jawline set hard. Only the way he carried himself was the same. That, and the mouth. Whatever else had died in Jens Friis, the gentle lines of his mouth had survived and tempted Alexei to rush over and embrace him. But he recalled the coolness of the letter.

"Thank you, *spasibo*." One thin woman kissed Igor's hand and set off on her own down the road in the direction away from the hangars.

"Don't be damn stupid," a short man shouted after her. "They'll hunt you down and shoot you." He swung around angrily to the rest of the group. "We'll all pay for this if she leaves."

"Maybe this is a test of our loyalty," another shouted.

Others joined in.

"Let's leave. This is our chance."

"No, we've been promised our freedom."

"We can stay here and go on working for them or we can escape. Decide quickly."

What would Jens do? Would he cling to his monster?

Where was he? The white mane had vanished. Where? Alexei started to stride rapidly toward the group, who reacted with shock at the sight of his uniform, but just then an engine roared into life. The rear car, the one with the dead soldier in its passenger seat and its door hanging open, lurched violently off the dirt road and veered into the black world beneath the trees. It was traveling at speed and its headlamps carved a dangerous zigzag path between the looming trunks. There was a nerve-scraping screech of metal as the door was ripped off its hinges.

"Jens!" Alexei bellowed.

A slight figure came hurtling out of the darkness. It was Lydia running onto the road just in time to see the NAMI-1 charge back out of the forest on the far side of the barrier of the fallen pine. For a moment its wheels scrabbled and spun on the dirt as it struggled to regain the road, and its engine threatened to stall, and then it was off at full throttle toward the hangar complex.

"Jens!" Alexei roared again.

Lydia looked from her brother to the car disappearing into the night, and the expression on her face froze into one of despair.

"Papa!" she screamed. "Papa!"

"HE'S GONE. HE DROVE OFF. I DIDN'T EVEN SEE HIM, HE WAS SO eager to get back to his *monster.*"

They were deep among the trees and Chang couldn't make out her face in the pitch dark, but he could hear her voice. That was enough. He drew her to him, held her close, and kissed her cold cheek.

"That's why we're here, my love. In case anything went wrong with your brother's plan."

Her head jerked back to look at him, but her face was no more than a pale blur with black holes. It looked unnervingly like a skull and sent a cold finger of dread down his spine, so that he swore fiercely at his gods under his breath. *Don't let it be an omen.*

"We go after him?" she asked. Her voice had changed. It was Lydia's again.

"If that's what you wish."

For answer she kissed him full on the lips.

Out of the undergrowth a lumbering black form rose noisily to its feet, smelling no better than a bear, and growled, "So what are we waiting for?"

It was Popkov.

THE STEERING WHEEL KICKED AND BUCKED IN JENS'S HANDS. He knew he was driving too fast over the rough road. Something could break. He wasn't used to cars. Years ago in St. Petersburg he'd owned a glorious gleaming Buick, and twice in twelve years he'd been called on to drive a truck in the timber yards. But this army car handled like an ill-behaved dog, pulling hard one moment, unresponsive the next. So he just jammed the pedal to the metal floor and kept it there.

He had to get there fast before those hard-faced rescuers took it into their heads to come after him. He should be grateful to them, he knew he should, but he wasn't. Dear God, those people had risked their lives! Good Russian men had died. *Oh, my dearest Lydia, why weren't you there? I looked for you.* As he plowed through the forest, he wondered what the other scientists and engineers would do now. Escape? Olga would, Jens was certain of that. But not Elkin. Maybe those who realized the alternative was . . .

A branch loomed out of the darkness and smashed against the windshield, cracking one end of it. He was skidding all over the road, but he kept his foot down and raced toward the yellow glow that was forming in the distance. An imitation sun. Jens grimaced. Such an illusion, as if the Soviet machine heralded a new dawn.

"DOKUMENTI? IDENTITY PAPERS?"

The soldier had come out of his sentry booth beside the gate with his rifle pointing straight at Jens's head.

"I am one of the engineers who work here. I have no papers. Listen to me, the truck bringing us here was attacked in the forest." Jens revved the engine impatiently. "Open the gates. *Bistro.* Quickly."

The soldier stepped back into his booth and spoke for half a minute into a telephone. Immediately the gates jerked open and Jens drove in. For one terrible half-minute he'd believed they would refuse him entry, but no, he was in. He studied the compound with different eyes this time, at the slow sweep of the searchlights as they probed the early-morning darkness, at the uniformed figures rushing around like chickens as word spread of the attack.

He was dragged into a stark room he'd never been in before, interrogated by an officer whose mouth remained in a severe line but whose blue eyes sparkled at the prospect of action. He dismissed Jens with a wave of the hand when he'd extracted all he could, and abruptly Jens found himself outside in the compound at the center of a hubbub of shouts and orders, soldiers running, while the piercing wail of an alarm siren split the night air like a cleaver.

The rest was easy.

"I'll start work anyway," he said to his escort.

"Is that what you were ordered to do?"

"Yes."

He strode off toward the large hangar. The soldier didn't know what else to do with the lone prisoner, so he was relieved to have the decision made for him. Outside the small door at the side of the hangar patrolled the two men in black who normally hovered like unwanted shadows inspecting the prisoners' every action with narrow-eyed interest. But today they waved him inside without following. Their spectacles glittered as the searchlight struck them, and Jens saw them smile for the first time. Not at him but at the frantic commotion of their comrades.

Jens knew he had to move quickly. The biplanes first. He ran the length of the vast hangar, refusing to look up at the beautiful silver creature that floated above his head, and hurried through the doors to the smaller hangar attached at the rear. It was bitterly cold inside, like walking into an ice room, the electric lights dim and gloomy because some of the bulbs had cracked overnight. It was always happening. He studied the two wood-and-canvas biplanes with affection and stroked a hand along one of the lower wings. Its skin felt almost human under his fingers.

"You'll soon warm up," he said, and heard the sadness in his voice.

He hesitated. For a second his decision wavered. He could turn back now; it wasn't too late.

"Lydia, would you think worse of me if I did?" he murmured.

"You know from my letter what I've done, and yet still you came today."

Suddenly without warning the generosity of her love overwhelmed him, and for the first time in more years than he could remember, tears welled in his eyes. He felt a rawness in his throat. A tightness in his chest. No, no turning back. Better this way. He couldn't let the men of Surkov camp die. From his pockets he drew two sleeves that he'd torn from his spare shirt. He walked over to a green metal drum of aviation fuel in the corner of the hangar, unscrewed the cap, and dipped half of each sleeve into the liquid inside. The fumes made his head ache. Or was that the sorrow?

It took no more than five seconds to finish the job. He pulled out his cigarette lighter and flicked up a flame, touching it to one sleeve and then the other. When they were burning like torches, he threw one into each of the open cockpits of the planes and instantly they crackled. Flames licked up the seats like greedy tongues.

He stood there for only a couple of seconds, watching his gleaming hopes burn. Then he headed for the airship.

Fifty-three

"ARE YOU COMING, ALEXEI?"

"No, Igor. You go. I'll tidy up here."

"Tidy up?" Igor looked around at the carnage on the forest floor. "Leave the bastards for the wolves."

"You go, Igor," Alexei said again. "You've done your job well. I'll report to Maksim."

"Our *pakhan* wants to know you are safe. I am ordered to bring you back to him."

Igor's words were courteous, but Alexei had no doubt what was really in this *vor*'s mind. He was astonished that one of Igor's bullets hadn't already strayed his way during the confusion.

"Thank you, Igor. But go home. I am aware that their army retaliation units will soon be here in force."

Alexei turned his back on the thief and bent down to check on the first of the dead who were strewn across the road. The forest was silent now, just the wind jostling the branches, and as he crouched he could feel it leaning in on him, snuffling his neck, its breath stinking of rotten wood and death. Battlefields were always sorrowful places, but a battlefield after a meaningless empty little battle was enough to rip a man's heart out, especially if you were the one who had engineered it.

The others had gone, the living. The prisoners who decided to escape had changed the flat tire on the truck and driven off on an uncertain path through the forest. Those who were stupid enough to believe they would gain credit for their loyalty had set off huddled together, nervously aiming for the hangars and a lifetime of imprisonment at best. The *vory* had faded away like rats in the night, leaving only Igor.

"Go home, Igor."

But when he looked up this time, the thief had gone and the road was empty. Just the black shape of the first car remained, its headlamps as pointless as the battle had been. With care he felt the pulse of each soldier and when he found none, he closed their eyes and their mouths, removed their rifles, and arranged their limbs in attitudes of peace instead of violence, as if he could cheat the devil of their souls. At one point he thought he heard something and swung around, peering into the shifting breathing darkness.

"Lydia?"

No response.

"Lydia?"

But there was no one. After their father had driven off, the car veering wildly as it bucked out of control from rut to rut, skidding on the packed snow, she had wasted no time.

"Why didn't you stop him, Alexei?"

That's all she asked. Before he could reply she was off and running, leaping with gazelle legs across the road and plunging back into the forest from which she'd appeared. How could she see in there?

Why didn't you stop him?

Why?

Because a father should choose his son. Not the other way around. Alexei had been standing there, waiting for his father to choose him, but Jens didn't. Failed even to recognize him. That shouldn't matter, but it did. For a long moment Alexei gazed one final time at the dead bodies, muttered a childhood prayer over them, then climbed into the NAMI-1 and started the engine. As a last thought he returned to the nearest corpse, a very young and very blond soldier who looked quietly asleep except for the hole in his chest, and lifted him up into the passenger seat. Then he climbed back into the driver's seat and steered a path through the trees around the fallen pine. Once back on the road he headed north, toward the brick wall and the monster behind it.

"GET OUT OF THE CAR!"

The order was shouted at full volume. The sentry at the gate was jumpy. Alexei got out of the car.

"Here, you fool, can't you see who I am?"

The sentry observed the elegantly cut uniform of a colonel in front of him and shrank nervously into his own ill-fitting coat.

"Here." Alexei thrust Dmitri's papers under the soldier's nose. "I am here with a message from Colonel Tursenov himself. But I stumbled on a massacre in the forest. What the hell is going on here? I brought one of the wounded back here for attention, so be quick, open up."

The soldier saluted and hoped he would not lose this month's pay. "Yes, Colonel Malofeyev. Right away, Colonel."

He opened the gate.

CHANG HAD LAID A CARPET OF BRANCHES OVER THE COIL OF razor wire at the base of the wall. The pine sap smelled fresh and tangy and brought the memory of her last Christmas with her mother crashing into Lydia's head.

"Why don't you cut the wire?" she asked in a whisper.

"It could be alarmed."

They were at the back of the compound, where the forest was at its closest and the searchlight beams farther apart. Chang was standing immobile, his eyes half-closed, focusing on the wall. Lydia watched him exhale deeply, drawing together his energy, but she didn't kiss him good-bye. Or tell him she loved him. That would be to tell his gods she knew he wasn't coming back, and she wasn't willing to do that. Popkov clambered noisily on top of the branches, stomping down the wire, and stood with his back to the wall, his hands cupped together in front of him. Lydia was relieved that her Cossack was here, but frightened for him and for the hole in his side that Elena had sewn up.

"Ready?" he grunted.

Chang breathed out one last time, and she knew he was about to set off. Her heart was in her throat, but he surprised her by turning his head slowly and taking a long look at her. As if it might be his last.

"Lydia," he said softly, "remain here. Let me go to your father knowing you are safe."

She moved closer, but only one step. She didn't touch him. If she touched him she wouldn't be able to let go.

"I am always safe with you."

"It is too dangerous in there."

"I can watch your back."

"And who will watch yours?"

"I am quick. I can—"

"No, Lydia. Remain here."

A wind rattled the pine needles, the chattering of the night spirits, and the darkness weighed heavier than a sheet of steel. Neither spoke, not with words. Lydia swayed toward him, leaned so close she could smell the clean male scent of his sweat mingled with the dank odor of earth on his shoes and pine sap on his clothes. She could hear the tension in his breath.

"Please, my love," she whispered, "don't ask it of me."

He touched her hair and she rested her head against his hand. They stood like that for a long moment until Popkov growled again, "Ready?"

Chang focused on the wall once more. "Ready."

CHANG AN LO MADE IT LOOK EASY. HE SEEMED TO FLY. HE waited for the searchlight to slide past, and then he took a leap onto Popkov's cupped hands and up the wall, twisting, curling, landing on his feet like a cat, either side of the strand of vicious razor wire at the top. He uncoiled the rope that was slung over his shoulders and fastened the middle of it to the metal fixing that attached the wire to the wall. One end he tossed down to Popkov, the other he dropped to the ground inside. By the time the searchlight crawled over that stretch of wall again, he was gone and Lydia could breathe.

She gave the Cossack an affectionate tug on his beard, scrambled up on his shoulders, and grabbed the rope. Hand over hand she hauled herself up, cursing her skirts. Clumsier than Chang, she felt the wire at the top slice a piece from her finger. But once up there, viewing the compound spread out before her in the semidarkness and the looming shape of the hangar so close, she felt an unexpected calm. The fear and the nerves and the trembling fell away. This was it. Her father was here.

"Lydia." It came from below. So soft it was barely a word.

The searchlight was coming. The wind was biting her cheeks. With scarcely a sound she slid down the rope and crouched on the snow-scattered ground beside Chang. He seized her hand and together they ran.

THE COMMOTION AT THE FRONT OF THE COMPOUND WAS frantic. A roar of vehicles and shouting soldiers, boots pounding the frozen earth, hounds on leashes whining with the scent of blood in their nostrils. They were getting ready to move out into the black forest, but no one expected intruders to be already inside. Chang skimmed along the small hangar that lay in deep shadow at the rear of the much larger one and felt that Lydia would be safe here while he scouted ahead. *Safe?* No, not safe. But in less danger.

He whispered in her ear, "Wait," and pointed to the spot she was standing on.

She nodded and didn't argue. She was making it easy for him. He slipped along the length of the small hangar until he reached the side of the massive wooden structure of the main hangar, but here he was exposed. The lights blazed. He crouched low and raced toward a small door near the front of it that stood open. A man was standing outside it, dressed in black, lean and wolfish in the set of his limbs, his back turned to Chang's approach, the glowing tip of a cigarette hanging from his fingers. He was watching two dog handlers across the yard ordering their animals to leap into the back of a truck, but one dog was more intent on savaging his companion's hind legs. Chang moved up fast.

Two meters, that was all that lay between them when the man sensed something and turned. Their eyes met. The man wore spectacles and the lenses magnified his shock, but even so he reacted quickly to the threat. His hand jabbed toward the revolver on his hip, but too late. Chang had launched himself into the air, striking out with a kick that caught the man full in the throat. He clawed at his collar, knees buckling, and before he hit the ground a second kick thudded into his chest, breaking three ribs and stopping his heart.

The body was heavier than it looked. While the attention of the soldiers was elsewhere, Chang dragged it quickly just inside the open door. He glanced with astonishment at the great silver leviathan floating serenely above him, tethered to a tall metal mast, and rapidly retraced his steps. Lydia was still where he'd left her, but now her ear was pressed tight to the wall of the small hangar, the whites of her eyes huge in the dim light.

"Listen," she urged.

He listened. A dull roar filtered through the timbers.

"It's fire," she warned.

JENS HADN'T EXPECTED THIS. THIS BURNING PAIN OF REGRET IN his chest. He'd climbed up the long ladder into the gondola that was attached to the underbelly of the airship and immediately just the smell of its raw varnish and its faint odor of loneliness made him hesitate. Up here it was a solitary world. Different things mattered.

The gondola was set out with mahogany tables bolted to the floor along each side, next to the windows. Up front was the pilot's cabin, but Jens resisted the urge to enter the control cabin one last time. He reminded himself instead of all the military chiefs who would have been sitting at these tables in a couple of days, swilling champagne as they watched first one plane detach itself from under the bow of the airship and then the other from under the stern. The gas canisters packed with their deadly cargo and Surkov camp within spitting distance. Hundreds of fellow prisoners choking to death because of him.

He unlocked the hatch to the body of the airship itself and pushed it open, pulled down the collapsible steps, and climbed up. The air instantly grew colder. A soft gray twilight rippled through the silver skin from the lamps outside in the hangar, and it felt eerily calm. The interior was huge, cavernous, like being in the belly of a whale, Olga always said, but to him, even though he'd engineered it himself, each time he stepped inside he could not rid himself of the sensation of being a tiny speck, a fly caught in a gigantic spider's web of fine metal girders. He tipped his head back and gazed above him. It was beautiful, unutterably beautiful. He was proud of it.

A sudden sound rose from below and set his heart racing. He dragged his mind back to what he was doing and rapidly made his way along the central planking to the nearest of the gas balloons. These were the great moons of hydrogen gas that kept the airship afloat, and it was the work of half a second to thrust a chisel through its pliable skin. He could hear the gas escaping, as angry as a cat's hiss.

"Prisoner Friis!"

Jens spun round. It was one of the Black Widows. Just his head showed above the hatch. "What are you doing up here, Prisoner Friis?"

"My job, comrade. Until my unfortunate companions join me once more." Jens pocketed the chisel and walked back to the hatch so that he was looking down on his interrogator's neat bald patch. Even the man's spectacles looked irritated. "I've been inspecting the fastenings of the gas bags. Nothing must be overlooked for the coming test."

The man's eyes registered suspicion, but there was nothing he could pick on, so he backed down the steps to allow Jens access to the gondola. The moment he was out of sight Jens removed his cigarette lighter from his pocket, flicked its flame into life, and stood it, still alight, on the walkway. He had seconds. No more. He slid down the steps and made straight for the gondola's door. To his surprise the Black Widow was seated at one of the tables, gazing out the window and smoking a cigarette.

"Aren't you coming?" Jens asked quickly.

"Not for a moment. I like it here, it's peaceful."

Jens didn't stop to argue. He opened the door and fell, rather than climbed, down the ladder. Before he hit the concrete ground, all hell's fury exploded around him.

Fifty-four

THE ROAR OF FLAMES RIPPED THE DARKNESS apart. A blast of hot air scorched the skin on Lydia's face and sucked the moisture from her eyeballs, so that it felt as though sand was jammed against her eyelids. She could barely lift them. Then the smell hit, stinging, acrid, suffocating.

Only a moment before, Chang had started moving toward the open door again, little more than a flicker of shadow along the wall. He was intent on learning what was on fire in the small rear hangar, but when flames erupted twenty meters up into the predawn darkness, Lydia saw him turn abruptly and race back toward her. The explosion had torn a hole the size of a house in the side of the main hangar, and fire engulfed the interior in an orange-and-black inferno. *Oh God, Jens is in there.* She was certain.

"No!" she screamed, and, before Chang could reach her, she ran into the burning building.

The smoke came at her like an enemy in great waves of black, swallowing her. It clogged her lungs and choked her till she couldn't see, couldn't breathe.

She dragged off her coat and wrapped it around her head and shoulders. Showers of burning wood and debris descended on her like shrapnel, but she fought a way through them, her arm up protecting her face. She screamed her father's name.

"Jens! Jens!"

In the smoke and the flames she couldn't see anybody. It was a nightmare world. Her head felt as though a band of iron were being tightened around it. She was gulping in smoke and there was a hot pain in her chest, and then something hard and heavy struck her back, knocking her to the ground. She couldn't focus her eyes any more and knew her brain was dying from lack of oxygen. With an effort of will she pushed herself off her knees and screamed.

"Papa! Papa! Papa!"

She could hear the sound of her own voice, but her lips felt nothing, unaware of making it, as if disconnected from the rest of her. She stumbled over something, a wooden panel that had collapsed onto the ground in flames, and it set fire to one of her boots. Frantically her gloved hands beat at it and she found herself staggering into a small empty space at the heart of all this chaos, a kind of clearing in a blazing forest. Flames leapt all around her but this small still spot was miraculously free of fire. Across it lay a ladder tangled up with metal girders and a large heavy section of polished wood that was blistering in the heat. Crushed under them lay her father. She saw his white hair. Only his head and one arm were visible and his hand was stretched out, his eyes fixed on her. They were smiling.

"Lydia."

She didn't hear the sound because of the roar in her ears, but she saw his lips make the word.

"Papa!"

She crouched down and clutched his hand. Their fingers entwined for a fleeting moment, the way they had in the snow so many years ago. She whispered, "My dear Papa," before she pushed herself to her feet, seized the wood, and tried to yank it off his back. Her lack of strength shocked her. Her vision filled with bright stars and she had no idea whether they were the real night sky opening up above or whether they were inside her head. Jens touched her ankle and she knelt down quickly beside his head.

"Lydia," he said hoarsely, "get out of here. Now." He pushed at her, but the gesture was so weak she barely felt it. "Don't cry," he murmured. "Just go."

She didn't know she was crying. She kissed his white hair, and it stank of oil and smoke. Blood was oozing from his ear. "Papa," she gasped, and tucked her leg under the edge of the slab that was crushing him, taking the weight of it. She forced herself to push upright with the other leg. The wood shifted a fraction, enough for Jens to drag out his other arm and attempt to crawl forward on his elbows. But he was caught, his legs pinned.

"Leave, Lydia."

"Not without you."

"We'll both die."

In response Lydia seized a fallen piece of timber, heedless of the flames devouring it, and jammed it instead of her leg under the polished slab. Then she bent down, gripped both of Jens's hands, and pulled with all her strength until her lungs seemed to rip apart inside her. For a moment nothing happened except the fire leapt several paces closer, but suddenly something yielded. There was a loud crack and Jens started to slide forward. He made no sound. But Lydia could see in his green eyes what this was doing to her father, yet she didn't stop until he was clear of the wood. Relief surged through her until she looked at his legs. Bones were sticking out in all directions through the flesh. Even in the billowing black air she couldn't miss the white of the severed bones and the red of the blood. One kneecap had been torn off.

"Lydia, I beg you to go." His face was robbed of all color, his lips ash gray. "Don't let . . . me kill my daughter too."

Lydia crouched beside him, bent low, and draped one of his arms over her shoulder. "You did this? This fire?"

He smiled, and she loved his smile.

"Ready?" she asked.

He struggled to release himself from her grip, but she refused to let him go. Instead she half-lifted herself, raising him with her, holding him on her bent back. Still he made no sound as his shattered legs dragged behind him, but he didn't breathe either. A sudden furious squall of sparks and fiery debris showered on their heads and she felt something burning her ear and the back of her neck, but her father knocked whatever it was from her hair. She swayed, her lungs screaming for oxygen, and took one labored step forward. Both of them knew the only way out of this inferno was to run, but she couldn't run. Not with her father on her back. She took another step.

"Put me down, Lydia," he ordered in her ear. "I love you for coming for me. Now put me down."

"Alexei came." Another step. "He stopped the"—three more steps, but each one smaller than the last—"stopped the truck."

"Why?"

"Because you're"—she gasped, dragging in smoke—"his father."

A wall of flames rose before her. This was it. She had to walk through it. She twisted her head sideways. "Ready?"

He kissed her cheek. "Lydia, I am not Alexei's father. Your mother always believed that I was, but she was wrong. He is not my son."

CHANG WOULD NOT GIVE UP. HE'D FIND HER. OR DIE. THERE was no middle path. He called her name without ceasing, but the flames swallowed his words. The smoke suffocated life. He could feel it dying in his own lungs, and his fear for Lydia tore his heart into pieces.

The gods had warned him. They'd sent him the omen, but he had refused to listen to any words but hers. He'd let her come over the wall with him and now he was paying for not heeding the murmur of the gods, for not keeping a balance of desires. He could live—or die—with that, but he could not bear that she should die for it too.

He called out. He roared her name into the fire and the flames roared back at him, their laughter in every crackle and explosion that they spat in his face. He could see nothing beyond the inferno towering around him whichever direction he turned, and quite suddenly he realized he was looking with the wrong sense. Eyes could lie and confuse and panic. So he closed them. He stood totally still and exhaled the poisons from his lungs.

He listened for her again. But this time he listened with his heart.

LYDIA KNEW HER HAIR WAS ON FIRE. JENS WAS NO LONGER moving on her back. As she stepped forward, one painfully slow foot after the other, she refused to let her knees buckle, but for all she knew, Jens could be on fire too. Her mind no longer functioned properly. Control of her limbs had ceased and her lungs were shutting down. She couldn't scream if she wanted to. How she was still on her feet and pushing through a tunnel of flame and smoke that never seemed to end, she had no idea. It occurred to her briefly that she was dead and that this was hell.

Chang, my love, I didn't say good-bye. I didn't say I love you. The thought expanded in her head and filled her whole mind, so that when she heard his voice she didn't know whether it came from inside or outside her skull. But hands were lifting her father from her back and a strong familiar arm encircled her waist, supporting her. Even if she was dead and in hell's torment for the whole of eternity, she didn't care because Chang An Lo was at her side.

The final moments became a blur and she felt herself trembling uncontrollably. Big paws were knocking her head from side to side, and the burning on her scalp stopped. Dimly she caught a glimpse of an eye patch and heard someone laugh. Laugh? How could anyone laugh if they were dead?

"You were supposed to stay on the other side of the wall," Chang said to someone. "You're sick."

"I was bored. You can't have all the fun."

It was Popkov's booming voice and the filthy smell of his overcoat covering her. She saw him drape Jens over his great shoulder like a doll, and without knowing how, she found herself on Chang's back. She laid her head against his and tried to inhale, but all she got was thick choking smoke. She coughed, vomited, and felt herself slide down into a black hole so deep and so suffocating, she knew she would never claw her way back up.

ALEXEI WATCHED THE HANGAR TURN INTO A FIREBALL. IT transformed the compound into a shrieking, screaming scene of chaos. The darkness was gripped by writhing shadows as the flames tore loose, and the noise was deafening.

Figures hurtled toward the burning building, black and jerky in their panic, while others were racing away from it as though a pack of wolves were at their heels. Alexei threw the NAMI-1 into gear and drove at full speed straight for the hangar. To hell with anyone in his way. The heat hit him from twenty meters out, and it struck so hard it was like driving into a wall.

He saw them coming, Chang and Popkov. Bursting out of the side of the hangar where half the wall was gone. What the hell were they doing here? Wasn't Popkov wounded? Then he saw something on Chang's back and realized with a shock that it was Lydia. Another figure with white hair lay across the big Cossack's shoulder. It had to be Jens. He slewed the car around and gunned it toward the blackened figures who were fully visible to all in the glare of the flames, but afterward Alexei could not recall which came first, the shot or the explosion. They seemed to occur at the same moment, yet in his mind it was the shot that lingered, the sharp crack of a rifle ringing forever in his ears.

They were still more than five meters from him. Silhouetted and defenseless. The shot came from the side, from a soldier whose adrenaline was running high, too high for him to keep a steady hand on his rifle. He'd aimed at Chang, who was several paces ahead of Popkov, but he hit Lydia. Alexei saw her body jerk on Chang's back, then hang lifeless, her hands flapping loose as he ran.

Alexei's heart stopped. That was when he registered the other sound, a dull boom that reverberated inside his head like a roll of thunder. The stench of fumes burned in his nostrils and a part of his mind recognized them—a gasoline drum had exploded. But all his eyes saw was the wall, the way it moved. What remained of the side wall of the hangar, with all its heavy structural timbers and solid planking on fire, blasted away from the building. For one second it seemed to hang in the air, choosing its victims, then came rushing down toward Chang and Popkov.

Alexei stamped on the pedal. The car flung itself forward in one final effort, and Chang hurled Lydia and himself inside it as the wall crashed around them. The windshield exploded. The canvas roof split as a blazing beam tore through it and embedded itself in the empty rear seat. Sparks and flaming debris rained down on the car's hood.

"Jens!" Alexei shouted.

Beside him on the passenger seat, clutching Lydia as if he would never release her again in this lifetime, Chang murmured, "Popkov."

Alexei leapt from the NAMI-1 and found them both. Popkov was half-hidden under the car's axle, where the blast had thrown him. The chassis had protected him except for a long gash on the back of his leg. Amid the flames Alexei discovered Jens's body. His head was half-severed, his chest and limbs crushed under a flaming mass of timbers. His hair was smoldering. Another rifle bullet slammed into the side of the car and voices shouted, yet Alexei couldn't move. He gazed down at his dead father's mutilated face and couldn't walk away. *Not like this. Don't let it end like this, Papa.* He didn't even feel the next bullet graze his ear.

It was Popkov who moved him. Physically picked him up, dumped him in the driver's seat of the car, and wrenched out the blazing beam from the rear seat. Half a second later Alexei was speeding toward the entrance gate with his three passengers crammed in the back. When the sentry challenged him, he swore viciously at the soldier and waved Dmitri's papers under his nose.

"Get out of my way, you fool. I have to report this incompetence to Colonel Tursenov immediately."

"*Da*, Colonel, *da*."

The gate swung back and the forest opened before them. He drove only until the compound was out of sight and then stamped on the brakes, swiveling around in his seat.

"How is she?" he asked.

Chang didn't reply, but he was crooning softly and it sounded like a death lament. In the corner the big Cossack sat hunched and silent, tears streaming down his blackened face.

Fifty-five

❧

"DON'T DIE."

From somewhere far, far above, the words drifted down to her. Like the tiniest flakes of snow that melt to nothing the moment they touch your skin. But these words weren't soft.

"Don't die, my love."

It's too late. Can't you see, I'm already dead?

There was no pain, no thoughts, no desires, no colors, just a nothingness. A hollow void. But if being dead was this, just nothing, what was the point of all the vital effort of life? And what happened to the future life she had planned? Did it still exist? Would it go on unfolding without her? An image of Chang slid into the void inside her, Chang An Lo going on, taking himself a Chinese wife and having bright-eyed Communist children. All without her. Would he weep? Would he remember? The strange thing was that even in death her heart wanted him to be happy.

But happy with *her*.

"Come back to me, my fox girl." His words floated down to her, yet they were sharp as needles under her skin and wouldn't let her rest.

No, my precious one, it's too late. She felt herself tumbling deeper into the hole, head over heels down into the void, its blackness swallowing her, sucking all the brightness out of her, her fingers uncurling and letting go. No pain. Not even the image of Chang anymore. Just the emptiness of the void now. *It's over.*

"Come back, Lydia, or I'll come down there after you and drag you back with my bare hands."

No, let me rest.

Something was grabbing her, physically shaking her until she felt her teeth rattle.

Teeth? How could she have teeth if she was dead? When you're dead, you're just spirit. Damn it, damn it! Teeth! That meant a tiny part of her was alive. Damn it! It took a gigantic effort of will, but she dug her fingernails into the wall of blackness and felt her body jerk as the falling came to an abrupt halt. It made everything hurt. It would be so much easier to let go.

Chyort! Inch by inch, hand over hand, she started to haul herself up.

THE BULLET, THAT'S WHAT SHE SAW FIRST WHEN SHE OPENED her eyes. It was sitting on the windowsill, proud of itself in the sunlight, shining as if it had been polished. Second came Elena's broad face. She was leaning over Lydia, the lines of her face rigid, and her fingers were stained scarlet. Red paint? Why was Elena messing with paint?

"So you're awake."

"Yes." Lydia's throat felt as though it had been skinned. The air inside her tasted black and rotten.

"I've just changed your dressing." The colorless eyes studied her intently. "Sore?"

"A bit."

"You shouldn't be. Your friend has been dripping God-knows-what filthy Chinese muck onto your tongue and telling me you'll feel no pain."

"Chang? Where is he?"

Elena's somber face broke into a smile. "You'll live."

"She'd better."

"Chang An Lo?" Lydia turned her head and found him there at

her side, sitting on the bed. His expression was one she'd never seen before.

"Was I dying?" she whispered.

He lifted her hand to his lips, kissed her palm and each finger, and held it to his cheek. "No, my Lydia." He gave her a smile. It was so full of a heat she could feel on her skin, it melted something cold and frightened within her. "You weren't dying. You are indestructible. You were just testing me."

His voice filled her head. He bent forward, still holding her hand as if it were part of himself, and rested his forehead in the curve of her neck. He remained like that for a long time, without moving, without speaking. His black hair grew warm under her cheek and she felt the thread that bound them together tighten as it spun a silken strand through their flesh and blood and bone.

"Chang An Lo," she murmured, and saw a glossy lock of his hair ripple with her breath, "if ever you die, I promise I'll come and find you."

THE ROOM WAS TOO FULL OF PEOPLE. WHITE-HOT SPARKS seemed to flicker in the air, stirring it into constant motion. Lydia was sitting up in bed when all she wanted to do was slide back into that black hole. They had told her about Jens.

She'd screamed, "No!" Then silenced herself. Crushed the pain into a hard ball.

She pictured him among the ruins of his grand dreams, his proud white head smashed to the ground by his own hand in the ultimate sacrifice. *No, Papa.* The tears escaped down her cheeks and wouldn't stop. When she tried to wipe them away she saw her hand for the first time and it was burned, an ugly red and covered in slimy ointment.

"It's disgusting," she murmured as she stared at it.

Someone laughed and she knew it was with relief because a burned hand was so much better than a burned life. But Lydia wasn't talking about her hand. It was her failure. That was disgusting. *Papa, I'm sorry. Forgive me.* Black dots fluttered on the edge of her vision, and she had the sick feeling they were pieces of the black hole that had followed her, biding their time. She struggled to see straight. There were words she had to say.

"I want to thank you, all of you," she said. "For your help." Her voice was raspy, scarcely recognizable as her own.

"We almost did it." It was Alexei.

"Jens was grateful," she whispered. "He told me so." She looked at Alexei, who was pacing the room restlessly, this man she now knew was not her brother. "Thank you. *Spasibo*."

Popkov was looking wretched, playing cards with Edik on the other bed while Misty lay on the pillow and chewed one of Popkov's stinking socks.

"You found each other," the Cossack growled. "At the end you and Jens were together." He threw down his hand of cards in defeat and shrugged his huge shoulders. "That's what matters." He shuffled the cards.

Lydia nodded. Couldn't speak.

Alexei stopped at the end of her bed. "He's right, Lydia. To have you there would have meant everything to him."

"And to me," she murmured. "But I was too late to stop him. He chose to destroy what he'd started, at whatever cost, to save other prisoners."

Alexei shifted uneasily, and she could feel his frustration and the depth of his need. She had to give him something. "Alexei, he loved you," she said simply. "Jens told me. When he was on my back, he was worried for you."

Alexei's green eyes, so like her father's, stared directly at her, and she could see that he didn't know whether to believe her. But she was too exhausted to fight him and closed her eyes.

"I want to speak to Elena," she said in a whisper. "Alone."

There was an awkward silence. But when she opened her eyes again the air in the room had settled like dust, empty except for the imprint of Chang's lips on her forehead and the big woman seated on the end of her bed.

CHANG WAS UNEASY IN THE COURTYARD. IT WAS TOO PUBLIC, too visible to eyes. Anyone behind the windows would report the presence of a stranger, particularly a Chinese stranger. He was supposed to be viewing a bicycle factory, but had sent Edik with a message to Biao to tell the Russians he was unwell. It was the truth. He was sick. His heart was so sick he could vomit it up onto the court-yard cobblestones beneath his feet.

"Chang," Alexei said, "I'm glad to have this moment to speak with you."

Till now they hadn't spoken. He turned and inspected Alexei. Lydia's brother was a tall man in his long coat, proud like his father but as complex as his sister. There was no doubt that he was a man of courage and decision, for Chang had seen both in abundance at the fire in the middle of all the terror and confusion. Yet at the same time . . . he could sense in him the kind of sorrow that could take several lifetimes to heal.

"Each of us," Chang said quietly, "has our own history."

Alexei frowned. "I'm not here to discuss history."

"So what shall we discuss instead?"

"Lydia, of course. What else would you and I have to speak about?"

Chang smiled and felt the snow soft on his face. "We could speak about life. About death. Or about the future." He placed his hands together and bowed formally over them. "I wish to thank you, Alexei Serov, for saving my life at the fire. I am in your debt."

"No debt. No debt at all. You saved my sister's life. That is enough."

Chang inclined his head in the faintest of bows. *That is enough*. The words were true. If Lydia had not been on Chang's back, this Russian would have left him to burn. They both knew that. A young woman hurried out of the building into the courtyard with a bucket in each hand and glanced at the two strangers with open curiosity as she crossed toward the water pump. The only sound was the laugh-ter of Lydia's stray pale-haired boy on the other side of the yard with the Cossack. Chang and Alexei listened for a moment to the laugh-ter, both willing it to last longer in the cold echoing air.

"About Lydia," Alexei said suddenly.

Chang waited, watching the boy. He could sense the brother deliberating as to how to start.

"It won't work, the two of you," Alexei said flatly. "It's impos-sible to make it work; the barriers are too high. If you care for my sister at all, you'll give her up and leave Russia. Let her stay with her own people. For God's sake, can't you see, you and she are oil and water, you cannot mix?" His voice was growing softer, lower, more intense. "If you love her, Chang An Lo, really love her, let her have her own life. With you her future will always be as an outsider wherever she is."

Slowly Chang turned his head and fixed his gaze on the dark green eyes. Again the boy's laughter crossed the courtyard, but this time they didn't hear it.

"You understand me?"

"What Lydia and I decide to do is none of your business," Chang said coldly.

"She's my sister, damn it, that makes it my business." Anger flared and Chang knew it had been there all along, lying in wait. "You took Lydia over the wall. For God's sake, why did you take her with you to search for Jens in the hangar? You almost killed my sister. How can I ever trust you? Do you expect me just to forget and forgive such a—"

"No." Chang felt the pain twist deep in his gut, sharper than a heated knife. "No, I don't. No more than I can forgive myself."

"WELL?" ELENA ASKED, RESTING HER ARMS ON TOP OF HER bosom as she sat at the bottom of the bed. Her eyes had shrunk to wary points.

"You know what I'm going to say."

"How could I possibly know what goes on in that crazy head of yours?"

Lydia smiled. Everything hurt and she badly wanted to sleep, but she had to say this. "First I want to thank you, Elena."

"For what?"

"For taking the bullet out of me."

The woman shrugged. "I've had plenty of practice."

"Thanks anyway." She hesitated.

"What else?"

Lydia took a shallow breath. "I want to know why you betrayed me."

"What?"

"Both times that Alexei and I went into the forest the soldiers knew we were coming. They sent in stalkers to track us and would have caught us if Chang hadn't been watching our backs. The second time there was an extra car to guard the truck convoy."

Elena sat very still. "You are mistaken, comrade."

"The only people who knew what we were doing were the *vory* and Chang, Popkov, and myself. And you."

"Any one of those thieves would sell you to the secret police as soon as slit his grandmother's throat."

"No, you're wrong. They do as Maksim tells them and he is besotted with my brother, so he would let them do nothing to harm him. The others I'd trust with my life." She leaned forward. "So that leaves you."

"No."

"Don't lie to me, Elena." The gaps between her words grew longer. "We both know it was you."

"If I said yes," Elena muttered, "what difference would it make?"

"It might to Liev."

Elena gave her a long hard look. "Haven't you hurt him enough? Leave him in peace now."

"Is that why you did it? To rid him of me?"

Elena sighed. "Girl, when I first met you I thought you and I could be friends, but in the end I saw clearly that you weren't good for Liev. How can he have his own life when he is always living yours?"

"I didn't ask him to."

"No, you didn't have to. It's in his blood, bred to belong to someone like in the old Russian serf system. Like his father before him. As devoted to you as Misty is to Edik, and if you needed him to perform tricks for you, he wouldn't think twice before doing them." She exhaled slowly, but there was a sorrowful note in her voice when she said, "I had to get rid of you, Lydia. For Liev's sake."

Lydia swallowed the bile that had risen to her mouth. "You could have just asked me to go," she said quietly.

"He'd never have let you."

Lydia nodded. Guilt, smooth and slippery, oiled her throat.

"So you betrayed me to protect your Cossack. Does he know?"

Color rose to Elena's plump cheeks and she gripped both hands together on top of her head, flattening her shapeless hair. "No," she muttered. "Are you going to tell him?"

"No."

The woman nodded, shrugged her heavy shoulders, and walked over to the window, where she stood looking out. In a thick voice she added, "What you did for your father was wonderful."

Lydia let her face drop into her hands. "He still died. I couldn't save him."

"Maybe. But he knew what you did for him."

"I couldn't save my mother either," she whispered through her fingers.

"I know. You aren't any better than I am at keeping your loved ones safe." She added, "Come over here."

Lydia eased herself carefully off the thin mattress and joined Elena at the window. She was surprised to find that it was snowing outside, not heavily, just a feathery dusting of flakes that drifted through the air and made the world look gentle. They stood in silence, side by side, watching the men in the courtyard below. Chang and Alexei were standing stiffly together, talking quietly, and she wondered what they were discussing. The fire? The weather? The latest church to be blown up on Stalin's orders? Maybe her? They had their backs to the window so she couldn't see their faces, but her eyes lingered on the firm line of Chang's shoulders and on the tension in his long limbs. A young woman from one of the apartments was breaking ice from the courtyard water pump and stopped for a moment with a smile on her face to watch the antics of Misty.

Popkov had tied a length of string around the dog's neck and was teaching her to walk at Edik's heel. Lydia hadn't realized before how good he was with dogs, but neither had she realized how tired he looked. She felt a rush of tenderness for the big man who had brought her father so close to freedom only to have him snatched away at the final moment. *Oh Liev, my friend, I'm sorry if I asked too much. Even from here I can see it has taken something out of you.*

A slow sigh escaped from the woman at her side, misting the glass and blurring the picture of the boy and his dog.

"He's asked me to go to live in the Ukraine with him."

Lydia's eyes darted to Elena's face. "The Ukraine?"

"Somewhere near Kiev. It's where he grew up as a child."

"Was Liev ever a child?"

Elena smiled for a fleeting moment. "It's hard to imagine."

"Are you going?"

Elena watched Popkov, the way he leaned over the tiny puppy and spoke gently to it. "He's worried about you."

"He needn't be."

"I know."

"Do you love him?"

"Hah! By the time you reach my age and have known more men than hot dinners, love is no longer what you think it is, Lydia."

"But do you love him?" Lydia persisted.

There was a pause, and Lydia wiped the window with her hand. *The Ukraine. Oh Liev, half a world away.*

"Yes," Elena admitted at last. "I suppose I love the dumb oaf."

They both smiled.

"Then go to the Ukraine. I won't breathe a word about . . ." She let it trail off.

"And you? Where will you go?"

The question tightened Lydia's throat so sharply she started coughing, tasting smoke in her mouth.

"You'll tear your stitches. Get back to bed."

She helped her stumble back to the mattress, but Lydia grasped the fleshy arm that supported her and wouldn't let it go. She pulled the woman close. "Elena," she said fiercely, "if you hurt him I'll come and I'll find you, and I'll rip your heart out."

Their eyes held, the tawny ones fixed on the pale ones, and Elena nodded. She didn't smile this time.

"You have my permission to do so," she said.

Lydia released her grip but saw something in the woman's expression, some anxiety that made her ask, "What is it, Elena?"

There was no response. Lydia's pulse thumped. The broad face was shuttered now.

"Tell me, Elena."

"Oh fuck, why am I telling you this? You've got to get out of here, girl. Sick or not."

"Why?"

"Because they're coming for you today."

"Who?"

But she didn't need to ask. Already she was throwing off the quilt, swinging her legs to the floor, mind and pulse racing.

"Who?" Elena echoed. "Those bastards from OGPU, of course, the secret police."

Fifty-six

LYDIA RESTED HER HEAD ON CHANG AN LO'S shoulder and concentrated on forcing her legs to function. He was tracking back and forth across the city, his arm tight around her waist, keeping her on her feet until he was certain no watchful shadows were padding behind them in the snow.

When finally he brought her to their secret hideaway, the small one that had replaced the crucifix room, she stumbled through the door and released her grip on him for the first time. She took a slow deep breath to keep the pain in her side at bay and pulled off her hat, but when she glanced in the mirror on the wall and saw her hair for the first time since the fire, she blushed lobster red. It was appalling. One whole chunk was burnt away and the rest was shriveled and charred. With the blisters on her forehead, she looked like a badly made scarecrow.

"Cut it."

"Rest first," Chang had urged. "You're exhausted."

"Please, cut it. Short as a boy's. Get rid of the . . . damage."

His black eyes had looked at her reflection for no more than a moment, but she realized in that flicker of time that he'd seen all the damage right down into the heart of her. He'd seen the void and the guilt and the fear, and she felt ashamed. Lightly he kissed the side of her singed hair, pulled the sharp knife from his boot, and sliced off the first handful.

"Better?" he asked.

She nodded. "It's only hair. It's not my limbs."

But as he continued to cut and the locks of hair fluttered to the floor like dead leaves, Chang's mouth curved down in a half moon of sorrow. He bent and gathered the charred copper curls from the floor and cradled them in his hands like a gift of flames for his gods. A memory of her mother hacking off her own long dark waves with a pair of blunt kitchen scissors came stamping into Lydia's mind, and for the first time she understood. That terrible need to punish oneself. The sense of relief it brought, that same relief she'd seen on Antonina's face the first day they met in the hotel bathroom.

"Chang An Lo," she whispered as she swung around to face him, "tell me where you hurt."

His pupils widened as thoughts seemed to ripple through him, creating purple flecks in his eyes. "My shoulders."

That wasn't what she meant and he knew it. "Show me."

He settled the flock of curls carefully on a chair and removed his padded jacket. It had brown holes scorched into it, and his tunic underneath was no better. He stripped it off and turned his naked back to her.

"That's colorful," she said. Her hand covered her mouth to seal in all other sounds that were battering to get out.

"Are you any good with ointment?" he asked.

"I'm an expert. Fingers light as feathers. Don't you remember?"

He twisted around. "Yes, I remember. As if I could forget."

"In the garden shed in Junchow when you were wounded and . . ."

He swung her up in his arms and laid her on the bed. "Hush, my love, don't hide back in the past again."

With infinite gentleness he removed all her clothes, just leaving the bandage around her waist where the bullet had entered her side. But despite Elena's stitches it was stained the colors of rotting fruit, reds and browns and oranges. He kissed the soft skin of her stomach, then wrapped her in the quilt.

"Come here and talk to me," she murmured.

"Sleep first and then we'll talk." From the battered old leather satchel Lydia had given him long ago in China, he drew a tiny bottle of muddy liquid and poured a drop onto her tongue. "Sleep now."

But she forced herself into a sitting position. "Ointment first." She held out her hand.

He didn't resist. A ceramic pot appeared from the satchel and she sat him down on the bed, knelt behind him, and smeared the creamy substance from the pot onto her fingers. With her touch as light as the promised feathers, she massaged it into the raw flesh of his shoulders. She didn't ask what caused the wound. A burning timber crashing down? A blast of white-hot flames? It didn't matter now. The ointment smelled strange, of herbs that made her eyes sting, and she felt her lids growing heavy. She kissed the good clean healthy skin in the center of his back, but when she opened her mouth to tell him that he was the bravest man on God's earth, before the words could form on her tongue she was fast asleep.

WHEN SHE WOKE IT WAS DARK. THE NIGHT SKY CLUNG TO THE windowpane, rattling it, trying to get in. Lydia felt Chang's warmth curled around her but knew instantly that he was awake. She felt stronger after the sleep and allowed her lungs to breathe in a shallow steady rhythm, clinging to the pretense of sleep because she was not ready for what lay ahead. The loss of her father had buckled something inside her, and she grieved for him and for the dream that was gone. It came as a shock to find that her cheeks were wet. Had she been crying in her sleep? She lay like that, nestled against him, for a long time. An hour, maybe more. Unwilling to give him up. She clutched each second to her and memorized the exact feel of his hand on her hip and his breath on her neck, the way it made the delicate nerves of her skin ripple with pleasure.

"When do you leave?" she asked at last in the darkness.

He didn't respond, except to tighten his grip on her.

"When?" she asked again.

He sat up and lit the candle that stood on the table next to the bed. Shadows, black and twisted, leapt around the room, as ugly as her fears. He rested his head back against the greasy wall and focused on the door. Not on her.

"You can't stay here," he said. "Now that they're searching for you, you must leave."

"I know. Though I suppose"—she smiled up at his profile—"I could become a street rat like Edik with my short hair, and work for the *vory*. I'm good at stealing."

She felt a shiver in his chest. He touched her cropped hair. "It looks like rats have already been at it."

She laughed and saw that it pleased him.

"Is the pain bad? Do you need more . . . ?"

"Hush." She put a finger to his lips. "It's not bad."

He raised an eyebrow at her. "More herbs?"

"No, I need a clear head. I want us to talk."

Gently he drew her to him, cradling her against his naked chest, and for a while both let the moment linger, knowing that things were about to change.

"You can't stay here," Chang said again.

"So let's talk about what we do next. It's what I've been thinking about and working for, a future for us together."

A little snort escaped from his nostrils. "Yet you risked it all for your father."

She said nothing, just stroked his chin.

"Ask me," he said.

"Ask you what?" But she knew.

"Ask me." He lifted her chin and made her look into his eyes. "Ask me again."

"No."

"Then I'll ask it myself. Am I willing to go to America with you?"

She didn't breathe.

"Lydia, my sweetest love, the answer is no."

She didn't gasp or cry out or cram the words back in his mouth, all of which she wanted to do. She studied his face in silence before asking, "What did he say to you?"

"Who?"

"Alexei, of course. You and he were together in the courtyard and I can just imagine what . . ."

She stopped because she felt him tense, heard his quick intake of breath. He was halfway out of the bed with his knife suddenly in his hand when the door burst open and crashed against its hinges. Five men crowded into the small room. They were all Chinese and they all carried guns.

"Get out!" Lydia yelled at them. She threw a quilt over her naked body.

The one in the front of the pack was young with a long face and dressed in a military padded jacket. The others looked to her like professional killers, all clothed in black with hard eyes that seemed disconnected from the human race. Lydia leapt from the bed, but Chang stepped between her and the intruders, and she was terrified he was going to attack.

"No!" she screamed.

But he didn't move. He remained frozen. Instead a torrent of words in rapid Chinese flowed from him, and the young man in blue answered in quick bursts, clearly unhappy. At one point the young man gestured at Lydia and her heart kicked under her ribs, but when the words stopped, Chang grew very still.

Without turning he said in measured English, "This man is Biao. He is . . . he *was* . . . my friend, a member of the delegation."

Her limbs shivered.

Chang's eyes were still fixed on Biao. "He is the person whom I trusted to find this room for us, the only person who knew where it was."

"Why is he here?"

She wished he'd turn. Wished he'd look at her.

"Biao has come with his companions to ensure that I return to the Hotel Triumfal immediately."

"Why? It's not even morning yet. What has happened?"

At last he turned and the look in his dark eyes drew all the shadows in the room to him. "Biao said that I should ask you."

THEY WAITED OUTSIDE THE DOOR. CHANG FORCED BIAO TO agree to it while he spoke to Lydia. He was tempted to slit Biao's worthless throat in payment for betrayal, regardless of the consequences for himself, but he was not willing to risk Lydia's life as well. As soon as the door closed he held her by the arms and refused to let her look away.

"Tell me." He sought out the truth in her eyes. "Tell me what you have done."

Her chopped hair stuck out at strange angles and her pale face looked wretched. But far worse was the fear in her eyes. What was she so frightened of? He eased his grip on her thin arms and saw his thumbprints remain on her white skin as though they'd rather be with her than with him.

"Tell me," he said more gently.

The words, when they came, rushed out of her. "The delegation is leaving Russia today and you haven't even told me. So go to them. Go. Go back to your China and to your Communists. Even though you despise their leader." Sudden fury made the amber of her eyes look burnt, the way her hair was burnt.

"Lydia," Chang said sharply, "how do you know that the delegation is leaving today?"

She had been breathing hard but stopped abruptly. He saw her fox teeth bite down on her tongue. How was it possible to love someone so much and yet not know the secrets hidden under her tongue? The blisters on her forehead glistened golden in the uncertain light from the candle, and his heart jolted for her. He wrapped his arms around her quivering frame and folded her to his chest. He kissed her smoky hair and felt her melt into him, so that all the fury and the questions were gone. Just a stillness remained at the heart of them.

A rap on the door made Lydia jump.

"Quickly, my love," he whispered into her hair, "tell me. Tell me everything."

She rested her head against his neck for a brief moment, then broke free and went over to the window. She pulled on her blouse but remained by the window, gazing out, as though what lay behind her was too painful to look at.

"How did you know," he asked, "that the delegation was leaving today?"

"Li Min told me."

"Li Min? Our delegation leader? How do you know him?"

She drew in a deep breath, as if she were drowning. "Listen to what I have to say, Chang An Lo, and then you can leave. Last year in China when I was about to set off for Russia to search for my father, a group of your people came to me."

"My people?"

"Yes, your Chinese Communists. They'd heard I was traveling to Siberia. Maybe they had informers in the railway ticket office, I don't know. But they came anyway. They knew from Kuan that Jens Friis was my father, and they told me he had designed a secret project to help the Soviet military. Obviously they must have their spies in the heart of the Soviet system, even in the Red Army, but they didn't know what it was he'd created or where he was being held—in a prison or one of those god-forsaken labor camps. Not even whether he was dead or alive. Chang, you have to understand, he was my father and I . . ." She stopped herself, snatched a breath and finished quietly, "So they asked me to find out."

Anger, heavy and unwieldy, was churning in his gut.

"And in return?" he demanded. "What did they offer you?"

"I asked for you."

"Me."

"Yes. I asked for you to be kept out of the civil war in China, far away from the Kuomintang army." She swallowed and he thought she would look around, but she didn't. "I wanted you safe. I had no idea they would send you here to Moscow, I swear. That came as a surprise." She twitched the buttons of her blouse. "A welcome surprise. It proved they were sticking to their side of the bargain."

He moved silently across the room until he was standing right behind her and could hear the catch in her every breath. "So that's why you went into the prison that day to get the letter? The one from Jens about the construction of the project. So that you could give it to Li Min."

She jumped at the sound of his voice so close but remained with her back to him. She nodded.

"Lydia."

"I know you're angry. That you feel I betrayed you and did a dirty deal behind your back. But the thought of losing your life to a Kuomintang bullet was . . . too much. I couldn't bear it. And now that your Chinese friends have what they wanted, they are leaving and taking you with them."

She leaned back till her head was touching his cheek, and just that

simple intimate movement of hers was enough to break his resolve
to give her up. The immensity of what she'd done for him took
his breath away. That she'd bargained her own life and that of her
father . . . for his. His arms encircled her injured waist and drew her
close against him, fighting to keep from crushing her into his own
bones where she would be safe.

"You're right, I am angry, Lydia, but not with you, my love. With
them." He smelled the blood on her and it made his heart weep. "I
should have realized it wasn't your past you were protecting."

"No," she whispered, "it was our future. Yours and mine. But . . .
Chang, we are both created by our past."

Another knock shook the door, and Biao shouted for them to
hurry.

Chang spoke urgently. "Lydia, you must decide now. If it's America you want, we can—"

She spun around, her eyes wide and intent on his. "No, not
America."

"My heart cannot beat without yours beside it."

"Is that what Alexei told you to do? To give me up?"

"He said that with me you would be an outsider."

She laughed, making the air in the room come alive. In the middle of all the fear and the pain and the danger she laughed, tossing
her shorn curls, and the sound of it mended something inside him
that was broken. "Oh Chang An Lo, I have been an outsider all my
life. I used to fight against it, thinking I wanted to belong, but not
now. It's being an outsider that has brought me you."

He took her face in his hands. "Your brother believes you must
stay here in Russia, and when I see you here, I know this country is
a part of your soul."

"Forget what Alexei says. He is not my brother."

"What?"

"Jens told me. He said that Alexei is not his son. That my mother
got it all wrong. Even Alexei's own mother must have lied about it."

The sorrow on her face flickered like the shadow of a night spirit
in the candlelight. "Oh my Lydia, in that fire you lost your brother
as well as your father."

She smiled at him, a fragile twist of her mouth. "Your gods

exacted a high price," she said. "And now they're stealing you from me again."

"Come with me."

Her eyes widened. "To China?"

"Yes."

"No," she said. "Have you forgotten? We decided long ago that while you are fighting for the Communists there is no place for a Western girl dragging at your heels. No world in which I could find a place."

"There is one."

"Where?"

"Hong Kong."

Fifty-seven

THE CAR WAS CROWDED AND ITS INTERIOR smelled of China instead of Russia. Lydia was pressed tight against the window with Chang An Lo seated beside her, a barrier between her and the others. His hand had clasped hers the moment they entered the car, and though he was arguing fiercely with the one he called Biao, his fingers never left hers.

Her canvas bag lay on Chang's lap on top of the satchel, as if he would hide her from the Chinese intruders. Biao and another of the ones in black were crowded on the far side of Chang on the rear seat, while the three others were in the front. The one in the driver's seat had a silvery scar where one of his ears should be.

Their voices sounded harsh to Lydia's ears, a flood of angry Chinese words filling the air between Chang and Biao, friends who were fighting like enemies. She longed to know what was being said, but she knew Chang would tell her only as much as he wished her to know. She leaned her head against the window and watched the snow and the streets dissolve behind the mist of her breath. She was frightened what else might dissolve.

"Lydia."

The words had stopped.

"Tell me what is happening, Chang."

His hand tightened on hers and he spoke in English, so that none of his compatriots would understand.

"Lydia." The way he said her name, she knew what was coming wasn't good. "I must leave you, Lydia. No, my love, don't look like that, it won't be for long. We agreed," he said softly, "that we shall meet in Hong Kong. I will be there, I swear. But I can't travel with you through Russia, they won't let me."

She glanced at the heads in front. "Not even if we run from these . . . ?"

"No, no more risks, Lydia. If you and I escape together from these people, they will hunt us down as we travel the thousands of miles back to China and I won't put you in that danger. This time"—he touched her neck—"I want you safe."

"So what are we to do?" She glanced at Biao, who was staring straight ahead, unwilling to look at her.

"It is settled." He held both her hands in his, and so she knew it was bad.

"Tell me."

"I am to travel with the delegation back to China and report to Mao Tse-tung. I have given my word that I shall give them no trouble."

She smiled at him. "Chang An Lo masquerading as a demure lamb, that will be something to see." But his eyes held no laughter. "What do we get in exchange?" she asked in a low voice.

"A guardian for you."

"I don't need a guardian."

"Yes, you do. The Russian secret police are searching for you, so . . ."

"Who? Who is this guardian?"

He glanced at Biao's sullen profile.

"No," Lydia said sharply, "I refuse to have—"

"Don't, Lydia, please don't fight this."

She swallowed the words on her tongue and saw his dark eyes follow the silent movement of her lips as she struggled to accept what he was saying.

"Biao will escort you all the way to Vladivostok. With him, you should have no trouble from the Russians. Then down south through China to Hong Kong."

"He hates me," she whispered. "Why would he do such a thing?"

"Because I have ordered him to do so. I know he will protect you with his life."

"Even though he hates me?"

"Trust him, Lydia. He will bring you safely to China."

She hung her head and he wrapped an arm around her shoulders, drawing her to him. "I would give my heart's blood to travel with you, my love, but it would just bring more danger down on your head." He kissed the side of her chopped hair.

"You'll meet me?" she asked. "You'll be there?"

"I promise."

"You won't change your mind and go off with your Communists again?"

"No. Not this time."

Their eyes held and she believed him. It was a risk, but she couldn't live with herself if she didn't take it. He leaned forward, seeing the belief in her eyes, and kissed her mouth, ignoring the others in the car.

"Now," he said softly, "where is your Cossack bear waiting for you?"

THE SNOW HAD STOPPED FALLING. AS LYDIA WALKED ON TO Moscow's Borodino bridge in the southwest of the city, cars rumbled past with chains on their tires and a pale watery sun sat low on the horizon as though it had no strength to struggle any higher. She felt a rush of relief when she saw the Cossack waiting for her, and he bared his teeth at her approach. Had he feared she wouldn't come? That she wouldn't keep their agreed meeting, here among the cast-iron boards listing the heroes of the 1812 war?

"I'm not locked up in the Lubyanka yet," she smiled.

Lubyanka prison was the nightmare of Moscow, a handsome yellow-brick mansion where interrogations in the dungeons took people apart piece by piece in ways they had never imagined possible.

"Don't mention that stinking place," he growled, and his single black eye studied her. "You look a mess."

She ignored him. "Hello, Elena."

The woman standing beside him had her arms folded and she was staring at the strands of hair poking out under Lydia's hat, but she made no comment. "You got here," was all she said.

"So, Liev. Off to the Ukraine?"

"*Da*. It's still got real people in it. Fuck Moscow. It's no more than a Soviet machine."

Lydia put out a hand and touched his granite chest with her fingertips. "Take good care of yourself, my friend." She looked up at him. "Are you feeling better?"

"Like a spring lamb."

She laughed.

"And you?" he asked, drawing his beetle brows together.

"More like an old goat."

He nodded, fingering his beard thoughtfully, and she noticed it was singed into a lopsided mat. Suddenly a narrow face popped out from behind his back.

"Whose car was that you came in?"

"Edik! What are you doing here? And Misty." She ruffled the pup's feathery ears. "The car belongs to some rather unpleasant companions of my Chinese friend."

Popkov scowled. "They've taken him?"

She nodded and stared down at Popkov's ancient leather boots with the howling wolf tooled on the side. "Liev," she said softly, "you knew about Alexei all along, didn't you?"

He grunted.

"That he wasn't my brother. You knew all along. That's why you were such a bastard to him."

He grunted again.

"You should have told me."

"*Nyet*. I couldn't. It made you happy."

Her throat felt too tight. She said nothing more. A horse and cart clattered past, scattering a spray of filthy gray snow over them, and Misty barked. The world was still moving.

"I'm going to grow wheat," Popkov announced.

"You?" Lydia smiled. "A farmer?"

"We'll learn," Elena asserted confidently. "Edik is going to help us, aren't you, boy?" She gave him a dig in his skinny ribs and he laughed.

"If you force me to," he grinned.

Lydia looked at the family of three, at the warm pride in Liev's battered face, and she envied them. "Be happy," she murmured, and found it hard to let him go. Liev kept staring at her before switching to gaze out at a laden barge lumbering up the Moskva River, and then staring at her again.

"What is it, Liev?"

The Cossack stretched his shoulders and rumbled something inaudible into his beard.

"The thing is," Elena said stiffly, "he won't come without you."

Lydia closed her eyes and swayed back and forth on her feet.

Elena hadn't finished. "He wants you to come with us."

Lydia rubbed her hands as if it were the biting wind swirling off the river that was making her shiver. "*Chyort!* Liev, are you out of your mind? Me on a farm? Don't be an oaf. I'm not a peasant with straw for brains. Go and play with your shovels and your hoes on your own; dig your holes without me."

It was fleeting, but she caught the look of relief on Elena's face.

"What will you do?" Popkov's deep voice was strained.

"Oh, I'll be safe, don't worry. I'm going back to China."

His black eye narrowed, and like an old bull he shook his head as if it had suddenly grown heavier. "You were desperate to get out of China. You said you hated it there."

"I lied."

"Let the girl be, Liev." It was Elena. She was assessing Lydia with a half-smile on her lips. "It's not the place she loves, can't you see? It's the person."

"But—"

"No *buts*! Stop fussing over me, you stupid Cossack," Lydia complained. She pushed him away. "Off you go to the Ukraine." She smiled brightly, surprising herself, and even laughed a little. "Have a good life. Thank you for everything."

She spun around and walked away. But she'd not gone more than ten paces in the direction of Smolensk Square before she was plucked off her feet. She was dangled over the icy ground, enveloped in a great greasy embrace, and with no breath in her lungs she clung to him. As each minute ticked by he crushed her harder to his chest, growling softly in his throat.

Just as suddenly he put her down. She thrust Dmitri's gold ring into his pocket. "To buy some land," she said, then walked away and didn't look back.

LYDIA STARTED TO WALK ACROSS THE CITY BUT SOON REALized she hadn't the strength to make it as far as the Arbat. So she climbed into an *izvozchik*, one of the horse-drawn taxicabs, and settled its thick rug over her knees, her arms wrapped around her bandaged waist. It was an uncovered vehicle, open to the elements, but that suited her. The snow had stopped and she liked the wind, cold in her face. The sky looked gray and old as it hovered over Moscow's roofs, and she felt a tug of dismay at the thought of leaving this city she'd fallen in love with.

The easy rhythm of the horse's hooves was slow and restful, and it gave her time to think. She closed her eyes and let her mind open the way Chang An Lo had taught her, but still the images of the raging fire pressed in on her, the flames leaping in her face and roaring in her ears. Instead she clutched at the feel of her father's hand in hers and the echoes of his voice when he said, *I love you for coming for me.*

"Papa," she whispered, "I'll come back."

One day she would. She didn't know when or how, but she would. Russia had entwined itself into the fibers of her being, and she could no more stay away from this city of domes than she could from the black soil Popkov and Elena would be churning up in the Ukraine.

A cart rumbled past in the street, and the sound of a car's klaxon brought her back to what lay ahead. She had to see Alexei. He was with Antonina in her apartment, and Lydia needed to speak to him. She was angry with him for telling Chang to give her up, but . . . she opened her eyes wide and felt her chest tighten . . . but despite Alexei, Chang would be waiting for her in China. She drew a deep breath and said aloud, "Be there, my love. Be there. For me." Once back in China she feared that his country and his gods might steal him from under her nose.

"Trust him," she whispered to herself, and felt the wind carry her words to their ears.

THE APARTMENT WAS IN CHAOS. BOXES EVERYWHERE. FURS AND candlesticks and even a silver samovar overflowed from their gaping mouths. Books were stacked in piles on the floor and paintings propped against the wall. It struck Lydia as obscene that a Communist had owned so much, and corruption seemed to writhe from box to box like the string that lay abandoned on the Persian carpets. She'd found it hard to walk through the door again, as the memories of the last time still weighed too heavy in her mind.

Alexei was surprised to see her. "Lydia, shouldn't you be in bed?" But he kissed her gently on both cheeks and did no more than raise one eyebrow at the sight of her hair. "I'm glad you've come because I have something for you."

He led her to the study, where Antonina was seated at the desk going through a drawer of Dmitri's papers. She looked up and her dark eyes brightened. Then she saw Chang's work with the knife and she frowned before coming over to the doorway where Lydia had stopped. She didn't care to enter that study again.

"Lydia, my dear girl, you're"—Lydia was sure the comment was going to be on her bizarre appearance but she was wrong—"so welcome." Antonina hugged her, and for once there was no smell of perfume.

"You look well," Lydia said.

"I am well."

In fact Lydia had never seen Antonina looking lovelier. But totally different. Her thick dark hair was tied loosely behind her head and she was wearing a plain blue dress and cardigan that had never been anywhere near Paris. But that wasn't the only change. Her face was free of makeup and she wasn't wearing gloves. There were shadows under her eyes as if she weren't sleeping, but her mouth was free of the tension that had previously kept it hard.

"Come and have coffee. Alexei, we'll be in the drawing room."

Tactfully she led Lydia away from the study, sat her down, and drifted off to make coffee while Alexei talked. Lydia found it unsettling to be with this man who was not her brother. She had to rethink him.

"Are you all right?" he asked with concern.

"Sore, but I'll live." She smiled at him. "Thanks to you."

He sat down in the chair opposite and stretched out his long legs in an awkward gesture, uneasy with her gratitude. She changed the subject.

"You're packing up, I see."

"Yes. They're starting to ask questions about Dmitri's whereabouts. It's too dangerous to remain here, so we're getting out today."

"Where are you going?"

"Antonina is changing her name so that they won't be able to trace her, and we've bought new identity papers. But we're staying in Moscow and moving to a different district."

"Of course, Maksim is in Moscow."

Alexei flicked a glance of annoyance at her, and she studied his eyes. It was their color that had misled her. It made her believe her mother's assertion that Jens was his father, but how stupid could she be? Jens hadn't been the only man in St. Petersburg with green eyes.

Suddenly she leaned forward. "I'm going back to China."

She heard his rapid intake of breath. "No, Lydia, don't. It will be a mistake. Listen, why don't you stay with us? Here in Moscow. We've found an apartment." He waved a hand around the high-ceilinged room. "Not desirable like this one, but it has two rooms, so . . ."

"No, Alexei. Thank you, but no."

"Please, Lydia, don't do this. It's all wrong. What are you and I without Russia? It's in our blood."

She shook her head. "I love Russia. But not enough."

Their eyes held. How could she ever have thought this man cold? The fire was there, deep in him, hidden behind the wall of pride. "I love you, my brother," she said softly. She couldn't rob him of his father by telling him the truth.

He rose from his chair and knelt on the polished floor in front of her, taking both her hands in his. "Stay in Moscow," he begged. "I would like to have you at my side. With Maksim's support I am going to remain one of the *vory* and intend to work my way up, so that . . ."

"When Maksim dies, you'll be there, ready to take over. My dear brother, you are nothing if not ambitious."

He didn't nod, but she saw his eyes shine and she recognized the thrill that rippled through him at some deep level. He wasn't a man to conform to Stalin's straitjacket, but she could already see changes in him and she was frightened for him. How much of what she loved most in him would disappear if he spent his life with these thieves? It was ironic. She used to be the one who stole and risked prison, not him.

"Or," she suggested, "you could return to China with me."

He frowned at her. "No. I'll not leave Russia."

Did he think her a traitor then? Is that what he meant?

"So what is it you said you have for me?" she asked.

He scrutinized her face, as though searching for something, before standing and removing some papers from a cabinet.

"Here, new identity documents."

Her heart thumped. "That was fast."

"A gift from Maksim."

"Thank him from me."

"I will." He stood looking down at her. "One last time, little sister. Give him up. You will make each other unhappy in the end."

"I can't. Any more than I can give up breathing."

"Very well." He held out a packet. "Here's a form with Dmitri's personal stamp on it to enable you to travel freely and buy tickets. And enough roubles—from Antonina—to get you to China."

She took them. Her hand trembled as she blinked back tears. "What can I say, Alexei? You are the brother I always wished for."

He smiled awkwardly, her words creeping under his guard.

"And I have something for you," she added. "I hope it will please you." From her pocket she extracted a small folded piece of paper and handed it to him.

He unfolded it. "It's one of Jens's notes."

It was the one in which he mentioned Alexei. "For you, if you'd like it."

Alexei nodded and turned away quickly, but not before she saw an emotion she couldn't read flood his face, making him look young and vulnerable. Carefully he refolded it and kept it in his hand.

At that moment Antonina entered bearing a tray. While Lydia

drank the strong coffee and ate one of the warm croissants, Antonina snipped at her damaged hair with a pair of scissors, creating something orderly out of the havoc. It occurred to Lydia that Antonina would always be good at that. She watched Alexei observing every nuance of Antonina's face as she worked, and she hoped they would be good for each other. Afterward she was taken to the main bedroom, where gowns and shoes and sable stoles were scattered across the bed.

"Help yourself to anything you want," Antonina said with an indifferent wave of her hand toward the bed and a black velvet box that sat open on the dressing table.

Even from where Lydia was standing by the door, she could see that the box contained jewelry. Unable to stop herself, she was drawn to it, revelling in the glitter of diamonds and the buttery sheen of gold, but she didn't touch anything. She might not be able to prize her fingers apart if she did.

"Thank you," she said. "For the roubles and now this offer. You are very generous. But no, I don't need more."

"We're going to sell it all. Getting rid of it through Maksim. Are you sure?"

"I'm sure."

"No desire for blood money, is that it?"

"Something like that."

"I don't blame you." Antonina came over and kissed Lydia's cheek. "At least let me drive you to the station."

LYDIA STEPPED OUT OF THE SLEEK SALOON AT THE STATION. The place was thick with travelers, suitcases, and porters' trolleys fighting for space, but she barely noticed them. What she saw were the uniforms. Gray with blue flashes at the collar, diligently checking papers and scrutinizing faces. Searching for someone.

"Security police," she murmured to Alexei.

"It's not too late to turn back."

The car door still stood open. All it would take was one step to be safe inside the car, but that one step would be a journey into her past instead of her future. Chang An Lo had offered her Hong Kong. It was an island teetering just off the mainland of China, but it bridged the gap that yawned between East and West, between his world and hers. A British colony, yet at the same time a thriving Chinese center of activity and growth. There he could still be part of his own country and could take his time to make his decisions. Whether to free his throat from the choking hand of Mao Tse-tung. And it might even be possible there for her to fulfill the dream she and her mother used to weave of her going to university one day. With a British passport in her possession, Hong Kong could be hers. Like an open door. All she had to do was push it wide and find Chang An Lo waiting for her.

She touched the quartz dragon at her throat. None of it would be easy, she knew that, because their love was fierce. It burned as well as bound them. Chang called her his fox; her mother had called her an alley cat; she was good at surviving. But their love? Would that survive what lay ahead?

Yes, she was determined they would make it survive. Each day they would breathe life into it, despite the dangers that circled them like wolves. She looked again at the officer in gray, at the gun holster on his hip, and she fingered the papers in her pocket. She knew that in China she would miss Russia the way she'd miss a limb, but to remain without Chang was impossible. She'd tried that. And almost died of the pain.

It's not too late to turn back.

The car purred behind her, smelling of leather and cigars.

"Lydia?" Alexei asked from inside.

Choose.

She closed the door and stamped her feet on the icy ground, smiling as she drew in a deep breath of Russian air and felt her heart race. There was a future ahead, one that she and Chang An Lo would carve together. It was a risk, but life itself was a risk. That much she'd learned from Russia, that much she'd learned from Jens. With a farewell wave to Alexei and a final touch of the Chinese amulet around her neck to tempt the protection of Chang An Lo's gods one last time, she looped her bag onto her shoulder and headed for the gateway.

Turn the page for an excerpt from
Kate Furnivall's novel

The Russian Concubine

The story of Lydia Ivanova's early years in China
Available in paperback now
from Berkley Books

One

Russia
December 1917

THE TRAIN GROWLED TO A HALT. GRAY STEAM belched from its heaving engine into the white sky, and the twenty-four freight carriages behind bucked and rattled as they lurched shrieking to a standstill. The sound of horses and of shouted commands echoed across the stillness of the empty frozen landscape.

"Why have we stopped?" Valentina Friis whispered to her husband.

Her breath curled between them like an icy curtain. It seemed to her despairing mind to be the only part of her that still had any strength to move. She clutched his hand. Not for warmth this time, but because she needed to know he was still there at her side. He shook his head, his face blue with cold because his coat was wrapped tightly around the sleeping child in his arms.

"This is not the end," he said.

"Promise me," she breathed.

He gave his wife a smile and together they clung to the rough timbered wall of the cattle wagon that enclosed them, pressing their eyes to the slender gaps between the planks. All around them others did the same. Desperate eyes. Eyes that had already seen too much.

"They mean to kill us," the bearded man on Valentina's right stated in a flat voice. He spoke with a heavy Georgian accent and wore his astrakhan hat well down over his ears. "Why else would we stop in the middle of nowhere?"

"Oh sweet Mary, mother of God, protect us."

It was the wail of an old woman still huddled on the filthy floor and wrapped in so many shawls she looked like a fat little Buddha. But underneath the stinking rags was little more than skin and bone.

"No, *babushka*," another male voice insisted. It came from the rear end of the carriage where the ice-ridden wind tore relentlessly through the slats, bringing the breath of Siberia into their lungs. "No, it'll be General Kornilov. He knows we're on this godforsaken cattle train starving to death. He won't let us die. He's a great commander."

A murmur of approval ran around the clutch of gaunt faces, bringing a spark of belief to the dull eyes, and a young boy with dirty blond hair who had been lying listlessly in one corner leapt to his feet and started to cry with relief. It had been a long time since anyone had wasted energy on tears.

"Dear God, I pray you are right," said a hollow-eyed man with a stained bandage on the stump of his arm. At night he groaned endlessly in his sleep, but by day he was silent and tense. "We're at war," he said curtly. "General Lavr Kornilov cannot be everywhere."

"But I tell you he's here. You'll see."

"Is he right, Jens?" Valentina tilted her face up to her husband.

She was only twenty-four, small and fragile, but possessed sensuous dark eyes that could, with a glance, for a brief moment, make a man forget the cold and the hunger that gnawed at his insides or the weight of a child in his arms. Jens Friis was ten years older than his wife and fearful for her safety if the roving Bolshevik soldiers took one look at her beautiful face. He bent his head and brushed a kiss on her forehead.

"We shall soon know," he said.

The red beard on his unshaven cheek was rough against Valentina's cracked lips, but she welcomed the feel of it and the smell of his unwashed body. They reminded her that she had not died and gone to hell. Because hell was exactly what this felt like. The thought that this nightmare journey across thousands of miles of snow and ice might go on forever, through the whole of eternity, that this was her cruel damnation for defying her parents, was one that haunted her, awake and asleep.

Suddenly the great sliding door of the wagon was thrust open and fierce voices shouted, *"Vse is vagona, bistro."* Out of the wagons.

THE LIGHT BLINDED VALENTINA. THERE WAS SO MUCH OF IT. After the perpetually twilit world inside the wagon, it rushed at her from the huge arc of sky, skidded off the snow, and robbed her of vision. She blinked hard and forced the scene around her into focus.

What she saw chilled her heart.

A row of rifles. All aimed directly at the ragged passengers as they scrambled off the train and huddled in anxious groups, their coats pulled tight to keep out the cold and the fear. Jens reached up to help the old woman down from their wagon, but before he could take her hand she was pushed from behind and landed facedown in the snow. She made no sound, no cry. But she was quickly yanked onto her feet by the soldier who had thrown open the wagon door and shaken as carelessly as a dog shakes a bone.

Valentina exchanged a look with her husband. Without a word they slid their child from Jens's shoulder and stood her between them, hiding her in the folds of their long coats as they moved forward together.

"Mama?" It was a whisper. Though only five years old, the girl had already learned the need for silence. For stillness.

"Hush, Lydia," Valentina murmured but could not resist a glance down at her daughter. All she saw was a pair of wide tawny eyes in a heart-shaped bone-white face and little booted feet swallowed up by the snow. She pressed closer against her husband and the face no longer existed. Only the small hand clutching her own told her otherwise.

THE MAN FROM GEORGIA IN THE WAGON WAS RIGHT. THIS WAS truly the middle of nowhere. A godforsaken landscape of nothing but snow and ice and the occasional windswept rock face glistening black. In the far distance a bank of skeletal trees stood like a reminder that life could exist here. But this was no place to live.

No place to die.

The men on horseback didn't look much like an army. Nothing remotely like the smart officers Valentina was used to seeing in the ballrooms and *troikas* of St. Petersburg or ice skating on the Neva, showing off their crisp uniforms and impeccable manners. These men were different. Alien to that elegant world she had left behind. These men were hostile. Dangerous. About fifty of them had spread out along the length of the train, alert and hungry as wolves. They wore an assortment of greatcoats against the cold, some gray, others black, and one a deep muddy green. But all cradled the same long-nosed rifle in their arms and had the same fanatical look of hatred in their eyes.

"Bolsheviks," Jens murmured to Valentina, as they were herded into a group where the fragile sound of prayers trickled like tears. "Pull your hood over your head and hide your hands."

"My hands?"

"Yes."

"Why my hands?"

"Comrade Lenin likes to see them scarred and roughened by years of what he calls honest labor." He touched her arm protectively. "I don't think piano playing counts, my love."

Valentina nodded, slipped her hood over her head and her one free hand into her pocket. Her gloves, her once beautiful sable gloves, had been torn to shreds during the months in the forest, that time of traveling on foot by night, eating worms and lichen by day. It had taken its toll on more than just her gloves.

"Jens," she said softly, "I don't want to die."

He shook his head vehemently and his free hand jabbed toward the tall soldier on horseback who was clearly in command. The one in the green greatcoat.

"He's the one who should die—for leading the peasants into this mass insanity that is tearing Russia apart. Men like him open up the floodgates of brutality and call it justice."

At that moment the officer called out an order and more of his troops dismounted. Rifle barrels were thrust into faces, thudded against backs. As the train breathed heavily in the silent wilderness, the soldiers pushed and jostled its cargo of hundreds of displaced people into a tight circle fifty yards away from the rail track and then proceeded to strip the wagons of possessions.

"No, please, don't," shouted a man at Valentina's elbow as an armful of tattered blankets and a tiny cooking stove were hurled out of one of the front wagons. Tears were running down his cheeks.

She put out a hand. Held his shoulder. No words could help. All around her, desperate faces were gray and taut.

In front of each wagon the meager pile of possessions grew as the carefully hoarded objects were tossed into the snow and set on fire. Flames, fired by coal from the steam engine and a splash of vodka, devoured the last scraps of their self-respect. Their clothes, the blankets, photographs, a dozen treasured icons of the Virgin Mary, and even a miniature painting of Tsar Nicholas II. All blackened, burned, and turned to ash.

"You are traitors. All of you. Traitors to your country."

The accusation came from the tall officer in the green greatcoat. Though he wore no insignia except a badge of crossed sabers on his peaked cap, there was no mistaking his position of authority. He sat upright on a large heavy-muscled horse, which he controlled effortlessly with an occasional flick of his heel. His eyes were dark and impatient, as if this cargo of White Russians presented him with a task he found distasteful.

"None of you deserve to live," he said coldly.

A deep moan rose from the crowd. It seemed to sway with shock.

He raised his voice. "You exploited us. You maltreated us. You believed the time would never come when you would have to answer to *us*, the people of Russia. But you were wrong. You were blind. Where is all your wealth now? Where are your great houses and your fine horses now? The tsar is finished and I swear to you that—"

A single voice rose up from somewhere in the middle of the crowd. "God bless the tsar. God protect the Romanovs."

A shot rang out. The officer's rifle had bucked in his hands. A figure in the front row fell to the ground, a dark stain on the snow.

"That man paid for *your* treachery." His hostile gaze swept over the stunned crowd with contempt. "You and your kind were parasites on the backs of the starving workers. You created a world of cruelty and tyranny where rich men turned their backs on the cries of the poor. And now you desert your country, like rats fleeing from a burning ship. And you dare to take the youth of Russia with you." He swung his horse to one side and moved away from the throng of gaunt faces. "Now you will hand over your valuables."

At a nod of his head, the soldiers started to move among the prisoners. Systematically they seized all jewelry, all watches, all silver cigar cases, anything that had any worth, including all forms of money. Insolent hands searched clothing, under arms, inside mouths, and even between breasts, seeking out the carefully hidden items that meant survival to their owners. Valentina lost the emerald ring secreted in the hem of her dress, while Jens was stripped of his last gold coin in his boot. When it was over, the crowd stood silent except for a dull sobbing. Robbed of hope, they had no voice.

But the officer was pleased. The look of distaste left his face. He turned and issued a sharp command to the man on horseback behind him. Instantly a handful of mounted soldiers began to weave through the crowd, dividing it, churning it into confusion. Valentina clung to the small hand hidden in hers and knew that Jens would die before he released the other one. A faint cry escaped from the child when a big bay horse swung into them and its iron-shod hooves trod dangerously close, but otherwise she hung on fiercely and made no sound.

"What are they doing?" Valentina whispered.

"Taking the men. And the children."

"Oh God, no."

But he was right. Only the old men and the women were ignored. The others were being separated out and herded away. Cries of anguish tore through the frozen wasteland and somewhere on the far side of the train a wolf crept forward on its belly, drawn by the scent of blood.

"Jens, no, don't let them take you. Or her," Valentina begged.

"Papa?" A small face emerged between them.

"Hush, my love."

A rifle butt thumped into Jens's shoulder just as he flicked his coat back over his daughter's head. He staggered but kept his feet.

"You. Get over there." The soldier on horseback looked as if he were just longing for an excuse to pull the trigger. He was very young. Very nervous.

Jens stood his ground. "I am not Russian." He reached into his inside pocket, moving his hand slowly so as not to unsettle the soldier, and drew out his passport.

"See," Valentina pointed out urgently. "My husband is Danish."

The soldier frowned, uncertain what to do. But his commander had sharp eyes. He instantly spotted the hesitation. He kicked his horse forward into the panicking crowd and came up alongside the young private.

"Grodensky, why are you wasting time here?" he demanded.

But his attention was not on the soldier. It was on Valentina. Her face had tilted up to speak to the mounted *soldat* and her hood had fallen back, revealing a sweep of long dark hair and a high forehead with pale flawless skin. Months of starvation had heightened her cheekbones and made her eyes huge in her face.

The officer dismounted. Up close, they could see he was younger than he had appeared on horseback, probably still in his thirties, but with the eyes of a much older man. He took the passport and studied it briefly, his gaze flicking from Valentina to Jens and back again.

"But you," he said roughly to Valentina, "you are Russian?"

Behind them shots were beginning to sound.

"By birth, yes," she answered without turning her head to the noise. "But now I am Danish. By marriage." She wanted to edge closer to her husband, to hide the child more securely between them, but did not dare move. Only her fingers tightened on the tiny cold hand in hers.

Without warning, the officer's rifle slammed into Jens's stomach and he doubled over with a grunt of pain, but immediately another blow to the back of his head sent him sprawling onto the snow. Blood spattered its icy surface.

Valentina screamed.

Instantly she felt the little hand pull free of her own and saw her daughter throw herself at the officer's legs with the ferocity of a spitting wildcat, biting and scratching in a frenzy of rage. As if in slow motion, she watched the rifle butt start to descend toward the little head.

"No," she shouted and snatched the child up into her arms before the blow could fall. But stronger hands tore the young body from her grasp.

"No, no, no!" she screamed. "She is a Danish child. She is not a Russian."

"She *is* Russian," the officer insisted and drew his revolver. "She fights like a Russian." Casually he placed the gun barrel at the center of the child's forehead.

The child froze. Only her eyes betrayed her fear. Her little mouth was clamped shut.

"Don't kill her, I beg you," Valentina pleaded. "Please don't kill her. I'll do . . . anything . . . anything. If you let her live."

A deep groan issued from the crumpled figure of her husband at her feet.

"Please," she begged softly. She undid the top button of her coat, not taking her eyes from the officer's face. "Anything."

The Bolshevik commander reached out a hand and touched her hair, her cheek, her mouth. She held her breath. Willing him to want her. And for a fleeting moment she knew she had him. But when he glanced around at his watching men, all of them lusting for her, hoping their turn would be next, he shook his head.

"No. You are not worth it. Not even for soft kisses from your beautiful lips. No. It would cause too much trouble among my troops." He shrugged. "A shame." His finger tightened on the trigger.

"Let me buy her," Valentina said quickly.

When he turned his head to stare at her with a frown that brought his heavy eyebrows together, she said again, "Let me buy her. And my husband."

He laughed. The soldiers echoed the harsh sound of it. "With what?"

"With these." Valentina thrust two fingers down her throat and bent over as a gush of warm bile swept up from her empty stomach. In the center of the yellow smear of liquid that spread out on the snow's crust lay two tiny cotton packages, each no bigger than a hazelnut. At a gesture from the officer, a bearded soldier scooped them up and handed them to him. They sat, dirty and damp, in the middle of his black glove.

Valentina stepped closer. "Diamonds," she said proudly.

He scraped off the cotton wraps, eagerness in every movement, until what looked like two nuggets of sparkling ice gleamed up at him.

Valentina saw the greed in his face. "One to buy my daughter. The other for my husband."

"I can take them anyway. You have already lost them."

"I know."

Suddenly he smiled. "Very well. We shall deal. Because I have the diamonds and because you are beautiful, you shall keep the brat." Lydia was thrust into Valentina's arms and clung to her as if she would climb right inside her body.

"And my husband," Valentina insisted.

"Your husband we keep."

"No, no. Please God, I . . ."

But the horses came in force then. A solid wall of them that drove the women and old men back to the train.

Lydia screamed in Valentina's arms, "Papa, Papa . . . ," and tears flowed down her thin cheeks as she watched his body being dragged away.

VALENTINA COULD FIND NO TEARS. ONLY THE FROZEN EMPTIness within her, as bleak and lifeless as the wilderness that swept past outside. She sat on the foul-smelling floor of the cattle truck with her back against the slatted wall. Night was seeping in and the air was so cold it hurt to breathe, but she didn't notice. Her head hung low and her eyes saw nothing. Around her the sound of grief filled the vacant spaces. The boy with dirty blond hair was gone, as well as the man who had been so certain the White Russian army had arrived to feed them. Women wept for the loss of their husbands and the theft of their sons and daughters, and stared with naked envy at the one child on the train.

Valentina had wrapped her coat tightly around Lydia and herself, but could feel her daughter shivering.

"Mama," the girl whispered, "is Papa coming back?"

"No."

It was the twentieth time she had asked the same question, as if by continually repeating it she could make the answer change. In the gloom Valentina felt the little body shudder.

So she took her daughter's cold face between her hands and said fiercely, "But we will survive, you and I. Survival is everything."